PUBLISHER'S PLEDGE

Sunrise in a Garden of Love & Evil

Dear Reader,

Blackmail, fetish clubs, murder and a blood-and-love starved vampire . . . every so often an editor has the good fortune to acquire a manuscript that wins him over from the moment he starts reading, like *Sunrise in a Garden of Love & Evil*. With its smoldering attraction between protagonists, sultry Southern atmosphere, burgeoning sense of danger, and unique interpretation of vampire mythology, the first book in Barbara Monajem's series enthralls from page one. Monajem's story is a delight in the same (ahem) vein as Charlaine Harris's internationally bestselling Sookie Stackhouse novels, and we proudly offer it up as a fresh new series into which you can sink your teeth.

Dorchester's Publisher's Pledge program is our way of identifying particularly special books by giving readers a risk-free guarantee. We feel so strongly about *Sunrise in a Garden of Love & Evil*, we're willing to pay a full refund to anyone who doesn't find it everything they want in a paranormal fantasy.

I sincerely hope that *Sunrise in a Garden of Love & Evil* captivates your imagination the way it did mine. See you in Bayou Gavotte.

Best regards,
Christopher Keeslar
Senior Editor

PROTECTION

Gideon left the headlights on and the engine running, got out and held the door open for his dog. "Put the gun away, Ophelia." He walked calmly toward her. "It's only me."

"I know who it is." Ophelia's voice broke, and a tear spilled treacherously down her cheek. She let out a scream of rage and fired, kicking up gravel far too close to Gideon's feet. He didn't flinch. He didn't move a goddamn hair. "Don't you get it?" she yelled. "I'm trying to protect you from yourself. I am not safe to be with!"

Gideon echoed her earlier words in bitter mockery. "'That's the stupidest thing I ever heard in my life.' You could at least come up with an intelligent lie."

Ophelia opened her mouth but shut it again. Pissing him off was what she wanted. Still, the disgust in his voice tore into her.

"Don't worry," he said. "I'm out of here, and I won't come back unless you need me." He turned to his dog. "Stay, Gretchen. Stay with Ophelia. Protect her." Gideon got in his car and backed into the turnaround, flinging his last words through the window. "What makes you think I give a damn about being safe?"

BARBARA MONAJEM

Sunrise in a Garden of
LOVE & EVIL

LOVE SPELL NEW YORK CITY

LOVE SPELL®

April 2010

Published by

Dorchester Publishing Co., Inc.
200 Madison Avenue
New York, NY 10016

ISBN 10: 0-505-52825-8
ISBN 13: 978-0-505-52825-4
E-ISBN: 978-1-4285-0836-1

The name "Love Spell" and its logo are trademarks of Dorchester Publishing Co., Inc.

Printed in the United States of America.

10 9 8 7 6 5 4 3 2 1

Visit us online at www.dorchesterpub.com.

ACKNOWLEDGMENTS

Thanks to my husband and daughters for everything from relentless support to flawlessly aimed criticism.

Thanks to Scott Simmons for cluing me in about landscaping in south Louisiana, and to Nancie Hays for answering my questions about guns. Needless to say, all errors are mine.

Thanks to the Internet acquaintances who pointed me toward sources about the kinky side of life. Again, misunderstandings and errors are mine.

Thanks to Chris Keeslar for being a delight to work with and for giving me the word "toothsome," which I *will* use somehow, somewhere.

Thanks to my daughters and sisters for brainstorming, reading and commenting; to Sheila Connolly and Jennifer Stevenson for their comments on the full manuscript in draft; to the many friends, relatives, critique partners and contest judges who read this story in bits and pieces, in part or the whole dang thing, just once or over and over again; to the members of Georgia Romance Writers and the Cherries for friendship and support. I couldn't have done it without you all.

Sunrise in a Garden of
LOVE & EVIL

CHAPTER ONE

Vampire: a human being with a genetic mutation characterized by, among other things, the appearance of fangs at puberty, an intense craving for human blood, and an irresistible magnetism for the opposite sex. Judging by legend, this particular mutation has existed for millennia, but is still sufficiently rare that most people don't believe such beings exist.

D. Tull, Society for the Protection of Not-so-mythical Beings

Ophelia Beliveau jammed her fangs back up where they belonged, puncturing her thumb, so the goddamned things slotted right back down. She sucked on the tiny cut and glared at her devastated garden. Insults? Just words. A dead cat on her doorstep? Disgusting, not to mention creepy, but she should have buried the poor animal earlier when she'd had the chance. But nobody—damn it, *nobody*—would get away with destroying her garden.

She sealed the wound in her thumb and pushed the fangs back more carefully into their sockets, at the same time running through her options. Smash the guy's garden in return? She couldn't do that to a lot of defenseless plants, although in their current state of neglect they'd soon be candidates for a mercy killing. Maim the bastard? That would just add to the burden for his wife and daughters. Kill him? That had its upside, but where would that leave her own plants while she rotted in jail? Trashed and lonely and unloved. No way. Her garden deserved better.

Ophelia thought and rethought and twisted up inside, and then did what she had sworn never, ever to do. She called the cops.

Gideon O'Toole yanked the cell phone away from his ear. "Artemisia, I can't investigate blackmail unless someone comes forward. Nowhere to start."

The speaker crackled with the force of his sister's voice. "She's scared to!"

"That's why blackmail works," Gideon replied, but Artemisia talked on and on. *I am a man of infinite patience,* he told himself as he sped down the straight-as-an-arrow Louisiana country road, letting his thoughts wander toward a late lunch at home, toward beer and a steak in the company of his three dogs. "Gotta go, Sis," he said, when she'd had long enough. "Vandalism call. Talk to your neighbor, get her to fess up. There's no other way."

At least his destination was close by: an old trailer on concrete supports with a flower garden, a highly tended lawn, a greenhouse with a row of compost piles stretching behind it toward the woods, and a lot of potted plants. And a shiny green truck with a magnetized sign on the side. *All the owner's money must be invested in that truck,* Gideon thought, *to make the business look prosperous whenever the dude goes to see customers.* He'd noted signs advertising Beliveau Landscaping in a few gardens around Bayou Gavotte. Healthy-looking gardens. Well, only an idiot would show off his failures.

Gideon turned his old maroon Mercedes sharply at the Beliveau driveway and pulled in behind the green pickup, startling a gray tabby from underneath to bound rabbitlike across the perfect lawn. Beyond the truck a woman stood in a patch of mud among shattered pots and scattered plants, holding a double-barreled shotgun in her apparently capable hands. She didn't exactly level it at him, but clearly wouldn't hesitate if the occasion arose.

Gideon studied her through the windshield and decided as usual to dispense with proper procedure; she wasn't going to shoot him. He turned off the car and opened the door.

"Who the hell are you?" the woman demanded in a soft, low voice. She glared at him with the coldest eyes he'd ever seen. But that was the only cold thing about her, and as he got out of the car and gaped, his reaction was immediate and overwhelming.

Uncharacteristically disconcerted, he reached awkwardly into his jeans and tried to pull out his ID. He couldn't keep his eyes off her, even while she watched him with patent disgust. "Gideon O'Toole, Bayou Gavotte Police," he said with a fair approximation of poise, and then gave up on that and laughed, bringing the slightest twitch to the woman's lips. Her eyes warmed a fraction, too, though her grip on the shotgun never wavered.

"I suppose you have this effect on all the men you meet, Mrs. Beliveau," Gideon guessed, trying to keep from squirming while he waited for his erection to subside. Ophelia Beliveau—if this was indeed who had called him in—wasn't what he'd call gorgeous. Pretty, with red-brown curls, ripe lovely lips, and a good figure. He liked the look of her, for sure, but she wasn't movie-star material. And she wasn't dressed to attract. She wore a sweat-soaked T-shirt, baggy shorts, and battered work boots, and had dirt on her face and hands, even under her nails. She didn't seem to be smoldering on purpose, unless this was a damn good act. But she gave off such heat, such an air of sexual promise . . . Jeez, her husband was a lucky man.

"Damn it," she said, interrupting his thoughts, the ice back in her eyes. "I wanted a uniform and a patrol car. Don't you at least have a flashing light to put on your roof?"

He collected himself. "Sure, but what difference does it make?"

"The difference," she said impatiently, gesturing with the shotgun, "is that I want my jerk of a neighbor who made this goddamned mess to see that I called the cops."

"You know for sure who did this?" Reluctantly, Gideon looked away from her to grimace at the chaos, then at the white contractor's truck next door, and finally at the house. A curtain at the window fell immediately into place. "He's watching us. Did you catch him at it?" Gideon reached through the open window of his Mercedes and retrieved a bubble to set on the roof, blue light flashing.

"Not that neighbor," Ophelia said. "Willy Wyler did it. Lucky for him I didn't catch him. He lives two doors down." She aimed the shotgun at an imposing Colonial house set back from the road, eyeing it through the sights. "I'd shoot him and get it over with, but unfortunately that's illegal, so . . ." She lowered the gun and shrugged. Beautifully. "I called you."

Thank you.

Gideon pulled himself together. What was he thinking? She was someone else's wife. He had a way with women, but not other people's. "Willy Wyler. Huh." *Lame, incredibly lame.*

The shotgun wandered in his direction. "I don't *believe* this," its owner said bitterly. Beautifully.

He must be going out of his mind. No, his mind was still here, harking back to the beer, the dogs, and the steak. It was his body that was totally screwed—or wanted to be. Damn it, this was a professional call! Stay cool. Ignore the gun. Get the hell out. He closed his eyes briefly. "What don't you believe?"

"I know the cops are in cahoots with the clubs in Bayou Gavotte, but I didn't think the protection extended to drunken has-been musicians. Fortunately, I don't expect you to really *do* anything." She waved the shotgun toward Gideon's Mercedes. "Do you have a crime-scene kit? All the paraphernalia for making plaster casts? Wyler's already a little scared of me, and if he sees I called the cops, if he sees you making a plaster cast of his tire tracks . . . Well, it won't hurt and it might help. So if it's not too much to ask—"

Way too much, under the circumstances. Although they tacitly accepted the fact because of Bayou Gavotte's resultant prosperity, ordinary citizens rarely understood the delicate balance between the cops and the club-controlling underworld. Which was fine, as long as they kept their mouths—luscious or otherwise—shut.

Gideon slowed his already-lazy speech into a thicker drawl. "Yes, I do have a kit in my car, because I make a point of being prepared. You lucked out. You got a detective, when all you needed was a patrol. But if you want my help, you'll drop the crap about police corruption. Right now."

The woman blinked at him with something resembling surprise. "Okay," she agreed pleasantly enough, and turned to walk up the driveway to the vandalized garden.

Laying the shotgun in the bed of her truck, she scowled at the havoc around her. Clay flowerpots sat devastated beside the driveway. Plastic ones had been stomped on and strewn halfway across the lawn. Plants dumped from their containers clung together in a pathetic heap of roots and dirt. "That used to be my vegetable garden," she said of a slew of crisscrossed tire tracks in the mud. "Good thing some of the inventory was inside the screened porch."

Gideon approached. "You keep a lot of stock on hand, Mrs. Beliveau?"

"Not usually. Last week the nursery cut a good deal." She squatted by the pile of dispossessed plants and separated them with strong, deft fingers. Gideon watched through half-closed eyes.

"Why don't you get on with that plaster cast." An order, not a question. Her voice cut into him.

He collected the plaster kit and camera from the trunk of his Mercedes and returned to Ophelia, holding two buckets out with his own unspoken command. Without a word, she took it. He let himself enjoy the sight of her striding toward the hose coiled neatly on the end of the trailer, then turned to survey the three hundred square feet of mud and crushed plant life. It was only the beginning of April, but the Beliveaus had started their new vegetables early and were still reaping the end of the fall plantings. Maybe a few turnips could be salvaged, Gideon decided, although they would probably be leather-tough. Only a few meager plants had been left undamaged. Gideon's eyes widened as he noted the plants at the edge of the garden. Marijuana. Well, well.

By the time Ophelia arrived with the water, he had taken two photos of the cleanest tire track from above and sprayed the track with fixative. He felt her eyes on him as he mixed the plaster, set a wooden frame around the track, and poured the plaster gently in, breaking the flow with his stir stick, adding leaves, pine straw, a few twigs, and other debris to the cast. Too bad the attention was nothing to get hyped about. Everyone thought plaster casts were cool.

"Relatively new tires," Gideon noted, frowning across at Ophelia's truck. "Unlike yours."

"I hope he's watching," Ophelia replied. "Maybe he'll get scared enough to waste four hundred bucks on some more new ones. Well, what do you know!"

A middle-aged, faded blonde, pretty in a haggard way, sidled across the next-door neighbor's lawn. She leaned tensely over the property line as if it were a cliff edge, and came out with a rigid, high-pitched babble. "Ophelia, I'm sorry to bother you if you have company, but I need a cup of sugar."

"Of course you do," Ophelia said. "Lisa Wyler, this is . . . What was your name, officer?"

"Gideon O'Toole, Bayou Gavotte Police Force," Gideon repeated, reflecting ruefully that he hadn't made much of an impression if she didn't remember his name. He stood up, stretching, and nodded at Mrs. Wyler, who returned a nervous smile fraught with meaning. She took in the plaster cast and slid her gaze over to the trampled garden, where it briefly lingered on the bedraggled marijuana plants before returning to his face.

"Somebody vandalized my garden," Ophelia said softly. Her tone almost made Gideon's flesh crawl, and it totally spooked Mrs. Wyler; the Beliveau woman certainly knew how to deal out cold and more cold. Gideon controlled the urge to laugh again and thoughtfully regarded the neighbor.

"This lovely policeman's making a plaster cast of the vandal's tire tracks," Ophelia continued, moving closer to Gideon and resting a playful hand on his shoulder. "Isn't that sweet of him?"

Gideon grinned at Mrs. Wyler. He hoped it passed as an evil grin and wondered what the neighbor expected him to do—clap handcuffs on Ophelia then and there because of some weed? Not likely. He had a feeling bondage wasn't her thing.

"I—I gotta go," said Mrs. Wyler, and ran off.

"What about the sugar?" Ophelia called after her.

"I'll . . . I'll make do without."

Gideon gave in to some low, delighted laughter, and continued to chuckle softly as he packed up his kit. He wiped the sweat off his brow and smiled at Ophelia. "In this humidity it takes a good while for the plaster to dry. How about if we sit down and you tell me all about it?"

The enjoyment vanished from Ophelia's face. "I don't need you to actually do anything with that tire print, officer. I just wanted to freak Wyler out a little. In case you haven't figured it out, that was his fool of a wife." A trace of regret crossed her features. "I shouldn't have scared her like that. She's a screwup with a drunk for a husband. I'm not usually so unkind."

"I suppose you don't usually call the cops to suit your own purposes, either?" Gideon started laughing again. "Well, you have the act down pat, lady. Right out of a horror movie. You sound like the devil, even if you look like love."

Her reaction was immediate. "Love? That's bullshit. Sex

is what I look like, and you know it and so does every other man in this goddamned world." Her eyes narrowed and her voice brimmed with anger—at him, at herself, at her neighbor or whomever, Gideon didn't know.

"Sometimes they go together, sex and love," he suggested, adding after a moment, "or so I've heard. But whatever you look like, I have to fill out an incident report. I'll need a little more information." He returned the kit to his car and brought out the appropriate forms, and she led him willingly enough to a couple of plastic chairs and a table out of the afternoon sun, under an awning at the end of the trailer. He settled himself across from her. "What makes you so sure Willy did this?"

"He's pissed off at me." Ophelia's eyes followed Lisa Wyler into the Colonial. "Looks like such a respectable place, doesn't it? But not all trash lives in trailers."

"He calls you trash? Is that why you're so bent out of shape?"

Ophelia responded with incredible cool. "Like I care what he thinks of me." She snorted, reached under the trailer, and pulled out a pile of half-gallon plastic pots. "I'm bent out of shape because . . . because he and his musician friends think they can have any woman they want. I have made it plain to them that this particular woman isn't available, but they don't like to take no for an answer." She separated the pots and set them in two neat rows beside her chair. "This mess is their petty revenge."

Gideon blinked, his brain starting to hum. Wyler and his friends might well want Ophelia—who wouldn't?—but he'd also seen her hesitation. "Is that the only problem?"

"That's not enough?" She was challenging him, smoldering on purpose now, just a touch, just to show him. Damn. Wars would be fought for this woman.

Still, things didn't add up. "What about your husband? Why would Wyler think he can sleep with you?"

"I'm not married," Ophelia said. "And no, I don't have a boyfriend either. I live here alone."

"Oh," Gideon said. "I thought—"

The icy stare was back, this time mixed with resignation. "Of course you did. *I'm* Beliveau Landscaping. Me, myself, and only I, with occasional help when I need it for installing fountains or planting big trees or laying sod."

"Sorry," Gideon said. "I assumed you were just into gardening, and that's why you're up to your elbows in dirt. I guess you just got back from work." He shifted and repeated with genuine contrition, "Sorry."

She gave a tiny nod that might have been acknowledgment. "Sexual stereotyping is the least of my problems. Anyway, that turd thinks I should be fair game, but I'm not, and he can't handle it. He's on drugs and he's a total dud, and I suppose even the musician mystique can't get him willing partners anymore."

"Trashing your garden seems like a stupid move. There has to be more to it."

"He's a stupid man," Ophelia said with a shake of her reddish brown curls. "I don't want to go into this any further. Thanks for your help. You can go now." Standing, she turned to watch a shiny red pickup head down Wyler's driveway to the road. It turned in the direction of town. "Well, what do you know? Maybe he *is* going to get new tires! It was worth it to call you, if only for that."

Gideon sauntered back to his car and got on the radio. "Jeanie," he told the dispatcher, "I'm still at Beliveau's place. If there's anyone between here and downtown, tell them to keep a lookout for a red Ford 350 pickup owned by Willy Wyler, who lives a few doors down from Beliveau. Follow him around, see what he's up to. If he tries to buy new tires, get the patrol to hover, make like he wants to see the old ones."

As he switched off the annoying blue flashing light,

Gideon turned to find Ophelia scowling at him. "What was that about?" she demanded. "I don't want you meddling in my business."

"You shouldn't have called me, then. Just arranging a little police harassment. If there's a car between here and downtown, he'll follow Willy around, make him nervous."

Ophelia smiled, a delicate flush spreading across her face, and it almost knocked his socks off. "Thank you," she said, but then backed off as if burned. "God, I'm thirsty. Do you want a Coke?"

Hell, yes. "Sure."

She looked almost flustered, and wonder of wonders, she didn't have a husband. Or a boyfriend. Not that he seriously expected anything from this woman but grief, but as he realized for about the thousandth time, she was so damn fine. Still, he had to take a dig. "Corruption's not so bad when it's in your favor, now is it?" He wondered for a moment if he was about to lose the soda and also whatever more time drinking it could wangle, but Ophelia merely snorted once more, a brief, cynical sound, and headed for her trailer.

She was lithe and purposeful and unusually muscular for a woman—hardly surprising, considering her occupation. As she entered the trailer, Gideon's cell phone rang. He read the display and sighed. "What now, Art?" he answered, the speaker prudently away from his ear. "Your friend ready to come clean?"

His sister launched into another rant. Gideon turned the volume low, tucked the phone under his chin, and started working on the Beliveau incident report, noting the devastation of the vegetable garden and the pots and plants. A bat house, currently occupied by wasps, hung askew above the shattered panes of the greenhouse. He itemized the damage, ignoring the marijuana.

"We—the police—have two options," he said when Art finally ran out of breath. "Either your friend or another victim comes forward, or we wait till someone gets fed up and offs the guy. Which wouldn't be a bad thing in itself, but then we'd have a murder on our hands, and unfortunately we have to try to solve those." He looked up to see Ophelia holding out a can of Coke and raised a finger. "Your friend also has two options: pay up or fess up." He paused. "Of course she's scared. That's why blackmail works. Now, I gotta go, baby. I love you, too." He closed the phone, took the Coke, and followed Ophelia back to the plastic chairs.

"Your wife?" His hostess popped the top of her soda and took a long swallow, head thrown back, her throat a graceful, naked curve. She had washed her face and hands while she was inside, probably not for his benefit, but because she wanted to be clean. He could always hope, though.

"My sister. I'm not married." Gideon did his best not to grin. "Don't have a girlfriend, either." What the hell. He grinned.

"Don't even think about it," Ophelia snapped. "I'm not available."

Not think about it? Was there any choice? He spread his hands. "Did I say anything?" He grinned again. "But now that you've brought it up, why not?"

The woman glared and ignored him. "Who's being blackmailed?"

"Some neighbor of my sister's." He smiled at her again.

"That poor woman. She must be so freaked out." His hostess eyed him with loathing. The gray tabby from earlier slipped out from under the trailer and eyed him, too. "And you're not going to do a thing about it."

Christ, thought Gideon, *they're all the same, even this one.* Why was he wasting his time? At his age, he should know better. "Not my problem until she reports it." He took a gulp of Coke and set the can beside his chair. It was time to finish the incident report and make his escape to the beer, the steak, and the three undemanding dogs.

He reached for the clipboard, but the tabby spat at him. "Psyche's not a friendly cat," Ophelia said, scooping the beast from under her chair. "Like me, she has a problem with men." Psyche purred and glared at Gideon with hot yellow eyes. "That's probably why she's still alive."

She sipped her soda, letting him figure that out. When he did, a cold claw of dismay clutched him. "You used to have another, friendlier cat, which your neighbor—?"

"Hung up on my front door a couple of days ago."

"What the hell?" Gideon half-rose, white-knuckle-gripping his chair.

The tabby hissed and dug claws into Ophelia's thigh, then took off under the house. She shuddered, eyes on the blood welling from the scratch. "Poor Psyche. You scared her." She licked a finger and wiped at the tiny red drops. Then, impatiently, without looking up, she said, "Don't get all worked up. It wasn't my cat. It was just an old stray and it was already dead. Hit by a car. I saw him lying next to the ditch when I left that morning, but I was late for a job so I planned to bury him when I got home." She sucked the blood off her finger, and Gideon thought he heard a small sigh. After a while, Ophelia raised her eyes. "I dumped the cat on Wyler's porch. Everybody's used to roadkill, and I figured the kids wouldn't understand the more sinister implications."

"Why didn't you report it?" Gideon stalked forward and barely stopped himself from grabbing her by the shoulders and shaking her. "What if he comes here when you're alone at night?"

"Oh, puh-lease," Ophelia said. "Wyler? Not his MO at all." She sighed again. "I regretted it right away. It was so disrespectful of that poor cat, which deserved a proper burial, and when I cooled down a little I realized it probably wasn't Wyler at all. He's childish and vindictive but not creepy."

She rose and turned away, but Gideon saw the shadow cross her face and pounced. "Someone else is, though? Damn it, Ophelia—"

She interrupted. "Unlike that poor blackmailed woman you're ignoring, I can take care of myself."

Christ. "I suppose you mean that shotgun. But what if he—whoever this is—breaks in and catches you asleep? Or comes over drunk with a bunch of his buddies? Tell me who this asshole is. I'll take care of him." He was burning to help.

"Nobody in particular," Ophelia said. She picked up a couple of trashed hostas, cupping their spiral roots in her hands. "Guys get a little fixated on me sometimes. No big deal."

"It's a big deal when they come over uninvited at night. It's an even bigger deal when they leave death threats on your door. You need to get a watchdog, at least. Do you have a cell phone in case someone cuts the wires?"

Ophelia scoffed. "Calm down." Tenderly, she lowered each hosta into a half-gallon pot. "I appreciate your coming here, but now you need to finish filling out that form and go away. I'll do fine."

Fine? Right. This was her problem, not his. Beer, steak, dogs. Then he looked at her again, at a tendril of curling auburn hair over her ear, at the swift passage of sadness as she tossed a damaged plant aside.

No, it was a huge problem, and definitely his.

"Ophelia," he began, then paused before giving it one more go. "What are you not telling me about all this?"

"Nothing you need to know." She grabbed the incident report form, tore off her copy, and shoved the rest back. "Don't forget your plaster cast. It won't look legit otherwise. You can trash it when you get home."

"It's not dry yet. It'll be at least another hour."

"I'll take care of it, then. Like I told you before, I just wanted to scare the bastard. Now, *go*." She scraped a spiderweb out of a plastic pot and replaced it with the last lonely hosta, then hefted all eight newly filled pots and carried them to her truck.

"No," Gideon said. He planted his butt on the plastic chair, ignoring Ophelia's outraged stare, and picked up his can of Coke. "You're not taking this seriously enough. I have

to take the plaster cast, and I have to make it clear to anyone who needs to know that you have protection now."

"I don't need—!" Ophelia began, but her words were
drowned by the screams of AC/DC as a purple Z-300 skidded into the driveway and blasted to a stop three inches
from Gideon's car.

CHAPTER TWO 🌷

The car rocked to the beat of Violet Dupree's favorite band. Violet's daughter, Zelda, leaped out of the passenger seat, fingers still in her ears. "We negotiated!" she shouted to Ophelia over the din. "AC/DC now, vintage Enya the whole way home!"

Thank God they're here, thought Ophelia, hurrying down the drive to hug her scrawny, freckled niece who, at almost thirteen, had begun to fill out but still showed no signs of the vampire gene. She held Zelda by the shoulders and scrutinized her face. The girl grinned. A nice grin, but not a vampire's. Not yet.

"Stop worrying," Zelda said. "What with Mom hoping for and you hoping against, I'm going nuts. What will be, will be. You got vandalized, huh? What a mess, but at least it got us back from shopping in New Orleans. Mom has no sense of style." Her eyes lit on Gideon, who was downing the last of his Coke. "Who's your friend?"

"He's not my friend. He's a very annoying cop. I'm so glad you guys are here." She grimaced. "How did Violet find out?"

"She's friends with the dispatcher at the cop shop, who said she was sending you a real babe." Zelda watched Gideon's approach with a critical eye. "Not bad looking for an old guy."

Violet got out of the car, swatted the radio off, and floated toward them in lime green chiffon and black lace. "Angel, baby, this is so dreadful!" She tossed herself into Ophelia's arms.

Ophelia hugged her half sister, inhaling deeply of her lavender scent. "Sorry your shopping trip got interrupted, but I'm so glad you came. I totally screwed this one up. Rescue me. *Please*," she whispered.

Violet smothered an exclamation, patted Ophelia on the back, and moaned artistically. "You're upset, poor angel! Well, no wonder, but . . . Hel-*lo*!" She favored Gideon with a long, lazy stare. "Just what the doctor ordered. So, you're the policeman Jeanie sent. *So* pleased to meet you, Officer O'Toole."

The detective took her in, suffered the inevitable reaction to a vamp, and chuckled. "My pleasure entirely," he said. "Miss . . . ?"

"Violet Dupree. I'm Ophelia's sister." She smiled, turning on her allure full force.

"Charm must run in your family," the detective said, blinking. "I'm Gideon O'Toole." He took Violet's outstretched hand and bent his head to kiss it.

Zelda grinned and stuck out her own hand. "I'm Zelda. Violet's my mom."

He bowed over Zelda's fingers and pressed them gently to his lips.

Violet cocked her head to one side for one more evaluation, then turned to Ophelia. "No? He's quite a hunk."

Here we go again, thought Ophelia, unaccountably depressed at running the same old scenario. She feigned an indifferent shrug. "He's all yours. If you want him, that is." She started back up the drive. "I have work to do."

Violet plucked at the wind tangles in her blazing orange hair. "Ophelia, are you positive? He's adorable."

Ophelia turned and made a face. "He's also the kind of creep who would hang around gawking at one woman, claiming he's there to protect her, while he ignores another one in genuine distress."

"Whoa," Zelda said. "Major dis."

Gideon's face darkened. "You have no idea what you're talking about, Ms. Beliveau, and no understanding of police procedure."

"Too bad I know so much about corruption and harassment," Ophelia retorted. She held his eyes for a long second and then had to let go. Work. She had to get back to work. Ignore the man. She headed toward her garden.

"Here comes Mr. Donaldson," Zelda remarked, her eyes on the neighbor's front porch. "Right on cue. Mr. Donaldson has the hots for my mom," she explained to Gideon. "Welcome to our soap opera. It's not your fault you're male. Be thankful you only have a bit part, because we're very hard on men."

She fished a grimy Pez dispenser from her pocket and offered Gideon a candy. He accepted it and said, "Thank you, Zelda." He watched the neighbor amble down his front steps. "Maybe he saw something. I'll go find out."

Ophelia whirled. "Don't you understand? I don't want you meddling in my life!"

"You shouldn't have called me, then." Gideon took the ditch to the next yard in one stride while pulling out his ID.

"You see?" Ophelia hissed to her sister. "Violet, I need to talk to you. Zelda, go inside and get some Cokes. Or tea. There's lemon in the fridge and mint around the back."

"He's just doing his job," Violet protested. "Which is awfully nice of him, considering how rude you're being. What happened to 'Violet dear, he's much more your type, I absolutely insist' or 'I still miss what's his name, I can't even look at another man' or even 'I'm coming down with mono again'?"

"I don't want him to do his job," Ophelia said. "He's already done everything I need. I want him to go away." Why had she told him about the cat thing? She followed Gideon with her eyes.

"But, angel," Violet said, "why not get some good out of

the situation? I was so thrilled to hear you'd called him. And it turns out he's as attractive as Jeanie said, and a charming flirt as well, and you have to start again somewhere. So, why not?"

Ophelia retrieved six pots of ham-and-eggs lantana, due to be planted in the morning, and dumped them in her truck. "Vi, I called the *police*. Generic. It could have been a woman or a well-meaning wuss or even a happily married man—I can handle all those. But what did I get? A god-damn *hero*. Thank heavens the vandal didn't get these." She indicated a flat of impatiens, which she set next to the lantana. "Not that they'll have much chance of survival at the customer's place, but—"

"Ah," Violet interrupted. "But he isn't a wuss or a woman, is he? He's a stud."

Ophelia hunched a shoulder. "He is pretty good-looking." Pretty well built, too, with a lovely calm voice and—

Can it.

Violet said, "Clearly it's a sign!"

Right. Fate again, flipping her the bird, dealing her another gorgeous male. Ophelia sighed and wiped the sweat off her brow, refusing to recall Gideon's strong hands mixing the plaster, the light breeze stirring the curls at the nape of his neck, the intoxicating aroma of pheromones in his sweat. Her eye alit on Gideon's bucket, three-quarters full of water, shining like a beacon in the afternoon sun. She picked it up and poured it over her head.

"Oh," Violet giggled. "I see."

Ophelia pushed her fangs back where they belonged and wrung out her T-shirt.

"You are a sorry mess," Violet said. "Turned on by your own blood, too, I suppose?"

Ophelia tossed two bags of cypress mulch into her truck. "I'm surviving. I've been hunting nutria."

"Ophelia, they're *rodents*! How vile!"

Ophelia shrugged. "They taste okay, and there's a bounty

on the pelts." She took a roll of duct tape and a pair of scissors from the bed of the pickup, letting her eyes roam once more toward Gideon, relaxed and calm as he questioned Donnie Donaldson. She shook her head. What was it about this cop? "It's probably just a hormone surge." She handed Violet the scissors and unrolled a length of tape.

Violet snorted. She cut the tape where Ophelia indicated.

"I've made it through twenty-nine ovulations without a man," Ophelia remarked, trying to sound proud. She caught Violet's eye and laughed. "I've kept track. Pathetic, I know." She stuck the tape around a cracked pot, good enough for a day or two's use, and unrolled some more.

"Angel, I can find you a donor, or better still, a transition man, at the snap of my fingers. The club's full of them. A little human blood goes so much further, and with some good lusty sex as well, you'll be able to think straight again." Violet cut a couple more pieces of tape.

"Vi, to be in transition you have to be transitioning *to* something. I'm finished with men. Done. And the duct tape's finished, too, damn it." Brightly, she added, "If I calculate twenty more years of regular periods, that's only two hundred forty more ovulations to survive without sex." Her half sister shuddered, but Ophelia went on. "Of course I have to add the hormone surges just before my periods and during menopause, so—"

"Stop!" Violet clutched her temples. "Just thinking about all that deprivation gives me a headache. How about a woman? You've never shown any interest that way, but there've been some lovely lesbians at the club lately—"

"Violet, I'm not going to sleep with anyone of either gender." Ophelia nestled a salvageable holly into one of the mended pots.

Violet shook her head and tut-tutted. "Angel, you simply must have either blood or sex. Depriving yourself of both is downright dangerous. You'll get careless and the wrong person will find out you're a vamp. It's not worth the hassle."

Eyes on Gideon, she asked, "Is he really a scumbag? Who is he supposed to be rescuing right now?"

Ophelia rolled her eyes, relieved at the change of subject. "It's a blackmail victim who won't come forward, and he's probably right that it's not officially his problem yet. But so what? He could at least make a push to find out who she is and help her, instead of hanging out here, pissing me off." *And turning me on.*

Violet giggled again. "I know, such an inconvenience. He could cause several hormone surges a day all on his own." She frowned. "How does he know about her, if she won't come forward?"

Ophelia arranged sixteen pots worth of monkey grass in a huge plastic tub. "She's a friend of his sister. It wouldn't be all that hard for him to find out who she is, even if his sister won't say. All he has to do is get hold of her phone for a few minutes, look at the recent calls, and go from there." She slung the plastic tub into her truck, set what was left of the monkey grass in a smaller tub for Donnie Donaldson, and set that aside. "The minute he got off the phone with his sister, he came on to me."

"Angel, you can hardly blame him for that. Everyone comes on to you. I know, I know, being irresistible sucks. What possessed you to call the police? You have other options."

"Temporary insanity," Ophelia said. "I came home and saw my garden and went ballistic. I suppose you mean I should have called Leopard, but I don't like the underworld's methods, and I'm tired of being beholden to him. I thought a cop would come by in a patrol car. I figured he'd go gaga over me and do what I told him and then leave—done, finished, a small but effective warning to my neighbor. No thugs, no violence, no crap. Instead I get a nosy detective in a frigging Mercedes." She uncoiled the hose and watered all the repotted plants. "I can't stand people meddling in my life. We have to distract him."

"You'll do it very nicely in that wet T-shirt," Violet laughed. "Especially since you're not wearing a bra." The other shoe dropped. "Your *neighbor* did this? Not Donnie, surely!"

"Of course not Donnie. Willy Wyler did it."

Zelda picked her way down the steps from the trailer, balancing a tray with a pitcher of iced tea, three cans of Coke, tall ice-filled glasses, lemon slices, mint sprigs, and the sugar bowl, and set it on the table with minimal clatter. "I am so good at this! Almost good enough to work at the club. What about Willy Wyler?"

"He's the one who trashed my garden." Ophelia shook open a green trash bag and shoved in handfuls of pine straw from a broken bale. "He lives in that big Colonial house."

"Willy Wyler, the guitarist?" Zelda's big blue eyes opened their widest. "That's Joanna Wyler's dad. In fact, there's Joanna in the yard with her little sister." She wrinkled her nose. "Is that really *her*?"

Ophelia looked at her niece, trying to keep her voice neutral. "Is Joanna a friend of yours?"

Zelda pursed her lips. "I've known her since kindergarten, but she's too preppy to be friends with me. I can't believe the clothes she has on. Nobody wears cutoffs anymore. And chartreuse? Majorly passé. I never would have believed she owned clothes like that."

"You're wearing cutoffs," Ophelia said. "And chartreuse."

"I'm ahead of the times," Zelda said. "I guess it would be tacky to go say hi. I mean, with her father vandalizing your place and all. Poor Joanna. Oh, she's seen me." Zelda waved wildly at Joanna, who raised a limp hand, then did a double take and dragged her little sister into the house.

"Whoa," Zelda said. "Major put-down. Soap-opera subplot: the tormented lives of troubled teens. Stay tuned for tomorrow's installment." She poured a glass of tea and offered it to her mother.

Ophelia tied the trash bag shut and tossed it into the truck bed. "Vi, I'll need to leave some plants at your place for a few days until this blows over." Damn, it burned her up to give in even an inch to harassment, but she couldn't let that cop get any more involved.

"Of course, angel. Here come the men. Don't hyperventilate, now. Maybe *you* could come and stay with us, too."

Ophelia glowered in response.

"That's an excellent idea," Gideon agreed as he came up, Donnie Donaldson following eagerly. The detective's eyes strayed over Ophelia and lingered on her breasts, then moved to Violet with scarcely a flicker. "Especially considering the dead cat."

"Jerk," Ophelia said under her breath.

"What?" Violet cried, slopping tea. "What dead cat? Not *Psyche?*"

"No, no, Psyche's fine. You're upsetting my sister for no reason," Ophelia growled through her teeth. "Not to mention my niece."

"Not at all," Gideon said, gaze back on Ophelia's breasts before coolly capturing her eyes. "They have every reason to be concerned about you, Ms. Beliveau." As if she were a mental case. Which was probably true, since she wanted to slug him and then fuck him into submission. But that was just her vamp gene speaking.

His phone rang and he flipped it open. "Yeah, Art, what is it now?" He retreated down the drive.

"Ophelia." Violet's voice had an edge to it now. "Tell me!"

"I'll frigging tell you later," Ophelia growled. "Better yet, ask Donnie. Zelda, pour Donnie some tea." She grabbed a Coke and popped it open, scowling in Gideon's direction. "Donnie, what did the cop ask you?"

Her neighbor dragged his eyes away from Violet long enough to take a glass. "Thanks, Zelda girl. Whether I saw anything, whether I thought Willy might have done it . . . That sort of thing."

"Of course he could have done it," Violet said. "He's been hitting on Ophelia forever."

"I told him that. Willy's a hot-tempered guy, too. But I got home just before Ophelia, so I didn't see nothing." He raised his chin toward a narrow driveway that disappeared into deep woods across the road. "He asked me who lives over yonder, and I told him Plato can't see nothing from his house, and he works evenings, so he's asleep all day."

Violet put an arm through Donnie's and steered him onto the lawn. "Tell me all about it. . . ." Smitten as always, Donnie let out a long ecstatic breath as they strolled away.

Zelda's eyes held a touch of moisture. "Am I allowed to give the cop some tea?"

"Oh, *sweetie*," Ophelia said. "Of course you are. Just because I'm pissed off with him doesn't mean you have to be rude." She put an arm around Zelda's bony shoulders and squeezed. "I'm being such a bitch, aren't I?" This was what fear did: screwed up everything, even the relationships with people you loved. "I can't think of a better way to get rid of him. I'm sorry about Joanna Wyler, too."

"No skin off my back," Zelda said. "I'll be nice to her. She'll get over being such a dope."

"You are really amazing," Ophelia said. "But don't be surprised if she's not nice back to you. Last week Wyler told me never to speak to his kids again. He wouldn't say why." She hunched her shoulders. "He and Lisa used to ask me to watch them sometimes. I don't know what's got into that family all of a sudden. This whole thing really stinks."

"Art, baby, no one's going to take her children away!"

Ophelia's heart clenched as Gideon's voice sounded clearly up the driveway. "Thanks for serving the drinks, sweetie," she told Zelda as the detective meandered back toward them, still talking. "I'd better get some work done."

She slopped through the mud into her ravaged garden and tossed a few woody turnip plants to the side, then worked her way along the flattened mounds row by row as Gideon spoke and listened and belittled his sister's concerns. Ophelia came to the marijuana just as the detective hung up, and she pulled back and gaped at the disgruntled little plants that she had certainly not put there. "Where the hell did these come from?" she muttered.

Gideon was suddenly beside her. "Your neighbor lady pointed them out to me." He ripped one from the mud and tossed it aside, sounding way too amused. "Of course, I have no proof either way who planted them, you or one of the Wylers, but—"

"If I had planted them, they would be healthy! So, are you going to arrest me?" She glared at him and bit her lip hard. Then her fangs slid down and she turned away.

"Of course not. I'm corrupt, remember?"

Her voice shaking traitorously, she said, "Right. I suppose I have to sleep with you instead."

"You'll *never* have to sleep with me."

Ophelia cringed at the disgust in the lawman's voice. Well, what did she expect? She had done her best to turn him off. Mission accomplished. She flung the remaining marijuana plants onto the mounting pile of debris.

Zelda, bless her, showed up with Oreos. "Help yourself, Mr. O'Toole. Are you gay?"

Ophelia sputtered, and Gideon blinked. "What? Why would you think that?"

"That person you were talking to. Art. You called him baby. That sounds gay to me."

"Artemisia." Gideon smiled down at her. "My little sister." He picked up two Oreos.

"Artemisia O'Toole," Zelda said. "Cool name. Have a cookie, Ophelia. Want one, Mom?"

Violet was hurrying toward them, the wriggling Psyche clutched to her breast and Donnie close behind. "Ophelia, are you sure you won't come and stay with me while this nice policeman takes care of things? Even better, why not sell your place to Donnie and move back to town? He'd be glad to buy it, wouldn't you, Donnie darling?"

"Be a bit of a pinch right this moment." Donnie glanced

at Violet, quivered deeply and visibly, and added, "But I can
find a way to swing it. Anything you need."

"Don't worry, Donnie," Ophelia said. "I'm not selling."
She couldn't.

Violet pouted. "You could run your landscaping business
just as well from town, and also come to the club sometimes.
It would be perfect!"

"No," Ophelia said. "I'm staying here."

Violet's sigh betrayed more than a hint of annoyance.
"When Ophelia speaks in that tone, it's a waste of time to
argue." She looked into Gideon's eyes with a gaze calculated
to enthrall. "Mr. O'Toole, before you leave, I need your advice about a suspicious visitor at my club."

Gideon strolled down the driveway beside Violet, wishing
he could brush her off the way she'd dismissed Donnie Donaldson, waiting for her to stop yammering so he could go
home. Not that he didn't sympathize with her. The clubs in
Bayou Gavotte were subject to endless scrutiny by moralizers
who believed they were dens of sin. Of course, some of the
clubs *were* dens of sin, but not, according to Violet, her pre-
cious Blood and Velvet.

"It's all tourists and posers, just silly people who want to
pretend they're vampires or watch other people pretend
they're vampires. What harm is there in that? We only serve
drinks and bar food. The only drugs are the ones the customers bring in, and of course we try to discourage *that*, but
what can we do? Certainly not confiscate every pill in everyone's purse or pocket! We have no whips and chains, no ju-
veniles, no spectator sex in back rooms like *some* places I
could name, and although vampire posers tend to get over-
excited and bite their dates, our emergency care is excellent."

"In other words," Zelda piped up from the side, "it's a sissy
club." In a darkling voice, she added, "But I still wish I could
work there. Five more long, long years."

Gideon grinned at Zelda. She was a nice kid, and her mother wasn't too bad, if only she'd lay off the sexy stuff, which was not only annoying but unnecessary, since she was drop-dead gorgeous. Maybe she'd been putting on this act for so long she didn't know how to stop. He tried to ignore the visceral effect it had on him, fortunately nowhere near as strong as Ophelia's. But Ophelia had gone inside, thank God, so now he could get his head straight and go home and never have to see her again.

At the thought of never seeing her again something twisted in his gut, but he ignored that, too. Never seeing her again was a consummation devoutly to be wished. Not the ideal to-be-wished-for consummation, but never mind. Once you got past the incredible sex, she'd undoubtedly be a bore. *Dogs, beer, steak.* That was the life.

"Get a private detective," he said, when Violet took a breath. "Some guy asking nosy questions at your club isn't a job for the police. He hasn't done anything disruptive or illegal, so start with a background check." He reached for the door handle of his Mercedes.

"We already did that," Violet said. "His story checks out. I hope he's not a Fed. They're such a nuisance, and we do *so* much better without them." She slipped her fingers through the crook in Gideon's arm and steered him back up the driveway.

That was for damn sure. Gideon didn't know by what means, fair or foul, the underworld had convinced the Feds to mind their own business. The arrangement with the local police was comfortable enough, although the chief still vacillated between unease at cooperating with Leopard and his goons and pride in Bayou Gavotte's reputation for safety.

"There's definitely something phony about him," Violet was saying.

"We're experts at spotting phonies," Zelda spoke up. "Like, you're not a phony. Like Ophelia's not. Like Lep's not. Like Mom acts like one but isn't. Like I bet preppy Joanna

Wyler wishes she didn't have to be. Like Constantine is, but he's okay underneath."

Christ. Teenyboppers hanging with vigilantes and rock stars. "You know Leopard and Constantine Dufray?"

"All the club owners do," Violet said. "And Lep does a wonderful job of keeping the clubs safe for tourists, but his idea of helping Ophelia would be to have that poor Wyler beaten up and thrown out of town. And no one in their right mind would ask Constantine for help."

"Actually," Zelda said, "it depends on the kind of help. He let me use him once for show-and-tell at school. That was a nonviolent activity, of course. We don't approve of violence, except when absolutely necessary." She spied Psyche under the truck and made kissy noises.

"That's why Ophelia called you," Violet told Gideon. "After Lep's thugs finished with Willy Wyler, they'd prowl around Ophelia's place, driving her crazy until they caught whoever did the cat thing"—she shuddered—"and do something *terrible* to him, which is probably what will happen now."

"He deserves to have something terrible done to him," Gideon said.

"I know, but you don't understand the effect Ophelia has on men!" Violet giggled. "Well, of course you do, but you're a stable person, not the type to get obsessed and violent and *stupid* about it." She sighed. "Ophelia's a sweet girl, although I suppose that's hard for you to believe, considering how she's treated you, but she's had some lousy experiences with men, and now she's moved out to the sticks with almost no neighbors and bought all these dreadful guns, and although I don't think she's ever actually shot anyone, I live in desperate fear that someday she will. And that would probably *destroy* her."

"Not to mention the dumbass she shoots," Gideon said. He guided Violet back down the driveway toward his car. And hers, which would have to be moved so he could get the hell out.

Violet stopped and cocked her head to one side. "No, she's an excellent shot. She'd just hit the poor guy in the foot or something, but she's naturally such a gentle person that . . . Try not to think too unkindly of her." She dimpled up at him. "Or to think of her at all. She's very stubborn. When she says no, she means it."

So am I stubborn, thought Gideon, moving inexorably toward the Mercedes. Not that stubbornness was likely to get him anywhere with Ophelia. Not that he wanted to get anywhere with her. Beer, dogs . . . oh, hell. He almost snarled, and Psyche hissed at him from the safety of Zelda's arms.

"Let me apologize on her behalf, too, because she won't. You can be sure of that." Violet let go of his sleeve and got in her car. "Please drop by the club as soon as you can. Take care of your sister's friend's blackmailer first, though. She's much worse off than we are."

"Right," Gideon said. "When the blackmailer's caught, you're tops on my list."

He drove away determined to put Ophelia, her sister, and his own sister firmly out of his mind, and within five minutes leaped up his front steps to the joyous welcome from the dogs in the fenced backyard. The phone was ringing, and he got the door open just as the answering machine finished its spiel.

Ophelia's voice came on, low and hesitant. He listened, transfixed, as she began her message, but by the time he reached the phone she had gone.

"I'm scum," Ophelia told herself as she turned on the shower. She had left the others in the driveway with a list of breezy excuses—an appointment for an estimate, a truck full of plants to deliver, and of course a life to get on with.

She squared her shoulders against the memory of the disgust in Gideon's voice. Which was ridiculous, as she should have been relieved at the success of her tactics, as well as grateful for Vi's efficient takeover. She soaped her hair and remembered Gideon walking beside Violet in total absorption, which just went to show he was scum, too, albeit gorgeous, sexy scum. She scrubbed her scalp furiously and rinsed with rage, and stepped out of the shower clean and still scummy and knew that whatever he might be, she couldn't leave it at that.

Both cars were gone, Gideon no doubt following Vi into town like a puppy on a string. Fine. Whatever. Ophelia toweled her hair and flipped through the phone book. *O'Toole, Artemisia . . . O'Toole, Gideon—Highway 43, Bayou Gavotte.* Far too close for comfort. She returned to the entry for Artemisia, which listed Olive Street, near one of her customers. Whatever.

She ran her finger under Gideon's number and picked up the phone. She only needed to show him she wasn't such a bitch as she had pretended. Which wouldn't change a thing, since he now viewed her with abhorrence, so what harm could one phone call do? Three rings and she heard his lovely, slow voice, but it was just a machine. She took a deep breath and waited for the beep. "Gideon—Mr. O'Toole, this is Ophelia Beliveau. I'm calling to say I'm sorry about that last remark I made. It was uncalled for and I apologize. Uh . . . good-bye." Pitiful, but at least she'd done it. Now, for that life she was so eager to get on with.

She dressed, gathered up her clipboard and a pamphlet on flagstone, and headed for her truck. Donnie Donaldson came across the ditch, carrying a two-by-four and a portable saw. "What's the cop gonna do?"

"Nothing," Ophelia said. "I told him to go away. You're going to fix my porch railing? Thanks!"

"No time like the present. Aren't you pressing charges?" He tut-tutted at the broken panes of her greenhouse.

"Of course not," Ophelia said. "I just want Willy to sit up and take notice. He must have been drunk or on drugs to do such a dumb thing. When he comes to his senses we'll discuss restitution." She dumped the clipboard and pamphlet on the passenger seat of her pickup, took the small tub of monkey grass and set it next to the ditch. "Keep this in your yard where Willy won't trash it, and I'll add it to your border in a day or two."

"Wonder why the cops sent a detective," Donnie mused, setting the two-by-four and the saw on one of the paving stones leading to her front steps. "I knew his parents. He lives down the river a ways."

Ophelia lifted her shoulder in a shrug.

"You know who he is, don't you?" Donnie took a tape measure and a pencil from his belt.

"Somebody or other O'Toole. So what?"

"He's *the* cop. The one who let Constantine Dufray off the hook."

"He didn't let him off the hook," Ophelia said irritably. She'd heard this nonsense far too often in the months since the rock star's wife had been poisoned. Considering that they owed them their safety, the people of Bayou Gavotte were ridiculously ready to believe the worst of Constantine and the other underworlders who often acted as the town's vigilantes. Come to think of it, her jibe at the cop this afternoon had been completely unwarranted. What had gotten into her? As a vamp she was hugely indebted not only to the vigilantes who protected her, but to the lawmen who turned a blind eye. "There was no evidence against Constantine to start with. He was hours away when his wife died."

Donnie shook his head. "I know he's a friend of yours, but where there's smoke there's fire." He scrawled dimensions on one of the boards.

Perhaps, but whatever deaths Constantine was responsible for, his wife's wasn't one of them. "Think what you like, Donnie," Ophelia said, "but watch what you say. Constantine's a friend of Violet's, too."

She got into her truck and headed toward a residential area fifteen minutes across town. Forty-five minutes later she escaped that prospective customer with a promise to return with a drawing of a winding path edged by flowering shrubs, and she drove into the crowded tourist area of downtown Bayou Gavotte. Her destination was the Impractical Cat, ostensibly to deliver plants for the patio, actually to warn Leopard off before he took matters into his own hands. By now Violet would certainly have called him.

Ophelia pulled the truck into the alley behind the restaurant. She entered the patio, still under construction, and deposited several pots of lantana in a corner. The door swung open. "Yee-haw, Ophelia!"

A rough hand whacked her on the butt, and Ophelia jabbed an elbow into the jerk whose paw was groping for her breast. "Fuck off, Burton." She kicked him in the shin for good measure. "Beat it, or I'll really hurt you."

Burton Tate laughed and rubbed his shin.

Inside, a waitress scurried by with pitchers of water and tea. "Hey, Marie," Ophelia called out. "Lep here?"

"In the office with Constantine." Marie motioned Ophelia aside. "Your number was in the men's again this morning. Lep had 'em paint over it, but . . ." She grimaced. "Sorry."

Ophelia shrugged. "Thanks for letting me know. Forewarned is forearmed."

"You can put my number up in the ladies' room anytime you want." Burton limped hurriedly past.

"Sure you want your number to be up, Burton?" Ophelia asked, and Marie guffawed. Ophelia continued down the hall to the lair of the drug-dealer-turned-drummer who controlled the underworld of Bayou Gavotte.

"Come in, girl." Leopard sighed, but Constantine Dufray shot her a grin. It was the Native American rocker's real smile, not the mesmerizing one his fans swooned over, which meant he was genuinely amused.

Leopard, on the other hand, was not. Ophelia threw herself into the easy chair in the corner and told him, "I left some lantana on the patio. I'll come back tomorrow or the next day to plant it."

"Uh-huh," Leopard said. "You're a pain in the ass."

"And you're a thug. So what?"

Constantine grinned again. "Cappuccino, vampire babe? Good elbow on Burton, by the way. Solid kick." He laid his guitar below the one-way glass that showed the back hall, stretched like a languid cat, and went to the espresso machine on a table by the wall.

"Thanks—and kindly shut up," Ophelia said. "Listen, Lep, I'm sorry if I hurt your feelings. I wanted to get through this without anyone beaten up."

"That lowlife Wyler deserves to be beat up," Leopard grunted. He tugged at his dreads and untied the grubby leather thong holding them back.

"Blood? Or just mocha?" Constantine pumped in some chocolate syrup.

"Shut up, Constantine," Ophelia repeated. "Lep, I want to stay on good terms with my neighbors. Also, Wyler's kids don't need to see their dad trashed. Let me handle this my way."

"When some moron's hanging death threats on your door? Not a chance." Leopard flicked the thong between strong brown fingers. "None of this matters. What matters is you dissed Gideon O'Toole."

Surprised, Ophelia said nothing. She sank lower into her chair and scowled. "I should have known he'd be a friend of yours. What'd he do, come whining to you?"

Leopard snorted. "You're the one doing the whining, girl. He's not a friend, exactly. He's the buffer between me and our sorry excuse for a police chief, and he deserves some respect. From what Vi told me, you treated him like dirt. Of course, she might have been pissed because he wouldn't play with her. Not one to be led around by his dick."

Ophelia tried to ignore the lightening of her heart. Not many turned down her half sister's advances. "I called and apologized. Left him a message."

Constantine whistled. He poised whipped cream over the coffee cup.

"Shut up," Ophelia responded. "Yes, please."

Leopard was grinning now. "Not your style, apologizing to a guy who comes on to you."

"I was way out of line," Ophelia admitted. She took a cream-covered cinnamon-sprinkled cappuccino from Constantine. "I freaked out. I was expecting some doofus I could dazzle and then send away. I didn't want a nosy detective."

"You shouldn't have called him, then," Lep said.

"I didn't call *him*," Ophelia snapped, then rolled her eyes. "Anyway, I got rid of him, so hold off about Willy Wyler. He didn't do the cat thing, and I want to talk to him and his wife before you send in your thugs. As for the cat—"

"You didn't get rid of him," Lep interrupted. "Gideon called a couple of minutes ago. Told me he'd take care of you."

Oh God, yes, thought Ophelia. *Oh God, no.* "I don't want a cop looking into my life . . . and I know, I know—I shouldn't have called him, then."

Leopard spread his hands. "Since Gideon wants to handle your little problem, and since I don't intend to step on his toes, you're on your own . . . unless he finds a reason to clap the cuffs on you."

"Of course, it depends *why* he's clapping on the cuffs," Constantine interjected. When Ophelia shot him the bird, the rocker laughed, retrieved his guitar, and fiddled with the tuning pegs. "Exactly. And why not? He's a red-blooded guy, and you need it bad."

She couldn't deny the last. "You can't expect me to jump into bed with some man I hardly know."

"I know him," Leopard replied. "He's a good guy. Go for it."

"What if I don't *want* to sleep with him?"

Lep and Constantine laughed so hard they almost fell off their chairs.

Ophelia fumed, waiting till they'd had their fill. "I see Vi's been busy today. I can't believe you're abandoning me like this."

"You asked for it," Leopard said, still chuckling. "I wish I could be there when he finds out you're a vamp. As far as I know, he's not into anything bent."

"Look on the bright side," Constantine added. "No thugs after Willy, just like you want. I may take care of the cat dude myself, though, once your cop figures out who it is. Just for fun." His fingers trickled across his guitar strings. "I need a break from the stress of rock and roll."

"Shut up," Ophelia said one more time, sinking farther into her chair. "What am I going to do? The last thing I need is a cop looking over my shoulder!"

Constantine shrugged. "For a vamp, you lead a hell of a clean life." When Ophelia said nothing, the rocker's eyes darkened a tad, and she wondered not for the first time how much he knew. Or guessed. "But since you're worried," he continued, "why not distract him with sex?"

"He's not that easy to distract," Leopard said. "He's a persistent dude."

"In which case, he'll persist about the sex," Constantine said. "Once he's fucked Ophelia, what's the chance he'll lock her up?"

"Zilch," Leopard said. "Not in jail, anyway."

"Since neither of you perverts has slept with me," Ophelia grumped, "there's no way you can know that."

The two perverts laughed themselves silly.

Ophelia waited for them to cool it and sipped at her coffee, terror and desire battling within her. She licked at the disappearing mound of whipped cream and contemplated licking Gideon. She thought about sinking her fangs deep inside him. She thought about Gideon sinking himself deep inside *her*. Then she remembered the last man she'd bitten, and nausea sucker punched her. She sat up and put the cup carefully on the floor.

"Oh, shit," she said, clutching her stomach. "I'm so scared."

"Gotta move ahead sometime." For a man with a rep for violence—not that he had ever been caught—Constantine's voice was surprisingly gentle. "You can't—"

"Be ruled by fear," she agreed. "I know."

CHAPTER THREE 🌷

Men and their dumb bondage jokes, thought Ophelia. *Not that Vi's much help. Oh God, what am I going to do?*

Definitely not whine that nobody understands me, she told herself, although she had a feeling that Constantine, brutal though he might be, understood all too well, especially after the death of his estranged wife and the media kerfuffle that followed. But face it: a pair of vigilantes and a sister with absent sexual mores didn't make the grade as life-choice advisers. Sleep with him, they all said. Why not?

Apart from the fact that I met him only a few hours ago? Because I can feel my past poised to destroy me.

Dumb and dramatic, but that didn't make it any less true. Ophelia drove away from the center of town, with its tourists and clubs, to one of the older, oak-lined residential sections of Bayou Gavotte. Even setting her appalling past aside, it was obnoxious to distract a guy with sex unless you intended to deliver. A rush of longing shot through her. Lord, did she ever want to deliver. But there had to be another way to distract him, to buy some time.

She puttered down Olive Street to her client Andrea Dukas's house, took a left at the cross street, and pulled around to the back gate to park beside their new minivan. The rear doors of the vehicle gaped wide, revealing a stroller, a folded baby cot, and several suitcases stowed any which way. On the ground behind the car stood five potted azaleas. Andrea had likely found a so-called bargain at the hardware store again.

"Miss Ophelia!" Two little girls tumbled across the lawn, ponytails flying, pink backpacks bumping on their shoulders. "We're running away!"

Ophelia settled her hostas and the flats of annuals in the shelter of the fence. "Sure you want to do that? Your sister and brother will miss you."

"They're running away, too. So is Mom."

The eldest Dukas girl tottered toward Ophelia carrying her year-old brother. She gasped a hello, dumped little Simon in his car seat, and hollered at the twins to get in the van.

Had Andrea and her husband split up? Impossible. "Where are you going?"

One of the twins began, "To G—"

"Shut up!" her older sister shrieked. "Mom said not to tell *anyone*." She sniffled woefully. "I'm sorry, Miss Ophelia. I didn't mean to be rude."

"That's okay." Now Andrea was staggering toward them with a cooler, while a tall, dark-haired woman who looked somewhat familiar juggled cups, sandwiches, three Tupperware containers, and an overflowing tote. Ophelia frowned at the tear tracks on Andrea's cheeks and the other woman's grim face. She said, "Sorry if it's a bad time. I came to drop the plants for tomorrow."

Andrea's face puckered. "Didn't you get my message? You'll have to take the plants back, because everything's gone wrong and I can't afford you anymore." She struggled to hold back tears. "I bought some azaleas and tried to return them, but they w-wouldn't take them and now you can't even plant them for me, so they'll die!" She slung the cooler into the van, sobbing, and slammed the doors.

First time ever, thought Ophelia: a good excuse to not plant stressed plants that had been overfed and would probably die anyway, and she couldn't use it. "Of course I'll plant them. At least then they'll have a chance of survival. I'll plant the ones I brought, too, and you can pay me whenever. No rush."

Tears gushed out as Andrea got into the driver's seat. "We'll never be able to pay you. We'll have to sell the house and live in a *trailer*." She blanched. "I'm sorry!"

"For cripes sake, Andrea, like I care about that." What the hell was going on?

Andrea yelled at her kids about seat belts while her friend distributed cups and sandwiches and lifted the tote through the window. Two dog-eared photographs fell out.

Andrea's voice rose in panic. "Oh, no! What if some fell on the lawn or in the house?"

Her friend retrieved the photos. "I'll check everywhere. Once you're gone, I'll call my brother and fess up."

"Not until I'm across the state line! What if he starts snooping and asks about me?" Andrea's red-rimmed eyes were drowned in tears.

The friend shot a glance at Ophelia and back at Andrea. "Unlikely. He never talks to me unless he absolutely has to."

"Anything I can do to help?" Ophelia asked.

"No." The friend followed this hostile monosyllable with a grudging "Thank you."

"I wish." Andrea gave Ophelia a wavering smile. "Your advice totally transformed my . . ." She mouthed "sex life" as she took the photos. "Come to think of it, Art, you should talk to Ophelia. About you know what. And you know who."

Art stiffened. "You'd better get going." She stood away from the car, and Andrea drove off. Ophelia took a good long look at Art, who glared back.

Perfect: a way to distract Gideon. With detective work, not sex.

"You're being blackmailed. *Both* of you, right?"

* * *

Gideon hung up the phone, picked it up again, dropped it back in its cradle and himself on the couch. The world slowed, stopped, and started spinning again. The right way this time.

"She won't apologize," Violet had said. She had been dead wrong. And he had been right. For once, his instincts hadn't let him down. But then, where sex was concerned they never did. In that long moment when Ophelia stared at him before turning away, there had been heat in her eyes. She'd been trying for disdain, sure, but the longer she'd looked, the more the desire had come through.

Hot damn, thought Gideon, but sobered himself immediately. This woman was nothing but trouble. He ran his fingers through his hair and tried to get his head straight. The yowling of the dogs penetrated his whirling brain. He let them inside and greeted them automatically, popped open a beer, and took a steak out of the fridge. Hot damn. He could use that kind of trouble.

Whistling, he took the charcoal and the lighter onto the porch to start the barbecue. *Take it slowly,* he told himself. *Check into the vandalism and the dead-cat thing. Find out who did what, and make sure neither happens again. Easy. Meanwhile, figure out what makes Ophelia Beliveau tick.*

While the coals heated, he cut a ripe tomato into thin slices and popped a potato in the microwave. He trimmed the fat off the steak and tossed it to the dogs. *First things first,* he decided as he laid the steak gently on the grill. He leaned against the porch rail and dialed the dispatcher at home.

"Uh-oh," Jeanie said when she answered the call. She chuckled. "Hi, Gideon."

"You set me up," he accused cheerfully. "I'll forgive you on one condition."

"Ooh," Jeanie said. "Anything you like. Is Ophelia as sexy as they say?"

"As who say?"

"Her sister. The guys that hang out at Blood and Velvet. The lowlifes who write her number on men's room walls."

"Jesus." He blew out a long breath.

"Violet says that'll stop if she gets a man of her own. She says Ophelia projects too much if she's not getting any. So when Ophelia called, naturally the first person I thought of was you."

"I hope you don't expect me to be flattered."

"Oh, no," Jeanie laughed. "You may look like a romance hero, but you're actually a pain in the patootie. We want you defeated. Roped and tied and helpless."

"I doubt if Ms. Beliveau's into bondage," Gideon said. "Listen, babe, did anybody follow Willy Wyler around?"

Jeanie switched gears briefly. "Nope. He never showed up on the road to town, but I found out he has a gig at the Chamber tonight. Maybe he turned off through the golf course they're building or one of the ritzy new subdivisions out there. That's real close to Ophelia's. You're interested in her, huh?"

"I'm sure every man who sees her is interested," Gideon said discouragingly. "She has a ton of sex appeal. Well, gotta go."

"She won't give you the time of day, right? Fabulous. You'll have to go through hardship to win her. I can hardly wait to tell Art. Which reminds me."

Here we go. He closed his eyes and held the phone away from his ear, picked up his fork, and turned the steak. *Women.* He looked at the three female dogs gazing patiently and adoringly up at him. No nagging, and so easily satisfied. On the other hand, no sex appeal whatsoever.

"If she does give you the time of day," Jeanie was saying, "which she probably will sooner or later—although God knows why, because you're so arrogant and obnoxious, and you'd better help that poor woman who's being black-mailed—"

"You *are* going somewhere with this, I hope?"

"If she falls for you, Gideon, you'd better treat her right. Violet says she's had bad experiences with men. Real bad."

"Jeanie, don't think I don't appreciate your efforts, but I'm comfortable being arrogant and obnoxious. Go find Ophelia some guy who's in touch with his feminine side. I'm not the therapist type. I can't even get through a phone call with my sister, much less a relationship with a woman who's sworn off men."

"If you knew what she'd been through, you'd be more understanding," Jeanie urged. "You keep saying you've lost your instincts for people, but it's your own lazy fault. How can you relate to people if you never have relationships? It must be so lonely out there with just a bunch of dogs. Tell you what. I'll find out all about her and let you know."

Gideon sighed. "Suit yourself, Jeanie. Gotta go." He hung up and put the perfectly seared meat on a plate, and the three dogs clustered close, tongues hanging out. "No way I'm lonely." He proceeded to share his steak.

An hour later, he left the two old German shepherds, Daisy and Belle, to sleep off their meal in the shade of the river birch that dominated his back yard, and whistled Gretchen into the car. She was a good companion on patrol, pretty patient if left in the vehicle, friendly with kids, disarming to most adults.

He turned out of his driveway onto the road and addressed his canine companion. "So, Gretchen, you're the closest I have to a feminine side. How should I play this?"

Gretchen turned her shaggy blonde face away and stared out the window.

"It's got to be a game. She played me the whole time. I'm not saying I didn't enjoy some of it, but still . . . it was definitely a game. The thing I don't get is why. If she wanted me, she could have had me. If she didn't, why suck me back in?"

Gretchen lolled her tongue out the window.

"She didn't have to offer me a Coke," he continued. "She didn't have to tell me about the dead cat."

Gretchen brought her head inside and nipped at her matted flank.

"Nervous as hell, too, but it's not like I tried to jump her. Pretty much all I did was smile." Gretchen snorted, and he said, "Most women *like* my smile. Should I try and impress her? And if so, how?"

Gretchen hunched a shoulder and returned to the window. "What about the vandalism? Willy or his wife?"

It doesn't matter. You need to show Ophelia your caring, compassionate side. Unless you want to end up like your old man.

Gideon squelched this thought as he did any suggestion, by himself or anyone else, that he resembled his father in anything other than build and hair color. He made a right off Highway 43, musing, "Lep says Willy's been cheating on his wife since day one, and she doesn't care as long as she's got her house, her fancy car, and designer clothes for herself and her preppy kids. It's not as if Ophelia's interested in the jackass."

As he neared Ophelia's place, Gideon's pulse quickened— dumb, since she probably wouldn't be home yet. He'd just drop by to see if the plaster cast was still there. Not that it mattered much, but if a woman could shake his composure to the extent that he forgot evidence, he needed to do some serious personal reevaluation. Or just have sex with her and get it over with.

"Lep usually knows what he's talking about," he told Gretchen. "He also told me if I do anything to hurt Ophelia, Constantine will kill me slowly while he cheers him on."

Gretchen yawned.

"And here I thought you cared. I guess that means I can't just have sex with her and get it over with." He scratched behind Gretchen's right ear. "I wonder what she is to Constantine. I don't like the idea of her having anything to do with him."

He slowed the Mercedes and turned into Ophelia's driveway. A girl of twelve or thirteen, dressed in a chartreuse tank and cutoffs uncannily like Zelda's but on a far more mature figure, whirled from a crouch in the wasted garden. A smaller girl cast in the same mold of creamy skin and blonde curls stood beside her. Trying his damnedest to look unthreatening, Gideon parked and got out. Gretchen lolloped over to the mud patch to say hello.

"Meet Gretchen," Gideon said.

The younger Wyler sister smiled angelically and threw her arms around the dog's neck, but the elder stared at Gideon, her lip wobbling. Jeez. The last thing he wanted was to scare her.

"You want the plaster cast?" he asked. "Hold on, I'll get a box for it out of my trunk so it won't get broken."

Tears welled in the older girl's eyes. "You don't want it? You're not gonna arrest my dad?"

"Nah." Gideon fetched a cardboard box, giving her time, praying she wouldn't cry.

"But . . . why not?"

He smiled. "Ms. Beliveau doesn't want me to."

The girl let out a shuddering sigh and fiddled with a pentagram on a gold chain against her chest. "Are you going to see Ophelia again?" The girl's moist eyes pleaded with him.

Hell, yes. "Sure." *Just don't cry.* "What's your name?"

"Joanna Wyler. That's my sister." Joanna fished a grubby tissue from her pocket and blew her nose. She scowled at the younger girl. "Connie, don't rub your face all over that dog. That's gross."

"Is not," Connie retorted. "Come on, Gretchen. Come meet Psyche."

"Dummy," Joanna said. "Psyche's a cat. Dogs and cats don't mix."

"Do too." Connie skipped toward the trailer, and Gretchen trotted cheerfully beside her.

Joanna said, "I'm not allowed to speak to Ophelia anymore. Tell her I'm really, really sorry, and can you give her this?" She fingered the delicate chain but didn't remove it.

"It's Zelda's. I found it in the driveway." Her fingers gripped the pentagram, and she took a deep, longing breath. "I wish I could be Zelda. She's so lucky. She's so cool."

"Psyche!" Connie cooed at the edge of the house.

The gray cat picked her way daintily from beneath the trailer, her yellow eyes lit on Gretchen, and she came to a complete stop. Stared. Took a few more steps, and Gretchen stretched forward, nostrils quivering. Elegantly, the two female animals touched noses. Psyche sidled past Gretchen's leg and meowed at Connie.

"Told you," the child said. "Gretchen's a girl. Psyche only hates *boys*."

Joanna's chin wobbled. "See, I'm wrong again. I'm such a failure. Zelda's never wrong. And her mom owns a club. I'll never get to go to a club."

God help me, Gideon thought, *she's going to blubber.*

"And she doesn't have these awful boobs," Joanna wailed. "My life is so over."

Jesus. Gideon blinked at Joanna's chest, which he had tried not to notice bulging in her too-small tank top. What the hell did you say to a kid? Nice rack? This was why he wasn't a therapist. "There's nothing wrong with your breasts."

The girl blushed. "I can't do gymnastics anymore. They bounce too much, and the boys stare at me at school." She blushed even more. Why had she picked him to unload on?

Joanna hurried on, unstoppable. "It absolutely sucks. I wish I was skinny like Zelda. She can wear anything she wants. She can *do* anything she wants."

"Give Zelda time," Gideon said. "Look at her mom and Ophelia." *Very nice racks.* "Genetics will catch up with Zelda sooner or later."

"She won't have to dress all preppy and boring," Joanna continued bitterly. "How old is old enough to have sex?"

Christ. Where were the girl's parents? "When you're grown up," Gideon said sternly. "When you find some guy you love. You shouldn't even be thinking about it now. Ignore the boys. They're gonna look, 'cause that's what boys do, but that's all they should be doing for several more years."

"That's what Ophelia said." Tears glistened in the kid's eyes. "She probably hates me now. Zelda hates me, too. Not that she was ever my friend, but now she'll never speak to me again." Resolutely, she pulled the necklace over her head. "Please take this to Ophelia. She can give it back to Zelda."

Gideon ignored her outstretched hand. "Why not give it to Zelda yourself when you see her at school? It's not your fault your dad vandalized Ophelia's place."

Joanna shook her head, lip wobbling. The tears rolled down her cheeks. Gideon dug in the side pocket of his Mercedes and handed Joanna a napkin. She blew her nose and wiped her eyes.

"Listen," Gideon said. "Ophelia doesn't hate you, and Zelda won't hold it against you." Memory thwacked him with inspiration. "She understands what a bore it is to be a prep. Go talk to her." *Go cry all over her. This is why I avoid domestic calls. Give me a nice clean homicide any day.* "You'll see."

Joanna clutched the pendant dramatically to her chest as if it linked her to Zelda's magic. Words tumbled out. "My dad didn't do the cat thing, I promise. That was really creepy. He'd never do anything like that. Please make sure Ophelia knows."

"I'll tell her," said Gideon gently. "Any idea who might have done it?"

Joanna shook her head. "No. No way. People like Ophelia. She's so nice." A spasm of misery crossed her face.

Gideon squatted in the mud, picked up the now-dry plaster cast, and turned it upside down into the box. "Did your mom send you to get this?"

Joanna nodded. "She's all mad 'cause my dad went to buy tires we can't afford. You're not gonna arrest Ophelia either, huh? Because of the marijuana, I mean. My dumb dad planted it. He figured if she called the cops, they'd see it and arrest her. My mom told him that was stupid."

Yep, thought Gideon. "Ophelia might not be so forgiving if this happens again. Can we get your parents and Ophelia together to discuss it?"

Panic flashed across Joanna's face. "No! We gotta go." A battered white van turned into the driveway two doors down. "Oh, no!" she moaned. "Did they have to show up now? I look awful when I've been crying!"

Yep, thought Gideon again, eyeing the vaguely familiar young man emerging from the passenger door.

"Joanna's got a *boyfriend*," Connie sang.

"I do not." Joanna scowled.

A second man, several years older and with daggers tattooed on each arm, appeared around the front of the van. "That's Burton Tate," Gideon said.

"You know him and his brother?" Joanna clasped her hands ecstatically in front of her breasts. "Aren't they fabulous?"

Nope. "I went to school with Burton," Gideon said. "The kid's his baby brother?"

"Gabe," Connie said. "Gabe's a babe."

Joanna rounded on her sister. "Shut up!" She blew her nose fiercely. "Our dad has a gig with their band. At a club. It's not fair!"

The younger man noticed Joanna, waved, and grinned. Joanna turned brilliant red and waved shyly in return. The older brother stared for a second, then whacked Gabe on the shoulder and led him toward the house. A few seconds later the brothers returned carrying a guitar case and a battered cardboard box. That idiot Wyler had clearly forgotten his equipment.

Gideon raised a hand to Burton, who nodded and swung back into the van. They drove off and Joanna said, "We better go home. Connie has gym class. Thanks for the plaster cast. It'll calm my mom down. She's a bit of a wreck right now."

Pathetic, thought Gideon, as he let Gretchen into the car and got in himself. He backed into the turnaround. Perfectly good kids stuck covering for stupid parents, trying to navigate puberty with no guidance at all. There were drugs involved, probably, but no way would he harass the children to find out.

He took a right onto the road and an immediate left into the gravel drive of the only other neighbor for a good quarter mile. He watched in his rearview mirror as the Wyler girls trooped home, Joanna cradling the box, Connie running back to pet Psyche three times before finally catching up. At the end of the long drive, which led into the woods, Gideon pulled up before a single-wide trailer of the same vintage as Ophelia's but in far worse repair. "You don't need to go across there," Donnie Donaldson had told him earlier. "Plato's real weird, and he can't see nothing from his place."

No vehicle stood before the house. Plato must have left already for the evening job Donnie had mentioned. Gideon strode up the steps to peer through the front door and knock. When no one answered, he turned his Mercedes around and rolled slowly back the way he had come.

About thirty feet before the end of the drive, invisible from the road but in full view from where he sat, was a deer stand high up in an oak. Gideon put on the emergency brake and followed a well-used path to the base of the tree. A rope ladder lay coiled on a branch twelve feet over his head. Gideon circled the oak, found the end of a single rope a foot above his head, and reached up to pull it. The rope ladder tumbled obligingly down.

The platform was tidy and bare but for a pair of rusty shears hanging on a nail. Thanks to careful pruning, the view of Ophelia's place was damn near perfect.

CHAPTER FOUR 🌷🌷

Art paled. "How do you know about the blackmail?" Her dark eyes and strong features, familiar yet different on a female face, hardened with hostility.

"Wow," Ophelia blurted. "You are so obviously Gideon's sister."

"Unbelievable!" Art fumed. "He's been blabbing to one of his bimbo girlfriends!"

Bimbo girlfriends? This was the kind of man who had finally caught her fancy? "I am not one of your stupid brother's girlfriends," Ophelia gritted out.

The woman's eyes narrowed. "My brother's not stupid! The bimbos are."

Ophelia fought annoyance. "I only met him this afternoon."

"So what?" Art said. "I've been told he moves fast."

Ophelia could imagine. "Whatever he may have done with any number of bimbos, he didn't blab anything to me."

"Then how do you know?"

"My garden got vandalized today, and they sent Gideon to check it out. I overheard him talking to you about someone being blackmailed."

"Wonderful." Art threw up her hands and stomped across the lawn toward Andrea's house.

Ophelia gave chase. "What are you going to do about it?"

Art whirled. "It doesn't matter. You can't help, so forget

it." She took the stairs two at a time, scooped a stray photo off the porch, and went inside.

Ophelia followed. "Of course I can help. Lord, what a mess."

"I promised I'd clean up," Art said. "It about killed Andrea to leave an untidy house."

"I'll do the bedrooms."

Ophelia set to work without giving Art a chance to object. Sooner or later, she would feel compelled to get whatever it was off her chest. Women with screwed-up love lives couldn't help confiding in vamps; it was one of the perks of the vampire gene. Not that Ophelia felt the least bit qualified to dispense advice, but blackmail she could deal with.

Art banged and clattered at the kitchen sink, but gradually the clamor lessened and the aroma of coffee wafted through the house. Ophelia put a load of towels in the washer and went to the kitchen. Gideon's sister slumped at the table over a mug of coffee, moodily gazing at a bowl of fruit. "It's not fair." She rearranged the apples and pears. "It's not illegal to pose nude."

"No," Ophelia encouraged her. "It isn't."

"I modeled for the art school to make extra money, and some creep took pictures without me knowing."

Ophelia poured herself coffee. "Icky."

"I'm a high-school art teacher. He threatened to tell the principal."

"The principal can't fire you for that."

"And send copies to all the male students at Bayou Gavotte High."

"Holy shit," Ophelia said, and dropped into a chair.

Art posed bunches of grapes over the apples. She took a long swallow of coffee and draped a banana along the side of the bowl.

"Did Andrea pose, too?"

"No!" A solitary apple remained on the table. Art took it

in one hand and the stem in the other, and twisted until the stem came off. "Big Simon took a picture of her nursing little Simon. She's naked and so is the baby. The blackmailer's threatening to report her to Children's Services."

"For what?"

"Using her baby for sexual gratification."

"That's crap!" Ophelia said. "They can't take her kids away because of one perfectly innocent picture."

"You'd be surprised. The world is full of prudish Neanderthals. I know. I was married to one." Art reached into a drawer for an apple corer. "We know the blackmailer's connected with the print and photo shop, but we're not paying him one red cent. Andrea's gone to her mom's. Big Simon's out of town on business. I'm going to tell my brother about me, nothing about Andrea, and he'll shun me even more than he already does, but he'll arrest the guy and it'll be over with." Her voice trembled. "If the pictures get out, I'll give up teaching. Maybe I really *am* an exhibitionist. My ex certainly thought ɔ. Oh, and I like hugging my students, too. That definitely makes me a pervert. I'll go tend bar in a vampire club, and my students can sneak in and leer at me, and the hell with everyone."

Ophelia grimaced. "You want to work in a club?"

Art banged a cutting board on the table. "You have a problem with that?"

"Of course not. My sister owns one." She frowned. "Do you like teaching? Do you really want to give it up?"

Tears glistened at the corners of Art's eyes. "What difference does that make?" She set the apple carefully in the middle of the board.

"It makes all the difference," said Ophelia. "You can't let some asshole destroy your career. I only met Gideon today, but I'm sure he wouldn't want that!"

Art poised the corer over the apple. "You want to know what'll happen when I tell him?" She lowered her voice and imbued it with obnoxious, patronizing patience. "'Why did you have to pose nude, Art? That was asking for trouble. In fact, why did you divorce Steve? He's a perfectly nice guy.' Shit. Shit!" She jammed the corer down on the apple and caught her little finger underneath. Blood welled up, red and juicy and irresistible.

Ophelia grabbed Art's hand and clamped her mouth around the bloody finger, closing her eyes to savor every drop. The cut sealed shut. It was the crowning moment of a perfectly stupid day.

Gideon stopped the Mercedes at a light. "What next? Her sister or mine?"

Gretchen opened one eye and shut it again.

"Fortunately, the pervert's watching Ophelia, not those kids," Gideon said. "Which I wouldn't have thought a positive, but at least Ophelia can defend herself." He ruminated a moment. "Joanna's a hormonal catastrophe. Add peer pressure, a hefty dose of guilt, and a crush on a dude in his twenties." Women. Life would be so simple without them.

It struck him, quite suddenly, that his father must have come to the same conclusion. He continued in uneasy silence to the main intersection in downtown Bayou Gavotte. Ahead was the Impractical Cat, but he didn't need to see Leopard yet. To the left were most of the clubs in his kinky little hometown, including Blood and Velvet, Violet's club. Not much happened till after dark, however, so he made a right toward the residential area where Artemisia lived.

As Zelda opened the door she saw Joanna Wyler flinch. *Wimp*, she thought, but she felt sorry for the girl and so bathed the poor preppy thing in a friendly smile. "Hey, come on in." She wiped her flour-covered hands on the frilly pink apron she'd had since she was a kid.

"I can't." Joanna gulped. "I just came to bring your necklace. I found it in Ophelia's driveway."

"Thank you!" Zelda took the pentagram on its chain and

gave Joanna a hug. "That's so sweet of you." She scanned the street. "How'd you get here?"

"Mom dropped me at the coffee shop. I'm supposed to do homework while my sister's at gymnastics." Joanna glanced nervously toward the street.

Zelda shrugged. Waited. Smiled.

"Mom would absolutely kill me if she knew I was here," Joanna added.

Go, then, Zelda thought, but she said, "What she doesn't know won't hurt her. Sure you don't want to come inside? I'm making cookies."

The other girl shook her head so fast that Zelda had to bite her lip to keep from laughing. Zelda waited again, wondering whether Joanna would speak or pass out from holding her breath. Finally, the words rushed out. "Can you give Ophelia a message?"

"No problem." Suddenly Zelda wished her mother were home, wished even more that Joanna didn't look so needy. "What is it?"

"It's 'cause my mom won't let me talk to her anymore."

"Big drag," Zelda said. "What's the message?"

"I feel so bad," Joanna mumbled. "I really *like* Ophelia."

"Everybody does," Zelda agreed, and then it hit her that Joanna's confessional mood might be something her mother had predicted. For some bizarre reason, screwed-up women had an urge to confide in vampires. Not that she knew whether she was going to be a vamp or not, but either way, she might be able to solve a mystery for Ophelia. "I could do with a coffee," she said. "The cookies can wait." She tossed her apron on the floor, wrote a note to her mom, grabbed her knapsack, and pulled the door shut behind her.

"Whoops," Ophelia said, feigning unconcern. "My bad. Look on the bright side. You won't need a bandage now." She sucked her fangs back into their slots while Art stared, eyes wide.

"Oh, my God." Gideon's sister glanced dazedly from Ophelia to her finger and back. "You're a vampire! That's so cool."

"Not particularly." Ophelia examined the apple and ate the slice stained with Art's blood.

"Does Andrea know?" Art still goggled.

"No, and neither would you if I hadn't screwed up just now. I don't exactly advertise." Through her vexation, Ophelia heard Vi's voice: *You'll get needy and then careless.* She'd been right. But Violet's proffered donor or transition man was not the right way to go.

Meanwhile, Art had turned into a goddamned tourist. "Show me your fangs again! How do you make them go in and out of your gums?"

Cripes. Ophelia showed her how the fangs worked. "I can slide them up and down on purpose, but they tend to come out on their own if I smell or taste blood." Or get angry. Or turned on.

"Fabulous! I always hoped vampires were real. Oh, my God, you just drank my blood! And the cut's totally healed. How did you do that?"

Ophelia sighed. "My spit heals small wounds pretty much instantly."

"Wow. You're not dead, are you? Will I turn into something weird?"

Ophelia rolled her eyes. "Of course not. It's just some genetic thing. Apart from the fangs, I'm completely normal." Except for the night vision and the ultrasensitive hearing and the exaggerated sense of smell. And the special spit. And—

"But you're irresistible, right?" Art giggled. "I knew the stories were true! For once, I was right and Gideon was wrong! He said it was just some dumb perversion."

Ophelia disregarded the lead weight punching into her heart. "Good. The more people who believe that, the better. We vamps have enough problems as it is." She paused. "I need you to keep your mouth shut."

"So . . . ," Art said, as if she hadn't heard a word. "What did Gideon think of you?"

"What difference does it make?" Ophelia asked irritably. "He had the same reaction as any other man. Since he's obviously not shy where women are concerned, he hit on me the first chance he got. I told him where to go. Now, promise you won't tell anyone I'm a vamp. It's for your own safety as much as mine."

"Does Gideon know?"

She glared at Artemisia's growing grin. "No, and he doesn't need to. I called the cops as a warning to the guy who vandalized me, period. I don't need any more help. But Gideon's not taking no for an answer. He's acting like I need protection, investigating stuff I can take care of myself. If he finds out I'm a vamp, he'll be even worse."

"Gideon? No way. It'll scare the hell out of him. He may look sexy, but he's very conventional." Art laughed, suddenly full of mischief. "If you want to get rid of him, show him those fangs."

"Fine." Just fine. But . . . "I don't want to scare him off yet. If we set a trap for the blackmailer, we'll need him to take care of the evidence against you and Andrea."

"Destroy it, you mean? That's illegal!"

"Maybe not, if the only charge is blackmailing me."

"You? No way." Art stood and poured more coffee. "It's not worth the risk."

"Why not? There may be a slew of other innocent victims. We'll give Gideon something more important to think about than whoever vandalized me."

"It's a lousy idea." Art set her mug down and paced back and forth. "What will you do, get someone to take compromising pictures of you? You're running a small business. You'll be as vulnerable as I am."

Ophelia shook her head. "I'll *look* as vulnerable as you. That's the beauty of it. We'll use film, so it'll look normal bringing it into the print and photo shop. We can put pictures of my landscaping signs in people's gardens on the same roll, without showing enough to identify their houses. He won't know most of my customers are too bent to care about kinky pictures." As Art shook her head, still pacing, Ophelia tossed in her ace: "My biggest client is Constantine Dufray. He'll think it's a hoot. If the bondage types find out, they'll just razz me about improper technique. I don't advertise my connection with the clubs, but I don't go out of my way to hide it, either."

Art was stuck a few sentences back. "You know Constantine Dufray?"

Dazzled again. "Yes, I know him, yes, I can get you tickets or backstage passes or a personal introduction, and will you please keep your mind on more important matters? Do you have an old-fashioned camera? Not digital, I mean."

"Sure. I teach photography." Art gazed dreamily out the window. "Constantine. Cool."

"We'll take some pics at Blood and Velvet tonight. I'll be a dominatrix. Vi will find someone to pose with me. We'll have to borrow supplies from another club, because my sister doesn't allow anything to do with bondage in Blood and—"

"Oh, shit," Art said. "My brother's at my place."

Ophelia's heart lurched as she went to the window. Gideon's Mercedes was behind a Toyota a few houses down.

"I wonder how long he's been there?" Art radiated uneasiness. "Since he caught me vacuuming naked, he doesn't drop by for no reason."

Good Lord. "It'll take him only a minute with the phone in your house to find out who you were talking to all afternoon. Damn it, he'll ruin our plans."

"Here he comes. No, he stopped to be polite to my neighbor. Maybe she'll drag him around her garden. . . . No, he's saying good-bye. I could *try* to fend him off." Art grimaced. "He'll drag it all out of me."

"Leave him to me," Ophelia said. "I can distract him."

"I'll bet you can." Art grinned.

"Come to my sister's for dinner and bring your camera and some color film. I'll let her know to expect you. Seven o'clock, the big purple Victorian behind Blood and Velvet. And for your own safety as much as mine, *please* don't tell anyone I'm a vamp."

Art grinned again. "Cross my heart."

Ophelia stationed herself by the front windows and watched Gideon stroll up Andrea's walk, calm and confident, a big blonde mutt with matted curls trotting at his side, rays of late-afternoon sun slanting behind them. She took a deep breath and told her thudding heart to chill. *So what if he's the first man you've responded to in years? He dates bimbos and would be terrified of fangs. Detective work first, and sex only if all else fails.*

Ophelia counted slowly to ten before opening the door. There Gideon stood, pheromones in jeans and a checkered shirt with rolled up sleeves. What was it about rolled up sleeves? Powerful forearms, strong capable hands . . . *Pull yourself together, girl!*

"What a surprise." She left the door ajar and leaned on the jamb, eyeing Gideon with what she hoped looked like lighthearted disdain and not naked, hopeless lust. For a second the detective appeared mesmerized. Then his gaze cleared and his lips twitched.

"Ophelia. What are you doing here?"

"Landscaping." She turned up the allure, but the answering heat in his eyes almost knocked her to her knees. She tore her eyes from his. "Nice dog." She extended a hand under the animal's nose.

"Meet Gretchen," Gideon said. "Landscaping. *Inside* the house?"

"I take care of all Mrs. Dukas's plants when she's away." Ophelia slipped out onto the porch and shut the door behind her. "And the Dukases are out of town. Sorry." She scratched behind Gretchen's ears.

"Really." A touch of annoyance crept into Gideon's voice.

"Yep." Ophelia busied herself with Gretchen's soft blonde curls, which sorely needed scissors and a comb. "You have business with them?" She steeled herself to glance up again.

"My sister will do just as well."

Ophelia tried a puzzled expression.

Gideon chuckled. "I'll talk to Art instead." He reached for the door handle, but Ophelia blocked him—getting way too close in the process. "Or not." He leaned closer without hesitation, nose to her nose, his hot breath bathing her lips. She closed her eyes and breathed him in, and her lips parted of their own volition. As his mouth brushed hers, a shudder ran over her. If she hadn't had that taste of blood, her fangs would have come down by now.

She shrank against the door. "No."

"No?" He was only a millimeter away. "Why not?"

"It's not a good idea." She slid to one side. "Don't go in the house. That's not a good idea, either."

"Why the hell not?" Gideon drew back, finally looking confused. Worried, too. "What's wrong with Art? Is she okay?"

"She's all right, but she doesn't want to talk to you." She could see that hurt him, so she added, "Let's sit down and discuss things."

Ophelia crossed the porch and sat on the top step next to a pillar. She tickled Gretchen toward her side, hemming herself safely in and away from Gideon's heat, and removed the secateurs from her belt. "This poor dog is covered with mats." She held a clump of Gretchen's fur between two fingers and clipped it off.

Gideon frowned down at her. "What do you want to discuss—dog grooming, which is irrelevant, my lousy relationship with my sister, which is none of your business, or that you're not attracted to me, which is a load of crap? I know you want me." He lowered himself beside Gretchen's other flank. "Go ahead, get it over with. Tell me I'm arrogant and obnoxious."

"Of course you're confident." Ophelia ran her eyes over him without a tremor, back in control. She clipped off more matted fur. "You're nicely built, pretty good-looking, have plenty of attitude . . . Women go for those things."

"Including you."

"I'm not immune, but that doesn't mean I'll hop into bed with you." Snip. "Therefore, I suggest you back off."

"Nope." He grinned. "I can wait out your little game."

"It's not a game," Ophelia retorted. Gretchen panted companionably beside her. "I can't believe I thought for a few short minutes this afternoon that you might be an okay guy. I suppose all your moves are about getting women into bed. After that, it doesn't matter how they feel. I bet you're a major disappointment." Reaching for a clump that was too close to Gideon's arm, she thought better of it.

"Not so," Gideon said. A laugh lurked in his voice. "I know what women want."

"You have no idea what I want." She grabbed the damned mat and sawed away at it. "Which is fine, because you wouldn't have the guts to deliver."

"Try me," Gideon said. "It's a win-win situation for you. Either complete and utter sexual satisfaction . . . or the satisfaction of being right."

"I don't get off on being right," Ophelia snapped.

"You won't be right," Gideon said. "You will get off, though. How about it?"

Snip. "You don't know the first thing about the female mind," Ophelia went on, determined not to think about getting off. "No wonder your sister feels abandoned, with a brother like you." Her eyes flew to his. "I didn't mean that! I'm sure you care about Art. I'm not usually so rude, although you probably find that hard to believe. Not that it matters what you think, since you're such a sleaze."

"I'm not a sleaze." Gideon shifted to give Ophelia access to Gretchen's other flank. "How about we call a truce? Play it straight with each other?"

She wished. What a deep, calm voice. What laughing eyes. Until he saw the goddamned fangs. Until he—She shut her mind to the memories. "It's not that simple."

"We'll see about that," Gideon said. "Is Art the one being blackmailed?"

Ophelia fought for an answer and came up with nothing. She gathered the discarded clumps of Gretchen's hair into a pile.

"Damn it," Gideon growled. "What's she done?"

Ophelia shook her head. "Nothing illegal, but she thinks you'll disapprove. If you go in ranting and raving, you'll estrange her even more. You'd better leave it to me."

"I don't rant and rave! I don't even disapprove. She's an adult. She can do what she pleases."

"Uh-huh." Ophelia allowed herself a tight little smile. Gretchen yawned and laid her head on her paws. "Even vacuum the house naked?"

Gideon's face darkened. "What, she told you her whole life's story in the last hour? She can do anything she likes naked, but not with the curtains open. That's just plain dumb."

"She's trying to say something, Gideon. She got out of a bad marriage, but she's lost whatever sexual confidence she had, which I suspect wasn't much to start with. She's fighting back, but she shouldn't have to fight you, too."

"She told you all this?"

"Not in so many words."

Gideon stared down at the steps, clearly fighting chagrin. "It's my fault if she's turning to strangers instead of me." A squirrel chattered along the branch of a live oak by the road. It started down the trunk, tail twitching, and Gretchen's nose came up. Gideon, too, was watching the squirrel. "What can I do for her? I admit it—apart from sex, I don't have a clue about women, and Art's not about to discuss her sex life with me."

"Be a friend. Hang out with her. When she looks good,

say so. And when you remind her to shut the curtains, make sure she knows it's not because you disapprove of nakedness, but because you care about her and want her to be safe." The squirrel reached the ground and Gretchen took off, barking joyfully, to scare it back up the tree. Ophelia chuckled. "What a darling dog." She smiled at Gideon, forgetting restraint.

He swallowed. "Lord, you're beautiful."

Ophelia flinched and stood up in a rush. "Art and Andrea Dukas are both being blackmailed. Andrea and her husband really are out of town, and you don't need to discuss it with Art, because I'm going after the blackmailer myself."

Gideon stood as well, his appalled expression everything she could have hoped.

Ophelia headed for the stairs. *Back to detective work, Mr. O'Toole. Thank God.*

CHAPTER FIVE 🌷

Gideon laid a hand on the retreating woman's arm. "Hold on a minute."

"Let go of me!" Ophelia ripped herself away from him.

Lord Almighty. "Look, Ms. *Beliveau*," Gideon tried, "I don't know what you've been through, or why you can't let yourself be pleasant with me, but my sister's at risk. If you won't tell me what you're planning, I have no choice but to take care of it myself."

Ophelia paced the porch, fists clenched, looking anywhere but at him. Finally she said, "This may seem irrelevant to you, but I'm trying to find a way that Art and Andrea don't have to accuse this guy and expose themselves. For sure, Andrea won't do it. She'd move halfway round the world rather than risk her kids going into foster care. And Art's talking about giving up her job."

"What? She loves her job! She's a born teacher." Gideon stifled the urge to slam his way into the house. "What's she being blackmailed for?"

Ophelia threw up her hands. "She was doing nude modeling at the art school, and someone took pictures of her."

"What's wrong with that crazy girl? If she was short of money, she should have come to me."

"You're behaving just like she said you would. There's nothing wrong with posing nude. Maybe she enjoys it. Maybe she likes people looking at her naked body. Many women do."

The whine of a vacuum came from inside the house, too close to be a coincidence, and Ophelia gave a tiny spurt of laughter. She cupped her hands around her eyes and peered through the narrow window beside the door, while Gideon stood well back. Women. All of them were insane.

"Scaredy-cat," Ophelia taunted. The beginnings of a grin tilted her mouth.

Gideon fought amusement. "If *you* want to clean house in the buff, honey, I won't be shy. You'd look cute with a feather duster." He leaned on a column and looked her over.

"That is so sexist." Ophelia returned his stare, hot and haughty. "But then, you're used to being that way. Your bimbos will do anything you ask."

Bimbos? "I suppose you got that from my sister, who doesn't know any more about my sex life than I do about hers." His eyes drank in the swell of Ophelia's breasts and the lush curve of her hips and he almost caught fire. Something pushed him in one smooth motion away from the pillar and toward those hot eyes and lips, something primal. He settled a hand on her waist, hard, cupped a warm breast with the other and fastened his lips on hers. Ophelia whimpered and pressed herself into his hand, parted her lips, and licked back at him with a hot, eager tongue.

"Gideon O'Toole!" A voice out of the past slapped at him. Gretchen barked, and sharp footsteps clomped up the steps. "You should be ashamed of yourself!"

Gideon pulled dazedly away as a hickory switch smacked his legs. Gretchen barked again and felt the switch in her turn, and Ophelia skittered down the stairs, saying, "Thanks, Mrs. Cotter," her face white, hands to her lips. "I don't know what got into me." She hurried toward the garden.

"Gideon's been like this since he was a boy," Mrs. Cotter replied. Twenty-odd years had left her unchanged when it came to dispensing untender care. "I caught him kissing the girls in first grade."

"Yes, Mrs. Cotter," Gideon admitted. "And they always enjoyed it—as Ophelia was doing until you came along."

"Sassy boy, making a display of yourself, kissing and fondling in public. Such things should be kept private." Mrs. Cotter clopped away down the walk. "As for you, Ophelia, be warned. This boy's been trouble from day one."

Ophelia was scanning the flower bed. "Thanks again, Mrs. Cotter. I really appreciate it. I have work to do. Here"—she marked with a trowel from her belt—"here and here." Dirt was soon leaping obediently into neat piles beside precise little holes. Gretchen snuffled at the aromatic earth. Mrs. Cotter continued briskly down the sidewalk, no doubt planning to call the chief of police.

"Kissing and fondling in private sounds like fun," Gideon suggested.

Ophelia's eyes remained on the ground. "No."

"You were enjoying it. I was enjoying it. Why not?"

"No," Ophelia said again. She pushed Gretchen gently away and strode along the flagstone path to disappear through a gate in the stone wall. A minute later, still not looking at him, she returned with two flats of impatiens.

You knew this was a bad idea, Gideon told himself, unable to walk away but needing to take care of Art. This woman was a mess. His sister was a mess. He wasn't a frigging therapist.

"What's Ms. Dukas being blackmailed about?"

For a long second, he thought Ophelia would refuse to reply. Then, "Her husband took pictures of her nursing her baby naked." When he made an impatient noise, she added, "You never know when some social worker will decide that's perverted. Andrea won't take chances with her kids."

"The blackmailer's someone at a photo shop? There's only one left in town. It's a print shop, too, as I recall."

"Yes." She sounded grudging.

"I suppose you're thinking of luring him into blackmailing someone else?"

She said nothing, but with quick, sure movements coaxed plants into new homes.

"But you've got some cockeyed notion about entrapment, so because I'm a cop, you've decided I can't be involved."

Ophelia offered him an exaggerated sigh. "We shouldn't discuss this. Why don't you just trust me?"

Gideon laughed out loud. "How do *you* feel about trusting *me*? Not so confident, huh? And yet I'm a very trustworthy guy."

"That's different!" Ophelia tamped earth around a couple of red impatiens. "I do trust you, more or less."

"Bullshit."

"It's not bullshit." She nestled the last plant into its home. "You don't understand."

"I'm more than willing to try."

Her words were soft and bitter, her face still averted. "I wish."

"What*ever* you wish, sweetheart," Gideon said. "Just give me a chance."

He was such a fool.

She brushed dirt off her hands and stacked the flats, then picked her way to the back of the flower bed. Gideon let the silence hang for a minute or two. "Honey, you haven't given me any reason to trust you. You're feeding me too many mixed messages. At the moment, however, what matters to me is that my sister gets through this okay. I need to know what's going on."

Ophelia fiddled with the timer on the Dukas watering system. "When I'm ready for you to arrest the blackmailer, I'll give you a call." She picked up her trowel and the flats and started walking.

Undeterred, Gideon strode beside her. "The hell with that. Say you convince some fool to set himself up to be blackmailed. Hopefully the dude at the shop falls for it and I arrest him . . . but what if your friend screws up and the dude gets wise? Even if the plan works, what about the photos of Art and Ms. Dukas? They could be in the shop, at his house, on his computer. I can't be sure of getting everything. But with more warning, the odds are better. I need to know everything you and Art know about this guy, so I can prepare in advance."

"I'll keep you informed." Ophelia slipped ahead of him into Andrea's backyard.

Gideon followed. "I can't take that for an answer."

"I'll call you tomorrow, then. Tomorrow morning. First thing." She headed for her truck.

"Not good enough. What the hell is wrong with you? Talk to me, damn it!"

"I don't want to talk to you. I don't need your help."

"Too bad." Anger slowed his voice. "You've got it whether you like it or not. We can skip the sex, even though you want it as much as I do, but you damn well better cooperate when it comes to the law."

Her fists clenched as she hurried ahead. "I have friends who can do the job just as well or better."

Gideon fought back surprise. "Calling in vigilantes? I thought you didn't hold with violence." Ophelia was almost running now. In his frustration, Gideon lashed out. "On the other hand, what could be simpler? Constantine Dufray can off the guy, and everyone will live happily ever after."

Ophelia whirled, eyes narrow, voice cracking. "Don't you *ever* dis Constantine to me!" She tossed the dirty trowel and the empty flats into her truck. "Now leave me the fuck alone."

Gideon waited as she drove away, rage churning his gut. Gretchen shoved her cool nose under his hand. He stalked across the street toward his car. Art could wait for later.

"Losing your touch, boy?" Mrs. Cotter cackled from her gate a few doors down. "She's too bright for you. You chased silly girls in first grade, and still do, by what I hear."

Gideon slowed. "If you say so, ma'am."

Mrs. Cotter rapped the gate with her stick. "Unless you're

thinking of marriage . . . which you should be at your age. Ophelia's an ideal choice: smart, pretty, kindhearted, an excellent gardener to boot. If anyone can tame that wilderness around your place, she's the one. My daughter drove me that way last Sunday to see all the fancy subdivisions and the new golf course. Your driveway's so overgrown it's a miracle you can get your car into it. Heaven only knows what condition the house is in. Your mother would turn in her grave."

"Yes, ma'am." Obviously she had more to say, so he waited with gritted teeth.

"Court Ophelia the old-fashioned way. Marriage first, sex afterward, as it should be."

That worked for him, as long as they got married tomorrow. Better still, tonight. He was going out of his mind.

Mrs. Cotter poked him with her hickory stick. "Otherwise, she'll think she's just another conquest."

"I never . . ." He wasn't getting into this with his first-grade teacher. "Yes, ma'am."

"Think you never hurt anyone? I'll bet there are broken hearts all over town. Silly ones, but broken all the same. Mind you don't hurt Ophelia, or you'll have to deal with me."

Not to mention Leopard and Constantine, and Violet and Zelda, and by now probably Artemisia as well. Gretchen and Psyche, too.

"Yes, ma'am." Gideon fled.

Dusk was falling as he arrived at the Chamber. Unlike Violet Dupree's Blood and Velvet, which catered to the faux-vampire crowd, the Chamber focused on the milder forms of punishment and mutilation. You could participate or just watch. You could get stripped, but only so far, tied and whipped or hung on chains, and of course pierced or tattooed or scarred if you so desired. Like Blood and Velvet, it was a sissy club, a tourist hangout. In the welter of striped velour and gold trim, whorehouse daybeds and gaping idiots, nothing much illegal or even remotely serious went on.

Gideon avoided a tussle and, far more inconvenient, a locked door, by choosing the employee entrance at the rear, and worked his way with little protest to the wings of the dance-hall stage. There being no sense in wasting any time, he marched onstage to where Willy Wyler was hooking up a wah-wah pedal and grabbed him by the throat. Wyler clawed at him, choking, and Gideon rammed the musician against the scaffolding and let him fall.

"What the fuck is going on?" Burton Tate dropped the mess of wires he was tangling with and hurried over, followed by his younger brother and a lanky guy on speed. "Get the hell out of here or I'll call the . . . Oh, yeah. You are the cops. What are you doing, dude?"

"Saving Willy from the tender mercies of Leopard's goons," Gideon said. "He should be thankful."

"Don't mess him up too bad, dude. We got a show tonight." It was the same wheedling, whining Burton as ever. "What'd he do?"

The musician on speed goggled, and Gabriel Tate, with a scared glance at Gideon, shoved a couple of groupies into the opposite wing.

"Vandalized the wrong person's garden."

Gideon waited while Willy Wyler dragged himself up off the floor.

"So I heard," Burton said. "Lisa was all bent out of shape about it." He scratched the dagger tattoo on his bicep. "Willy shoulda known better. Ophelia don't put out for no one, 'cept Constantine and Leopard. Why else would they protect the bitch?"

Gideon took Willy by the arm. "I won't hurt him unless I have to."

He guided the guitarist over to the bar and balanced him on a stool, then picked a cigarette from the packet in Willy's shirt pocket and lit it for him. "Okay, Willy, now listen. We both know you didn't vandalize Ophelia's place because she won't fuck you. That would be dumb, and although you're not one of the world's bright bulbs anymore, you're not that dumb either. Why'd you do it?"

Willy grabbed the cigarette and took a long drag. The silly fuck was trying to think.

"Don't waste your time," Gideon said. "We know you did it. All I want to know is, why?"

Willy cleared his throat and cleared it again. "Fuck, man, why'd you have to choke me? I woulda told you without that."

"Because, Willy, I want you and everyone else to leave Ophelia alone. Just talking doesn't leave enough of an impression."

Willy stared. "Fuck, man, you're not falling for that dyke, too, are you?" He blanched. "Don't hit me, man! It's true, I swear!"

Gideon, who hadn't moved a muscle or changed expression, sighed. "Christ, Willy, not jumping in the sack with every turd that makes a move on her doesn't make her a dyke."

Willy Wyler took another drag of smoke. "Promise you won't hit me?"

"I promise I *will* hit you if you don't tell me what I want to know."

"You're not gonna like it." He flinched as Gideon leaned forward. "Okay, okay. The thing is, man, she likes kids. I ain't got nothing against dykes, fags neither, but they gotta stay away from kids, and my kids in particular."

Gideon held his breath, gripped Willy's shirt, and yanked him forward, though getting in the smelly old dude's face was the pits. "Tell me the truth, asshole."

"I swear," Willy babbled. "She took nudie pictures of my girl Joanna, real disgusting stuff. The kid's only thirteen, man, and she's got her posing like some slut. There's even one of little Connie in the bathtub. No big deal, but still, who knows what she'll do next? I couldn't put up with that!"

What smelled like genuine anguish had bled through the stink, and Gideon eased up, frowning. "Go on." He motioned to the bartender, who had wisely decided to wipe the far end of the bar first. "Bourbon, straight up."

"I told her to stay away from my kids. That was a couple weeks ago." Willy paused, evidently trying to think again and succeeding to a limited extent. "Long story short, I was all coked up this morning and I sorta lost it." He slumped. "But goddamn it, she's got no right touching my girls!"

Gideon let go of Willy and leaned back far enough to take a proper breath. "How'd you happen to see these pictures, Willy? Ophelia come by one day and show them to you?"

"You don't believe me, man, but it's true. Ophelia dropped off some of Lisa's CDs to be printed at the photo shop, and she must have mixed up her roll of film with our stuff. In fact, I know she did, because my name was on the fucking envelope, and—"

"And what?" As if he needed to ask. While Willy tried thinking again, Gideon traded the whiskey for a five and offered it to Wyler. "Did Joanna say Ophelia took the pictures?"

"Of course she—" Willy's eyes flicked this way and that. "She didn't have to, poor baby. She cried her eyes out and said she was sorry and . . . She didn't say Ophelia *didn't* take them!"

Gideon lifted his eyes to heaven. "Who put the dead cat on her doorstep? One of your jackass friends?"

Willy downed the shot of whiskey. "No clue, man. Lots of guys are pissed off at her, and maybe she's been messing with other people's kids, too. I dunno." He shook his head. "I don't want nobody thinking that was me. Or that it was me took those pictures." His voice rose close to panic. "I'm a druggie, man, but I'm no pervert. My career would be in the toilet, and they'd ship the kids off to foster homes and Lisa'd kill me."

"Your career's already headed for the toilet," Gideon said.

"Look who you're working with. Not getting as much session work as you used to, either, but you could fix that if you got off the drugs. Have some pride. While you're working on that, keep your head down, don't trash anybody's place or beat anybody up—blackmailers in particular. You hear?" He grinned as Willy's jaw sagged in surprise. "I'll take care of the blackmailer and find out who really took those pictures, but you better clean up, or those kids'll end up in foster homes regardless."

He escorted Wyler back to the band and signaled to Burton to accompany him to the door. "Get rid of the underage chicks," he said when they were alone in the corridor. "You know the law."

"I know, dude, I know, but my kid brother—"

"Your brother's not a kid anymore. You want him to keep his nuts?"

"Jeez, Gideon, c'mon!"

"This isn't me talking, Burton. When it comes to the clubs, the underworld applies the rules. One, no one under eighteen. And two, no unwilling participants."

"They're my brother's girlfriends, dude, and he wants them here. I need him in the band. He's got the voice."

"You looking for a soprano? That's what he'll be once Leopard's goons cut off his balls."

"Jeez, Gideon, kids get into some of the other clubs, so why not here?"

"People sometimes die violently in those other clubs, Burton. You want to take chances, take your brother and his groupies and get a gig there."

They emerged into an open area that held the tattoo, piercing, and mutilation facilities and gift shop, where workers were gearing up for opening time. Above the bustle rose a laughing voice. "It's a cute flogger, Joe, but pink? I need something macho."

"Whoo, baby!" Burton stuck out a paw. "I'm all the macho you need."

Ophelia whirled, brandishing the flogger. Burton held up his hands, giggling, to fend her off. Her foot connected instead, and he fell gasping to the floor, hands to his crotch.

"You should have listened to me earlier, Burton." Ophelia dropped the flogger on the counter. "And so should you, Gideon O'Toole. Show the cop what I came for, Joe."

The man in the gift shop snickered, pulling items out of a silver shopping bag one by one: handcuffs, fake fangs that were weapons in their own right, weights, clamps, and chains.

What an act. Gideon chuckled, folding his arms.

Ophelia snapped, "Give me a proper whip."

Joe handed her a leather monstrosity that would cut through elephant hide. "There you go, darling. Gonna be a big night?"

"You bet." She dropped the bullwhip in her bag. "Pack it all up."

"Almost makes me wish we were of the same persuasion," Joe said. "Can I come watch?"

Ophelia laughed. "How about that pink vibrator at the back? The one with the feathers."

Gideon felt a flush of anger and something ridiculously like hurt. He leaned against the gift-shop counter, hoping he at least looked cool. His voice came out calm enough. "What did Burton do to you earlier?"

"He groped me." She didn't look at him. "As he has done too goddamn many times." She took the end cap off the vibrator. "Batteries."

Joe dug under the counter and handed her two double-A's, looking appreciatively from Ophelia to Gideon and back.

Gideon said, "I seem to recall doing the same thing, honey."

"Just because you're in a different class from Burton doesn't mean you're up to scratch." Ophelia twisted the bottom of the vibrator and said, "A nice gentle buzz for some nice gentle girl. Go find one of your bimbos. You can be damn cute together in the buff." But as she turned the vibrator off and finally raised her eyes to his, something must have shown in his face, because her expression changed to sadness and her voice filled with regret. She put the vibrator in his hand and closed his fingers around it. "You're a good guy, Gideon, but I'm not what you need. For your safety and mine, please stay away."

Then she picked up her shopping bag, said, "Put it on my account, Joe," and left.

CHAPTER SIX 🌷

Ophelia dumped the bag on the mauve marble tiles of her sister's kitchen floor and reached for a cookie. Violet slapped her hand.

"They're Zelda's! Anyway, we have to ice them first."

Ophelia sat down. "I don't know what's gotten into me, Vi. I look at that damn cop and go weak at the knees."

"Nothing's gotten into you." Her half sister set an elegant Japanese cup of steaming green tea down before her. "Or, rather, no*body* has. Sorry, angel, but I'm running out of sympathy. I could see doing without when none of them turned you on, but you wanted this guy at first sight." She poured tea for herself. "I almost envy your desperation. I'm so jaded, I'm considering sleeping with Donnie. I've been toying with the poor man for years. It would be an act of kindness, and I have to do it with *someone*. Who knows, he might be interesting."

Ophelia made a face. "I doubt it."

"On the downside, he might be impossible to get rid of afterwards. It's safer to stick to my regulars." Violet took the fake fangs out of the bag. "Just like the good old days." She peered deeper and sucked in a sharp hiss. "You know I don't like anything to do with bondage in the club."

"No one will see it but us," Ophelia said.

"Yes, but you look marvelously sexy just dressed as a vamp, angel. You used to draw scads of customers. . . ."

Ophelia suppressed a retort about scads of nutcases following her around. Instead she said, "I don't want to look as if I'm going to a costume party. I need to look like a dangerous domme. Halloween isn't blackmailable, but BDSM is."

Violet set the paraphernalia on the table among three plates of cooling cookies, the whip last of all. "Eww. Why not get a cute little flogger?"

"Because Gideon showed up at the Chamber. You know what he was doing there? I didn't figure it out till after I left. He was harassing Willy Wyler, when I expressly told him not to. He's impossible. He doesn't listen. He doesn't give up. You know who he is? Donnie told me." She ignored the tea and eyed the cookies. "He's the cop who took all that flak from the media when there was no evidence Constantine killed his wife. Everyone said he'd been scared away or bought off, but he wouldn't budge."

"That should make you like him even more. You go for the morally upright type."

"I think he resents Constantine. Constantine got to exploit the bad-boy thing for his image, but Gideon was left looking wimpy." Ophelia's fingers hovered over a cookie. Violet pulled the plate away just in time. Ophelia sighed. "I was so pissed off to see him again when I hadn't had time to recover from that amazing kiss—"

"He *kissed* you? And you *let* him? You didn't tell me that when you called."

It had been a miracle Ophelia had even been able to talk at the time, thinking of Gideon.

Her half sister giggled. "How'd he deal with the fangs?"

"He didn't get that far." Ophelia heard her own disappointment and tried to be thankful instead. No point getting a taste of his blood and then having to deal with him freaking out. "I'd barely got myself calmed down when he showed up at the Chamber. They had some nice red leather floggers at the gift shop, but I thought the whip would scare him off." She curled her fingers around the teacup to keep them away from the cookies.

"And?" Vi twinkled at Ophelia while drinking her own tea.

"It didn't work." She scowled. "He thought it was funny, so I insulted him instead. I gave him a pink vibrator with feathers on the end."

Violet gaped. "He must have thought you were insane."

"No, he knew exactly what I meant, and I put it in words to make sure . . . and it was such a lie, and I felt like slime for the gazillionth time today." She clutched her teacup and gazed hungrily at the bare, boring cookies and knew she was losing her mind. "I've always been in control before. I've always been able to say no and mean it. I've learned not to care about whatever guy I'm brushing off, because I can't afford to." She took a gulp of tea and swallowed down the tears that threatened, inexplicably and out of character, to overcome her. "But with Gideon I do care, and even when I say no, I mean yes, please. Even when I'm enraged. Even when I'm terrified."

"Yum. Go for it!" Violet said. "You can't ignore chemistry like that. And don't worry about the vibrator. He'll bounce right back and use it on you." The buzzer on the oven went off. "Where is Zelda? She's supposed to be making these cookies. I've told her not to stay out after dark until she gets her fangs."

"*If* she gets her fangs," Ophelia corrected, grabbing a cookie unnoticed and scarfing it down.

"*When*," Violet said with finality. She took the baking sheet out of the oven and shoveled cookies onto a fourth plate.

The front door banged open and shut, and Zelda careened into the room. "Hi, Mom, Ophelia. Sorry I'm late." She took in the cooling cookies and said, "Mom, you're the absolute best. I'll get the icing." She beckoned to someone in the front hall. "Come on, don't be shy. Welcome to our den of sin."

Artemisia O'Toole came slowly into the kitchen, nervous as all get-out.

"Hel-lo," Violet said. "You certainly do look like your brother. I hear you need sex. Have some tea. Don't worry, I'm not after your blood. I only do men. Are you any good at icing?"

Artemisia took the chair Ophelia pulled out for her. "Um, sure," she said. "I won a cake-decorating contest once." She stared as Violet repacked the shopping bag. "Cripes, Ophelia. Couldn't you have got a cute little flogger?" She blushed up to the roots of her hair.

"My, my, you really *do* need work," Violet said.

"We're not doing cute," Ophelia said. "We're doing twisted. And scary." She poured Art some tea. "Not that it bothered your pain-in-the-butt brother," she muttered. "You told me he'd be scared of fangs. He didn't even blink at a whip!" Defiantly, she took another cookie, snapped it in two, and shoved it into her mouth.

"Hey! Those are for school!" Zelda set three bowls of colored icing on the table, along with parchment cones and tips. She surveyed the three women and sighed. "This is about sex, right? Or lack thereof. Mom, hurry up and sear Ophelia a steak. I can only spare a few cookies, and Ophelia's already had one."

"Two." Violet went to the fridge. "How would you like your steak, Artemisia? We eat them extremely rare."

"Lightly singed," Zelda said. "I'm actually beginning to like it that way."

"Of course you are, sweetie. It's the vamp gene, just like I told you." Violet threw Ophelia an I-told-you-so look as she cut into a thick, juicy steak. "But this is an emergency." She put a thin slice, red and bloody, into Ophelia's mouth.

Delicious, Ophelia thought, licking her lips ecstatically.

Would Gideon would laugh at this, too, or turn away in disgust?

Art didn't seem to mind. In fact, she was blushing. "Make mine medium."

"Sweetie, what you really need is raw," Violet said. "Or very, *very* well done."

"Well done," Art repeated, squirming but clearly determined. "You're absolutely right." She palmed her cheeks and glanced uneasily at Zelda. "Golly, this is so embarrassing."

"Don't mind me," Zelda said. "I am old beyond my years. Do you want to do roses? Leaves?"

"I'll take the green." Art snatched thankfully at the icing with the leaf tip on the end. "What's the occasion?"

"Spring festivals around the world," Zelda said. "Easter, Ostara, Naw-Ruz . . . Our teacher's a blast."

"I can do tulips and daffodils," Art said. She topped a cookie with broad, flat tulip leaves and a stem. "And irises, but if you want purple ones, you'll have to make more icing."

"Coming right up." Zelda hauled out the shortening, sugar, and food coloring.

"Give me the pink," Ophelia said. She did a tolerable rose on one cookie and then another. *Boring.* She drew a heart. *Dumb.* Painstakingly, she constructed an erect pink penis piercing the heart. She glowered at the cookie. Violet snatched it up and showed it around. "Symbolism, anyone?" Ophelia grabbed for the cookie, but Violet had already eaten it.

"Yum," she said. "Do you suppose Gideon's is pink?"

Ophelia choked on a laugh. "He's quite a bit darker than Art."

"Purplish, then. You can eat his when Zelda gets the icing done."

"Too bad there's no black icing," said Art in a strangled voice. "I've always wanted one of those."

"Double yum," Violet said. "I'm sure we can arrange something."

Art blushed again and said to Ophelia, "I thought you weren't interested in Gideon. What got into you on Andrea's porch?"

"He's a hunk," Ophelia said. "I'm a horny vamp." She shrugged. "No biggie." Though maybe it was. It looked like a biggie, from what she'd noticed.

Art said, "I have some news for you. I still can't believe it. Mrs. Cotter says Gideon wants to marry you!"

"You see?" Ophelia banged her fist down. The cookies jumped and angry pink icing squirted onto the table. "It's the same damn thing all over again!"

"What same thing?" Art swooped a finger into the pink icing and smeared it on her tongue, then went back to drawing leaves. "I think it's a great idea."

"Calm down, angel," Violet said from the grill. "She may be right. You'd get plenty of sex. Good sex, too, I bet."

Art executed a last set of tulip leaves on her plate of cookies and took Ophelia's depleted icing sac. "That's what all his bimbos say, even after he dumps them and breaks their hearts. They say, 'Oh, Art, I'll die without him, he's so much fun in bed.'" She drew a tight little tulip. "Why can't *I* get a man like that?"

Violet dropped a steak on the grill, put some rolls into the cooling oven, and came over to look. "You will, sweetie. Think open. Think uninhibited. Look at that sorry little flower you just drew. Not happy. Not having fun."

"Right." Artemisia swiped the icing into her mouth and tried again.

"As for you," Violet told her sister, "Gideon is exactly what you need. You take everything too seriously. It's about time you had sex with someone fun. Well, it's about time you had sex, period, but if you don't enjoy it, it's not much fun."

"Very profound, but how can I have fun when the whole time I'm thinking down the road? If he doesn't freak out afterward, thinking he's got HIV or been bitten by the devil, he'll get possessive, and then when I tell him to leave me alone he'll get depressed and suicidal, or obsessed, and he'll start stalking me or—"

"Gideon would never stalk anyone," Art inserted, offended. "If you want to get rid of him, all you have to do is talk too much." She grimaced. "Our mother talked all the time, like me, and our father was a pigheaded old grump. Gideon's terrified that's where he'll end up, so his relationships never get past having sex."

"What could be better, angel?" Violet said. "Indulge yourself and then dump him without a second thought. He'll handle it. He looks perfectly stable."

"My father looked stable," Ophelia said icily. "Then he killed himself."

Art's hand froze in midair. "Oh, my God. I'm so sorry!"

Violet made a disgusted noise. "Your father was a jealous fool, Ophelia. We're half sisters, by the way, Art. My father was Mom's first husband. Ophelia's dad was her second. He was obsessed with the thought that she was cheating, although she never looked at another man until the day she left him. After that, of course, she went wild, until she married a religious pervert who thinks drinking blood is a sin. Fortunately, he's willing to put his soul on the line to have sex with her." She flipped the first steak over and put three more on the grill.

"I'm not marrying anyone," Ophelia said.

"Speaking of perverts," Zelda remarked, looking uncharacteristically solemn, "I had coffee with Joanna Wyler this afternoon." She set down a bowl of neon purple icing.

Ophelia glanced up. "Did you find anything out?"

"Sort of," Zelda admitted. "It doesn't make any sense, though. She says her dad says you're a bad influence. Does he know you're a vamp?"

"I don't think so," Ophelia replied. "That would make him even more persistent. And it's not like I can turn Joanna into a vamp. You're either born with the gene or you aren't." She searched Zelda's face. "What? Does he think I'm lesbian because of my rep for hating men?"

Zelda shifted uneasily. "Something like that."

"So what?" Violet turned three of the steaks over. "It's not a crime. Not that a law would stop any of us. But Willy's not a gay-basher. Lisa's sister is lesbian. They have gay friends." When Zelda still held back, she added, "Spit it out, for God's sake!" She reached into the fridge for a salad.

"It's majorly dumb," Zelda said. "Put the salad down, Mom. Step back from the counter."

"Tell me!"

Zelda planted her hands on her hips. "I mean it, Mom."

Her mother rolled her eyes and complied.

"Okay," Zelda said. "He thinks Ophelia's . . . into kids."

Violet surged forward, stopped, returned to the stove, tossed the steaks onto plates, then stalked out the back door onto the porch. She slammed the door, screamed, then stormed back inside to grab the phone off the wall. Her voice was low and furious. "I'll have Lep beat him up. Then I'll have Constantine kill him. No, I'll kill him myself." She mashed numbers with a trembling hand.

"No!" Ophelia made a grab for the phone, tripped over the shopping bag, and landed on her knees. Vi grabbed the whip and kept moving, running it through her free hand. "First I'll make him beg for mercy. Lep? Constantine! Perfect. I need you over here right now. That disgusting, low-down, no-good Willy Wyler's been calling Ophelia a child abuser!"

Ophelia grabbed the phone and dodged around the kitchen table with an enraged Violet just behind. "It's no big deal!" she hissed into the receiver, and "Don't you dare!" and "We don't need any help!" Then, as the screen door opened and shut, "Tony's here. He'll calm her down. No, don't come over. Stop laughing, damn it! Good-bye!"

Tony Karaplis walked across the threshold and took Violet in his arms. Burly and in his fifties, built like a bruiser, with hairy muscular arms and a luxuriant mustache, he invariably radiated calm control. Violet beat her fists against his chest and screamed while Ophelia put the phone back on the wall, Zelda stood resigned, and Art stared aghast, the yellow icing cone dangling from her hand.

Tony waited like a rock until Violet was done. "Better now, baby?"

"No." Violet scowled. "But thank you."

"Who have we here?" Tony gave Art a long, appraising look and an irresistible smile. The icing cone dropped to the floor. Art flushed and stared and finally smiled slowly in return.

Zelda picked up the icing. "Tony, much as we love you, you're mesmerizing my best cookie decorator. I have to get these done for school!"

"This woman needs it bad," Tony said simply.

"Not now, and not from you." Ophelia pushed Art back into her chair. "He's a vampire, Art, and a playboy as well. Is that what you're looking for, or do you just want a normal guy with some skills?"

Art sighed, as if at some blinding revelation.

"Now she knows how her brother feels." Violet put the steaks on the table and tossed the salad. "Are you hungry, Tony?"

"Not for steak and salad," Tony twinkled. He took the basket Zelda had filled with warm rolls, pulled out a chair, and turned to Ophelia. "What was all that about?"

"Promise you won't go out and kill anyone?" Ophelia said bitterly.

"Hey," Tony said, "I've been respectable for years now. I'm practically a senior citizen."

"Well, I'm not." Violet viciously attacked her steak. "I am seriously enjoying imagining this is Willy Wyler I'm chopping up."

Tony grimaced, and Ophelia explained. To which he remarked, "Hurting Willy won't help."

"Thank you," Ophelia agreed. "None of this makes any sense. I've known the Wylers for two or three years—I even babysat their kids once or twice—and I've never done anything to make them think I was a child abuser. There's something weird going on. I have to find out what." She served salad onto Art's plate. "Eat, or I'll make Tony leave. We have work to do."

Art pulled herself together. "Let me finish the icing first." She took the cone and did the last three daffodils. "Poor Gideon. He must be feeling totally whacked."

"Exactly. His judgment is skewed because of who I am."

"Maybe not." Art put the yellow cone down and picked up the one Zelda had just filled with purple. "I mean, Tony is amazing. . . ." She glanced at him and blushed again. "But I know he's not the man for me. He's more like a promise—a promise that something I never believed was possible." She bent her head to the icing again. "Gideon's the level-headed one in the family. He's not likely to do anything dumb."

Tony chuckled. "I've gotta meet this guy."

Violet, soothed by a couple of bites of bloody steak, said to her sister, "If you won't let me kill Willy, you'd better sleep with Gideon."

"For cripes, sake, Vi! That makes no sense at all!"

"Purely as a preventive measure, angel, to avoid calling Leopard in if you're accused of child abuse or something else. Since this particular cop is yours for the asking . . ."

"I can't think of a worse reason to sleep with him," Ophelia said. "Anyway, what else would I be accused of?"

Violet gave her a strange, uneasy look, and Ophelia thought, *Oh God, what now?* Then Art spoke, and Ophelia vowed to confront her sister later.

"I agree with Violet," said Art. "That you should sleep with my brother, I mean. But for a purely selfish reason."

Ophelia frowned.

"You like him, he likes you . . . and maybe I'll get to have you for a sister-in-law." Then Art whipped off irises, one after the other. "You all are totally weird, and I love it."

"Thank you," Violet said. Tony and Zelda just laughed.

Art finished the last iris with a flourish. "Anyway, why not?"

CHAPTER SEVEN 🌷

Gideon glowered at the ridiculous pink vibrator in his hand.

"You want a sack for that?" Joe smirked across the gift shop counter. He flipped open a small silver shopping bag with pink handles. "You wouldn't want anyone thinking you're gay or anything."

"Nobody ever thinks Gideon's gay," a warm voice said from across the room. A tall, bright-eyed black man strode forward. "For sure not the bimbos he hangs with."

"Darby Sims!" Gideon clasped his friend's hand. "Jesus, Dar, what do you know about who I hang with? You've been gone for years. Long enough to be married with a passel of kids."

Darby chuckled. "No, I'm still free as a bird—and stand by the fact that all the chicks I ever saw you with were brainless ninnies. Not good for anything but sex."

"They weren't that bad," Gideon said uncertainly. He put the vibrator on the counter. "How about you gift wrap it for me, Joe?"

"Who's the lucky lady?" Darby asked.

"Ophelia Beliveau, the lady who just gave it to me."

Burton Tate dragged himself up off the floor, clutching his testicles, and shot a sick, angry look at Gideon before stumbling down the hall toward the stage. Gideon didn't react.

Behind the counter, Joe shook his head. "Don't get hung

up on Ophelia. Big mistake." He pulled out silver tissue paper with glitter and magenta stars.

"So, that was the famous Ophelia," Darby said. "From what I hear, she's no bimbo."

"Famous in what way?" Gideon asked.

Darby staved him off with a hand. "Not saying a word against her, bro, but have you seen the statue in her sister's garden? She's dressed as a vampire, fangs and all. She's plenty dangerous in real life, even without the fangs. Look what she did to poor old Burton."

"He shouldn't have touched her," Gideon said. "She doesn't scare me."

Joe nestled the vibrator in the tissue paper, leaving a few feathers peeking out. "Gideon the cop, you are in for one nasty surprise. She won't let you down so easy next time."

She wouldn't let him down at all, Gideon decided. Not if he played things right.

Joe shook his head again. He unraveled a length of silver ribbon from a spool under the counter. "She has her choice of any stud she likes. Major studs, like Constantine Dufray. You're cute, but"—he took his time appraising Gideon—"a cop for Ophelia? No."

Yes, Gideon decided, knowing he had gone insane, and not caring. "We'll see about that."

"Your funeral," Joe replied, snickering. "At least Ophelia will get a top-quality vibrator for her collection. But she'll think about Constantine when she uses it, not you."

"I'll wean her off Dufray." Gideon shrugged.

Darby rolled his eyes. "You always were a crazy man. Stick to the bimbos. From what I've heard, Ophelia's hot, but she's also bad news."

"Ophelia's a sweetie!" Joe said fiercely. "Watch your mouth, if you want to hang out here. Everybody in the clubs loves that girl."

"Except the poor bastards she drives crazy." Darby

frowned down at his watch. "I'm here for an interview. Tattoo artist." Then he paused, visibly tense. "How's your sister these days? Still with old Steve? Two-point-something kids?"

"Didn't you know? She divorced him a while back."

"Say what?" Darby stood straight.

"She's been going through some rough times," Gideon admitted.

Darby glowered. "What, did the bastard cheat on her?"

"Not that I know of. She won't talk about it. She up and filed for divorce one day, citing irreconcilable differences, and he went along with it. Got hitched to another chick not long ago."

"Good riddance. I never did like Steve." Darby took a longer look at his watch. "I hope she finds someone better."

"She might like to see you, Dar," Gideon suggested.

"I don't think so." The man's face hardened. "Gotta go." He headed into the tattoo parlor. "See you around."

One mystery at a time. Gideon turned back and eyed his gaudily wrapped package. "Ophelia drives men crazy, huh? Tell me about it, Joe. Forewarned is forearmed."

Joe shifted a shoulder. "Nothing to tell. Guys get obsessed. They go nuts and stalk her." He whirled a spool of magenta ribbon.

"Do you know of anyone who's obsessed with her right now?"

"Apart from you?" Gideon received a smarmy smile. "There's Burton, but he's just a dumbass. I hear Willy Wyler dumped a dead cat on her doorstep, but he knows he won't get to first base. There are guys who hang at Blood and Velvet hoping she'll turn up. And Plato Lavoie, who lives across the road from her. He's been loopy about her for years."

Plato, noted Gideon. Finally, something seemed to be going his way.

"There are always new ones," Joe went on, "but if they don't learn to back off, she has friends to take care of her.

She doesn't want you, so be one of the smart ones and stay away."

"Nope," Gideon said. "By the way, Willy Wyler didn't do the cat thing. If you get any inkling of who might have done it, let me know." He held out a card, which Joe took with the tips of his fingers and a pained grimace. "If you can't stomach tattling to a cop, get word to Leopard. Either way, whoever did it has to be stopped."

A blonde in a black sequin-spattered dress minced up on a pair of four-inch heels. Gideon looked her up and down. Good figure. Discontented face.

"Who are you looking at?" she asked in a shrill voice, then noticed Gideon properly and changed gears. "Hey, you're cute." She shifted again. "Did you see a tall black man wearing"—she shuddered—"jeans and a purple T-shirt?"

"In the tattoo parlor," Gideon said.

"Oh God," the woman replied. "Still? I need him now!" She eyed Gideon. "The club's just opened. Wanna have a drink? You look like good company."

She didn't. And if this was what Darby called free as a bird, Gideon wondered what caged would be like. "Thanks, but I have an appointment with another lady." He took the silver gift bag and handed Joe a five.

The blonde wiggled her claws at the package. "What's in there?"

"A top quality feather-duster vibrator." Joe smirked. "Let me show you my other wares."

Back in the car, Gretchen was waiting patiently. Gideon gave her a good scratch behind the ears.

On the way to the Impractical Cat, his cell phone rang. It was Jeanie. "I've got some gossip for you," the dispatcher said.

"Hold on." Gideon circled the block, realized from the crowd gathering outside that this was likely one of Leopard's famous poetry nights, and parked in the tow zone across the street. "Shoot."

"I'm so brilliant. I thought of my memaw! She knows everything about Bayou Gavotte for the past seventy-five years." Jeanie paused for a deep, dramatic breath.

Gideon sank low in his seat and got comfortable. Gretchen put her head on her paws. "Go on, babe. You've got me where you want me."

"Ooh, I wish," crooned the dispatcher. "Memaw says Violet and Ophelia were both born here in Bayou Gavotte. Their mama was a beautiful girl from New Orleans. Violet's daddy was the gangster who started Blood and Velvet. He and their mama split up when Violet was a kid, because their mama wanted a normal life, no clubs and weirdos and all that. She married Ophelia's daddy, a college professor, and Ophelia was born. Which would have been fine, except Mr. Beliveau turned out to be totally paranoid. Memaw says he thought everyone at the college and then everyone in town was sleeping with his wife." She paused again. "Gideon?"

"Go on, babe, I'm all ears."

"Not quite, I hope. You have other useful organs." She giggled. "They up and moved to Atlanta, but he got even worse there, 'cause there were so many more people to be sleeping with her, and one day he went off his rocker and shot himself."

Gideon let out a long breath. "Sounds like a blessed release for his wife."

"Memaw says she married again soon after, so who knows?—maybe she really was messing around. Violet came back here right out of high school to learn to run the club, and her daddy left it to her in his will. Ophelia didn't move back till after college, maybe three years ago."

He thanked her for the info and turned off the Mercedes, leaving Gretchen silently protesting another stretch of boredom, and went through the patio entrance of the Impractical Cat. He cursed at the chaos inside. Poetry night or not, Leopard would have to spare him a minute or two.

He slipped onto a barstool and ordered a beer. "Leopard around?"

"Who wants to know?" asked the pimply recruit behind the bar. Twerp.

"Gideon O'Toole. Tell him I need to talk to him."

"Next you'll be saying you want to see Constantine Dufray." The kid picked up a joint from an ashtray and took a long drag.

"That would work, too." Gideon grabbed the joint and dropped it sizzling into a dirty shot glass. "You know the rules about toking up on the job. Give Leopard my message, and maybe I won't turn you in."

The kid behind the counter glared, just as Leopard's bellow blasted through the bar. "What the fucking hell is Ophelia's number doing in the fucking men's room again?" Leopard slammed through the doors to the kitchen, bellowed some more, and swung out again, whacking Gideon on the shoulder on his way past. "Come the fuck on over here."

Gideon followed, Leopard elbowing the crowd out of his way and nodding to the bodyguard at the restroom door. After one glance at the restroom wall, Gideon came out possessed by such rage that he could barely speak. A busboy with a can of spray paint scurried past, and Gideon shoved his way down the hall to Leopard's office. Inside with the door closed, he recovered his power of speech in a stream of curses. Finally, he took a deep breath and sank onto the couch.

"Second time today," a rough voice said from the far corner.

Gideon stiffened, appalled at his lapse of awareness. Women. They really screwed with your head. Small comfort, that he hadn't reacted further. Most men were downright terrified by Constantine Dufray's air of carefully suppressed violence, not to mention his even worse reputation. But the rocker was Leopard's friend, which counted for a lot—even if, God forbid, Ophelia was in love with him. Yet if she loved Dufray, a man who it was said dealt summary justice on whomever he saw fit, sent tormenting dreams to his enemies (not that Gideon believed a word of it), and was thought to have murdered his wife, why was she so unnerved by Gideon? He was relatively harmless.

He pulled himself together. "How often does this happen?"

"From time to time," Constantine said. He laid down his guitar and ambled to the espresso machine. "Espresso? Cappuccino?" Eyes hard, the man's voice was mocking. "No sense getting all bent out of shape." He motioned to the coffee machine again, an amused question in his glance.

"Espresso. Single shot. Thanks." Gideon fixed his eyes on the one-way glass to the hall, automatically noticing the patrons entering from the patio, the waitresses scurrying by. But watching wouldn't do much good now.

"I wonder if it was the same dude both times." Constantine scooped coffee into the filter and tamped it down. "Murder has been done for less."

For the second or third time in their acquaintance, Gideon found himself in complete agreement with the vigilante rocker. "Lep needs to put a camera in there."

"Illegal. Am I lucky you weren't so lax when it came to evidence against me?"

"You're lucky you were two hundred miles away when your wife was killed," Gideon said. "And so am I."

Leopard came in cursing and slammed the door. "We need to get a goddamn camera in there, and fast."

"Tonight after close," Constantine said wearily. "But it's only a Band-Aid. So we catch this creep and waste him. There'll be others soon enough. She'd attract a lot less attention if she got herself laid." He grinned offensively at Gideon. "You up for it, sport?"

Leopard chuckled. "Constantine's right. You'd be doing a public service. Makes me look bad, assholes getting away with scribbling on my restroom walls. Still, only if she wants you."

"She wants me." Gideon accepted an espresso from Constantine. "But any time she catches herself warming up to me, she backs off like she's been burned."

"Not used to rejection, sport?" Constantine's voice held more amusement than insult.

"She's not rejecting me." Gideon sipped his drink. "She kissed me." Into the loaded silence that followed, he added, "But she's scared of something."

"Not so dumb after all." Constantine retired into the corner and picked up his guitar. "We should have found her a detective years ago."

Gideon let out a long, slow breath. "What was it? Rape?"

Leopard snorted. "God help the asshole that tries to rape Ophelia." He shrugged. "Guys see her, they fall hard and fast and out of control. Scares her."

"So . . . that means no one can fall for her? Her first reaction is panic, so she runs?"

Leopard sighed and shook his head. "What'd you do? Tell her you love her, that shit?"

"Not quite. It's a long story. . . . She's setting a trap for a blackmailer."

"Go, Ophelia," Constantine said. A raunchy riff emanated from the guitar.

"Don't tell me," Leopard said. "You tried to stop her."

"I made it clear that if she didn't cooperate, I'd harass her until she did."

"You dumbass. What'd she do, knee you in the nuts?"

"She said if she needed help, she'd get it from you. Then she drove away."

"Shit, Gideon, you're better with women than that."

"Not this one." Gideon was rueful. "Should I let her go ahead and trap the blackmailer?"

"Better not get in her way," Leopard said, laughing. Constantine echoed him from the corner.

"Too late. She looked like she wanted to bite me."

"Not much doubt about that," Constantine said, and Leopard cracked up.

Gideon stretched. "Too bad I can't let her run this thing on her own. Get back to my peaceful life." Nonchalantly, he added, "If it were only Ophelia, I'd say lump it, she's not worth the bother, but my sister's involved."

"Lump it?" Constantine's tone bordered on a threat.

Leopard merely sounded incredulous. "Ophelia's 'not worth the bother'?"

"Hell, it's not you like you two are falling all over yourselves to get her. Or if you already have her, why would you offer her up to me on a platter? If she's too screwed up to appeal to a couple of rock musicians . . ." He took a contemplative sip of his espresso. "Either that, or she's playing some game."

"Ophelia's not screwed up," Constantine said. "And she doesn't play games."

"She's way-high maintenance," Leopard proposed. "Sex at least twice a day."

"And she doesn't approve of violence," said Constantine. "She'd never do for me."

"Not only that, she reminds me of my mom," Leopard added. "No way."

"So, since she's got the hots for you, you poor sucker—"

"You're the sacrificial lamb."

"If she's so hot for me," Gideon asked, "why is she running away?" He drained his cup and folded his arms with an air of endless patience. "It has to be more than a few obsessive boyfriends and a father who killed himself over his wife's supposedly imaginary lovers."

Leopard spread his hands. "I hear they really were imaginary. The guy was nuts."

"Ophelia can't possibly think every man will be the same. Her mother got married again."

"To a religious fanatic," Leopard reminded him. "Not sure whether that's a plus or not."

"I'm not a thug," Gideon said, ticking off one finger. "Not a vigilante, either. I'm not a lunatic. Not a fanatic." He ticked off three more fingers. "What else do I have to not be? A lowlife? A slanderer? No problem. In the few hours since I met Ophelia, she's been called bad news, a bitch, a dyke, a child abuser, the best gangbang in town . . ." Gideon took a deep breath. "And yet, a lot of people love that girl, from her sister to my first-grade teacher to the guy in the gift shop of the Chamber."

"Child abuser?" Constantine's tone chilled even Gideon's heart. "Who said that?"

"Some idiot who was fool enough to believe it," Gideon replied. "It doesn't matter. What matters is who put the idea in his head."

Leopard stood. "You two duke this out. I gotta take care of some last-minute shit." He disappeared into the noise and lights of poetry night.

"You may get off on being judge, jury, and executioner," Gideon said to Constantine, "but let me find the culprit first."

"So long as you find him," Constantine replied. The phone on the desk rang and he picked it up. "Hello, Violet," he said, and after ten seconds started laughing. "It sounds serious," he chuckled, and "Willy Wyler, huh?" An obnoxious grin. "I'd better come over and save you." Finally, doubled over with laughter, he managed, "Good-bye, Ophelia," and hung up. "You're right," he told Gideon. "Willy wouldn't have the guts or the imagination to come up with that. You could have just told me."

"It's a frigging blackmail case. I didn't want to turn it into a murder."

Constantine grinned. "Gotta satisfy my bloodlust somehow, sport. Either I wipe whoever said that about Ophelia, or I wait till you hurt Ophelia and then wipe you."

"Why would I hurt her?"

Constantine shrugged. "People do, and they're mostly the men who fall for her. You're up shit creek now for better or for worse. I sure hope I won't have to kill you."

Gideon laughed and played a hunch. "You're a jackass, Dufray."

"Uh-huh," Constantine agreed. "Let's get out of this hell-hole. Poetry nights are the pits."

CHAPTER EIGHT 🌷

Gideon and Constantine left Tony's Greek and Italian restaurant by the back door. They had eaten on a private patio, where Gretchen was treated to enough scraps to renew her patience. The owner of the restaurant, Constantine's friend, hadn't appeared during their meal.

"Meet him some other time," the Native American rocker said. He pulled his long black hair into a ponytail and stuffed it under a ball cap. Together they walked across a deserted alley and through the yard of a vacant house to the parallel street where Gideon had parked the Mercedes.

"Ophelia will be pissed if you mess with Plato Lavoie," Constantine said, as they drove toward Blood and Velvet through the clear spring night. "She knows all about the platform in his tree."

"I won't mess with him," Gideon replied. "Only ask him a few questions. If he didn't do the dead-cat thing, maybe he saw who did."

"Not likely." Constantine shook his head. "He works evenings and sleeps till afternoon, and by then Ophelia's home. Nights he's not working, he hangs at Blood and Velvet."

"I still have to ask."

Constantine snorted. "You want to size him up. See if he's a threat to your woman."

"That too," said Gideon amicably.

A block from Blood and Velvet, Constantine jerked his

head to the right. "Park at the back. Maybe we should see if your woman's a threat to you."

Gideon did a mental eye roll and pulled around behind the club. Constantine directed him to park across the alley next to an eight-foot brick wall surrounding a huge purple Victorian house—Violet's, evidently. Gretchen sighed and lay down in the back seat to wait once again.

Constantine unlocked a gate in the wall and led Gideon into a small back garden. Exterior lights tripped on, revealing a deck ringed by pots of dangling vines and a short flight of steps to a brick patio crowded with plants in dingy pots. Ophelia's inventory, Gideon guessed, in its temporary home. In the shadows near the gate stood a stone statue of a woman.

Constantine led the way to the deck. "Ophelia wouldn't let her display it in Blood and Velvet. After weeks of threats and tantrums, Violet compromised and put it here." He reached under the deck and flipped a switch, indicating the statue with a sweep of the hand. Ophelia stood in wind-blown glory, curls and cape billowing behind, naked but for flying fabric at her nipples and crotch, forever aflame in artificial stone. One raised arm brandished a whip; the other hand cradled a ball whose chain coiled next to her bare, restless feet. And then there were the fangs—slender, sharp, and deadly, glistening in the harsh light.

"Lord Almighty."

"Sure you want to take that on?" Constantine asked roughly.

Gideon strode across the patio and down an azalea-lined path toward the statue, which was set on a short pedestal and sheltered from prying eyes by the garden wall. "I want the living, breathing version. What was this, a publicity stunt?"

Constantine came up behind him. "When Ophelia moved here, Violet assumed she would join her in running the club. Ophelia tried for a while, but she'd rather be up at dawn mucking in the dirt than out at midnight with a horde of screwed-up partiers. They had some vampire pics done, and Vi had a sculptor model this statue on them without telling Ophelia. They had a bloody fight about it, Ophelia being stubborn as hell and Violet unable to see any point of view but her own, but they made up and parted ways soon after. Vi still has hopes Ophelia will change her mind." He paused. "Not likely. Ophelia inherited the trailer with several acres going down to the river, as well as the tract where Plato lives, from her old man."

"She's Plato's landlady?" Gideon ran his eyes over every detail of the statue, but he kept going back to one particular feature.

"Yep," Constantine said. "Not too thrilled by the fangs, huh, sport?"

"They're ridiculous." Gideon shrugged and tore himself away.

Constantine reached for the switch. "Not sexy? Not scary? They're a little out of proportion, but the sculptor wanted them to show."

"They're like the fake fangs she picked up at the Chamber tonight. Really dumb."

Constantine returned Ophelia's likeness to the cool, forgiving darkness, and five minutes later they walked through the candlelit anteroom of Blood and Velvet.

A bartender greeted Constantine, while his eyes stayed on Gideon. "What'll it be—blood and tonic?" He whipped a knife out from under the bar and made as if to slit his wrist. "The blood is very fresh." He threw back his head, showing incisors sharpened to points, and laughed like a maniac.

"Blame Vi," Constantine told Gideon. "She says the customers like it."

"Sure scared a blonde bitch a minute ago." The bartender gave Constantine a put-upon look, swiped his rag around the bar. "But not enough to get her to leave."

Constantine cocked his head. "Problems?"

"Vi and Ophelia are in the photo studio. Plato got wind and went upstairs."

"Ophelia can handle Plato," Constantine promised. "She wouldn't thank me for interfering."

"It's not only that," the bartender said, his eyes sliding to Gideon and away.

"He's a cop, but he's family," Constantine said. "Say what you have to, Al."

Al spoke just loud enough to be heard above Violet's elegant taste in jazz. "It's this Sims character, the one Vi's suspicious about. He's been asking nosy questions and acting like he's hot for her, but she knows he doesn't have it bad. Now he's here with this blonde with an agenda, and they took off after Plato. If they see Plato with Ophelia . . ." He spread his hands. "It's not the kind of publicity Violet goes for."

"Darby Sims?" Gideon spoke up. "The blonde's in a black sequined dress?" When Al nodded, he said, "Dar's a friend of mine. He'll tell me what's going on."

"A word of warning about Plato," Constantine said on the way upstairs. "He sees himself as Ophelia's love slave. He'll be slobbering all over her."

Gideon swore.

"You'll have to get used to it, sport. There'll always be guys like him getting off on her."

"Idiots. How did your wife like it, with all those fans fantasizing about you?"

Constantine sneered. "Whenever my wife emerged from her drug-induced stupor, she broadcast to the entire world that sex with me was a nightmare—on a mission to save my female fans from a like fate. Not that I was likely to sleep with any of them, but how was she to know? Fortunately, most of the little fools either thought she was delusional or that she wasn't woman enough to take me, whatever that means."

At the third floor they turned down a long corridor. At the far end, Darby and the blonde rounded a corner.

"It's a good thing my wife is dead," Constantine said.

Gideon had no answer for that.

"Can we get on with this?" Ophelia lisped. "These fake fangs are killing me."

"I have to get it right." Artemisia adjusted one light and hurried across the room to another. "If I have to quit teaching, you could hire me to take kinky pictures."

"You won't quit teaching," Violet said.

Ophelia shivered in the black teddy and fingered the whip. "This is not supposed to look professional. The pictures can be crap, as long as I'm clearly visible with some unidentifiable male. Damn it, I can't talk properly with these fangs in the way!"

"So shut up," Tony said. He shifted his hairy legs on the chaise lounge upholstered with fake leopard skin. In only boxers and a pink blindfold, he still looked far from vulnerable. He pulled the scarf over his eyes. "Wake me when it's time to go home."

"If you fall asleep, we really will tie you up," Ophelia warned.

"Go ahead and try," Tony replied.

Violet stood back, nodding approval. "Angel, you look magnificent! Oh, I *do* wish you'd come work in the club again."

Ophelia snarled, and Art flashed one picture, then two, then three.

Violet said, "Hold on, Artemisia, her stockings are crooked." She adjusted a garter and let Art shoot more. "Since you won't wear heels, angel, how about wind in your hair? That's one of the best features of your statue."

"I refuse to freeze my boobs off," Ophelia said.

A gentle knock sounded on the door, followed by a much sharper one. "It's probably for me," Violet said, heading for it.

"Two more," Ophelia suggested. "That'll leave room for

some garden pictures on the roll." She straddled Tony and hovered above him, brandishing the whip.

Violet opened the door a crack, and the murmur of voices came through. Art snapped a picture from the side and went to the head of the chaise to get the last one from the front. "I'll be out in two minutes," Violet said.

"I want Ophelia!" A strident female voice was followed by a growled male protest.

Violet said, "Our photo session is almost done. Oh, hello, Plato. Now, you know Ophelia doesn't like it when you—"

"She's in costume! I have to see her!" Plato burst past Violet and flung the door wide.

"Shit." Ophelia leaped off the chaise lounge and advanced on Plato, whip raised. He whimpered and cowered into the corner, grinning like a fool. "Stay!" she ordered, and the man crumpled happily into a heap on the floor. Ophelia swiveled toward the doorway, where a tall black hunk and a slinky blonde stood gaping. Then Constantine showed up, and—no surprise, considering her luck today—Gideon.

She spat out the fake fangs, scowled at the appreciative grins on the faces of her dearest male friend and would-be lover, and took in the gawping black stranger and the blonde. What a goddamn nuisance.

"Great job," she told Art, who flushed deep red and glanced at her brother.

"You *bitch*," said the slinky blonde.

CHAPTER NINE 🌷

Gideon took in the situation and the room, which was twenty by thirty or so. A small cloth-covered table by the door held a silver tray of bottled water, a box of tissues, and a white ceramic lamp. A large folding screen enclosed the room's far-left corner, and curtains on the far wall covered the doors to a balcony at the back, if he recalled the building exterior correctly. Violet was enraged and squirming in the grip of a burly man wearing only boxers and socks. Artemisia stood beside them, blushing and clutching a camera to her chest. A scrawny balding man who must be Plato crouched against the far wall, and Darby Sims had his back to the door. At center stage, staring each other down, were the blonde from the Chamber and Gideon's very own Ophelia, gripping that ridiculous whip.

"Marissa, you are way out of line," Darby said, his voice rife with embarrassment. "Cool it or they'll call the cops."

"Already here," Gideon said in his ear. "Whatever happened to your taste in women?"

Darby snorted. "Man, I'm glad you showed up. What do we do?"

"Nothing for the moment. Wait. Watch."

"Watching's no problem at all." Darby sucked in a tight, appreciative breath, murmuring, "And I thought Violet was impressive."

"For fuck's sake, Vi," Constantine spoke up. "Let Tony get dressed. Ophelia can fight her own battles." In a smooth, practiced move, he wrapped an arm around Violet as Tony let her go.

"Bitch!" Marissa screamed, oblivious to everyone but Ophelia. "Say something, goddamn it! Bitch!"

"Many people would agree with you," Ophelia answered, rocking on her stockinged heels, feet spread in an aggressive stance.

"It's no surprise that men flock after you, the way you dress," Marissa sneered. "Slut."

Ophelia ran eyes over the blonde's own attire. "They flock after me no matter how I dress. I send them all away. Then their women come crying." She yanked on the bullwhip, snapping it, and Marissa yelped and backed away. "Whose poor, helpless, neglected woman might you be?"

"You don't know, do you?" Spittle flecked Marissa's mouth. "You stole my husband and didn't even think about what it would do to me, you home wrecker, you thief, you witch, you—"

Ophelia cut into the abuse. "I don't steal. If your husband, whoever he is, was jerk enough to come on to me, I told him to fuck off. Some men don't listen." She paced the room and back, toying with her whip, hot as hell but playing it cool. It took all Gideon's concentration to notice anything but her.

"'Whoever he is'!" The blonde threw up her arms. "Did you all hear that? Whoever he is! As if anyone could forget Johnny!"

Ophelia stiffened but let go of the tension so quickly that Gideon almost missed it. She went on walking, turning, the whip coiling through her hand and lashing behind her like a tail. "I've known a lot of Johnnys."

"Johnny Parkerson," Marissa said. "Well? Where is he?"

Ophelia stopped, a tight smile on her lips, her fingers clenched around the handle of her whip, but then recommenced pacing. "Crazy Johnny. Blond like you, lady, and I don't usually go for blonds, but incredibly good-looking. I haven't seen him for ages. Maybe you should try one of the clubs he worked at." She threw her sister a furious scowl.

Violet stopped struggling in Constantine's arm and glared back.

Constantine deposited her on the chaise next to a bewildered Artemisia. "I remember him," he said coolly. "You know, Vi, the exotic dancer. Called himself the Blond Bomb."

Violet made a face. "Oh dear, yes. Anything would set him off." Beside her, Art let out a nervous little titter. "Darby mentioned him just the other day, but Johnny left Bayou Gavotte years ago, and Ophelia's right. He never worked in my club."

"I kicked him halfway to Atlanta," Ophelia said with satisfaction. "I did you a favor, lady. I could have turned him into something like Plato here if I'd wanted." She motioned toward the loony crouched against the wall. "Instead, I sent him home."

"You did a rotten job of it, bitch, because he left me again and came right back here to dance with you in your club."

"True, he did come back again, more than once, but I sent him away every time. As for dancing, it must have been with someone else. It's been years." Ophelia appeared to have lost interest. She began coiling her whip.

Violet stood, saying crisply to the blonde, "I really must get back to work. I have no idea why you've come to harass Ophelia, but I can't have this kind of disruption in my club."

Marissa planted her hands on her hips and shrilled, "I'm here to find my scum-sucking husband! Darby's tried in every club in town, but I know you've got him hidden someplace!"

"Why would we hide Johnny? Ophelia told him to go away—and when she says go away, she means it." Violet glanced at Gideon. "Usually. In Johnny's case, definitely. He's a very unstable man. We were relieved when he left."

"But he never came home!"

Ophelia looked up from the whip, that tight smile back, her voice tense and clear. "What do you bet he found someone new?"

"Ophelia!" Violet said. "Don't be catty!"

A muscle quivered at the corner of Ophelia's mouth. "Her current escort doesn't look too thrilled."

"Hard to believe the poor bastard could find anyone to equal you, baby," Tony said unexpectedly. "It's been entertaining, but I've gotta go." He slid his feet into his loafers and left.

Violet gathered the clamps and chains from the photography session and stowed them in the silver shopping bag from the Chamber. To Marissa, she said, "Girl, it's obvious you did a rotten job of holding on to him, but look on the bright side: He's crazy. He got on everyone's nerves. He must have been impossible to live with." She turned away. "Constantine, please walk Artemisia to her car. You've made your arrangements with Ophelia, haven't you, Art?"

Art dragged her eyes from Dufray. "Um, yeah." She glared at Gideon, daring him to object.

Violet smirked. "Don't worry about your sister, Mr. O'Toole. Constantine can be a perfect gentleman when he chooses."

Gideon was doing his damnedest to keep a blank expression, but the struggle must have shown. Or not. Nobody in his right mind would cheerfully watch his sister waltz away with Dufray.

"Hey!" Marissa howled. "You can't brush me off. My husband has disappeared, and I don't know if he's alive or dead, and—" She gaped. "My God, that's Constantine Dufray!"

"I'm sure he'd be happy to give you an autograph," Violet said.

"An autograph!" Marissa screeched. "From a murderer?"

"Tsk." Violet shook her head, and Constantine grinned.

Marissa's face was suffused with rage. "I've looked for Johnny all over, and I haven't been able to find hide nor hair of him, and now I know why. He got on your nerves and you had a nice convenient murderer right here in town. You had Constantine Dufray kill him!"

An astonished silence fell. The coils of the whip slithered out of Ophelia's hands. Gideon stared at her, Darby hissed with chagrin, and Violet wound herself up to speak. Constantine started to laugh. Plato against the wall pitched in, a high hysterical sound, and Ophelia gathered the whip and stalked toward him.

"Shut up!"

He clamped his hand over his mouth and rolled onto his back like a dog. One leg wagged out of control.

Still laughing, Constantine laid a hand on Art's shoulder. She jumped, her eyes flying to his. "Don't worry, babe." He pushed her gently toward the door. "You couldn't have a safer escort. I'll kill anyone who gets in the way." He tapped her on the rear and they went out.

"I'll go to the cops," Marissa spat. "He won't get away with this. None of you will."

"Cops?" said Ophelia coolly. "There's one right here in the room."

Oh, no she didn't. "I'm off duty," Gideon said. "Go to the station in the morning and file a missing-persons report."

"Bullshit. That's all I hear in this town." Marissa sneered. "Did your girlfriend like her vibrator? Obviously that matters more than whether my husband's alive or dead."

"When I'm off duty and it's not my case? Of course it matters more."

"They say the cops in Bayou Gavotte are in bed with the clubs, and you're the proof. You'll all be sorry!" Her heels clacked across the floor as she stormed away. "Come on, Darby."

Gideon's friend blew out a breath. "Later, man," he said. "I'm really sorry, Violet."

Violet folded her arms and tapped an irritated foot.

"Come *on*." Marissa stomped out the door. Darby threw up his hands and followed.

Ophelia stood over Plato, fingering her whip, and for a brief appalling moment Gideon envisioned himself in Plato's position as a love slave. Then he returned to sanity.

"You'll have to do without your smile this time, Plato," Ophelia said, her voice tight but not unkind. "Now get out." The man whimpered and shambled backward toward the door, eyes still fixed on her every move. Ophelia threw down the whip and scowled at Gideon, as if to order him the same, but her lip trembled treacherously.

"Gideon, I expect you to see that Ophelia gets home safely," Violet said. "Turn off the lights when you leave. Plato, *move*." She pushed the man out and softly closed the doors behind them.

Ophelia ran across the room, parted the curtains, and lunged onto the balcony. Gideon didn't want to talk to her, hurt and angry as she was, but Violet had left him little choice. At the very least, he should . . . what? Apologize for being such an insensitive brute? If he'd known about Johnny . . . No, the magnitude of the problem hadn't sunk in. Factor in the Platos of the world, and no wonder she was running scared. Sure, he'd been a jerk, but this evening's crap wasn't his fault. No apologies, then. And he couldn't promise never to touch her again, either. . . .

He turned off the spotlights, leaving only the small lamp burning on the table by the door. Slipping between the drapes, he pushed out onto the balcony. It extended the length of the room. A row of window boxes massed with petunias adorned the wrought-iron railing, flanked by a row of potted ficus trees. Some sort of fern dangled overhead. Music from the club dance floor drifted up through the heavy darkness. For a cold second he couldn't find Ophelia, but then he heard small, distressed sounds from the far right. She slumped between a ficus and the railing, head and half her torso over the edge, retching.

"Oh, hell," Gideon whispered, but this he could handle.

He went for tissues and a bottle of water. Returning, he hovered while she heaved, spat, and shuddered. Then he laid one hand on hers that clutched the railing and said, "Here, take these."

She accepted the tissues and wiped her face, took the water he held out, spat some more, and finally sagged back, shivering all over. Gideon removed his shirt and laid it over her shoulders. Tentatively, he put an arm around her. She didn't lean into him but didn't pull away either, just shivered and then shivered less, and finally took a long, deep breath.

"Better?" Gideon asked.

Ophelia shrugged under his shirt. "I'm all right, thanks. You can go now." But she didn't sound all right, and she made no effort to escape.

I can't just back off, honey, he thought. *That won't solve anything. Not for me, not for you, either.* He gazed across the roof of Violet's house and the rooftops beyond, into the deep purple sky of Bayou Gavotte, and prayed for inspiration.

From three stories below came a mournful howl. "Poor Gretchen," Gideon said. "She's wondering why she's stuck down there with your statue while I'm up here with the real thing."

"I suppose Constantine took you to see it," Ophelia said bitterly. "How dare Vi order you to take me home!"

"She's concerned for your safety," Gideon said. "So am I."

Ophelia shifted out of the circle of his arm. "She's trying to force me into bed with you. It's not going to work."

"Of course not," Gideon said. "I can woo you without any help from Violet or Constantine."

"Oh God," Ophelia replied, "Please don't be one of those." She pushed shakily from the railing, and the shirt slipped off her shoulders.

He caught it and put out a hand to steady her. "One of what?"

"A romantic. Wooing me. Everything smelling of roses."

"Right now you smell of vomit, honey. No worries."

Ophelia gave a small sound, almost like a laugh, and tripped slowly toward the doors. Gretchen bayed miserably below. "Go get that poor dog. You don't have to take me home. I must have eaten something bad, but I feel fine now."

"Gretchen can wait," Gideon said.

"Do I have to spell everything out? I don't *want* you to take me home." With obvious effort she added, "You've been very kind. Now, please go away."

Gideon followed her inside, shutting the balcony doors and pulling the curtains. "Screw kind. We need to talk."

"You don't give up, do you?"

"No," Gideon agreed.

With a dazzlingly abrupt shift of gears, Ophelia perched on the edge of the chaise lounge, unsnapped her garters, and rolled her stockings deliberately down her tanned, shapely legs and off her toes. She picked them up between thumb and forefinger and carried them to a silver trash basket by the screen. "Help yourself, if you're into souvenirs. I don't see any barf on them." She let the stockings fall.

Gideon felt blood crawl up his face. "No, thanks."

Ophelia disappeared behind the screen, which Gideon now saw was decorated with Oriental erotica. No surprise. A few seconds later, her black teddy flew over the top. "If you don't want the teddy, I suppose I could give it to Plato. He'll get off on it for weeks."

He would not let her get to him. Gideon struggled between something akin to fury and the urge to grab the flimsy black fabric and bury his face in it, risking the smell of vomit for one whiff of Ophelia. When he knew he could control his voice, he said, "What's your arrangement with Art?"

He watched her feet at the bottom of the screen: Underwear on. Shorts. A few seconds later, she came out carrying her socks and sneakers, sat on the chaise again. "If I don't tell you, I suppose you'll go harass her."

"Reluctantly, yes, I will do exactly that. I'd rather not

jeopardize my already-shaky relationship with my sister by giving her the third degree, but you leave me no choice."

"Oh, so you're not looking for a relationship with me, then," Ophelia said. "You're just harassing me for a quickie. What a relief. Nothing to jeopardize. Of course, you won't get the quickie, either, but at least your emotions aren't involved." She jerked her sock straight and shoved one foot into a shoe. "I hope the lucky girl who gets the vibrator also gets a better deal."

"Ophelia," Gideon said gently, and she threw him a hot glare and looked away again, tugging on the second sock. He said, "I can pussyfoot around with my sister and try not to hurt her feelings. I can't and won't do that with you. The vibrator is yours and you know it. Now, please tell me what's going on."

Ophelia tied her second shoe and let out an exaggerated sigh. "First thing in the morning, she's going to take pictures of some gardens I did, complete with signage, to finish the roll and show the blackmailer where I'm vulnerable. I'm going to stop by her school to pick up the film and drop it off at the print and photo shop." She stood up. "Will that do?"

"It's a mite obvious, but worth a try. How does he contact his victims?"

"By mail. Art said it was a computer-generated fill-in-the-blanks form letter. She's supposed to put the money in the kind of envelope you put film in and leave it in the night drop."

"He's not worried about being caught." Gideon's eyes strayed toward her teddy. "You're not really going to give it to Plato, are you?"

Ophelia scooped the garment up. "Of course not. It belongs to Vi. Now, go."

CHAPTER TEN 🌷

Half a mile from home, Ophelia realized the car behind her was Gideon's. He really wouldn't give up so easily. He wouldn't give up at all. A surge of longing and despair took such hold that she could no longer control the tears she'd battled the whole drive home. She had the best of reasons to suck this cop into her web, to attach him so firmly that . . . *No*. She couldn't. She liked him far too much. She had to keep pushing him away.

Flicking away the tears, she turned into her driveway. Psyche bounded before the headlights to hover under the porch. Ophelia turned off her truck and in one quick movement got out, gripping her shotgun tightly so she wouldn't shake.

Gideon left the headlights on and the engine running, got out, and held the door open for his dog. "Put the gun away, Ophelia." He walked calmly toward her. "It's only me."

"I know who it is." Ophelia's voice broke, and a tear spilled treacherously down her cheek. "Go away!"

"Sweetheart—"

"Don't call me that! I am not sweet."

She watched Gideon control himself and start again. "I will leave in a minute. I brought Gretchen to stay with you. She's good company, and she'll warn you if there's any danger."

"There is no danger I can't handle myself." How had he come up with such a blessed idea? "Take your dog and go home." Ophelia bit down hard, piercing her lip, ignoring the blood, fighting tears, wanting the dog like crazy. She felt so alone.

Anguish in his voice, Gideon said, "Ophelia, don't cry. Honey, you can't think I'd harass you after what you've been through tonight."

"You *are* harassing me," she choked out. "I am not honey. I am poison. Get the hell away." She sniffled hard, clutching her shotgun, and Gretchen trotted up and stuck a cool nose under her other hand. Ophelia's fingers moved by instinct toward the dog's curls, but she yanked her hand away, clenching and unclenching her fist, needing and wanting the animal so much it hurt. "Gretchen doesn't want to stay with me. She's yours. Take her and go away."

"I discussed it with her on the ride over, and she agreed to stay with you."

"That's the stupidest thing I've ever heard in my life." Ophelia cocked the shotgun hammer, but it didn't have the intended effect—Gideon just stood there. She added, "Get off my property and don't come back."

Gideon swore under his breath. "Stupid or not, Gretchen is staying with you." As if on cue, the dog planted her butt on the drive.

"Damn it, Gideon!" Ophelia let out a scream of rage and fired, kicking up gravel far too close to Gideon's feet. He didn't flinch. He didn't move a goddamn hair. "Don't you get it?" she yelled. "I'm trying to protect you from yourself. I am not safe!"

"That's the stupidest thing I ever heard in my life," Gideon echoed in bitter mockery. "You could at least come up with an intelligent lie."

Ophelia opened her mouth but shut it again. Pissing him off was what she wanted.

Still, the disgust in his voice tore into her. "Don't worry. I'm out of here, and I won't come back unless you need me. Stay, Gretchen. Stay with Ophelia." Gideon got in his car and backed into the turnaround, flinging his last words through the window. "What makes you think I give a damn about being safe?"

The dream came as it always did, hard and fast and exploding with fangs and the intoxicating, horrifying smell of human blood. But this time a dog's shrill whine cut through the dream and Ophelia jolted awake, fangs out, hands curled into claws, as Psyche hissed from a corner and Gretchen whimpered and shoved at her, then skittered away. Ophelia sucked in a deep, sobbing breath and found herself bathed, as always, not in blood, but in sweat and tears.

She sat up, her head throbbing. The light was on. She had cried herself to sleep on the carpet with Gretchen huddled next to her—a frightening sign, since never in the last few years had she shed more than a tear or two, except in her dreams, or slept anywhere except showered and clean in her bed. She had been in control. And now she wasn't.

She began to rebuild control, first with a shower, then with tea and cheese toast shared with the cat and dog. She climbed into bed and buried her feet under Gretchen's flank. If Gideon kept sticking his nose into her business, she'd keep distracting him, with sex as a last resort. If Gideon were her lover, Leopard and Constantine wouldn't harm him no matter what. He'd be safe. Except from her.

Every which way, things looked bad. But while she didn't have a hope in hell of controlling random events and people, she could at least try to control herself. And who knew? She might, as Violet suggested, get some excellent sex before everything blew up in her face. On that dubiously cheerful thought, she snuggled gratefully next to Gretchen and forced herself back to sleep.

"You'll never guess what happened last night," Artemisia said the following morning. She stood outside the high-school art room, glowing in the sunshine. Softer and sexier. Transformed.

"What?" Ophelia knew what was coming.

"Gideon called me."

Okay, so she didn't know. "He wasn't supposed to harass you!"

"He *apologized* to me, Ophelia. He said he'd been a poor excuse for a brother and that we should spend more time together." She bit her lip. "You must have said something to him."

"A little," Ophelia admitted.

"It almost killed me not to tell him you're a vamp. Guess what?" Art said.

Here it came. "What? Where's the film? I have to get going."

Art fished the film out of the pocket of her smock. "I *really* like Constantine. How can people believe he's a murderer?"

Ophelia said nothing, because there was no acceptable answer that was also the truth.

Fortunately, Art was perfectly ready to do the talking. "He was so sweet to me last night, even though I blabbed my whole life story to him. He says my ex was a frigid prig and that I'm a lovely, sensual woman. He says if I want Dar, I should go sweep him off his feet."

"Dar?"

"The black guy who was with that horrible woman last night. He's a friend of Gideon's. I had a huge crush on him in high school, but I was already going out with Steve then, and in any case Dad would never have let me date a black guy. But now I can do exactly as I please, except that it wouldn't be right to steal him from another woman. Except that she's married to someone else, unless he's dead, but either way, it's not right to poach. And she's gorgeous and sexy, and I'm only his friend's little sister. . . ." She trailed off, flushing. "Guess what?"

Finally.

Art leaned closer. "Constantine gave me an orgasm!" She blushed fiercely red. "It's not like it sounds. I didn't sleep with him. He just touched me, and boom!"

Ophelia smiled. "He's good at energy manipulation. He must like you."

"Or feel sorry for me," Art said philosophically. "He said he did it to prove to me that I was sexy, which makes no sense, because he was the one who made it happen, but you know what? I really *feel* sexy now. He says Dar kept looking at me, and that the other woman was only sexy on the outside, and she was screwing even that up by being such a bitch." Uneasiness crossed her face. "He said she won't be in town long, but how can he possibly know that? He sort of scared me for a bit, but then he was sweet again, and he made me give him my number."

Damn. What was Constantine planning?

"Anyway, I've decided to at least *try* for Dar, but I wish I hadn't done the nude modeling. What if Dar finds out?"

"If he minds about the modeling," Ophelia said, "he's not worth a minute of your time."

"But—"

"No buts. I don't know why you even considered paying the blackmailer. What about the drawings the students made of you? You have no control over what happens to those, any more that you have over the photos. You're already out there. Just forget the whole thing."

Art looked dubious, but then Gretchen appeared from foraging in the school grounds and nuzzled her. "That's Gideon's dog!"

"He loaned her to me," said Ophelia flatly.

"Gideon loaned you *Gretchen*? She's his absolute favorite dog. He says she's the only woman he can talk to." Art grinned. "I thought he'd given up on sleeping with you. He told me you said no."

"It's never that simple," Ophelia said.

* * *

In the print and photo shop, Ophelia resisted punching the slime wearing a Constantine T-shirt and focused on being an innocent, friendly dupe. Such a small shop couldn't have more than three or four employees, and this guy was here in the morning to open the night drop. He probably lived in the apartment overhead; he'd appeared via the stairs in the back room when she'd come into the store.

She handed in the film she had picked up from Art and paid for some prints she had ordered a few days before. "That'll be seven sixty-three," the slime said, playing with his tongue ring. A strand of dirty blond hair caught at the edge of his mouth. "Nice flower pictures. Did you take them?"

"Yeah, I'm a landscaper, and those are some of the gardens I did," Ophelia said politely. You never knew what might drum up business, although she wouldn't touch this creep with a fifty-foot hose. She handed him a ten-dollar bill and his fingers touched hers. *Eew.*

"I bet you photograph real well, ma'am," he said slowly, with a widening leer. "You're quite a flower all on your own."

"Fuck off, asshole." So much for friendly and innocent. This did not bode well for success at self-control.

"Don't even *think* about her, if you value your life." Donnie Donaldson ambled up to the counter. "Ophelia wields a mean shotgun."

Crap. Why had he shown up now? "Hey, Donnie."

Donaldson grinned. "Saw you pull it on that cop last night."

"Donnie, you're such an old woman, peeking out the window at your neighbors."

"Nothing else to do. Think he'll stay away? He's got plenty of guts, I have to say that for him. He didn't budge when you shot at him."

Ophelia shrugged as if it didn't matter. "He said he wouldn't come back. He knows I'm not interested."

"Why'd he give you the dog, then?"

Shit. Ophelia rolled her eyes. "I'm thinking of buying her from him," she improvised. "She's a great dog. Well, I gotta go." *And get out of here before my plan is totally screwed.*

"That hot little cunt shot at a *cop?*" The slime's lascivious voice pursued her out the door. "Man, I could use a shot at her!"

That afternoon in the middle-school art room, Joanna Wyler tiptoed to the table where Zelda was snipping pictures from magazines. She whispered, "Shawanda's not here, so can I sit with you?"

"You can sit with me even when Shawanda *is* here." Zelda scooted her stool over. "There's room for three."

"Thanks," Joanna muttered, "but Shawanda scares me to death." She set her own magazines down.

"You'll have to stop being a wimp if you want to hang with me," Zelda said. "If that really is what you want to do." The scissors flew through and around a garden, and roses littered the table. She fixed a challenging gaze on her would-be friend. "What's the deal?"

Joanna flipped jerkily through the top magazine in her pile. "I need advice."

"From me?" Zelda grinned evilly. "First thing, no more preppy button-down shirts." Joanna reddened, looking so miserable that Zelda took pity. "Just joking. What you wear is your business. Or your mother's, in this case. But what kind of advice can you possibly want from me?" She handed a pair of scissors to Joanna. "We'd better look busy. Cut some stuff out."

Joanna started snipping at random. In a low voice, she said, "I need advice about sex."

Zelda struggled to ignore a surge of fury; she might not care whether she turned out to be a vamp, but she absolutely refused to inherit her mother's temper. She hadn't tamped it down quickly enough, judging by the alarm in Joanna's eyes.

"Wait till tomorrow," she said evenly. "Shawanda knows more than me. She's older. She's done it."

"I'm sorry." Joanna cut jaggedly around the fork in a silverware ad, her hands trembling. "Your Mom has a club, so I thought . . . God, I'm such a loser. I can't say anything right."

Zelda put out a hand to pat Joanna's. "Calm down. I'm not pissed off at you, and even if I was, what does it matter? I'd still be your friend." She tore out a page of daisies.

"Thanks." Joanna's whisper was barely audible. "I didn't mean you were sleeping around. I didn't mean your mom's a whore or anything awful like that. But you're different, and my friends are so useless. Some of them have had sex, but they're all such . . . such . . ."

"Sheep?" Zelda suggested. Daisies carpeted the roses.

Joanna let out a hysterical giggle and clamped her hand over her mouth. "Uh-huh, and you can't trust grownups, and—"

"Depends on the grownup," Zelda said. "Who do you want to do it with? Him?" She waved the scissors in the direction of a hunky eighth grader named Rick, whose collage of a multicolored goddess had begun to take shape. "It's obvious sex is on his mind."

"No!" Joanna hissed. Hurriedly, she cut out a carving knife.

"Maybe those are your boobs he's putting on his collage," Zelda murmured. Rick raised his head, first looking blankly in their direction and then unexpectedly fixing on Zelda. She grinned at him and turned back to littering the table with flowers. "They're definitely not mine."

"You're so lucky. I hate the way guys look at me," Joanna said. She snipped around a cross studded with diamonds.

"Ignore them," Zelda said. "And to answer your unspoken question, don't have sex."

"That's easy for you to say, but you don't care what other

people think. I need a good reason why not. And don't tell me it's illegal until I'm sixteen or I might get pregnant or an STD. I already know all that." Joanna found a photo of a pair of garden shears and cut them out.

"How about because you don't want to?"

Joanna blinked.

"Having a guy look at your boobs is part of sex," Zelda said. "If you don't want that, you don't want sex. And then, of course, there's love. It's better if you're in love."

"That's what Ophelia said. That's what her policeman said, too."

"They were right. The only way to not care what other people think is to just not care."

"But—"

"Think about it," Zelda said. "You don't have to be a wimp if you don't want to."

A minute later, Joanna looked up from the vodka bottle she had cut from an ad. "They may not be your boobs," she told Zelda, "but Rick is definitely looking at you."

Zelda raised her eyes coolly to Rick's. His mouth hung slightly open, and his eyes widened when Zelda's gaze fenced with his.

Zelda shrugged and turned back to her friend.

At the nursery that afternoon, Ophelia stood by while a sturdy guy named Bob loaded Japanese maples onto her truck. She could have done it fine herself, but Bob was dying to help, to gaze at Ophelia and brush by her any chance he could. The last-ditch option of jumping Gideon was looking better by the second. Hot sex would take the edge off her allure.

Stop planning on sex. That's only a last resort.

Stop hoping for a last resort.

Late in the day, when all Andrea Dukas's plants, including the stressed azaleas, had homes in the ground, Ophelia parked in a small gravel lot off the river road and wandered with Gretchen down a path to the river. "I'm not exactly planning to sleep with him, but I'm incredibly nervous," she told the dog. "What if he doesn't like the fangs?"

Gretchen grinned, showing a delightful set of teeth.

"Sure, but you're *supposed* to have magnificent canines. I don't want a man who has sex with me because he can't help himself and then freaks out afterwards." Gretchen hared off down the trail, and a minute later an angry quail rose from the underbrush. The dog lolloped expectantly back, but Ophelia's mind was elsewhere. "I know it's old-fashioned and impractical for a vamp, but deep in my unrealistic heart, I want someone who loves me—me *and* my fangs."

Gretchen nudged Ophelia and took off again. Ophelia reached the edge of the woods to see two wild turkeys flap noisily away. The dog returned and butted the shotgun tucked under Ophelia's arm.

"A hunter, are you? I'm not hunting today, Gretchen. The only prey I need is a man."

They stood by the river, their respective curls ruffled by a fitful breeze. *It's my nature,* thought Ophelia. *I'm a frigging man hunter. Nothing more.*

A solitary fisherman appeared upriver on the opposite bank and raised a cordial hand; men were so much more pleasant at a distance. Ophelia waved away a cloud of gnats and picked her way disconsolately downriver. At a flicker of movement beside a log, she and Gretchen both stopped dead.

Slowly, very slowly, Ophelia laid down the gun, pulled a slingshot out of her pocket, loaded it with a convenient pebble, took aim, and let fly. Bingo! The nutria toppled into the river, and Gretchen bounded past, almost knocking Ophelia into the water. She returned with the rodent, neck neatly broken. "Supper," Ophelia said. "Gretchen, you're the best."

They hiked up an overgrown trail toward the road, pushing vines this way and that, dipping under a fallen ironwood, climbing over a rotting pine. They came out of the woods a short way down the road from her truck. Gretchen yipped excitedly and trotted toward the parking area, bounced partway back to Ophelia, and took off again. Ophelia gave up on justifying herself, saw the flashing blue light from a police car, heard voices, and arrived in the parking lot to find Gretchen licking a uniformed policeman.

"Down, Gretchen!" the cop protested. "Where's Gideon? He can't be here yet. He was twenty minutes away five minutes ago." The man's eyes fell on Ophelia and stayed there.

Ophelia glanced from the cop to his car, which partly blocked the entrance to the lot, to a stunned, sick-looking couple propped up by a silver Toyota, and finally to her truck. To two bare feet hanging off the back of it. "What the hell is going on? Who is that in my truck?"

The policeman stopped gaping and remembered his job. "That's your pickup, ma'am? The green truck?"

"Of course it's mine," she snapped. "Is there any other truck here, green or otherwise?" Ophelia marched over to her vehicle, the policeman hurrying alongside, protesting feebly.

Dumped among the maple saplings lay a body. A horrendous pulpy mass had once been the man's face. Blood—there was blood everywhere: on his straggly dark blond hair, on his belly beneath a ripped Constantine shirt, dried and crusted on his jeans. His thigh lay across a helpless, broken maple twig, and his butt had demolished another tree entirely. Her mouth twisted in the effort to keep back her fangs. She pressed a hand to her face and stumbled to the edge of the woods, where she laid her shotgun and the nutria to one side and tried like hell to be sick.

CHAPTER ELEVEN 🌷

From the reception area of Bayou Gavotte's cheerful little police station came a shrill, unwelcome voice. "Who do you think you're looking at?" Marissa said, and then, "This place is a dump," and finally, "I want you to arrest Constantine Dufray." In the back, with a view through a partially open door, Gideon propped his feet up and waited for the inevitable.

"Woo-hoo!" Jeanie clapped her hands. "That's thirty-three whole weeks!"

The chief, unfortunately clad in his oldest overalls today, set the plywood he was staining on a newspaper-covered bench by the wall. He laid his paintbrush beside it, took out his wallet, and handed the dispatcher a five. "Damn it, Jeanie, I can't afford this bet anymore."

"Hey!" the blonde said. "Didn't you hear me?"

"Sure did, ma'am. That's thirty-three straight weeks of complaints about Constantine Dufray. Ever since his wife was poisoned, the psychic researchers have had a field day." He pulled a battered notebook from his hip pocket and sat on the bench. "He been sending you nightmares? That's the most common complaint, followed by sex dreams, suicidal depression—"

Jeanie snorted. "It can't be sex dreams. Women never complain about those. It's their stodgy old husbands who do."

"You don't look suicidal, ma'am," the chief said. "You look

pissed off." He clicked his ballpoint. "What kind of nightmares? Wild mustangs trampling you?"

"That's a sex dream," Jeanie said. "One of the best."

"Tied to a super-size dream catcher?"

"Sex dream." By now, Jeanie would be buffing her long copper nails. "Lame. How about eagle-feather tickle torture?"

"Now, now, Jeanie," the chief said. "This is serious to our visitor, if not to you."

Marissa spat, "He's not sending me nightmares. He killed my husband!"

Jeanie laughed with delight, and the chief threw up his hands. "That's what, twelve?"

"Thirteen," Jeanie said, "and you know it." Grumbling, the chief gave her a twenty. He flipped several pages farther and made a notation. "Are you reporting a murder, ma'am?"

"Goddamn right I am!"

"Not my department," the chief said happily. "Gideon!"

Gideon took his sweet time, emerging to find Marissa pacing the floor in an animal-print bodysuit and a snarl. "This is a missing-persons case," he said. "Nothing to do with me."

"She said it was a homicide," the chief replied blandly.

"It's not a homicide without a corpse," Gideon said.

"Find the frigging corpse, then, and it will be!" Marissa splayed her hands on shiny, leopard-skinned hips. "This is your detective? I want someone else, not Vibrator Man."

Jeanie choked on a giggle. She glanced from Gideon to Marissa and back. "Ooh, what's our resident sex god come up with now? A new interrogation aid?"

"What kind of man gives his girlfriend a vibrator?" Marissa made a face. "An inadequate one."

"You have a new girlfriend, Gideon?" Jeanie bounced up. "Who? Is it *her*?"

"No girlfriend," Gideon said. "It was a gag gift." He leaned across and clicked on Jeanie's keyboard. "Mrs. Parkerson, I checked into your husband's disappearance this morning. We handled it close to two years ago."

Jeanie scanned the computer screen. "John Parkerson, exotic dancer from Atlanta. According to the report of a local pharmacist, Mr. Parkerson filled a prescription for painkillers, mentioning in idle conversation that he'd found a job in Houston. The pharmacist went outside for a smoke immediately afterward and recalls seeing Mr. Parkerson get into his car and take the ramp for Interstate 10. All other inquiries drew a blank. Parkerson's vehicle never surfaced under his name or any other, and Parkerson has not been seen in Bayou Gavotte since that time."

The chief said, "Have you tried Houston, ma'am?"

"Of course I've tried Houston," Marissa snapped. "I've tried everywhere. After he left here, Johnny dropped out of sight, and I bet it's because he never left at all. He was way too hung up on his stupid Ophelia Beliveau for that. But he's not at Blood and Velvet. I spent a fortune to have it checked out every day for two whole weeks."

"They don't have exotic dancers at Blood and Velvet." The chief spread stain on another piece of plywood with slow, smooth strokes. "It's an elegant sort of place. Try the Chamber or the Oubliette. If your husband's still working in Bayou Gavotte, that's where he'll be."

"Get your ass whipped at the Chamber while you're there," Jeanie advised. "A never-to-be-forgotten experience."

"That's enough, Jeanie," the chief said. "Gotta have some standards of decorum."

"Sorry, Chief," Jeanie returned unrepentantly.

"You're the *police chief*?" Marissa sneered down her nose at his paint-spattered overalls.

He dropped his brush into a bottle of spirits. "That's me."

"Then *you* look for Johnny, damn it! And when you don't find him, I want you to arrest Constantine Dufray. He's in cahoots with those bitches at Blood and Velvet. They got pissed off at Johnny, and Constantine killed him. I'm sure of it!"

Jeanie grinned. "Ooh, death by Dufray. Very sexy. Have you seen him in person, hon? Definitely to die for." The phone rang and Jeanie elbowed Gideon away to answer it.

"Yes, I've seen him," Marissa said. "He's creepy. He laughed like he was the devil himself when I said he killed Johnny."

"He always laughs like that." The chief thumped the lid onto the can of stain. "Likes to mess with people. Can't say I like him much, but he generates a lot of publicity for Bayou Gavotte. Nowadays we get as many tourists as New Orleans." His brows drew together. "You publicly accused Dufray of killing your husband?"

Marissa hunched a shapely shoulder. "Why not? Everybody knows he's a murderer."

The sergeant shook his head. "Not a good idea to mess with Dufray. Thirty-three weeks of allegations, and plenty of similar stuff in his past. Mostly it's people's imaginations running wild, but some of it might be true. Why take chances?"

"You believe that bullshit?" She added uneasily, "What could he possibly do to me?"

"Hard to say till it happens, ma'am. If you have any nightmares, if you get the feeling of being haunted or pursued, let us know."

"So you can do what?" cried Marissa.

"Take note," said the chief. "Gather all the information we can."

"This town stinks!" Marissa swept toward the exit. "Everybody in the whole place is perverted or insane. I'll find Johnny if it's the last thing I do."

"Not if Constantine killed him, you won't," Jeanie said as the front door closed behind the blonde. Back at her desk, she took another call. Her voice caught Gideon as he reached the door to the back. "This one really *is* yours."

"What are you setting me up for this time?" Gideon demanded. "After yesterday, I'm really not in the mood."

"You have to be for this one," Jeanie said quietly. She handed him a slip of paper to read.

Gideon blanched. "Shit."

"She's not there, though," Jeanie said hopefully. "There's no reason to suppose anything's happened to her. Oh God, poor Vi."

"Get a crew over there." Gideon slammed the door behind him.

Jeanie's voice floated in pursuit. "This totally sucks. And I didn't even get to tease him about the vibrator."

Ophelia sat on one of the logs ringing the small parking lot and waited for Gideon to show up. The sickening smell of death, the horrifying, enticing aroma of blood, and the fury over her trees roiled inside her brain. No one except another vamp would understand; her turmoil wasn't like a normal person's, and she hadn't even been able to vomit. The cop had come to check her out and all she'd been able to manage was "Lucky thing I had lunch hours ago."

"Luckier than those folks over there who called me," said the cop, a bashful young man named Turlow. "I hate to have to bother you with this, ma'am, but can you identify the body in your truck? Gretchen, sit!"

Ophelia suppressed the urge to scream. *Who cares who he is? He ruined my trees!*

Normal women didn't freak out because a dead body had broken a few branches. Normal women probably fainted at the sight of so much blood. But then, normal women didn't sprout fangs at twelve years old, either. And sensible women didn't evade police questions.

Well, she'd never earned either descriptor. She shuddered. "You saw that god-awful mess. His own mother wouldn't recognize him."

"All right, ma'am, if you'd just sit down over there and

wait, please," the cop began. He eyed her shotgun warily, ignored the nutria, and because he clearly couldn't help it, blurted, "What are you doing with Gideon O'Toole's dog?"

"He loaned her to me," Ophelia answered. And felt terrible.

"He's a . . . a friend of yours?" A flush crawled up the poor man's ears.

"Oh, yes," she said with a sweet smile that told a lot of lies. And she felt even worse.

She sent him away and sat with the dead nutria across her knees and Gretchen beside her, unaccountably on edge as she waited for Gideon to show up. She'd have to tell him, of course, and if her assumption was correct he'd be pissed as hell with her for getting involved in the blackmail case in the first place, but how could she have known? And why should she care? It wasn't as if she had anything to do with this murder. Pure coincidence, that some bozo had dumped the body in her truck.

Goddamn it, why had some bozo dumped a body in her truck?

Far more unsettling, why was she so uncomfortable about seeing Gideon again?

When he arrived, he left his car by the road and strode onto the scene like some cool, dark, and capable god. Ophelia's heart leaped, and Gretchen's whole body hurtled toward him. He greeted his dog with a firm hand, gave Ophelia the briefest of businesslike nods, sent Gretchen back to her, and turned to the other cop.

Ophelia sat on the log and stroked the furry body of the nutria as Gideon conferred with Turlow, with the couple who had found the corpse, then with the crime-scene people when they showed up. The couple was allowed to leave, and Turlow got a roll of yellow tape and began laboriously ringing the parking lot. Gideon never once looked Ophelia's way, just directed the crime-scene people and poked at the body and probably hurt her trees even more, until Ophelia longed to strangle him.

Gretchen edged closer and snuffled anxiously at the nutria. "Your priorities are so right," Ophelia said. "The hell with him. Let's have supper." She grubbed in her pocket for a jackknife, sawed off the nutria's tail for the bounty it would fetch, and slit the corpse from throat to anus. More blood and gore. So there.

She scooped the entrails behind the log for scavengers to feast on, then hacked off the head and tossed it to Gretchen. "Help yourself," she said, and suddenly Gideon was standing over her.

"What are you feeding my dog?"

"Nutria head," Ophelia said without looking up. "Yum."

"Gretchen certainly seems to think so."

He was pissed off, she realized. "Be thankful I didn't give her the guts."

"Turlow thinks you're my girlfriend."

Ophelia glanced up long enough to see that the expression in his eyes matched the sarcasm in his voice. Okay, *that* was why she was on edge. She'd sure screwed up this one. "Because of Gretchen. He implied you wouldn't loan her to just anybody."

"I can see why it might be convenient for you to pretend to be my girlfriend under the circumstances—"

"What circumstances?" Ophelia said hotly. "I didn't kill that guy!"

"—but this is a murder investigation, Ophelia. It's best to stick to the truth."

Ophelia's insides heaved, but she came up with a shrug. "Says the corrupt cop. Anyway, I didn't exactly pretend to be your girlfriend. He made an assumption, and I couldn't see any advantage in denying it."

For way too long, Gideon said nothing, and Ophelia felt

lousy and said nothing either. She sawed at the nutria and took a deep breath. "Listen, I'm sorry I shot at you last night. I know you meant well."

"I'm sorry I harassed you," he replied immediately. "You can pretend to be my girlfriend if you like. Even if I don't get to sleep with you, it makes me look like one hell of a stud."

Ophelia responded with a tiny chuckle.

"Turlow also says you don't know who that is in your truck."

Ophelia peeled the hide away from the nutria's belly. "Unfortunately, that's another impression I gave him."

"What the hell?"

"Since he's not easy to recognize in the condition he's in," Ophelia said, her voice tensing, "and since I wasn't a hundred percent sure, and since Officer Turlow had already said you were coming, I thought it best to wait and tell you. In case you wanted to handle it your own way."

"Damn it, Ophelia. Move over." He sat on the log next to her, his warm, firm body touching hers. She closed her eyes to sense him better and sighed. "Who is it?" he asked.

"Judging by his size, his hair, and his clothes, it's the guy who was manning the photo shop when I dropped off the film this morning. The only thing I couldn't check was whether he had a tongue ring. It was hard to tell whether he even had a tongue."

"Fuck," Gideon said.

"That's what he suggested," Ophelia said. "He was a bit of a slime, and he might have been the blackmailer, but I don't suppose he deserves to be dead, and for sure not like that." She sliced off a strip of bloody meat and fed it to Gretchen. "On the other hand, I would cheerfully gut the bastard who put him in my truck and killed one of my new trees and damaged another."

Gideon said, "I wish I could deal with it my own way, but this is a murder. A bloody, brutal murder. I need you to put the rest of that animal down and come look at your truck again. I know it will be unpleasant, but—"

"I can handle it," Ophelia said in a tight voice. "If I put the nutria down, Gretchen will eat the rest. It's my supper."

"You eat nutria?" Gideon's expression said it all.

"Sorry. Yes." Ophelia licked her fingers, one by one. *You want the truth, well, here it is.*

"Whatever floats your boat." A laugh crept into his voice. "Let me get you a bag for it. Come on." He led the way to his Mercedes, and she picked up the shotgun and followed. He held open an empty Wal-Mart bag for her to put the nutria in. She licked off the knife and returned it to her pocket.

"Put the nutria in the trunk," Gideon said. "The shotgun, too."

"Why?"

"Because you shouldn't be shooting nutria here. This is a public park."

"You know perfectly well I was carrying it for protection," Ophelia retorted. "And I did not shoot the nutria." But she supposed it wasn't the right moment to make a fuss, so she laid the gun in the trunk. "Damn it," she added, back at her truck. "Those maple trees cost me eighty bucks apiece. I can't sell damaged trees!"

"Forget the trees for the moment," Gideon said. "Look over the whole truck bed and tell me if you see anything that doesn't belong to you."

"Besides the body?"

"Of course, besides the body."

"I can't forget the trees," Ophelia said. "That's money wasted, money I don't have." She surveyed the bed. "The tools are mine. The cypress mulch and pine straw are mine. The empty pots and flats are mine. Those bits of foam rubber sticking to his clothes are not mine. The dirt and debris in the bottom is, unless some of it was on his body before it got dumped here. The goddamn broken trees—"

"When was the last time you saw the truck bed without the body in it?"

"At the nursery where I bought the healthy, uninjured trees," Ophelia said. "I drove straight here, but I didn't look in the back when I arrived. However, I think if someone had dropped a body from on high, I would have noticed the thump."

"Let's hope so. Nothing that's not yours, then?"

"Not as far as I can tell unless I take everything out of the truck, but it's getting dark and I have to go home and do an estimate."

Gideon put an arm around her shoulders and steered her away from the pickup. "I'll take you home. We'll have to keep the truck for now."

"What?" Her rage was enough to turn every head of the crime-scene crew, as if they hadn't been turned already. Well, except maybe the one woman on the team, but even she was gawking now. "Gideon, I need my truck! This is my livelihood you're talking about, not to mention two trees I need to plant tomorrow. You can't just take it away!"

"I'm sorry," Gideon said, "but the bed of your truck is evidence. We'll process it as quickly as we can. And we'd better get moving"—he raised his voice—"because it's getting dark and it's about to rain."

"For fuck's sake, Gideon—"

"For fuck's sake, Ophelia, I have no option here! Give me your key. I said I'll take you home."

"Thank you very much," she replied, her voice quavering. "But I don't want you anywhere near my home." She stormed toward his car. "Give me my gun and my nutria. Do I get to take my notes out of the front seat of the truck, or are you confiscating those, too?"

"The whole truck. I'll bring you what I can in the morning." He made no move to open his trunk. "In the meantime, I need your truck key."

"In the meantime you can fuck off. Give me my shotgun. I'll walk home."

"I haven't finished questioning you," Gideon said.

"You . . . you . . ." She couldn't find words. "Questioning me? You know perfectly well I didn't have anything to do with this. That's the most blatant excuse for harassment I've ever seen!"

"Ophelia, I don't want to bring you to the station. I'd much rather go eat with you somewhere pleasant where we can have a discussion instead of an interrogation."

"That's bullshit and you know it. You have no right to take me to the station. You have no probable cause—"

"A body in your truck and your lack of cooperation give me plenty of probable cause."

She gaped at him, dizzy with the shock. "You—you actually suspect me of killing him?"

"Of course not, Ophelia, but this is a murder and I have to follow procedure. Either way, you leave this scene without your truck and with me."

"You bastard!"

"If you say so."

Ophelia stamped her foot and glared at the gravel, fighting the fangs, her breath coming way too fast. "You leave me no choice."

"I'm glad you recognize that." Gideon unlocked the Mercedes and opened the passenger door. For the third time, he asked for her key.

She separated the truck key from her ring and, letting her breath out in a long, slow hiss, controlled the urge to throw it across the parking lot into the gathering dusk. She dropped it into his hand.

"Thank you," Gideon said. "Get in. I won't be long. Gretchen!" He whistled, and the dog hopped into the backseat. He handed Ophelia his own keys. "Turn on the radio if you like. There are CDs in the holder, too."

He shut the door, and once again, unaccustomed tears filled Ophelia's eyes. She swallowed them and turned in her seat to dig her fingers into Gretchen's fur. The dog snuffled and licked the tears off her cheeks. Ophelia blew her nose on her T-shirt and sank back into the soft leather upholstery. She took a deep breath. And another. And one more.

Maybe it was the removal of all options for control over anything but herself, maybe it was the comforting male scent of Gideon's car, maybe it was because it was Gideon's scent and Gideon's car and no one else's, but when finally he got into the driver's seat, Ophelia was fast asleep.

She clawed up out the depths of despair with a long, eerie whine that made the hair stand up on both Gideon and his dog. "Oh God, no—I didn't, no please, no please!" she cried, the words tumbling one over another in a harsh, anguished voice. She sat up, her eyes flashed open, and her face and body twisted and arched toward Gideon in a wide-mouthed roar of terror.

"Ophelia, wake up!" Gideon rotated the steering wheel and grabbed at her flailing arms. Gretchen launched into a fury of barking and flung herself at the gap between the seats. The seat belt slammed Ophelia back into the seat just before she tore someone, anyone, to bits.

"Oh God oh God oh God what happened what did I do what did I say?" Her hands flew to her face. What with the rain and the glare from the headlights and trying to watch the road, surely he hadn't seen!

"You had a bad dream," Gideon said slowly, pushing his dog out of the way as the car lurched to the side of the road.

Think! "It wasn't a dream, it was a night terror." Her heart beat frantically. She had almost killed him. If not for the seat belt . . . "It's not about anything, or—or at least I never remember anything. I just wake up completely psyched out. What did . . . what did I say? What did I do?"

Gideon told her. Her chest heaved and her heart battered against her ribs, but she hadn't said anything that mattered.

"Does this happen often?" he asked.

"It depends." She huddled in her seat, half-turned away. "Usually it means I'm . . . oh, emotionally overwrought. I never know when to expect it, but it's not that big a deal."

Gideon got the car back on the road. "Where do you want to eat?"

Somewhere safe. "Tony's," Ophelia said.

CHAPTER TWELVE

Tony hadn't looked like a wuss in only boxers and a pink scarf. Now, in jeans and a black tee that emphasized his heavily muscled arms, he was formidable. He left a gaunt, black-draped woman at the bar and boomed, "Ophelia!" He wrapped a strong arm around her and, with only a flick of the chin to acknowledge Gideon, led them to the private patio off the kitchen where Gideon and Constantine had dined the night before.

"What's going on?" Tony kicked the door shut, holding Ophelia way too close for Gideon's taste, a tender smile on his battered, ex-bruiser's face.

Ophelia laid her curls on Tony's broad chest. "It stinks. This is Gideon O'Toole. He's a cop and I'm sort of under arrest."

Tony bellowed a curse, let Ophelia go, and rounded on Gideon, who stood his ground.

"She's not anywhere near under arrest, and she knows it." Gideon's eyes left Tony's alarmed scowl to settle on the exasperating girl he at times liked far too much for his peace of mind. Other times, like now . . . "Grow up, Ophelia."

Tony glanced from Ophelia's furious face to Gideon's impassive one. The door opened and the woman in black came through, nostrils flared, a sinister hiss issuing from scarlet lips.

"Beat it, Sonya," Tony said. "I'll get back to you."

"Tony," Sonya said, "I *need* you." The hiss morphed to a pitiful whine. "I need you now."

Tony shoved her out and slammed the door in her face. "What's this all about?"

"He forced me to come here," Ophelia said. "He said the alternative was going to the station to be interrogated."

"Here was a better choice." Tony tossed a menu in front of Gideon and fixed the scowl back on him. "You ate here with Constantine last night. Then you showed up with him at Vi's." When Gideon nodded, Tony added, "Order something. Drink?"

Gideon ordered a pesto pizza and a beer.

"Aren't you on duty?" Ophelia mocked.

"You're driving me to drink," Gideon replied.

Tony laughed and said, "Your usual, baby?" and left to place their orders.

Ophelia perched on the edge of a chair and looked at her hands, and Gideon slouched on the other side of the table, watching. He couldn't ask her about what he thought he'd seen—which was impossible. It was dark. It was a trick of the light from the dash. She had him so fucked up he was imagining things.

"Stop staring at me," Ophelia said pettishly. "You're giving me the creeps."

And what was she giving him? Something between the creeps and a hard-on. "I'll get Gretchen." When he returned, Tony had brought a Coke for Ophelia and a beer.

The ex-bruiser turned a chair away from the table and straddled it, hands on his knees. "Shoot."

Gideon looked at Ophelia. She hunched a shoulder. In clear, precise language, Gideon explained about the corpse and his reasons for questioning Ophelia and confiscating the truck.

"Someone sure has it in for you, baby," Tony said finally.

Ophelia, who had sucked down an entire sixteen ounces

of Coke during Gideon's brief explanation, was wide, wild awake. "Couldn't it be a coincidence?"

"No," said Tony and Gideon in unison.

Ophelia pushed her empty glass away. "Why not? Someone desperately needed to get rid of the body, saw a truck parked in a secluded and otherwise-empty lot, and dumped it."

"If you were an ordinary person, maybe."

Gideon saw her stiffen. Damn. Smoothly, he added, "If nothing else was going on, maybe. But we already know someone has it in for you."

"The dead-cat thing." Tony flapped a hand when Ophelia bristled. "Yeah, Vi told me about it. You should have told Leopard when it happened."

Ophelia crossed her arms and glowered.

"Even if the guy saw the truck by accident," Gideon continued, "he knew it was yours. There are magnetic signs on both sides."

"Why dump a body in your truck, though?" Tony asked. "It makes no sense. If he was pissed off 'cause you turned him down . . ." He shook his head. "Anyone who would beat some poor bastard to death like that would just as likely rape and then kill you."

"He could *try*," said Ophelia darkly. "Maybe it was a woman."

Obligingly, Gideon asked, "Can you think of any woman whose guy has the hots for you?"

Ophelia shook her head. "There have been plenty, as I'm sure you realized last night, but not so many lately. It was a lot worse when I worked at the club. I've been keeping to myself." The look she gave Gideon said it was his fault she wasn't still doing so.

He took a swig of beer, but his eyes never left her face. "How about business competition?"

"My business is too small to threaten anyone. Not only that, half the work I do is for Constantine. He wouldn't hire someone who harassed me out of business. Which reminds me." She opened her cell phone and dialed. "Constantine, can you loan me a truck for a few days? Gideon confiscated mine because someone dumped a body in it."

At the other end they heard Constantine's voice and then his laughter.

"I'm at Tony's. Thanks." Ophelia slapped the phone shut. "I have my own ride home."

"Good," Gideon said. "That lets me off the hook."

Tony looked between them and chuckled. "Young love. What fun." He twisted the ends of his mustache, and a moan came from the other side of the door. He opened the door, stuck out a hand to stop Sonya, spoke a few low, terrifying words, and slammed it shut again. "Women. Enough to drive you nuts."

Amen, thought Gideon. "Then there's the child-abuse thing."

Ophelia paled. "I don't know where Willy got that idea! I never touched those girls!"

This really bothers her, realized Gideon. Like the bitch last night did. Like the blood and gore today didn't.

"Of course not." Tony straddled the chair again and reached across to caress Ophelia's cheek. "We all know that."

Ophelia threw him a grateful look and clipped her cell phone on her belt. "You talked to Willy last night, didn't you?" she demanded of Gideon. "What did he tell you?"

Gideon tried to look compassionate and reassuring. And deprecating. Fat chance. "Willy said the dirty photos of Joanna came back with other pictures you dropped at the shop for Lisa. He said you accidentally mixed up your stuff with theirs. The guy at the photo shop saw them, and now Willy's being blackmailed, too." Gideon spread his hands. "Willy's an idiot, but when we add it all up, you're right in the middle of this mess."

"I did not take those pictures!" Ophelia flamed.

"Of course not," Tony said again.

Gideon said, "The question is, who did?"

"Joanna must know," Ophelia said.

Gideon sighed. "When I spoke to her yesterday, she didn't want me to talk to her parents or try to get you to talk with them."

Ophelia glared. "When was this?"

"When I went to pick up the plaster cast, Joanna and Connie were there. Mrs. Wyler had sent them to get it."

Ophelia muttered something sarcastic.

"Joanna went on and on about her boobs and wanted to know when she would be old enough to have sex."

Ophelia shifted from annoyance to concern. "She's scared to talk to her parents, so she dumps on anyone who's nice to her. With the dirty pictures, I guess it was easier to let me take the blame." She bit her lip. "Unless Willy's into his own kids and is mad at me for telling her she's too young? I don't believe it! I'm not crazy about Willy, but he dotes on those girls."

"I don't think it was Willy," Gideon said.

"Must have been a boyfriend took the pictures," Tony said. "How old is this girl?"

"Thirteen," Ophelia replied.

Tony spat.

"I know."

"Too much doesn't make sense," Gideon said. "Why did whoever took the pictures drop them at a public photo shop? How could he not know they amounted to child pornography? Is he being blackmailed, too? How did the blackmailer know whose kids were in the pictures? Come to think of it, who took the nude pictures of my sister? Assuming he turned them in to be developed at the shop, how did the blackmailer recognize Art?"

Nobody had an answer, so Gideon went on. "There are plenty of avenues to explore, but you're in the spotlight, Ophelia, especially since you handed in that film this morning. He could have developed the film, contacted you immediately, and you could have freaked out and murdered him. In order to keep you off the suspect list, I need to know all about your day. What you did, who you were with, the whole bit."

"All right. After I pee." She shot him an I-dare-you-to stop-me look and went inside the restaurant.

Immediately, Tony loomed close. "Do you have any idea what will happen if you put Ophelia in jail?"

"She's not going to jail," Gideon said.

"I mean it, kid." Tony got right up in his face. "Do you have any idea?"

Under the table, Gretchen growled.

"I'll tell you, kid. Since there's no lockup in Bayou Gavotte, she'll go to the parish jail. She's not your average girl. No matter how disciplined the guards usually are, I guarantee you that one at least, maybe more, will find her so irresistible they'll get her alone somewhere and—"

Gideon stood slowly and spoke through his teeth. "I said she's not going to jail." He eased back slightly and hushed his dog. "I'm doing my best to keep her safe. If you could convince her to cooperate with me, it would be a hell of a lot easier."

Tony relaxed a bit. "You're the cop who let Constantine go. He says you're okay."

"I didn't let him go. I never arrested him. There was no evidence against him."

Tony waved a hand. "Ophelia's bitching at you because she's scared. She has to be sure she's safe with you, and there's only one way to—"

An unearthly howl came from the kitchen. Tony plunged through the door, and Gideon followed across the kitchen and into the back hall. The woman in black lay sprawled in the doorway to the ladies' room, bleeding sluggishly from a wound on her arm.

From inside the restroom came the sound of Ophelia spitting. Her voice followed. "She attacked me. So I bit her."

She spat again, emerged, and threw a pile of paper towels at Sonya. "Staunch it, you stupid woman. Tony's not interested in me." She went back into the restroom.

"Christ, Ophelia. What got into you?" Tony called.

"Sorry. I'm a little overwrought." More spitting. "She tastes disgusting."

"To you, maybe. Not to me." Tony swept Sonya off the floor. "Your food's ready," he told Gideon. "Go eat." He carried the weeping woman into an office at the rear of the store.

Gideon returned outside, schooling his face to hide the progressively more bizarre thoughts he was having. Ophelia came back looking even more uneasy than when she left— which made two of them. The humor struck him, and he grinned at her and felt better.

"Your sandwich is far more edible than Sonya. Dig in," he said, slicing up his pizza. "Honey, this'll be easier all around if you stop viewing me as a threat. I'm no danger to you, cross my heart."

"All right," Ophelia replied, not in the least reassured, judging by her demeanor, but she went to work on a sandwich filled with bloody lamb and beef and answered his questions between feeding Gretchen and herself. Alibi-wise, she did pretty well: she'd spent an hour gossiping with old Mrs. Cotter while she planted azaleas in Andrea Dukas's garden, then lunched at the Impractical Cat after planting lantana on the patio there. In the afternoon she'd done a couple of estimates and finished at the Dukas place, where she'd spoken briefly with Mrs. Cotter about spring planting. Then on to the nursery, where the saleswoman and an admirer named Bob would vouch for her. She'd even waved to a fisherman across the river before returning to her vehicle.

On his third piece of pizza, Gideon said, "What do you want me to get from the truck?"

"The clipboard with my notes on it. I can't do the estimate without my notes. My work boots would come in handy. And my pocketbook. I have no wallet, no checkbook, no driver's license . . ." She eyed him defiantly. "Don't you dare say I can't drive because of that."

"Of course not," Gideon said.

Constantine appeared outside the fence surrounding the patio, with Artemisia clinging to his hand. Gideon cursed under his breath, and the rocker flicked open the gate and pulled her inside. "Art didn't want to come say hi to her disapproving big brother, but you've got other things on your mind, don't you, sport?"

"Sure have, Dufray." Gideon rose. "Murder tends to take center stage." He smiled at his sister—a damn good smile, considering whom she was with.

Art's mouth twitched nervously. "Ophelia, are you okay? Constantine told me about the body in your truck."

Ophelia shrugged. "I'll survive."

Gideon said, "Art, baby, were you at school all day today?"

"Of course."

"No quick trips out at lunch or in your planning period?"

"No, I even stayed late for a staff meeting. Why?"

"Thank God," Gideon said, sitting down again. "I'll tell you why, but you have to promise to keep it under wraps. Can you do that?"

Art flushed and planted her hands on her hips. "I'm not six years old anymore, Gideon. I can keep a secret." Her eyes found Ophelia's. "Can't I?"

"Definitely," Ophelia said. "I think the body in the truck was someone who worked at the photo shop. It might be the blackmailer."

Art squeaked, "I'm a murder suspect?" She gasped. "Is Ophelia a suspect?"

"No, baby, no, of course not," Gideon said. "Neither of you are, but it's a relief you both have alibis." He forced another smile. "Have a good time tonight. I'll take care of things."

His reward was immediate: Art flung her arms around him. "Oh, Gideon, I love you! Thank you!" When he hugged her back, she whispered in his ear, "It's not what it looks like, I promise." He tightened his arm and kissed her hair, unaccountably grateful for the affection and reassurance, and watched her hurry to hug Ophelia as well. *If only*, he thought. *If only Ophelia would let me offer her comfort, too.*

"Gideon will find the murderer," Art said, and Ophelia nodded wearily.

I will take care of you, sweetheart, Gideon told her in his mind, so of course she didn't hear him.

Constantine tossed Ophelia a set of keys. "I parked my big new truck out front. You'll look macho and prosperous. Anything else you need, let me know."

"Thank you," Ophelia said.

"There's a rifle on the rack. Best I could do on such short notice."

"Thank you," Ophelia said again. "I'll be fine."

"Love you, babe. Come on, Art, we've got some serious clubbing to do." Constantine blew Ophelia a kiss and then they were gone.

Ophelia gritted her teeth at Gideon. "Don't you dare harass me about the rifle."

"Ophelia, for God's sake—" Gideon stood. "I give up. Listen to me. I'm glad Constantine loaned you a truck. I wasn't looking forward to driving you home. I'm thankful I don't have to."

Tony walked in. "What gives?"

"She has a good alibi, so no worries," Gideon said. "I'm out of here. I have work to do."

"Hold on," Tony said. "I have something for you." He bolted back into the kitchen, and Ophelia and Gideon were left not looking at each other—or at least Ophelia wasn't. Gideon, no matter how angry and unwanted he felt, couldn't help it.

"Maybe we should exchange cell numbers," he said after a while. "Since I can't come to your place. I'll call and arrange to drop your belongings somewhere."

"All right," Ophelia said, surprising him. She accepted the pen he offered, carefully wrote her number on a napkin, and pushed it across the table. She took the business card he held out, tried to stuff it in her pocket, and pulled out a slingshot. "This is how I got the nutria."

"Impressive."

"Gretchen fetched it from the water and broke its neck." She put the slingshot away.

"She's impressive, too," Gideon said—then gave in again. "You can keep her for a while longer, until we've sorted all this out."

"All right," Ophelia said once more, clearly dying to get away from him. But surprising him again, she added, "You were great with Art. Constantine won't hurt her. He just pretends to be a jerk."

"I know." *Ask her, you dummy*, Gideon told himself, but he couldn't, not until he'd thought it through himself. If it wasn't just his eyes playing tricks, if he'd really seen fangs in Ophelia's mouth . . .

He had a lot of thinking to do.

Silence returned, and at last Tony came bustling in holding a small pizza box and a menu. He eyed Ophelia, cast a glance at Gideon, sighed, and packaged up the remains of Gideon's dinner. "Here."

Gideon took the box and turned to go.

"Take this menu, too. We deliver."

"I never order takeout," Gideon said.

"Seriously, you need this," Tony said. But as he held out the menu, he grabbed Gideon's reluctant hand and, with a knife that came out of nowhere, slashed Gideon's thumb. Blood appeared, alive and brilliant red, rolling over Gideon's wrist and down his arm.

Gideon flung the pizza box at Tony's face and sprang away. "What the fuck was that for?"

"Tony, you traitor!" Ophelia cried. At the same time she leaped for Gideon, grabbed his thumb, and sucked it into her mouth, jamming his arm between the warm, lush curves of her breasts, backing him up to the wall. He sank against it, the sensation of her tongue against his bloody thumb making him so weak he could hardly stand. Her mouth swirled around and over his thumb and down his wrist, lapped up the blood on his arm, then returned to the wound, painting out the pain and offering pure pleasure instead.

Tony picked up the pizza box and put it on the table, then retreated laughing to the kitchen. He shut the door softly behind him, and the light on the patio went out.

Ophelia let go of Gideon's thumb and sagged against him, all soft, pliant curves and hot breath on his chest. She shivered and let out a tiny moan. Her fingers burned across his skin, seethed up his neck and into his hair, and he shuddered in turn as she raised her head and latched her mouth to his. He groaned, yielding to the hunger and intoxication of her lips and tongue, returning the heat with an ardor as needy and demanding. He ran a hand down her spine, licking at her lips, fencing with her tongue, aflame to explore and discover and possess.

She broke the kiss and made as if to withdraw. *No!* His heart hammering, his loins insistent, Gideon held her hard against him, breast and belly and thighs—*No, don't go!*—and bathed his senses in her glory. *Stay with me forever.*

Ophelia pulled away. "Come on, Gretchen." She opened the gate to the dark alley beside the restaurant and turned back to Gideon, left breathless and bereft against the cool brick wall. "You won't need a bandage," she said.

CHAPTER THIRTEEN

"So now he knows you're a vamp." Violet grinned.

"He'd have to be an idiot not to." Ophelia slumped deeper into the billowy beige couch and messed with the remote.

"How did he taste?"

"Magnificent." Ophelia gave up on the TV and all but disappeared into the cushions.

Violet primped before a mirror with a bloodred stained-glass frame. "Go get him, then."

Ophelia almost tossed the remote across the room. "I don't want a love slave! Why didn't you warn me about that Marissa woman? That's why you gave me that look at supper, right?"

"I didn't know she was going to show up, angel," Violet said. "But Darby had been asking questions about Johnny, and I wondered if I should tell you. Not that it matters, after all. Setting aside the annoyance—"

Ophelia blinked. Annoyance? Blind panic was what she'd felt.

"—you impressed the hell out of Gideon."

This time, Ophelia did throw the remote. It bounced off a cushion and slid under a chair.

Violet continued. "And who cares what happened to Johnny, anyway? I wonder what the woman's really after. Insurance? An inheritance? She seemed way too pleased to assume he was dead. In that respect, she has all my sympathy. Do you suppose Constantine really killed him?"

Ophelia pulled herself together and retrieved the remote. "Why would Constantine kill some dancer he hardly knew?"

Violet shrugged, picking at a nonexistent blemish. "I have to run to the club. Donnie Donaldson's coming by, and I promised I'd be there. He wants to tell me about his construction business. How boring is that? Maybe I'll distract him with a kiss or two. Or maybe not." She turned from the mirror as her daughter came down the stairs. "Zelda, make Ophelia some tea. Something to improve brain function." She regarded her sister with a pained expression. "Angel, you're behaving irrationally. Someone's got it in for you. Dead bodies in your truck are no joke. Here's this gorgeous cop lusting after you, and you're spurning him. So what if he ends up a love slave? Better to have him protecting you because you're a vamp than not protecting you at all."

"That sounds awfully sordid to me," Zelda offered.

"Thank you." Ophelia slouched into the sofa again.

"It *is* sordid, darling," Violet said. "But it's the way of life, so make the best of it." She planted her butt on the arm of the couch and spread her hand. "See what Art did for me this afternoon?" Shocking pink spiders on black fingernails.

"Lovely," Ophelia said.

Violet stretched out a shapely foot. "Tomorrow, my toes. Art told me all about her ghastly ex and his puritanical notions. I think Darby will do nicely for her. There's nothing the least bit stodgy about *him*. It's so sweet of Constantine to help her out."

Again, Ophelia wondered what Constantine was up to. He wouldn't hurt Art, but he might frighten her badly. Unfortunately, there wasn't much Ophelia could do about that.

"Actually, I doubt if Gideon's the submissive type," Vi said.

"He's not. I want to throttle him. He pushes me around, he insists on his own way, he turns things to his advantage . . ." Ophelia arched herself against the cushions and groaned. "He's so *hot*, and I want him so much it's killing me."

"You sound like a sex-crazed sixteen-year-old."

"Hey! Don't malign the younger generation!" Zelda showed Ophelia her nails: rust-colored cockroaches on a green background. "My new method of creeping out the guys."

"Something happening?" Violet's mouth quirked up.

"*Mo-om!*" Zelda headed toward the kitchen. "Every time a guy says hello, I don't wonder if I'm a vamp."

Ophelia and Violet's eyes met.

"Even normal women have to fight them off at times." Zelda's voice, high and clear and a little unsure, carried from the next room.

"Well," said Violet.

"We don't know for certain," Ophelia said, but her eyes betrayed her. "Okay, okay, you may be right about Zelda, but not about me. I'm not sex crazed. I know I can get a love slave just by crooking my little finger. I don't want that. I don't want it to be just about the sex." She fought for words. "He has to really like *me*."

"Oh. My. Lord." Violet gaped at her sister. "I do believe you're falling in love!"

Gideon's cell phone rang as he drove back toward Bayou Gavotte. After dealing with the crime-scene people in a haze, he had taken the slow country roads to New Orleans, along the bayou and through the swamps. Once there, he'd spent an hour prowling the Quarter, thinking until his mind was ready to implode. At least he had control of his temper now.

He read the display. DARBY SIMS.

"Gideon? You've got to do something about Artemisia. She's out clubbing with Dufray."

Christ. "So?"

"I don't like the way he looks at her," Darby said.

A shrill voice in the background was surely Marissa. "What about me? Are you talking to that jerk of a cop?" An echo told Gideon the phone was now on speaker. "Constantine looked like he wanted to kill me! What are you going to do about it, Vibrator Man?"

"You're imagining things, Marissa," Darby said. "Dufray hardly spared a glance for you. He was all over Artemisia."

"He's the creepiest person I've ever seen! He makes me think of axes and thumbscrews!"

"You *saw* axes and thumbscrews—in the decor there." Ah. The Oubliette. "Gideon, Dufray looked like he wanted to *devour* Artemisia."

"Maybe she'd like that," Gideon said callously. He had enough worries of his own. At least Dufray wasn't a vampire. He hoped.

Darby groaned. "He's all wrong for Artemisia. She's just been through a lousy marriage."

"What about me?" Marissa snapped. "I had a lousy marriage, too!"

"Sounds like you've got enough on your hands, Dar," Gideon said. "Art's a grown woman. She's not answerable to either of us."

"Get off the phone with that useless cop and go look for Johnny!" Marissa's bitching was followed by grunts and muffled curses.

"I thought better of you, Gideon," Dar panted. "I guess I'll have to—"

Marissa hollered, "Oh, no, you don't! I'm not going back in there because of some stupid girl who deserves whatever happens to her."

Gideon hung up. When he reached Bayou Gavotte, he went straight to the Impractical Cat and stalked into Leopard's office.

"She's a goddamned vampire! Why didn't you tell me?"

Gideon made himself close the door without slamming it. A couple of hours earlier, he'd been so pissed off at Lep he might well have shot the door off its hinges. This was calm. This was controlled.

"It's just not done," Constantine said. He didn't look up from the riff he was working on. "Generally, it's up to a vamp to tell or not. Their secret, their risk. Bad things tend to happen to people who betray a vamp's confidence."

Gideon rolled his eyes as an alternative to breaking Constantine's guitar over his head.

"Nothing 'goddamned' about her," Leopard said. "Not undead, not evil, not allergic to crosses and garlic, nothing like that. Think of her as a hot chick with fangs."

"You know I didn't mean it that way," Gideon growled. He leaned against the door and glared at the one-way glass showing the back hall. The day after poetry night, even the usual bustle seemed slow. To the left of the glass, a video screen had been bolted to the wall, and shots of stalls and restroom walls flicked by. He doubted if watching other men take a dump was Leopard's idea of entertainment. Served him right. "Tony didn't leave it up to Ophelia. He slashed my thumb right in front of her."

"Tony's an older guy," Leopard said. "He takes liberties. Of course, he's a vamp, too."

Not done, huh? Gideon barely prevented himself from snarling. "I wondered, after Ophelia overreacted and bit his girlfriend, and they exchanged opinions on how she tasted." He pushed away from the door and wished he didn't sound so bitter.

"That explains it," Leopard said, kicking back in his recliner. "He figured Ophelia was too close to the edge, so he forced the issue."

"You 'wondered'?" Constantine mocked. "I thought you didn't believe in vamps." His fingers traveled, hesitated, traveled again on the strings of his guitar.

Gideon retreated to the couch, giving up on maintaining a front. With these people, it took too much work. "You know how it is. All the rumors, the stories . . . You think you don't believe in something, but you sort of wish you could." He choked on a laugh. "Jesus. The damn fangs glow in the dark!"

"You're okay with it?" Constantine's pick poised in the air.

"Of course I am!" Then, guessing: "How could she imagine I wouldn't be?" No way would he tell them about the hours of turmoil leading up to this visit. There had never been a doubt about the outcome. He found himself staring at his wholly healed thumb for perhaps the thousandth time. "Jesus. Are there a lot of vamps around?"

"Compared to so-called normal people, no," Lep said. "It's a rare gene. On the other hand, there seem to be more vamps now than there were in the past. It's getting harder to keep them secret, that's for damn sure. There are even on-line vampire help groups nowadays, although most people think it's just a game." He gave Gideon a hard, meaningful look.

Gideon tamped down his annoyance. "Don't threaten me. You know I won't tell anyone."

Constantine played the same riff he had been messing with ever since Gideon had shown up. Again. And again. Louder.

Leopard narrowed his eyes. "If you're not okay with the fangs, you need to back off right now. You gotta like 'em or you gotta leave. If there's one thing that'll mess with a vamp's head, it's when the asshole she just laid throws up because he can't handle the fangs. That happened to Ophelia at least once. It better not happen again."

"I'm fine with the fangs." Gideon pressed his thumbs against the bridge of his nose. "Lep, I almost hauled her in to the station. If she hadn't agreed to go to Tony's instead . . . What if she'd ended up in jail with a horny guard in charge? Too many guys have no control when she's around."

Leopard spread his hands. "She's not stupid. She knew what would happen if she went to jail. Between giving in to you and ripping some guard to bits, what choice did she have?"

"If she'd just *told* me—" Constantine's goddamned riff came again and almost split Gideon's skull. "For fuck's sake," he shouted. "Do you have to play it over and over?"

The rocker's fingers stilled. "You were the one who busted in here while we were writing a song."

"Busting in is what I would have done a couple of hours ago when I was *really* pissed off," Gideon said more evenly. "I came to see Lep. You were supposed to be painting the town with my little sister."

"Artemisia has work in the morning." Constantine's fingers caressed the strings. "She's a ripe little cutie. Wants to shed all her inhibitions at once."

"I don't see how you could be any worse for her than her ex," Gideon said irritably, mentally congratulating himself for not shooting the bastard then and there. Because he wasn't really a bastard.

"I've already been considerably better for her," the rocker announced with an obnoxious grin.

Definitely a jackass, though.

"Don't be a jackass, Constantine," Leopard said. He cocked his head at Gideon. "If you're here for advice, I can't help you. My mom's a vampire and I love her to death, but I know better than to get involved with a vamp myself. Not fucking worth it."

Constantine snorted. "Much as I love our Ophelia . . ." His fingers wandered lazily across the guitar strings. "I was only sixteen when I slept with a vamp. Way too young for common sense or self-control or any idea of consequences. Lep warned me, but it turned out the opposite of what everyone predicted. Instead of me getting obsessed with her, she got obsessed with me."

Gideon stopped himself just in time from asking what

had happened. Instead, he watched a busboy with a pile of dirty plates dodging Burton Tate at the entrance to the restroom hall.

Abruptly, Constantine stilled the guitar strings. "What next, sport?"

"Next I get back to work. I find out who killed that dude. I find out who has it in for Ophelia and why. I figure out how to keep her safe. Either of you know where Plato works?"

"Ophelia won't thank you for harassing Plato," Leopard said.

Constantine chimed in. "Told you so."

"What Ophelia wants is irrelevant right now. He may have seen something. He may still see something." Gideon cut his eyes to the video screen. Burton Tate banged into the restroom, glanced around, and immediately banged out again.

"Plato's a pharmacist," Leopard said. "He could lose his job if they find out he's bent."

"They won't find out because of me."

"You're treading on thin ice," Constantine said. "What Ophelia wants is critical to your chances with her."

"Whether Ophelia lives is even more critical," Gideon retorted.

"You're a man of remarkable restraint, sport. You're holding off on Ophelia, and you haven't tried to deck me. Not that you'd succeed, but any red-blooded American boy would at least try. Or are you saving your blood for Ophelia? Don't worry, she won't drain you. Just a taste should satisfy her—as long as she gets laid."

"She's hardly talking to me," Gideon said. "She sealed this goddamn cut because she had no choice." Burton Tate passed the one-way glass in the direction of the patio. What was that in his shirt pocket?

"That's one way of putting it," Leopard snickered. He put his hands behind his head and leaned way back, grinning up at the ceiling.

Constantine said, "You've got a lot to learn, sport. You had her right where you wanted her and let her go."

"The patio at Tony's is not where I want her," Gideon said. "She ordered me to stay off her property. I have no alternative for the moment but to show restraint." He stood up. Burton Tate's arm, with its familiar dagger tattoo, hovered at the edge of the one-way glass. A hand reached out to pinch a waitress, and he came into the picture again. "It *is* a permanent marker," Gideon said.

"Burton Tate," Constantine said, and Leopard leaped out of the recliner. Burton headed back toward the restroom.

"That weasel." Leopard pushed the intercom button, but Constantine reached over and punched it off again.

"I'll take this one," Constantine said. "Unless . . ." He motioned to Gideon. "She's your woman, after all."

"Tempting," Gideon said smoothly, feeling no compunction to save Burton from Constantine's revenge. "But I got to rough up Willy Wyler yesterday. I'd better get on with the murder investigation."

"Plato works at the All-Nite," Leopard said.

Ten minutes later Gideon parked at the drugstore in the outparcel next to Albertsons supermarket. Five minutes after that he had an appointment with Plato Lavoie for half past midnight. Another two minutes, and he found the officer doing surveillance across from the photo shop slumped in his car, fast asleep.

Ophelia dragged herself out to Constantine's truck, intending a quick trip to the supermarket on the way home. No amount of talk or endlessly circling thoughts made any difference. It wasn't necessarily love—or so she'd attempted to convince Violet earlier. Haltingly, she'd tried to explain her feelings. "He's up front about what he wants. He doesn't take no for an answer." Which made absolutely no sense, considering that drove her crazy in any other guy.

Violet smirked. "I told you it was love."

"And he has a sense of humor, and he doesn't let me bullshit him, and—and I just *like* him a lot." An awful lot. "I want him to feel the same way."

"Love," Violet insisted. "You lucky girl."

Right. Love, liking—whatever it was, she couldn't explain to Vi why it would never work, so she drove morosely through town in the macho truck high up on its oversized wheels and wished, not for the first time, that she could have fallen in love with Constantine and gotten it over with. If anyone understood her predicament, Constantine did, but his methods were as unacceptable to her as Violet's take on sex.

Ophelia turned the truck into the strip mall that included Albertsons, grateful for the normality of shopping for food. Her eyes traveled automatically toward the print and photo shop, which would have closed hours ago. *Crap.* Artemisia hovered in front of the shop, surreptitiously trying the door. Dumb, because obviously the place was closed, and even dumber for other reasons. Gideon's sister shifted indecisively on the sidewalk, the breeze ruffling dark hair into her face. Then she scurried to the end of the strip and turned the corner toward the rear.

Damn. Ophelia wrenched the truck around, cut a wide swath past the cluster of cars next to the buildings and slipped between the far end of Albertsons and the bank next to it. She turned left behind the strip mall, careening by Dumpsters, vehicles, and debris. At the final turn at the end of the mall, she shut off her lights and inched forward, glad of the excellent night vision that formed part of her genetic heritage. Not that she needed it, for a wavering flashlight beam marked Art's progress up the metal staircase that led to the apartment above the shop.

Ophelia cut the motor, leaving the window open a few inches. "I won't be long," she told Gretchen. She climbed down from the cab and softly shut the door.

"Art!" she hissed. Gideon's sister sobbed, and the flashlight beam flew erratically across the dirty pavement. "It's me, Ophelia. Put that light out!"

Art ignored the command or maybe didn't hear it, and the flashlight beam swept back and forth like a goddamn beacon until Ophelia, leaping up the stairs in a fury, grabbed it and switched it off.

"Are you insane? What if the murderer comes back to ransack the store? Not only that, I'll bet a hundred to one Gideon has the shop under surveillance. Do you want to get arrested? Let's go!"

"I have to get inside," Art squeaked. "I know there's a way from the apartment. I've seen the stairs in the shop. I'm wearing latex gloves so I won't leave prints." She picked her way obstinately upward in the dark.

"Why do you have to get in there?" Ophelia scowled at her friend's back and followed. "Don't tell me. It's not just nude art poses. What is it, porn?"

"Of course not! I would never, ever . . ." Her voice quavered and sank.

They reached the platform outside the apartment and Ophelia shoved herself ruthlessly between Art and the door. "Tell me the truth."

"It's not intentionally porn!" protested Art. "I didn't know my picture was being taken!"

"Spit it out, Art."

"It was in the women's locker room at the art school. There must have been a camera in one of the cubes, and oh God, this is so embarrassing, but I took my clothes off and I was looking at myself in the mirror, posing, trying it on, getting my nerve up, which was dumb, since I knew from friends in art school how boring posing nude really is. But anyway, he *sent* me one of the pics, and I'm bending over, totally exposed, with this sassy expression on my face. Nobody will believe I didn't do it on purpose, and the other pictures may be worse! I went out with Constantine tonight to make Dar jealous, and I could tell Dar was totally shocked, and I just know he'll never want me if he finds out about the pics!"

"For cripes sake, Art—Shh!" Ophelia raised an urgent hand. Vampire hearing came in handy, too. "Good thing I know a little about B and E." She wrenched out her key ring and inserted a picklock into the keyhole. "Turn the handle when I say."

In fifteen seconds flat, they were inside the apartment with the door locked behind them. Art whispered, "That was so cool! Where did you learn to pick locks?"

"Tony taught me." Ophelia surveyed the messy living room, steered Art around a couch and across a sheepskin rug, pressed the flashlight into her palm, and indicated the kitchen, dimly lit by the streetlights in the parking lot below. "Take this and go through that doorway into the kitchen. Do *not* turn the flashlight on. There's enough light in there from outside."

"There's hardly any light at all! How can I search if I can't see?"

"You're not going to search," Ophelia said. "Leave that to your brother. There's someone outside. We have to get out of here."

Art spoke in a panicked whisper. "I can't let Gideon see those pictures!"

"They may be embarrassing, but they're not worth risking your life over. Go hide behind the kitchen door." She heard Gretchen bark and then howl pitifully, and wondered if every damn cop in the city knew Gideon's dog. On the other hand, the prowler might not be a vigilant cop.

"It might be the murderer!" Art cried. "What are we going to do?"

"You're going to wait in the kitchen. *I'm* going to get us out of here."

Gretchen barked again, howled, and barked some more.

"If he gets past me, go down the inside stairs and through

the shop, and run for help." Ophelia turned Art bodily toward the kitchen and pushed. "Move!"

Ophelia crept back to the door and positioned herself. A light flashed briefly below and went out. She heard unhurried footsteps and noted that Gretchen, after a last few sharp whines, was now silent. She waited some more, and a hand tried the door handle, then a key or a pick slipped into the lock. She focused and prepared herself. Sometimes, being a freak was all you had going for you.

The door opened wide. Her fangs gleamed with their own lurid light as her foot flashed forward, but Gideon sidestepped and launched himself at her—laughing now, goddamn it, laughing at her—and she went down under him, down, down, onto the sheepskin rug. Then he was kissing her, hot and hard and demanding, searing her mouth with his tongue, scraping it across her fangs, drawing his own blood, and Ophelia moaned as she tasted him, digging her nails into his shoulders, twining her legs around him and arching closer. The kiss went on and on and Ophelia flew with it, forgetting everything but what she needed from this man, breathing in his strength and his scent and his flavor and his goddamned sense of humor. His tongue plunged again for her fangs as his hands took her everywhere, rough and perfect, assessing her breasts, fondling her waist, slipping under her shorts in an unerringly intimate caress.

His lips slid away from hers and his tongue stroked her ear. "Let's make a deal," he whispered, spreading her slick juices, poising his fingers to do more. "A better kind of B and E. You break and enter me, and I enter you."

She chuckled and nipped at his throat, lapped up a drop of blood, and sealed the cut. Damn. "Gideon . . ."

"Ophelia. Sweetheart."

His breath came fast and hard. His heart hammered against hers, and a huge regret rose in her throat. She forced her hands between their bodies and pushed. "Not now, Gideon."

"Yes," he replied, licking hotly at her lips. "Here. Now."

He didn't know Art was there. "No." She pushed again. Gideon's groan pierced her heart. "Ophelia, please—"

"We can't." She pushed again. "Your—"

From below came a crash and the sound of shattering glass.

CHAPTER FOURTEEN 🌷

Gideon was off her and asking questions in impressive time. "Where are the inside stairs?"

"Next to the kitchen." Ophelia took off through the doorway to show him the path and slammed to a halt as a sharp aroma hit her nostrils. "Wait a second."

"Why?" Gideon whisked a towel off the counter and went for the door to the stairs.

"There's something . . . Don't go diving down those stairs!"

Gideon opened the door, and the odors of stale blood and death assailed them both. A woman lay sprawled on the staircase, head toward the bottom, arms flung wide. "Shit. Stay here." He flashed his penlight on and off and crept noiselessly down, pausing only long enough to be sure the woman was dead before he disappeared, gun drawn, into the photo shop.

Ophelia turned. "Art. Come on. Time for you to go home."

"That was *Gideon*?"

"Playing games with me," Ophelia said. *Good games. Damn.*

"You two were breathing mighty heavily for a game." Art appeared from behind the door. "Are you going to sleep with him?"

"It looks like it." She shook her head. "Art, this is serious. There's a body on the stairs."

Art gasped. "What if the murderer's down there? What if Gideon—?"

"Gideon's a cop," Ophelia said coldly, but her breath was catching in her throat and her heart thudding way too fast. "It's his job." She grabbed Art's hand. "First we get you out of here, then I'll go make sure he's all right."

In the truck, Art clung to Gretchen. "Oh, my God. Oh, my God."

Ophelia asked sharply, "Where's your car? You need to go home. I'll call you as soon as I know what's going on."

"The next row." Art pointed. "The old Toyota, but I'm not going anywhere until I know Gideon's okay. Do you know who the dead person was?"

"No." Ophelia pulled forward into a space a few cars away from Art's. "Stay here with Gretchen. I'll be right back." She jogged across to Albertsons and along the strip to the photo shop, letting out a long breath of relief as she heard Gideon's voice. He opened the door to the shop, saying, "Thanks, Lep," clicked his phone shut, and without missing a beat asked her in a harsh tone she had never heard before, "How did you know about the body on the stairs?"

He didn't look the same, either. He looked pissed off. He looked like a very angry cop.

Ophelia stared at him. "I smelled it. My sense of smell is very acute."

"Especially when it comes to blood, I'm sure." His voice made her wince. "What were you doing in the apartment?"

Ophelia's fangs begin to shift. She swallowed and strove to keep her own voice low and calm. "Andrea's and Art's pictures might be in there."

"There's nothing in there. Not in the store or in the apartment. No films, no prints, no CDs. The computers are gone, too."

He radiated such icy fury that Ophelia had to struggle to control her fangs. "Who made that noise downstairs?" she asked.

"One of the blackmail victims, doing the same stupid thing as you. You had no business messing with a possible crime scene and you know it."

Ophelia's chest heaved and her fangs bucked. "You weren't so unhappy about me being there a few minutes ago."

"I fucked up," Gideon said. "This whole case is a fuck-up. Two people dead now. If I could have got a positive ID and a search warrant earlier . . . And then the man on surveillance falls asleep!" He flapped a dismissive hand. "It probably would have been too late anyway. The girl's been dead for hours. You don't happen to know who she is, too?"

Ophelia jammed the fangs up with her thumbs and tried to be civil. "She might be the girl who works there afternoons."

"Did you touch anything in the apartment? Anything at all?"

"Apart from you?" Ophelia gave up and let her goddamn fangs slot down. "I'm not the one who was ready to spill my DNA all over a possible crime scene, mister."

Gideon's voice grated. "Like I said, I fucked up. I can't afford that. It won't happen again. I suppose I should thank you for bringing me to my senses." The ugly, bitter words lashed at her, and then it got worse. "Get the hell away, Ophelia. Go home."

Ophelia clenched her fists and snarled at him, fangs full down and gleaming. "Who the hell are you to tell me what to do?" She shot a wave of allure at him so strong he reeled.

But he immediately collected himself. Disgust flooded his face, and he stood his ground, his voice calm and flat. "Go home, Ms. Beliveau. Lep's sending Jabez to keep an eye on your place tonight."

"Lep doesn't have to—"

"You're in way too much trouble to call the shots. By rights you should be under arrest like that poor sucker I found searching the shop. Now get out of here before my crime-scene crew arrives." He flipped open his phone and walked back inside the shop.

Ophelia strode across the parking lot to Constantine's truck. No way was she going home just because some asshole cop said to. "Your stupid brother's doing just fine," she told Art as she ripped open the door—and then, horror of horrors, her chin began to tremble.

"Hey," Art began, "he's not stupid." And then she gaped at the tears in Ophelia's eyes. "What did my rotten brother do?"

"If *I'm* stupid, he's even stupider," Ophelia heaved. She swiped at the tears with the back of her hand and dug in her pocket. Only a grubby dollar bill. "Can you loan me ten bucks? I need to do some shopping and I don't have my wallet."

"Of course." Art got her pocketbook from the Toyota. "My brother called you stupid?"

"It doesn't matter," Ophelia said, wishing she'd had the presence of mind to keep her mouth shut. She took the ten Art held out. "I'll pay you back tomorrow. You'd better go home now. Don't you have school in the morning?"

Art hurried along next to her. "What made him say such an awful thing? That's not like him at all! I mean, *really* not like him."

Ophelia shrugged. "Whatever. I don't care. I hope I never see him again." She stormed into the supermarket.

Art followed her to the produce section and cringed when she tossed apples into a bag. "You're bruising them. Calm down! Why did he say that?"

"Because I went into the apartment when I knew it might be a crime scene." Ophelia knotted the plastic bag around her fist and swung the apples menacingly back and forth.

"You're scaring me, Ophelia." Art grabbed at the apples and Ophelia blew out a long breath. Gently, Art took the bag away.

"Sorry." Ophelia picked up a loaf of whole-wheat bread with quivering hands. "This is what happens when a vamp gets pissed off. I'm the mild-tempered version. You saw what Violet's like."

"But you went into the apartment because of me! That's so unfair of him."

"Like I said, it doesn't matter." Ophelia led the way down the next aisle for a jar of peanut butter. "That's all I need for now. Let's go."

"Didn't you tell him it was because of me?" Art cried. "You didn't! That's not right. It was my fault, not yours!"

"Let him think what he likes. I never want to see him again, so why get him pissed off at you, too?"

Art shifted from one foot to the other and bit her lip through the wait at the register. "No," she said the instant they hit the cool night air. "We can't leave it like that."

Ophelia opened the door of the truck and tossed her groceries onto the seat. "Yes, we can. He doesn't want to see me either, so it doesn't matter what he thinks of me. In fact, you can take Gretchen with you right now. That way he'll never have to darken my door again."

"Oh, come on, Ophelia." Tears glistened in Art's eyes. "Of course he wants to see you. He's just stressed about this murder case. His job's important to him. He wants to do it right."

"Fine, let's give him a woman he can talk to." Ophelia opened the passenger door. "Out, Gretchen. You're going with Art. She'll take you back to Gideon tomorrow."

Gretchen didn't move.

"Dumb dog." Ophelia whacked her on the butt. "Get down."

Gretchen still didn't move.

"Oh, for cripes sake. You call her, Art."

"Nope." Art gave a tremulous smile. "She never listens to me."

Ophelia grabbed Gretchen by the collar and tugged. The dog growled and showed her teeth, and Ophelia jumped back. "What's wrong with her? Doesn't she like you?"

Art giggled. "She likes me okay, but I guess she likes you better. I guess you'll have to keep her. I guess you'll have to see my brother again, whether you like it or not." She grinned at Gretchen and the dog grinned right back.

"Oh, shit," Ophelia said despairingly, and Art flung her arms around her and hugged her hard. "You don't understand," Ophelia cried. "This thing between Gideon and me would never have worked. In the first place, he doesn't really like fangs. In the second place—"

"He found out you're a vamp?"

"Yes, but that doesn't matter. There are a zillion reasons why it'll never work."

Art hugged Ophelia again and clambered into her little car. "You may be right, because it's your relationship, not mine, but I do know that when you're exhausted and angry is the worst time to make important decisions. Go home and get some sleep. We can talk again tomorrow."

Ophelia watched Art drive off and turned to Gretchen. "Obnoxious," she said. "That's what you are, dog." She trundled the truck slowly across the parking lot and onto the main drag, filled with a sudden longing for home—and also, now that she was alone and could admit it to herself, for Gideon.

Gretchen sighed and laid her head on Ophelia's thigh.

"You understand, don't you? You love him, too."

Gretchen licked Ophelia's knee.

"You get to go back to him, though," said Ophelia. "I don't." Tears choked her throat. "You didn't see the expression on his face. Just my luck, I finally fall for someone and he resists my allure because he hates fangs"—Gretchen stuck her muzzle next to Ophelia's butt—"and dumps me back on Lep. I should be relieved. He won't snoop into my life anymore."

On the country road toward home, Ophelia let the big macho truck have its way. A cop pulled her over, so she turned up the allure and sent him away dazed and blissful. "At least I've still got it," she told Gretchen as they drove off.

The dog snorted and scratched behind her ear.

"Not that it's much use, if the one man I want is immune."

Gretchen gave a cavernous yawn.

"For a minute there he really *did* seem to like them," Ophelia continued pitifully. "Guys usually just wait to be bitten. Gideon drew his own blood. And it was so damn good!"

But it hurt too much to think about Gideon's tongue and his blood and his capable hands, so she focused hard on reality instead. "I guess he was so turned on that he didn't realize until afterwards that the whole thing made him sick." Gretchen faced the window, eyes closed, evidently bored with the gig as confidant.

"Too bad," Ophelia said. "You had your chance to get away."

As she turned into her driveway, Ophelia braked and rolled down the passenger-side window to greet a bodyguard she might need but surely didn't want. Just like old times.

"Evening, Ophelia." The soft, low voice came from the big sycamore off to the right. Leopard's bodyguard was darker than the night, and so quiet and still that even she could barely see him.

"Thanks for coming, Jabez."

"My pleasure," the man said. "Some kid's waiting on your porch."

Gideon left the crew at the crime scene for his appointment, still in a cold rage directed mostly at himself. His desire for Ophelia simmered in some corner of his gut, stowed until the investigation was over and he could quell it properly. An appointment at the house directly across from hers didn't help, but since he would have to pass her place every day going home for the rest of his life, he might as well start getting used to it.

Her house was dark except for the porch light, and her driveway was empty, but a deserted pickup a quarter mile earlier told him Jabez was already in position. Nobody ever saw Jabez unless he wanted to be seen. Gideon dropped a hand in silent acknowledgment and gave thanks, not for the first time, for the Bayou Gavotte underworld. Separately, neither the cops nor the underworld could keep a handle on things. But with the underworld taking care of transgressions in the clubs and the cops handling the rest, they kept their kinky little tourist town safe. The murder rate for innocent people was at an astounding low.

Except for today. Not the blackmailer—better for everyone he was out of the way—but that poor girl in the staircase. Shit. *But it's not my fault,* he reminded himself. Yet his own appalling behavior was eating holes in his brain. Which he couldn't afford during a murder investigation.

When this is over, he told himself, *I will regain my sanity. Maybe I will even recover that tiny bit of instinct that got me laid now and then. It won't get me Ophelia, but . . .* Oh, hell. What was the goddamn use?

He parked behind Plato's old Chevy pickup and composed himself. Ophelia's neighbor waited in the doorway, drawn and desperately uneasy.

"I appreciate your agreeing to talk to me here, Officer O'Toole," he said. He stood back to let Gideon into a room full of baskets.

Really, really full. All over the walls, ovals and rounds mostly, with the occasional rectangle or square to break the monotony. Piles of baskets nested together, crammed against the ceiling, almost blocking the narrow entry to the bedroom hall. Delicate and intricate, thick and rustic, tall hampers, squat picnic baskets with hinged lids: every available surface was covered with baskets, except the kitchen table and one wooden chair. Tangles of green wisteria hung across the table, and beside them lay a yellow utility knife.

Plato tenderly removed a pile of baskets from the other kitchen chair and balanced them on the end of the counter.

"Please sit down." He stood rigid, hands twining together, even when Gideon took a seat.

"Relax, Mr. Lavoie. I didn't come to give you a hard time."

"I can't afford to lose my job," Plato said, clasping and unclasping his hands. "Even in Bayou Gavotte, there are plenty of people who wouldn't be able to forgive my oddities. But I'm a good pharmacist. I don't make mistakes. I double-check everything. I'm scrupulously careful about contraindications. My oddities have no effect whatsoever on my performance at work."

"Mr. Lavoie, I don't question your competence. Your lifestyle is your business, not mine. Consider this a friendly conversation about the safety of Ophelia Beliveau."

Plato's face darkened to rust. "I may be a basket case, but I've never done anything—*anything*—to hurt Ophelia."

"I'm not suggesting you have. Please sit, Mr. Lavoie." When the man did, fidgeting helplessly, wringing his hands in his lap, the poor bastard, Gideon added, "Feel free to work while we talk. You weave your baskets from wisteria?"

Plato picked up his utility knife and a strip of wisteria, tearing off the leaves in long, ragged strokes. "Some of them. In the spring mostly, when it's green and easy to work with." The strokes grew smoother.

Gideon sat back. "Mr. Lavoie, someone has targeted Ms. Beliveau with some nasty attacks. A dead cat was hung on her door several days ago. Her garden was vandalized. Today, a badly beaten corpse was planted in her truck."

The color in Plato's cheeks ebbed. "Donnie told me about the cat and the garden, but . . . Whose body?"

"It hasn't been identified yet. Willy Wyler has admitted to the vandalism, and he's given a plausible explanation for his fit of rage. Both he and Mr. Donaldson deny any knowledge of the cat, and although I haven't spoken to Mrs. Wyler, it seems unlikely she was involved."

Plato let out a breath of dry laughter. "Lisa Wyler soil her lily-white hands touching a dead cat?" He pushed the leaves onto the floor and set the cleaned vine carefully aside. "It doesn't fit her obsession."

"Which is?"

"Never to be trailer trash again. She had an impoverished childhood, and what with Willy going down the tubes lately with too much drugs and alcohol, she's likely to end up broke in her old age, too."

"Are you being blackmailed, Mr. Lavoie?" Gideon asked the question without preamble, but Plato didn't seem surprised.

"Most of my paycheck," he said. "It's been going on for years. I used to think it was someone I'd known a long time ago, because the money went to various mail boxes in New Orleans, but lately I've had to send it to a local shop." He selected another vine. "And no, I haven't reported it to the police. I don't need money, but I do need my job. I need structure in my life. It's what keeps me sane."

Gideon didn't laugh. "Don't send another payment without first checking with me. We know about your blackmailer; he's targeted quite a few people. We'll get him before long, and you'll be a free man again."

Plato relaxed even more. "I suppose you want to know if I've seen anything that would help you. Unfortunately, I haven't. Ophelia's up and out at dawn and comes home in the early afternoon, and I'm asleep most of the time she's gone. That way—"

Gideon waited, and Plato twisted his hands together, and Gideon took pity. "You have an hour or two to watch her before you go to work."

"I just look." Plato's expression was a plea for understanding. "That's all I do. I spend my free evenings at the club, but she hardly ever goes there anymore. Wasn't she amazing last night? Such beauty, such flashing eyes! And that whip! She's never carried one like that before." His face drooped. "I wish she'd exert her power over me more often."

"Maybe you should consider patronizing a dominatrix, Mr. Lavoie," Gideon said, "or join one of the BDSM clubs. Find someone looking for a good bottom."

"I'm not into *bondage*," Plato said distastefully. He picked up his knife and got back to work. "I'm a devotee. It was his fault, you know."

Gideon leaned back in the chair. "What was whose fault?"

"That Johnny fellow. He's the reason she left the club for good. She could handle all the other fools, but Johnny was crazy. You were there last night. You heard. If he'd really loved Ophelia, he would have been faithful to her."

"He was a married man," Gideon said. "What about being faithful to his wife?"

"It's different with a supernatural being," Plato said. "Ophelia's a goddess." Something must have shown on Gideon's face, for Plato gave him a pitying look. "Didn't you know? Goddesses require allegiance far above and beyond what ordinary people merit. These baskets"—he swept the knife in a grand gesture—"are my offerings. Don't you see? They're all O for Ophelia. Ovals and rounds, mostly, but even the squares and rectangles are stylized Os."

Christ.

"She's all I think about," Plato said, "so of course it shows in my offerings." He set the next clean vine by the others and sent another pile of leaves to the floor. "Worshippers have to be patient and submissive, like me."

"And Johnny wasn't?"

"Johnny wanted to have sex with her. That tawdry exotic dancer wanted to sleep with a goddess. Can you imagine the gall?" He chose another length of wisteria.

"But he didn't get her."

"No one does. She's above us all." He ran his eyes and hands up and down the vine. "Then one day he drove off in his fancy car and we never saw him again."

Huh. Something niggled at Gideon's brain. It felt like instinct. Or maybe just crap.

"No loyalty at all," Plato said. "No staying power. What's your obsession?"

Gideon eyed him. "Mine?"

"Everybody has obsessions, just some are considered more normal than others. Is it truth and justice? Your reputation as a cop? Or is it Ophelia Beliveau?"

"I can't afford an obsession at the moment," Gideon said. "I'm working a murder case."

"Obsessions don't just step aside, detective. If you don't acknowledge their power, they put you in your place, often in highly unpleasant ways."

"I'm used to dealing with unpleasantness," Gideon said. "Do you have any idea who might have a grudge against Ms. Beliveau?"

Plato methodically stripped another vine, and his response was both evasive and chilling. "A goddess has many enemies, but Ophelia knows I'll be watching her place. He'll make a false move, and I'll be the one to see it. You and a thousand other men may obsess over her, but my loyalty is what will count in the end."

CHAPTER FIFTEEN

"Oh, crap," Ophelia said, staring at the lonely figure waiting on her porch.

"Kid's upset about something," Jabez said from his post in the sycamore. "Didn't want to scare her away, so I kept out of sight."

"Thanks," Ophelia said. Gretchen sat up, thumping her tail gently against the car seat.

"Bit of a throw-down two doors down."

"Willy's drunk again, I suppose. Hopefully that's all."

"Next-door neighbor brought the girl a coffee, then went to break up the fight."

Joanna Wyler slumped under the light on Ophelia's tiny porch. Insects flitted around her, and she scratched at her arms. *Next, her parents will say I gave her West Nile.* Ophelia moved the truck forward and parked at the top of her drive. Gretchen burst out and bounded to the porch to say hello.

Ophelia retrieved a mosquito coil and a lighter from a box under the stairs and set the coil on the porch rail. She lit it. "Have your parents been arguing?"

Joanna sniffled and nodded. Gretchen licked the tear tracks off her face.

Ophelia sat down and patted the step beside her. "I don't know what to do with you, sweetie. You're not supposed to come here anymore."

Joanna burst into loud sobs. "Ophelia, I'm sorry! Please don't hate me!"

"I don't hate you." She motioned the girl forward, and this time Joanna obeyed. *What the hell,* thought Ophelia, *I have a witness.* She put an arm around Joanna's shoulders and gave her a squeeze, then let go and brought her hand back around to scratch at Gretchen's ears. "However, I'm not happy about being accused of taking dirty pictures."

"I'm sorry!" Joanna rooted in her pocket and passed a tattered tissue across her nose. "I never said that, I promise. My parents just . . . just decided it must be you, because some pictures that weren't supposed to be there came back in one of the envelopes you dropped off for them at the print and photo shop. They figured you got things mixed up."

"So why didn't you tell your parents it wasn't me?"

"I couldn't think of anything else to say," Joanna groaned.

"How about the truth?"

"I can't tell the truth!" Joanna wagged her head back and forth. "Zelda's right, I'm a hopeless wimp. My life is so over!"

Drama queen, thought Ophelia uncharitably, and encountered a look from Gretchen. *All right, all right, but I've got a good reason. All right again, maybe Joanna has, too.* "Zelda called you that?"

"No," Joanna said miserably, "but that's what she was thinking." She blew her nose into the soggy tissue. "Zelda said I can't be a wimp if I want to hang with her."

"That's Zelda's way of saying she likes you. Her friendship challenge, so to speak."

"Zelda's so cool. But I can't tell. I just can't."

"Are you scared of someone? Is somebody threatening you?"

"No," Joanna said sullenly.

Two doors down, the screen door slammed open and shut. "Joanna!" Lisa Wyler's voice rose in a wail that showed clearly whose mother she was.

Ophelia stood up, and so did Joanna, to see Lisa stomping across the lawn. The door of the Colonial opened again and

Willy Wyler stumbled down the steps, howling obscenities, followed by Donnie Donaldson.

Joanna moaned. "I can't *stand* my father! He's so *embarrassing*. He gets so *stupid* when he's drunk."

"He'll get sober in a big hurry." Ophelia unlocked the door of her trailer, flicked on the spotlight, which illumined the top end of the drive, and came out a few seconds later with a pellet rifle and some tissues. She handed the tissues to Joanna, who gaped at the rifle with frightened eyes. "Don't worry, I won't shoot him. If he won't stop for me, he'll stop for my backup. You might want to meet Jabez so you don't freak out."

On cue, her protector appeared from nowhere. Joanna clapped a hand over her mouth to stifle a shriek. Jabez nodded and vanished into the shadows beside Constantine's truck.

Willy lumbered bearlike across the ditch at the edge of Ophelia's property, Lisa babbling hysterically beside him, and now Donnie Donaldson hustled behind, protesting. "Come on now, Willy, don't get all het up."

"Goddamn bitch touching my little girl, lu-lu-luring her out at midnight!"

Lisa Wyler's face contorted. "Joanna, baby, are you okay? Did she hurt you?"

Joanna stepped down onto the drive. "Mom, I'm fine!"

Donnie put a hand on Wyler's arm. "Come on now, Willy, Ophelia didn't do no luring. She just got home, for chrissake."

"Made a—a—'ppointment to lure her." Willy knocked Donnie's hand away and crashed across the mud that had once been Ophelia's vegetable patch. But when the rifle in Ophelia's hands veered in his direction, he staggered and stopped dead.

Lisa halted behind her husband and peered around his bulky form. "Joanna, honey, you've been crying! Come away from that evil woman. What she did was wrong, and she'll pay for it. You're just an innocent baby."

"It wasn't Ophelia," Joanna said, her lip wobbling. "She didn't take those pictures."

Lisa glared. "There's no call for you to lie! We're here. She can't do anything to you now."

"I'm not lying!" Joanna sniffled. "Ophelia didn't do anything, I swear!"

"Okay then," Willy bellowed. "Who did?"

Silence dropped into the pool of light on the drive, and all eyes focused on Joanna. She opened her mouth, but only a squeak came out.

"Ophelia did it!" Lisa spat. "For years she sucked up to us and pretended to be nice, and it was all part of her evil plan to corrupt my baby's mind and body. And now she's controlling her with threats! She has her in her thrall!"

Willy gave an exasperated snort. "Shut up, Lisa! Let the girl talk!"

"You shut up!" Lisa hurled back. "No-good, drunken has-been! Can't even protect your own daughters!"

"Gotta know who to protect them from first!"

Lisa stomped up to her husband; they stood nose to nose. "Can't even make enough money to keep them in house and home!"

"Come now, Lisa," Donnie said. "Calm down."

Lisa rounded on Donnie with a stream of curses. "If you were really Willy's friend, you wouldn't lend him money for booze. He's drinking the house out from under us!"

"If you're so freaking worried about the freaking house, get a job!" Willy turned from his wife to his daughter. "Who took the pictures, Joanna?"

Joanna erupted into noisy sobbing. "I can't tell you! I'll die before I tell!" She covered her face with her hands. "Torture me if you want, boil me in oil, all I can hope for is to die!"

Willy threw his hands up in the air. Ophelia avoided Gretchen's eyes. The damn dog might think this was hysterically funny, but her own head had begun to throb.

The stalemate was interrupted by low, eerie laughter.

"Who's that?" Lisa bleated. "Who's laughing?"

Donnie Donaldson figured it out first. Jabez glided into the light, and Lisa screamed. Joanna rolled her eyes, and Willy looked just plain scared.

"Party's over," Jabez said. "Everybody go home." He leaned nonchalantly against Ophelia's truck and waited.

This time, Willy made no protest against Donnie's guiding hand. Lisa skittered forward and clamped her fingers around Joanna's arm. "Sweet baby, let's get you away from this place." She marched her daughter across the mud. "Once we get you safe, we'll call the cops and you can tell them all about what that evil woman did to you!"

"She didn't do anything!" Joanna hollered. "I won't accuse Ophelia, because it's not true. Kick me out in the street if you want, dump me in a ditch!"

"Cop's already here," Jabez said. "Good friend of mine. He'd be happy to set you straight." He waved as a car came out of the driveway across the road.

Lisa glared at him and dragged Joanna away. Donnie prodded Willy along behind.

Ophelia watched Gideon's car pull into the end of her drive and stop. "Why has that goddamned cop been bothering Plato?" she asked.

Jabez shrugged. "Better ask him."

"Not a chance," Ophelia replied. "Tell him he's not wanted here."

At the bottom of the drive, Jabez grinned. "She's pissed at you, man."

"Nowhere near as pissed off as I am at her," Gideon replied. "I take it I'm not needed?" The depressed little party had almost reached the big Colonial house.

"I've got it covered." Jabez adopted a belligerent note. "I'd like to teach her lunatic neighbors a lesson, but knowing Ophelia, she'll say no way. Kid mighta confessed who took some dirty pics, too, but the parents showed up."

Gideon fled back to town, burning rubber as he left Ophelia's drive, shaking the dust of her off his wheels and the thought of her, cold and bright in the porch light, from his mind. He sort of didn't think of her during the rest of the night as the crime-scene crew worked the print and photo shop and the apartment, and he set her aside while he questioned the ordinarily respectable citizen he had found stumbling through the shop in the dark. He made phone calls and verified his alibi, and eventually let the man go. Shortly before dawn he sped past Ophelia's again on the way home for a shower and an hour's sleep, allowing himself a glance at her dark and silent house, the glance of a cop who had a job to do, not that of a former would-be lover.

He'd been such a jerk.

Yet she'd deserved it. Her lame excuse about pictures of Art and Andrea still burned him up. Ophelia wasn't that dumb. She wouldn't risk being arrested, risk her life even, when she was 99 percent sure the blackmailer was dead. For some foolish reason, he had expected her to tell him the truth. He was an idiot to think he knew the first thing about Ophelia Beliveau. Or about his sister or anyone else, for that matter.

He turned into his lengthy overgrown driveway, the bushes trimmed barely enough so he could pass without scratching the Mercedes, and pulled up with a curse next to an old Toyota that for sure didn't belong there. Letting himself into the house, he found his little sister curled up on the futon bed in the living room in her T-shirt and undies, with Daisy snoring on one side and Belle sprawled on the other. *Shit,* he thought, *I don't have time for this.* He took off his shoes and tried tiptoeing to the stairs, but Artemisia had never been a sound sleeper.

"Gideon, we have to talk."

He put his right foot back on the floor instead of the first stair, where it had been headed. *Patience. You're a patient man, remember? In some far-distant past.*

He turned to face his sister. "Art, baby, I'm on a murder case. I don't have time for chitchat. Can it wait?"

Art's dark eyes, wide-open now, blazed at him in the low light from the end table. She swung her legs over Daisy's and sat up. "This is not chitchat, Gideon. I know you think I'm a silly little thing. I know you found another body and you're busy. I wouldn't have waited here all night if it wasn't important."

Gideon set his teeth. "Ophelia told you about the body? She had no call to go blabbing police business. Why can't you women keep your mouths shut?"

"You butthead!" Art yelled. "I know about the body because I was in the apartment, too."

"Unbelievable." What had he done to deserve this? "If anything else could go wrong—"

Art's face puckered and she began furiously to cry. "I was going to break into the apartment so I could search the store, and Ophelia tried to stop me, but then she heard someone coming and we went inside to hide. After you went to find out who was downstairs, she got me out of there. And then you called her stupid!"

Gideon ran a hand across his face and groaned. He nudged Daisy onto the floor and sat on the futon beside Art. "Christ, I'm even more of a jerk than I thought."

"Gideon, how could you?" Tears flowed down Art's cheeks. "We made a pact, Gideon. We promised each other. Doesn't that matter to you anymore?"

"Of course it does, baby. I screwed up big tonight in more ways than one. But I have to concentrate on the murder case for now. I can't afford to dwell on my own stupidity."

"Don't say that! Never, ever!" Art agitatedly looked around. "How come men never have any tissues?" She snuffled hard and wiped the tears with the back of her hand.

"Sorry," Gideon said. He put an arm around her. "Would you mind making coffee while I have a quick shower? Don't you have work this morning?"

Apparently that didn't matter, next to talking things out, so Gideon went slowly upstairs for a shower and thought about Art being there in the apartment and Ophelia pushing him away, trying to tell him something at just the moment the blockhead in the store had knocked over a lamp, and although he felt like a cad and a fool, he came downstairs a bit more cheerful to the welcoming aromas of coffee and bacon.

"Pancake egg?" He watched Art pour a dollop of beaten egg onto the pan.

She nodded. A tear trickled down her cheek and splashed on the stove. "I really miss some of the family stuff, Gideon. Not Dad calling Mom stupid, but things like pancake eggs and Mom's biscuits." Carefully, she poured two more dribs of egg onto the pan.

Gideon mussed her hair. "Me too, kiddo." He eyed the egg. "Teddy bear?"

"For my big teddy bear of a brother." Two more dribs became the feet, then a couple more the ears. "I thought we could be family again, you and me. And I thought you could marry Ophelia and she would be part of our family and we could be part of hers. And maybe I could get married to, uh, some really nice guy, and . . ."

Gideon dropped two slices of bread in the toaster and got out mugs for coffee. "It sounds idyllic, Art, but I'm already behaving like Dad, and I met Ophelia only two days ago."

"But you still want her, right?"

"I don't know what I want. But I have to ask you some cop questions now, baby. Why were you at that apartment?"

"To get my pictures, of course," Art said belligerently. "Andrea's, too. Listen, one little fight with Ophelia is no reason to forget about her."

"Did you touch anything while you were there?"

Art narrowed her eyes. "So you're going to run away from the first intelligent girl you've fallen for because you're afraid you might turn out like Dad? Grow up and control yourself instead."

"Please answer my question," Gideon said.

Art sighed elaborately. "I watch TV. I read books. I wore latex gloves."

"Thank God for that, but I want the truth about those photographs. Why would you panic about a couple of photos, when everyone in the art class drew pictures of you? You might find them embarrassing, but breaking and entering, maybe risking your life, to get them? You knew the blackmailer was probably dead. The chances the pictures would get out were minimal. I don't pretend to understand the female mind, but isn't breaking and entering a little over the top?"

Art flipped the teddy-bear egg gently over, her eyes firmly on the pan. "They weren't exactly nude modeling pics, and I don't feel like explaining it to you."

"This from the woman who vacuums naked?"

"I can vacuum any way I like!" Art flamed.

"With the curtains closed, sure," Gideon said. "As long as you don't endanger yourself, you can do whatever you please. Did I make a fuss about you going out with Dufray?" He popped two more slices in the toaster.

"No, and I appreciate that, but these pictures might sort of maybe look like"—her voice went softer—"porn, and I could lose my job, and . . ." It trickled away to nothing.

She's an adult, Gideon reminded himself. *What the hell has she been doing?* He forced himself not to grit his teeth. "And what?"

Artemisia got a stubborn look he remembered well from their childhood. "None of your business. It's nothing to do with these murders, and I'm not involved with anyone who shoots porn. I know you're killing yourself not to yell at me, but it would be better if you let me live my life and fixed your relationship with Ophelia instead." She scooped the egg onto a plate, placed two raisins for the teddy's eyes, and poured more egg into the pan. This time she gave it eight little legs. "Will you be able to get the pictures back? Please, *pretty* please?"

"Eventually, I hope so. For the moment, they're all missing. Computers, CDs, negatives, prints . . . gone." Gideon ran a hand through his damp hair.

"That's awful. Poor Gideon," Art said. "There's a lot of pressure on you to solve this, right? Especially after not being able to arrest Constantine last year."

"Baby, the only pressure is to get this guy before he kills someone else. Nobody will try to bribe me to plant evidence in this case."

Art gawped. "People wanted you to make up evidence against Constantine? They offered you money to prove he killed his wife?"

"You bet. Almost turned me off being a cop." Gideon watched his sister smoothly flip the egg. "A spider. That's gotta be symbolic." He tossed the toast onto a plate.

Artemisia blushed. "I have issues, and I am not going to explain them to you."

Good. "Just don't go thinking of catching Dufray in your web. He didn't kill his wife, but he's a dangerous man."

"I won't." Artemisia blushed again. "He's fun, but awfully scary. You know those rumors about him sending bad dreams? I think they may be true." She flapped a hand. "I don't expect you to believe me. And don't start worrying I'll sleep with Tony the vampire, because I won't. Although I totally understand why you can't keep your hands off Ophelia."

Gideon looked up from pouring the coffee. "So that's the secret you were so proud of keeping." He set the two mugs on the table, along with a carton of milk and a canister of sugar.

"Yeah, but now I don't have to, at least from you, and I

can even say I told you so, but I won't. Isn't it cool? She has fangs!"

"Yeah, the fangs are definitely cool." *Even more definitely, hot.* He pulled a chair up to the kitchen table. *And I can't afford to think about them now.*

Artemisia served the spider egg with its own two beady raisin eyes and sat opposite him. "You have to apologize to her."

Gideon cut his teddy bear into quarters and then eighths before he answered. "When I get a spare moment, I'll give her a call."

"A call? You have to go see her! Apologize in person!"

"Sis, I don't think she ever wants to see me again." He speared two pieces of teddy bear and washed them down with a swig of coffee. "I can't say I blame her."

"Of course she does. Gideon, you hurt her. She was crying last night."

Gideon wondered how much worse he would feel before this was over.

"She's not the weepy type, Gideon. Not like Mom. Not like me. Ophelia's tougher than that. She gets mad instead, but last night she was mad and crying, too. She even tried to get me to take Gretchen." Art rolled up her spider egg and cut it in pieces. "Gretchen wouldn't."

"Good for Gretchen, but I can't go see Ophelia. She's . . . Even if she'd listen to me, she's too distracting. I've got to keep my mind on my work."

"Gideon, you *have* to."

"Artemisia, butt out."

"Oh, how wonderful!" Art shouted. "You'll go back to dating bimbos just for the sex, and everything will be hunky-dory!"

"Now you're acting like Mom." He felt like a jerk again at the crestfallen look on his sister's face. "Sorry, but if you get to handle your issues, then I get to handle mine."

The phone rang. Gideon leaped gratefully to get it and hung up on a wrong number ten seconds later.

"Your message light's on," Art noted. She crammed in a mouthful of egg and toast.

Gideon fast-forwarded through the saved message from Ophelia; the last thing he needed was to give Artemisia more ammunition. He erased the next two irrelevancies, and Darby Sims's voice came on.

"Damn it, Gideon," Darby said, "pick up if you're there." Pause. "Listen, bro, we *have* to talk about your sister and Dufray. It's after midnight, and she's still not home." Art gasped, coughed, and gasped again. Gideon strode over and whacked her on the back. After a longer pause, Darby spoke again. "She's too sweet and innocent to hang with that dude. Call me."

Artemisia spat out a hunk of toast. "Thanks," she rasped. She took a swallow of coffee and coughed again.

"What the hell does he expect me to do?" Gideon slathered raspberry jam on his toast. "Forbid you to see Dufray? Challenge him to a duel?"

In a husky voice, Art said, "Does he think I'm a baby?" She ripped off a bite of toast. "I am so *enraged* at him." She glowered down at her plate.

Huh. Casually, he asked, "You had a thing for Dar way back when, didn't you?"

"A high-school crush on a college student," Art said, reddening. "I can't believe this." Her voice shook ever so slightly. "He talks like I'm still sixteen." She washed down her toast and, in a tone she probably thought sounded as casual as Gideon's, asked, "Has he moved home, or is he going back to Atlanta with that awful woman?"

Gideon gulped down the last of his coffee. "He was interviewing to be a tattoo artist the other day, so I guess he's staying. What do you want me to tell him?"

"I don't know," Art said grumpily. "Whatever brothers tell nosy, irritating, well-meaning friends." She gathered up the dishes and dumped them in the sink. "I've got to run, or I'll be late for school." She hurried out the door.

In a minute she was back. *Just like Mom*, thought Gideon almost affectionately.

"Go see Ophelia. I mean it." She banged out the door again. This time she drove away.

CHAPTER SIXTEEN

Ophelia woke unrefreshed after a night of fruitless thoughts and turbulent dreams where Gideon told her she was stupid and Constantine offered an endless line of gleaming, macho trucks. She swung out of bed and glared at Gretchen. "I suppose you slept just fine."

The dog's jaw creaked as she yawned.

"Today you're going back to Gideon, like it or not." Ophelia showered and dressed in shorts and a blatantly cheerful yellow tank top. She pulled her hair into a ponytail and rinsed one of last night's bruised apples. Early sunshine filtered through the bedroom blinds. It was perfect spring working weather, but the police had her two remaining usable maple trees.

Gretchen whined at the front door. Ophelia unlocked it and took a bite of the apple, resigning herself to another trip to the nursery. She followed Gretchen onto the porch and down the stairs to the yard . . . and saw that the front garden was dead. Dead impatiens, dead hostas, dead elephant's ear. The winding border of liriope? Dead. Two recently rescued azaleas, verging on dead. Yellow patches of grass splotched the still mostly green lawn.

In a few quick steps she reached the back garden. The small expanse of grass behind the house contained not one green blade. A drooping swatch of dead mint ringed the lawn. The flowerbeds next to the house were wilted and brown, and she didn't have to go into the greenhouse to see that not much green remained there, either.

Her fists clenched and her fangs slotted down. Useless, since whoever had done this was long gone. Probably days gone. It was a no-brainer to figure this one out. Ophelia peered under the house, and sure enough, the weed-killer bottle was empty. Who could possibly hate her so much?

She bit her lip hard, drawing blood and keeping back the tears until she was indoors with the door shut behind her. Then, huddled on the couch, shutting out the image of all the dead plants, the thoughts of all the wasted effort and all the work required to restore the garden, she tried to focus on what really mattered: Who had done this? And why?

Gretchen scratched on the screen door. She let the dog in and, on autopilot, made peanut-butter sandwiches for both of them. "Blame your stupid Gideon that you're not getting more of that nutria," she told the dog, her voice shaking, but with which emotion she wasn't sure, wishing she could call Gideon about this catastrophe but knowing she wouldn't. She managed to swallow two bites of her sandwich before tossing it to the dog. Gretchen gulped down the food but watched Ophelia with huge, reproachful brown eyes. *Don't call him stupid,* she seemed to say.

"I'll call him stupid all I want," Ophelia retorted, not meaning it, feeling plain lousy. She grubbed around for a pair of old sandals and filled the water bowl for Gretchen, then latched the outside door and locked the dog in the screened porch. She scooped up her pellet rifle and a handful of pellets and let herself out the front, ignoring the dog's indignant howls. "Too bad," she called as she walked around the side of the house. "I need some alone time, so you can't come."

Donnie Donaldson's screen door opened with a slight squeak, and Donnie appeared on the back porch with a can of lubricating oil. "What happened to your yard?" He screwed off the red top of the can.

"Somebody poisoned my garden," Ophelia said. She kicked at the dead impatiens. "Have you seen anybody—anybody at all—hanging around my yard in the past week?"

Donnie shook his head, making sympathetic noises. "Willy again, you think? He was mighty pissed off last night." He dripped oil into the upper hinge.

"Willy wouldn't know enough to do this," Ophelia said. "Anyway, it was probably done several days ago. All my weed killer is gone. Somebody who knew about gardening, or at least had the patience to read the directions, must have mixed it properly and used all I had left to cover so much ground." She ripped an elephant's ear out by the roots and dumped it at the edge of the drive.

"Jesus." Donnie oiled the lower hinge. "Sort of makes you want to give up, don't it?"

"Give up?" Ophelia stared at him. She tossed another elephant's ear to the side. "What are you talking about?"

Donnie made a broad sweep of his hand. "You been fixing up your yard for close on two years now, got it looking real beautiful. Now your soil's poisoned. Everything's ruined." He swung the now-silent door back and forth.

"No, the weed killer breaks down quickly," she said. "I can plant again right away. I'll try something new. Customers always want the same old thing, but I can experiment at home."

Donnie digested her words. "Better find out who did it first, or he might come do it again. Or something even worse." He set the can of oil inside his back door, picked up a couple of half-full green trash bags, and ambled down the steps. "Vi really wants you back in town. She went on and on about it the other day. Told me how good you were for business in the club, and how much she misses you."

"She's conveniently forgotten how much we fought," Ophelia said. "Vi and her club do perfectly fine without me."

Donnie stuffed dead leaves from a pile on the lawn into one of the trash bags. After a minute, he asked, "Who was that fella last night? New boyfriend?"

Ophelia gave him a wilting look. "Jabez is just a friend." She surveyed the front garden, trying to feel enthusiastic about starting over.

"You dumped the corrupt cop?" Donnie knotted the top of the trash bag and nestled it against a roll of carpet cushion in his truck.

Ophelia swung round. "He is not corrupt, and I was never going out with him. And in case you've forgotten what I said yesterday, Constantine did not kill his wife."

Donnie raised his hands in mock horror. "Whoops, I forgot. Vi might not sleep with me if I dis Dufray. Like she'll sleep with me anyway. Gotta be a lot richer than I am to touch Vi." He set to work on the next trash bag.

"Whatever gave you that idea? Vi's not interested in men with money. She has plenty of her own. She's a tease, Donnie, but if you persist she'll come around."

"If I have money she'll come around," Donnie replied. "It's the way of the world. I've been doing good lately. Another year or two, I'll be in her league." He crammed the leaves down in the bag. "You really gonna buy the cop's dog? Why's it howling like that?"

Ophelia blinked at him and then remembered what she'd told Donnie and the photo-shop guy only yesterday or a century ago. "Because I'm going for a walk, and I don't want her along."

"Doesn't sound like you're keeping her," Donnie said. "Maybe you should buy another dog, then. Violet's right, it's not safe here." He hooked his thumbs in his belt and frowned. "You're too stubborn and ornery for your own good. Think of how Vi would feel if something happened to you."

"I like it here," Ophelia said shortly. "So I'm staying."

"I don't know whether I'm glad to hear that or not," Donnie said. He knotted the top of the garbage bag and tossed it into his truck.

* * *

Next week, Gideon told himself as he neared Ophelia's house. *Or tomorrow.* Maybe even by tonight something would have opened up, and he could think straight enough to make that call. In the meantime, he'd drop Ophelia's belongings at Violet's house and get on with interviewing everyone who might have seen something at the photo shop yesterday afternoon.

Without really looking, he noticed Donnie Donaldson loading a bag of trash into his white contractor's truck, while Constantine's bright blue pickup hulked in Ophelia's driveway. Jabez must have left at first light.

But something about Ophelia's house and Ophelia's presence there sucked his gaze to the side, and he really looked.

He swerved into the driveway, Ophelia and her guns and her prohibition be damned. Before he had even opened the door of the Mercedes, a melancholy howl sounded from behind the trailer. He got out of the car and saw the extent of the damage, and an almost physical pain gripped him. "What the hell happened here?"

Donnie Donaldson balanced a TV-sized box on the tailgate of his truck and shifted an orange trash bag to make room for it on the bed. "Someone poisoned her garden. Weed killer."

"Where's Ophelia? Inside?"

Donnie shook his head, tsk-tsking. "She went for a walk. Wanted to be alone. She's all shook up, poor thing. Coupla years' work shot, just like that." He straightened a pile of two-by-tens next to a roll of carpet cushion and tied a red rag around the wood where it hung off the end of the truck. "Stinks, don't it?"

"Why didn't she take my dog with her?"

"Like I said, she wanted to be alone. She's putting up a good front, but if you ask me . . . This shit, on top of Willy and Lisa threatening to call the cops last night 'cause they think she molested Joanna. I heard she was caught with a dead body in her truck. That's not true, is it?"

"Where'd she go?" Gideon demanded. Gretchen yowled inside the screened porch.

Donnie motioned with his chin past the dead back lawn and the greenhouse to the row of compost piles leading toward the woods. "There's a path to the river. She took a rifle, so you better watch your step, officer. It's all her property, the whole way down. She didn't want to see you last night, and she sure ain't gonna want to see you now."

"I can't just drive off and ignore this," Gideon said.

"Don't say I didn't warn you." Donnie climbed into the white truck and drove away.

Gideon took a chisel from the trunk of the Mercedes and pried open one of the screens to free his dog, then strode down the path and into the woods after the departing Gretchen. The trail twisted through the trees for close to half a mile, and at any other time Gideon would have noted the dappled beauty of the woods in the early-morning sun, and maybe even appreciated the labor of love that kept the path clear, but all he could think of was Ophelia crying after he'd been such a jerk, and then going home to Willy's hateful accusations, and finally waking up to a dead garden.

He came out of the woods high on the riverbank not far from a bat house tacked on a metal pole. Another bat house stood in a cleared spot thirty yards downriver. At this point, the water picked up from its usual meander, passing a flurry of rocks and snags, till it rounded the bend farther down and quieted again close to Gideon's place. Upriver a few old farmhouses like the one Gideon had inherited perched not far from the water. Directly across from where he stood, behind a thin layer of trees, several houses abutting the new golf course were being built.

The path turned abruptly right upriver and descended between water oaks and pines toward the water's edge. A flower garden twined in and out of the trees. Gideon heard Ophelia's voice admonishing Gretchen and let go of a long breath. He came into the open a foot or so above the river.

Ophelia stood barefoot below him on a snag, a wreath of ivy and tiny blue flowers resting on her curls. She clutched a rifle in one hand, and her eyes dared him to wrong her again. Gretchen nosed upstream along the water.

Gideon cleared his throat. "Donnie told me you were here," he said. "Art spoke to me this morning. I owe you an apology."

Ophelia nodded. Her grip on the rifle slackened while she watched him, saying nothing. He stepped carefully down the slick mud of the bank, feeling his heart would burst at her beauty, the water sparkling behind her, the sunshine splashing the trees across the river.

Instinct clapped him hard between the shoulder blades. He sprang forward and toppled Ophelia into the water as a bullet whined. A knifelike pain slapped across his thigh. The two of them plunged underwater in a tangle of limbs as another shot cracked the water, and Ophelia kicked away and disappeared, the wreath bobbing and twirling in her wake.

Gideon launched himself after her, hampered by the drag from his clothes and shoes, fighting to stay under until they rounded the first bend. The sniper was on the far side of the river; of that Gideon was sure. Across from Ophelia's, the man had had cover, but he would be hard put to shoot at them unseen from the construction site and the half-finished golf course, which stretched below Ophelia's along the opposite bank. Gideon came up for air at last, hopefully out of sight of the sniper, and made for the flash of her yellow top, but when he got there Ophelia had taken it off and was already diving ahead. He kicked off one shoe as he dove again, rolling downriver, cursing his thigh as he ripped off the second shoe. He hauled his shirt over his head and kept going.

Several breaths later, Ophelia surfaced next to him by the bank. "Where'd you get hit?" Her naked breasts floated enchantingly at water level. "How bad is it?"

"Not so bad I can't enjoy the view," Gideon said, but Ophelia was already underwater, widening the rip in his trousers and licking at his thigh.

She surfaced again a few seconds later, pushing her fangs delicately back into place. "It's just a graze. Around the next bend, there's a little alcove under the bank where I can fix it properly."

"I know where that is," Gideon said. She must have done something properly already, because his thigh no longer burned. He plowed downstream beside her until they passed the cypress that marked the bend, then pulled hard toward the bank. Ophelia shimmered ahead of him under the willows. She peeled off her shorts and underwear, wrung them out, and stashed them at the back of the alcove.

"Take off your clothes," she said.

Whatever you say, honey. Gideon stripped off his trousers and boxers, then his socks, and followed Ophelia's delectable naked behind onto the soft mud bank under the trees, instantly harder than he'd ever been in his life.

"Lie back," Ophelia said, and Gideon propped himself on his elbows and watched with half-closed eyes as she licked the trickle of blood off his leg, as blissful as if he'd died and gone to heaven. He gave a fleeting thought to the condom in the wallet in his pants, but where Ophelia was concerned he had long ago abandoned all caution and common sense, and as for the future, he simply didn't care.

I don't care whether he likes the fangs or not, Ophelia told herself, *he's mine.* He looked ecstatic, of course, leaning on his elbows as he watched her work on his thigh. *I'll make him like them,* she vowed, and then realized that she was pleading, eyes closed as she tidied the graze. *Oh God, please let him like them, please let him like me.* As if in answer to her prayer his hand came lightly to rest on her head, playing with the damp strands of hair, brushing her cheek.

She breathed in the musky scent of his penis and ran a

hand up over it, caressing it gently, gliding her fingers over the tip, longing to run her tongue along the shaft, to savor him in her mouth. *Goddamn fangs*, she thought. *Why can't I just be normal?*

He wouldn't be this hot for you if you were normal, she reminded herself.

She crawled up and straddled him, taking control, touching her tongue to his, aflame with lust and a longing for something more, and he licked eagerly into her mouth, fearlessly negotiating the fangs. One hot hand fondled her butt, the other cupped a breast, rubbed and pulled at her nipple, shooting a sizzle straight to her sex, and she shivered with pleasure.

"Thank you," she whispered, surprising herself. "Thank you for saving my life."

"Instinct," Gideon replied, looking so happy it hurt, and then his expression changed. His hands ceased their wandering to grip her shoulders. He pushed her slightly away. "If you're doing this out of gratitude . . . ," he said, clenching his teeth, struggling with himself so valiantly it stole her breath. "If you're doing it out of gratitude," he said again, "don't do it at all."

"I'm grateful to be alive so I *can* do it." Ophelia teased herself lightly across his penis, nuzzled and scraped her fangs against his throat, worked her way back to the intoxication of his mouth. "You taste so good." She ran her nose past his armpit and the zing shuddered all the way to her clit. "You smell spectacular. So strong, so alive." So hers.

"As long as you won't regret it afterward." Gideon ran his teeth along her lip and tugged gently. The corner of his mouth lingered against hers, and his breath shivered hot on her cheek. "As long as you really want me."

The hell with caution. The hell with consequences, too. Ophelia reached down and poised him against her opening. "You want the truth?"

He smiled up at her, a crooked adorable smile, and his hands clamped hard on her hips. He nudged the tip of his penis gently into her, teasing back. "Tell me, sweetheart."

"I've wanted you from the moment we met." She took his face in her hands and kissed him hard. "When you started arguing with me, I wanted to throw you down on the mud and have my way with you then and there." She clutched him, aching with need. "It was torture keeping my hands off you."

"Mud, here and now," growled Gideon into her mouth. "Hands all over each other. My way, your way. Fuck me *hard*." His words dissolved into an inarticulate sound of pleasure as he thrust himself deep inside her.

She heard her own moan through a burst of heat, rocking against him, coming already, way too soon. "Oh, damn!"

"Bust it out all over me, honey. It'll be good. It'll be fine." Gideon held her still and tight as she shook, then brought her back up fast before she'd hardly gone down, his hands tasting every inch of her, playing at her breasts and spreading her ass, his slick fingers and hot breath sending her soaring as he drove up into her, shooting them both toward another glorious peak.

"Oh God," Ophelia said, "I *deserve* this!" She thrust herself hard against him.

"Hell, yes," Gideon panted, gripping her ass cheeks, licking her fangs.

"Do you realize how long it's been?" Ophelia gasped. "I'm a *vamp*." She thrust at him again. "It's my right!"

"Inalienable, honey. All yours." He laughed and pulled back, and his voice came out hoarse and harsh. "Bite me." He gripped her hips and rocked deep into her. "Do it now."

"Not yet." Ophelia writhed in his musk and his heat, rode him up the crescendo, and then her fangs took over, extending all the way, drawing her relentlessly toward him.

"Please," he gasped. She sank her fangs into his shoulder.

His blood seared through her. He shot hard inside her, over and over, with a long, tortured groan.

This time, there was no coming back. She pulled out her fangs, licked the tiny puncture wounds, and fell immediately into a warm, relieved darkness.

CHAPTER SEVENTEEN 🌷

Gideon woke first to an overwhelming contentment, then to the rueful knowledge that he'd screwed up even more now than before. He hadn't slept long, by the position of the sun through the willow leaves, but the sniper had had plenty of time to cover his tracks. If he'd tried to follow them down-river, there might have been telltale signs in the mud of the construction site, but by now, an hour or so into the work-day, they'd be covered and mingled with those of workers and trucks. He put his arms around Ophelia, knowing he should be hurrying over there, rushing to town to deal with the murder case before the trail went cold, but not really caring about anything except Ophelia asleep on his shoul-der and that his instinct was back at last.

But instinct had a mind of its own, and it gave him no clue how to deal with Ophelia now. She slept so peacefully, her breath light on his chest, her eyelashes lush against her cheeks. She stirred, and his response was so immediate that he had to laugh at his own helplessness. Another instinct knew what it wanted, that was for damn sure.

Ophelia's eyelashes fluttered. She squirmed languidly. "Mmm."

Mmm, indeed. Gideon rolled her under him, kneed her legs apart and entered her with one smooth stroke.

"Thank you," Ophelia murmured, twining her legs around his and arching toward him. "I need this." She moved with breathtaking voluptuousness. "Vamps aren't supposed to do without."

So hot, so ready. He needed this, too. "You don't have to do without anymore."

Ophelia sighed and opened her eyes. "Shouldn't you go to work?"

Gideon pulled almost out of her and slid easily back in. "Uh-huh." He set up a slow, lazy rhythm. "I'm completely screwed."

"Might as well enjoy it," Ophelia said, pulling his mouth down to hers. And they didn't speak again until they lay once more, sated, on the mud under the willows.

A soft whimper on the bank above broke the spell.

"Gretchen came home. Good."

"Home?"

Gideon pulled their soggy clothing out from under the bank. "This is my property. You can't see much from the river, but we're only fifty yards from my house."

"You own the weeping garden?" Ophelia scrambled naked up the bank behind Gideon and followed him into the tangled mess she had coveted for at least a year. With deep woods on either side and across the river, Gideon's garden was a secret paradise. Or had been, years ago.

"The what?"

"Weeping garden. It's crying out for care and attention." Ophelia picked her way gingerly up the twisting pathway past more poison ivy than she had ever seen in her life. "It used to be a beautiful garden."

"How can you tell?" Gideon turned to survey the jungle, but inevitably his eyes rested on Ophelia instead. "Honey, I can't think about plants even under ordinary circumstances. I hate to have to find some clothes for you."

"You do have a fig tree," Ophelia said, motioning ahead to the right. "But this isn't the Garden of Eden. Not any longer, that is."

"It wasn't an Eden before, either," Gideon said dryly. "It

was my mother's refuge from my dad. The plants didn't walk away when she talked to them. They flourished under her care."

"Maybe they listened to her," Ophelia said.

"She drove him nuts with her yammering," Gideon said.

"Maybe if he'd been listening to start with, she wouldn't have had to yammer."

"Chicken and egg," Gideon said. "All I know is, by the time Art and I were old enough to understand, she was a nag and he was a pigheaded old bastard, and it was way too late for any remedies. I swore then that I would never become my old man." He opened the gate, where Gretchen waited on the outside and two German shepherds paced in a small fenced yard shaded by a mature river birch. "Meet Daisy and Belle."

She followed Gideon and the milling dogs to the house, an elegant old Victorian with fresh sea green paint and cream trim. They strode up a flight of steps to a wide back deck with wooden benches, a barbecue, and yards of planking asking for potted plants. Gideon stopped. "Whatever my father believed was right, regardless of the consequences, regardless of others. Everybody else was stupid." He shook out his wet trousers, fished for his key ring, which had miraculously stayed in the pocket, and opened the back door.

The interior shone, tiled and painted and clean. Well, except for a few dirty dishes in the sink, but for a bachelor home with three dogs . . .

"You like it?"

A sense of oppression that had been creeping up ever since they had stepped onto the riverbank blanketed itself over Ophelia. "I'm not much into houses, but yeah, I do. I really do." The ideal lover with the perfect garden—but she was nowhere near ideal or perfect or even safe.

Gideon tossed their wet clothes into a laundry basket. "I enjoy taking care of the house, but I can't stand yard work."

Unbelievably perfect . . . but I can't do it. She waited

bleakly for him to bring it into the open so she could tell him no, but he didn't, merely led her up the stairs to a vast bedroom with a skylight above in which danced leaves and the sky, then through to a bathroom with a toilet, sink, and hexagonal-stall shower. The other half of the room was sealed off with plastic sheeting.

"Theoretically, it's for a tub, but I never take baths, so it's last on my list." He turned on the shower and motioned her inside. "What's wrong?"

"Real life," Ophelia said. "Intruding on our little idyll."

"We can do some more idylling later," Gideon said. He poured shampoo into Ophelia's hand and then his own. "Still no idea who might have it in for you?"

Oh, right. Someone had tried to kill her. "No." She noticed the shampoo and halfheartedly lathered her hair.

Gideon scrubbed vigorously. "The poison in your garden. Is that something permanent? Does it ruin your land for years, anything like that?"

"No, I'm pretty sure he used my nontoxic weed killer. I can plant again anytime." *But I don't want to. Not there. I want to plant here. And to plant here, I have to get away from there. And there's only one way to do that.* "It absorbs through the leaves and kills the plants, but it breaks down within a few days."

"Still, why dump a body in your truck yesterday afternoon, poison your garden last night, and try to shoot you this morning?" He took the showerhead off its hook and rinsed her hair.

"Weed killer doesn't work that fast." Ophelia stood quiescent under the warm flow. "Judging by how much I had left in the bottle and how many plants he killed, and taking the weather into account, he did it at least three days ago."

"Huh. Still, it looked like vengeance or intimidation up till this morning. It's a big jump to attempted murder. What happened to change his mind?"

Ophelia shrugged, a far grislier problem than an attempt

on her life exercising her mind. She wanted this garden. She even wanted the house, as long as she didn't have to take care of it. And she definitely wanted this man.

You know what you have to do first, she reminded herself. *You were planning it anyway, deep down.* But that had been planned for some time in the unforeseeable future.

"Do the Wylers have a rifle? Does Donnie Donaldson? Plato? Hello?"

Ophelia dragged herself back to the present. "Everybody has a rifle out here. Well, maybe not Plato, but he would defend me to the death. Why were you harassing him last night?"

"I wasn't harassing him." Gideon lathered up the soap and handed it to her, then quickly soaped himself all over. "He told me he intends to keep an eye on your place."

"Like he doesn't do that already. You don't mind him— uh—worshipping me?"

"His problem, not mine. I have his goddess in my shower." He took the soap from Ophelia, lathered it up again, and set to work on her. "Do you go down to the river regularly?"

"Most evenings. Mornings, too, if I'm not busy." She closed her eyes, but the images of what she had to plan, what she had to do, wouldn't go away. She leaned her forehead against Gideon as he soaped her, his big gentle hands comforting and kind. A dream garden. Excellent sex. Seemed okay with the fangs. Not prone to jealousy. Liked housework. She had to go through with it. The unforeseeable future was now. "Ooh." She sagged against him.

"Hello?" Gideon's hand left her clit to take down the showerhead. "Are you listening to anything I'm saying? Now I know how my mom felt."

Ophelia chuckled. "Maybe she was using the wrong methods to get your dad's attention."

"Jeez." Gideon rinsed her right armpit and then her left. "Not something I want to think about. Bend over."

Ophelia obliged. "Why not? They must have done it more

than the twice it took to produce you and Art. Coming from such a screwed-up, inhibited family, I'm amazed you turned out so well."

"I planned it that way." He tapped her lightly on the rear, turned off the water and hung the showerhead on its hook. "Who, besides your neighbors, knows you go down to the river?" He handed her a huge, fluffy white towel.

"The people who live in the houses across the water from my property. We wave hello now and then. Sometimes the construction workers whistle at me, but none of them have gotten close enough to get hit by my allure, so they don't see me as anything but another attractive woman." She pondered a moment. "A real-estate agent who's selling homes in the new subdivision next to the golf course. He insisted on a tour of my land, although I told him I'm not planning to sell anytime soon." She shrugged. "None of these people have any reason to harm me. You can't possibly expect me to wear only that!"

Gideon grinned down at the oversize T-shirt he was holding out: a double-extra-large Constantine Dufray shirt, of all things, the back sporting an iron-on photo of a shirtless, wild-haired Constantine on stage. "Art won it, but it was too big for her, so she gave it to me."

"How am I going to get home? I can't walk down the highway half-naked, and your car's at my place." She pulled the T-shirt over her head.

"I'll get someone to pick us up. There, see? Constantine's covering your ass, which I assume he's done many times in the past. Is that why you're so blasé about somebody trying to kill you?"

Ophelia scowled. "He's been a good friend to me. Don't you dare dis him!"

Gideon calmly pulled on khaki pants and tucked in his shirt. "I'm not dissing him. But you're not taking this situation anywhere near seriously enough, honey. I want to know why."

Ophelia shifted a shoulder. How could she run this game? Because that's how she had to see it. She had to make a game plan and carry it through, and stay as close to the truth as possible.

"I guess I assume you'll take care of it, just like Constantine and Lep have done in the past. I have other things to think about. I have to buy more maple trees and plant them for a customer. Unless you got my trees out of jail?"

"Not the trees, no, but your pocketbook and clipboard are in my car. Not the work boots. Theoretically—and no, this is not my idea—there may be evidence on the soles."

Ophelia narrowed her eyes. "You know perfectly well—"

"I know perfectly well that if I don't appear disinterested, the chief will take me off this case. People will find it way too easy to start with the 'corrupt and incompetent' crap again, after that fiasco with Constantine last year. Which will piss me off, because this case is my business, and which will piss my boss off, because in order to keep his cushy job, he'll have to do the work himself. We're a small outfit. We don't have to investigate many homicides, because when your underworld friends are annoyed with someone, they just make him disappear."

Ophelia muttered something unconvincing about corruption, her mind elsewhere already. Trees, estimates, and a major purchase, all today. "Do you have a computer? Can I get online?"

When Joanna Wyler's bus pulled up in front of the middle school, thirty minutes late due to a breakdown, Zelda Dupree experienced a miraculous turn for the better.

"The cramps are gone," she told the nurse. "Sometimes a little horizontal time is all it takes." Never mind that she had spent most of the last half hour bolt upright, glaring out the window of the school clinic, the only room at the front of the school to which she had access at this hour of the day, and had only started her period two months ago and been so far cramp free. She grabbed her hall pass and zapped out of the clinic and through the front doors of the school, pushing herself neatly in beside Joanna as she exited the bus.

"You said you liked my aunt Ophelia!" Zelda said. At the sight of Joanna's blotchy face and swollen red eyes, her tender side reluctantly emerged. "What's wrong? You look terrible."

Joanna burst into tears and walked faster.

"Don't cry, dummy," Zelda said. "You'll look even worse." She rooted in her jeans for a tissue and found nothing. All the better. She couldn't afford to soften yet.

"I can't help it." Joanna wiped her nose on her sleeve, and the books she carried slipped askew. She clutched them against her unwieldy chest and hurried ahead.

"Wimp," Zelda said cruelly, feeding on her anger, knowing Joanna couldn't take it and not caring. She kept up with the other girl, stride for stride. "You are in big trouble. Do you know how many people told me this morning that Ophelia had sex with you? Sixteen!"

"Oh, no!" Joanna scurried around the end of the building. "Everyone will think I'm a lesbian slut!"

Zelda grabbed Joanna Wyler by the scruff of her preppy striped button-down shirt and yanked her against the dull cinderblock wall of the middle school. Joanna shrieked and dropped her books. Her homework danced away on the breeze. "I don't care what people think about you. Nobody lies about Ophelia and gets away with it. You hear me?"

"I never said Ophelia did it!" Joanna cried. "My homework! It's getting away."

"Your homework won't matter when you're dead," Zelda hissed in Joanna's face. "Which you will be if you don't fix this, right now!" She scowled at the small crowd that had gathered. "For God's sake, stop gawking. Somebody go pick up her homework!" She rounded on Joanna again.

"My parents just assumed it," Joanna squeaked. "I told them Ophelia didn't touch me. I told them she didn't take those pictures, but they didn't believe me. It's my mom's fault. All she ever does is sit on the phone and gossip."

"What pictures?" Zelda broke in.

Joanna's gaze shifted from side to side and a flush crawled up her cheeks. "Dirty pictures," she whispered.

"Ooh," said a boy. "I wanna see them. Will I get to see your tits, Joanna?" Some girls giggled. One solitary kind-hearted boy was chasing around the parking lot after Joanna's homework. Zelda considered slugging the hoverers and decided against it. Joanna deserved humiliation, so humiliated she would be.

"Well then," Zelda said, easing her grip slightly, "this is easily solved."

"It is?" Joanna sucked in a deep, throbbing breath.

"You're going to tell your parents who *did* take the pictures. Better yet, you're going to tell me, right now. Tell all of us"—she glared at the semicircle of rubberneckers—"so we can spread the truth around instead."

"I can't!" Joanna howled. "I can't tell anyone, ever!"

"Is somebody threatening you?" Zelda demanded. "If they are, telling us is the best thing to do. There are six of us as witnesses. Seven," she amended, as Rick from art class showed up with Joanna's homework. He crammed it at Joanna, his eyes glued to Zelda's face. *Some do-gooder.* "They can't threaten us all. Who did it?"

"No!" Joanna's chest heaved. "I'll never tell! I'd rather die!" Her eyes flickered up and behind the crowd, and her voice rose. "Leave me alone, you bully! It's not my fault!"

Fury such as Zelda had never before known swelled inside her. Her jaw ached, her lips contorted in a snarl, and she drew back her fist to deck this girl good.

"Wow, Zelda," Rick said in an awed, worshipful voice. "You're so hot when you're mad!"

Zelda got in one solid punch at Rick before the administrator took her arm.

* * *

When the red Cadillac pulled up in front of the house, Gideon held his breath, waiting for the storm. It didn't come. Ophelia stiffened at the sight of the car and its buff blond driver, and then abruptly, immediately relaxed.

Huh, thought Gideon. *Seen this before.*

Her tone was disgusted but placid. "I guess I shouldn't be surprised."

"You need protection," Gideon said, "and I can't provide it. No budget for attempted-murder victims, and I have work to do. What choice did I have but to call Lep?" He watched the bodyguard check himself out in the side mirror before heading gracefully toward the front steps. "That dude belongs on the cover of one of Jeanie's romance novels."

"That's what he thinks, too. Let's go. I have work to do, too."

"You're not going to freak out? Argue? Yell at me?"

"I might yell at you next time I see you," Ophelia said placidly. "Several hours of Reuben's tall, blond, and hypermasculine presence should get me good and pissed off."

Gideon's lips twitched. "You're not acting like the Ophelia I've gotten to know."

Ophelia hunched a lazy shoulder and yawned. "I got laid. It relaxes me. Takes the edge off my allure, too, so poor Reuben won't have to fight himself so hard not to come on to me. However, I refuse to get into his car without a little more clothing." She snatched a throw off an old rocking chair in the corner and wrapped the fabric around her bare hips.

"You don't seem any less alluring to me," Gideon said, closing his eyes to shut out the view. He had to work.

"Thanks." Ophelia yawned again. She knotted the ends of the throw, sarong-style.

"Sure you'll be okay with this dude?"

"He won't kill me."

And that was that. She parted from him amicably, even

absentmindedly, and yet . . . and yet something warned him of tension hidden underneath that pleasant, distracted exterior.

Good old instinct, thought Gideon. *I'll figure her out.*

The blonde bitch was at the station when Gideon hared through a few hours later, between one set of fruitless interviews and the next. Her strident voice carried all the way to Gideon's office in the back. "I heard it on the news. There was a body in Ophelia Beliveau's truck. You knew it might be my Johnny, and you didn't call me!"

The chief regarded her blearily. "We had no reason to believe the victim was your husband. We now have a tentative ID, someone else entirely."

"Tentative? What good is that? You're deliberately hiding him from me. If it's Johnny, I have to know! How else can I collect on the insurance?" As Gideon came through the door from the back, Marissa eyed the chief. "Well, if it isn't Vibrator Man. He's protecting that Ophelia bitch because he's got the hots for her, just like Johnny."

The chief put three shingles and a utility knife on the bench by the wall and bent an annoyed eye on Marissa. "Do you have a reason for your visit, ma'am, other than to disrespect my detective?"

The blonde kept right on going. "He's wasting his time, because she's sleeping with Constantine Dufray. Otherwise, why would she be carting dead bodies around for him?"

"If you wish to view the body, I can arrange it," the chief said. "But since the height, weight, and coloring don't match those of your husband, and the face was beaten to a pulp and is unrecognizable, you might want to think twice."

Marissa's color faded under her makeup, ghastly against the tight purple spandex that enveloped her ripe curves. "My Johnny was beaten to death?" Her hands flapped to cover her mouth, her eyes wide and aghast. Jeanie made concerned sounds.

Gideon and the chief exchanged glances. "Not your Johnny," the chief said. "Someone else." He retrieved a tape measure from under the counter.

Marissa moaned. "Constantine killed my Johnny, and if you'd seen how he looked at me in that club last night, you'd know I'm in danger, too! Oh God, what am I going to do?"

In an ideal world, thought Gideon, *you'd leave town and never come back.*

Jeanie got up and put a hand on Marissa's arm. "Hon, you're exaggerating this all out of proportion. If Constantine killed everybody who got on his nerves, we'd all be dead by now. His bark is way worse than his bite." The blonde snatched her arm away. Jeanie shrugged, her duty done. "His bite's pretty doggone fantastic." She ambled back to her desk and picked up her current romance.

The chief said, "Ma'am, there's no evidence Dufray killed your husband or anyone else. It's all hype. Publicity for his bad-boy image." He set a square against the shingle and cut it smoothly in two.

"What about his wife? He poisoned her!"

"No evidence whatsoever." He measured and cut another shingle. Yesterday's plywood was now a box shaped like a lean-to. The chief placed a strip of shingle on the slanted top of the box and nailed it squarely, then set another shingle in place. "Looks good, doesn't it? The little critters will love it."

Marissa made a face. "What critters?"

"Bats," the chief said. "They keep the insect population down, and they're delightful to watch in the evening sky. Not only that, but—"

Marissa inhaled deeply, clenched her fists hard against her thighs, and screamed.

"I've got to run," Gideon said disgustedly. "Thank God for genuine homicides." He tossed a credit card at Jeanie as he headed out. "Get me a new cell phone. Same number, pronto. Mine's at the bottom of the river."

"In the cause of true love, what's a cell phone?" Jeanie said.

"This *is* a genuine homicide!" Marissa was shrieking. "You know how I know? Because Johnny always came back to me. He always called me when he was away. Sure he was crazy, sure he was fixated on Ophelia Beliveau, but he needed me! He fixated on other girls, too, before Ophelia, but he came back then, too. That's how I know, in my heart and my soul, that he's dead. That woman is suckering you, Vibrator Man, you and your no-good chief and this town!"

An instinct nagged at him, but he shrugged. "Without a body, there's nothing I can do." Gideon left by the back door.

Marissa's voice pursued him. "It'll be my dead body next! Constantine Dufray's planning to kill me!"

So help me, thought Gideon, *I almost wish he would.*

CHAPTER EIGHTEEN 🌷

Ophelia pulled to the curb in front of her sister's house, the red Cadillac close behind her, just as Artemisia parked her Toyota across the street. *Okay*, Ophelia told herself, *pretend to be normal. Calm, composed, living an ordinary life.*

"What's that monster machine you're towing?" Art asked.

Help me out, why don't you? "It's a chipper." Ophelia jumped down from the cab of the big macho truck, trying not to sound surly. Trying to sound . . . cheerful. Competent. A business owner pleased with a purchase. "I just bought it today."

"Eew," Art said. "The kind of thing that chops branches up into wood chips?"

Hopefully that's not all it chops. "That's why it's called a chipper."

"It looks like it's falling apart," Art said. "Are you sure it's safe?"

"I got it cheap for one special job," Ophelia said. "It doesn't have to last long." *God, please let it last long enough.*

"Did you see that movie *Fargo*?" Art shuddered. "Just looking at that thing freaks me out."

Like Gideon's sister had any concept of freaked out. Ophelia pasted on a serene face as Reuben came around the truck, sweaty, gorgeous, and pissed off. "Your brother decided I need protection, so poor Reuben's been stuck hanging with me all day."

"Whoa." Art blushed. At least she'd forgotten about the goddamned chipper.

A howl of fury came from behind the house.

"I will not be you!" Zelda screeched. They hurried toward the back, and Violet came into sight, dripping wet in a transparent red robe. She battled with the nozzle on the hose she held and sent a harsh spray across the garden at her daughter.

"You are my child!" shrilled Violet. "Have you forgotten everything I taught you about violence? Manage your anger, Zelda. Fight it and control it!"

Zelda sent an even stronger spray from her own hose, knocking Violet into the petunias, and Ophelia sprang forward before some plant that mattered was destroyed. She vaulted the gate and sprinted around the back of the house.

"Damn it, Zelda!" Violet shoved herself up, seething, groping for her hose, but Ophelia got there first and snatched it away.

"I am not a child! I will not be you!" cried Zelda again, her voice suffused with unaccustomed misery and rage. She sprayed the hose furiously across the garden, drenching Ophelia and spattering Reuben and Art as they rounded the corner of the house.

"Pax!" called Ophelia. She turned off the nozzle of Violet's hose.

"Okay, pax," Zelda said on a bitter little sob. She tossed her hose onto the flagstone and threw herself at Ophelia's chest and dug her fingernails into her arms. "I so totally screwed up," she wept into Ophelia's shirt. "Tell me what to do!"

Ophelia peeled Zelda's fingers away and closed her arms around her niece.

Violet flung up her hands in disgust. "I. Give. Up. From day one I've told her violence is never the answer, and the minute she hits puberty she starts beating people up."

"Like you don't lose your temper, Mom," Zelda burst out. "Like you've never slugged some guy who came on to you."

"Only when I had no choice," Violet said. She caught sight of Reuben and perked up.

Ophelia's bodyguard stared happily at Violet, dripping wet and nearly naked. "Need a hug?"

"No, I'm perfectly under control, you delicious, pheromone-rich hunk of meat. Ophelia put you to work, did she? Go take a shower, darling. I know you can't stand that sticky feeling."

Reuben grinned at Violet and raised his eyebrows.

"Sorry, darling, I'd love to join you, but right now Zelda's my priority. If she would only listen to me!" Violet's eyes flashed.

Zelda's flashed right back. "Maybe you should try listening to *me*, Mother!"

Art hovered uneasily at the corner of the house. "I'd better go home."

"Not at all," Violet said. "Come into the kitchen for tea. You're so much older and wiser and more cooperative than my adolescent child, of whom I expected much, much more." She saw Reuben hanging indecisively at the foot of the steps, his eyes on Ophelia. "Go! Girl-talk time. You're not wanted."

"For heaven's sake, Reuben, I'm not going anywhere," Ophelia said. "Have I tried to escape you even once today?"

"See?" Violet said, once the bodyguard was on his way up the stairs. "Even Ophelia's cooperating. And thank God for that, since her life is in danger. I'm glad to see at least one of my family acting sanely." Tears spilled onto Violet's cheeks. Ophelia sensed Zelda softening and grabbed her by the arm.

"Zelda and I will have a little talk." She hauled the teenager onto the back porch and settled beside her on the swing. "I am frigging well *not* cooperating," she said under her breath. "I am biding my time. And don't you dare tell Vi I said that. Now tell me what happened."

"Mom doesn't understand at all," Zelda said, when she had finished explaining the incident at school. "So what if I got suspended? So what if I was mean to Joanna? She deserved it. And please, please don't be mad at me for defending you. I couldn't *stand* what they were saying."

"I'm not mad, I'm grateful." Ophelia squeezed Zelda's shoulders. "But I think if we give Joanna a chance, if we make her feel safe with us, she'll tell the truth."

"She's already called twice. I refused to talk to her." She raised stubborn eyes. "It's not like Mom was an angel in school. She got into all kinds of trouble."

"Sure, but she never let it get past the administrator's office. I was more like you. But that's not the issue, is it? And neither is Joanna or the boy you slugged."

"No," Zelda agreed, and sniffed and bit her lip and finally released a couple of tears and then a couple more. Ophelia hugged her hard, and for a long time they sat together in silence.

Zelda sighed. "I didn't think it would be like this. I *swore* I wouldn't have a vamp's temper. I love Mom, but it drives me crazy when she throws things around and breaks dishes until some dumb guy holds her down. It's so childish! The water-therapy thing's sort of fun, but I don't want to be out of control when I'm thirty-five. I don't want to be out of control *now*, but I lost it, Ophelia! I don't even remember what happened. I was *blind* with it. What got into me?"

"Your mom's not out of control," Ophelia said. "The drama works for her, so she uses it. Has she ever hurt anyone when she throws things around?" Zelda shook her head. "When she breaks something, does she expect you to clean it up? No, she takes care of it herself. And you may have noticed that she gets a lot more irate when there's some guy around to grab her. Violet *likes* being squeezed into submission."

"Ick." Zelda drew in a throbbing breath. "What am I going to do?"

"Find your own way to control it, sweetie, and don't beat yourself up in the meantime. Have you sprouted your fangs yet?"

Zelda rubbed her gums. "No. Maybe I'm not a vamp. Maybe I'm just a violent bitch."

"Wishful thinking, I'm afraid," Ophelia said. "The main thing is to have control over your fangs once you do sprout them, and to use them only in the direst emergency. You could do a lot of damage." *God, yes.* "Not just to the person you attack, not just to yourself because you'd feel terrible, but to the safety of vamps in general. Maintaining our privacy without harming others is a huge challenge. In Bayou Gavotte, with any luck, you'll be all right, but there won't always be a Lep or a Constantine around to keep you out of jail. *God, no.* Slugging people isn't good, but it's a better option until you've learned some control."

"But why do we have such terrible tempers?"

"Because when some really bad guy comes along, and unfortunately there will be plenty, your temper will be exactly what you need. An enraged vampire with her fangs out terrifies ninety-nine bad ones out of a hundred, and with your wits and some self-defense training, you can hopefully handle the hundredth, too." *God, yes, please.*

"Ta-da!" Violet flung open the back door and motioned Art forward. A new, elegant Art in a long, slinky electric blue dress and impossible heels.

Art tottered forward. "This is so not me!"

Ophelia laughed. "You look fabulous."

"And definitely not sweet sixteen," Violet said. "Tonight will be so much fun."

"I'm dressed too much like Marissa," Art said mutinously. "If this is what Dar wants, I'm not right for him at all!"

Violet twitched the flared hem into place. "This is just an *occasional* you, snaring your man being the occasion. Tonight, the aim is to show him you're all grown up. Once that's sunk in, we'll wallop him with something else."

Inside the house, the phone rang. Zelda jumped off the swing and stopped dead. She glowered at Ophelia. Ophelia shrugged.

"Oh, all right," Zelda said. "If it's Joanna, I won't hang up on her. But that's all I promise."

It wasn't Joanna, though. It was Gideon.

"He sounds serious," Zelda said. She handed Ophelia the phone.

"Thank God you're there," Gideon said. "You're not answering your phone."

"I left it in the truck. What's wrong?" She saw Violet's eyes on her and knew what her sister was thinking, knew what she had now realized and would have realized earlier if not for other overriding concerns, but Gideon's next words drove all other thoughts out of Ophelia's mind.

"There's been another murder," Gideon said. "Plato's dead."

"Why?" Two tears rolled down Ophelia's cheeks at the pathetic sight of Plato on the forest floor with a hole in his chest. Dead leaves and pine straw clung to his clothing, and an army of ants marched efficiently under his once-crisp white shirt. She felt Gideon's eyes on her, as they had been ever since she parked at the side of the old country road across the river from her property. Gideon had nodded his thanks to a relieved Reuben, and since the red Cadillac had driven away, his focus had been unnervingly upon her, and the attention had nothing to do with sex.

She shook off an uncomfortable feeling of being tested and tested again. "He must have seen something," she answered herself slowly. Her eyes traveled through the trees toward the river. "Whoever shot at me, maybe?"

"What's the likelihood he would have been down at the river at dawn?"

"Close to nil," Ophelia said.

"If he saw something at dawn, he had all day to report it, but he didn't try to call me till close to two." Gideon sounded horribly grim. "He called three times within a few minutes. The third time he left a message, saying he needed to talk to me and only me, that he thought he had something but wasn't sure. At two thirty-five he tried me again and was cut off before he finished identifying himself. Shot at close range with a small-caliber pistol is what it looks like. By then I guess he was sure, but it was too late."

"Why didn't you answer your phone?" Ophelia couldn't hide the anguish in her voice.

"My phone was at the bottom of the river. I picked up messages every chance I had until I got the new phone an hour ago. This killer has sheer dumb luck."

"Plato was ready for work," Ophelia said irrelevantly. "He always wears a starched white shirt to work. He always wore black to the club." She bit back a sob. "He was crazy, but he was *good*. There aren't enough good people around. What was he doing over here?"

For too long, Gideon said nothing. Ophelia looked at Plato again, at the mess of churned-up pine straw around him and the dearth of it to one side, at a drawn and trampled patch of poison ivy and a broken native azalea. "You think maybe he wasn't shot here," she said. "That he was dragged—or dragged himself—from over that way."

Gideon still said nothing but led her slowly through the trees, parallel to more signs of disturbance, toward an old brown farmhouse nestled in the woods.

"The people who live in this house are on vacation," Ophelia said.

He waited some more, and again she felt obliged to explain.

"They asked me to take care of their lawn while they're gone. The people next door commute to New Orleans every day." She nodded at a green Victorian similar to Gideon's in size and shape. "I did some perennial beds for them last year. It wouldn't be hard to get in and out of here unseen. He could have parked on the driveway, dragged Plato through the woods, covered him with dead leaves and pine straw . . . The body might not have been found for ages. And of course, whoever shot at us this morning might have been here, too." Now it was her turn to ask questions. "Who found him?"

"One of the construction workers came down here after his shift to scope out the river for fishing. If he'd been an hour earlier, I might have had a witness."

"If he'd been an hour earlier, he might have ended up dead," Ophelia said. "This guy doesn't let witnesses live. Have you made any progress on the other murders?"

"A lot of negatives," Gideon said. His phone rang. Ophelia watched him listen. "Huh," Gideon said. "Makes sense." Ophelia tried not to be irritated at his terse sentences and veiled eyes. "Thanks, Jeanie."

Ophelia started walking. "I need to go home and take a shower."

"Busy day?" Gideon asked politely.

We had sex this morning. Polite doesn't fit anymore. "This morning Reuben and I went to the nursery to buy more Japanese maples. We dropped the trees at the customer site, prepared the ground for planting, and went to lunch. I have the charge slip." If he wanted proof. Goddamn it, what was going on? She waited, but Gideon said nothing, and his expression conveyed even less.

Ophelia forced her fangs to stay quiescent and her tone to remain neutral. "During lunch, I prepared a drawing for one of my estimates. Then we drove all the way to Baton Rouge to pick up some equipment, came back to plant the trees, which just about killed Reuben, and then went to Vi's house, where you found me. Reuben won't want to bodyguard me for a while. Poor baby, he didn't even get to sleep with Vi as a reward."

Gideon looked a polite question, and Ophelia pondered which one to answer. "Zelda got sent home from school for fighting, so Vi wasn't in the mood."

Gideon looked another question.

"Zelda was defending my honor. Lisa Wyler's been spreading word via the gossip tree that I molested Joanna, and although Joanna denies it, she won't say who did take those pictures. Vi spread word via another network entirely that Children's Services needs to leave me alone or they'll be sorry. Sometimes I'm grateful for my underworld contacts, but what if Joanna's in danger? She says she isn't, but whoever took those pictures must know she'll break down and tell somebody sooner or later." They reached Constantine's truck, parked behind Gideon's Mercedes. Gretchen came out from underneath and yawned. "You should be protecting Joanna instead of me. Now that I'm on my guard, I'll do fine."

"We're trying to keep an eye on Joanna," Gideon said. "Like I told you, we're a small outfit. In a mess like this, we have too much work and too few people." He gave her evil new machine a once-over. "A chipper. Be careful with that sucker, honey."

Ophelia rolled her eyes, trying for nonchalance, hoping the sick feeling didn't show on her face. Gretchen panted her way to Ophelia's side and yawned again.

"I worked for an arborist in college," Gideon said. "Did you pay good money for this piece of junk?"

"I only need it for one project," Ophelia said. "It'll do." She had to get away from there. "I have to go home."

Gretchen pushed a cool nose under her hand. "Take Gretchen. She's bored here," Gideon said. "She'll keep watch."

"All right," Ophelia agreed.

"I'll try to find somebody to keep an eye on you," Gideon added.

Surveil me, you mean? Ophelia kicked a stone into the woods, fought her fangs, and forcibly relaxed her hands.

The crime-scene van showed up. "Will you have dinner with me?" Gideon asked, and Ophelia tried her best to read him, but still she could see no sign of a desire for sex.

She shivered. It felt so *wrong.* "You're asking for a date? What about all these murders? What about Joanna?"

"Not eating won't help me sort this mess out. Talking it through with you might."

More interrogation? No way. Ophelia shooed Gretchen into the passenger seat and started Constantine's truck. "Call me when you're free. I might be feeling more sociable then."

"You don't have to be sociable, honey. You just have to be there."

Be there for what? Ophelia drove away, the ancient chipper clunking along behind. *You're not supposed to discuss police business with me. And why aren't you looking for sex?*

And yes, I'm a shallow bitch to be thinking about that, but I thought we had something going here. I thought you were different.

You didn't ask me to marry you. You didn't even ask me to move in. You didn't ask me to restore your garden.

And you sure as hell didn't say you love me.

She reached her driveway five minutes later. Gideon or no Gideon, she would ditch her past and move on. She drove around the house and across the dead back lawn to the edge of the woods and unhitched the chipper, then returned the truck to the driveway and hurried inside for a quick sandwich. No bodyguard showed up, so maybe even Lep couldn't always dish one up at a moment's notice. If only this would happen when she really needed to be alone. She cleaned the chainsaw, gassed it up, and put phase one of her plan into action.

But action left room for grief, and she kept seeing Plato, shot down because of her, dear crazy Plato who had given her unquestioning help when she'd needed it. Plato dead, while Gideon focused on her for no good reason and Plato's murderer went free.

An hour, a pile of branches and saplings ready for chipping, and no bodyguard later, she decided to take a hand in solving the mystery herself. Maybe Plato'd been killed at his place while he was watching hers. With Gretchen at her heels, she took her spare shotgun and marched across the road and up Plato's drive.

It didn't take long to find the patch of dried blood and the disturbed gravel, and tears threatened again, followed by rage at the thought of Plato dying in the dirt. She batted Gretchen away and ordered the dog to wait, carefully skirted the path into the woods, and climbed up to the platform where Plato had so faithfully kept watch.

Plato had done more clever pruning. The view had expanded from her own house and garden to include Donnie's and Willy's on one side and the woods on the other, and unless you were looking for it, you wouldn't see the changes from across the road. Nothing seemed different from usual. No one was at Willy's, but he probably had another gig tonight, and Lisa and the girls might be anywhere. Donnie's truck was gone, too, but the TV flickered through his uncurtained front window, which meant he'd probably run to the corner store for milk.

She let her eyes rove around the contents of the platform itself: Plato's telescope on its tripod, pointing toward the floor, his old shears on a nail, a half-empty package of potato chips, a pile of wisteria leaves, and the utility knife he used to strip the vines. A stack of three baskets in a corner and the uncharacteristically misshapen bottoms of two more, set against the wall.

A tendril of wisteria hung untidily over the edge of the roof, brushing Ophelia's face. Automatically, she reached up to snap it off, but the squeak of a screen door distracted her. She whirled, fangs slotting down, ready to leap for her life.

A rotund uniformed officer of the Bayou Gavotte police fended Gretchen off and hurried up the gravel drive. "Excuse me, ma'am?"

Ophelia jammed the fangs into place. "What the hell are you doing here?" She clutched her shotgun and drummed up some allure.

Ponderously, the cop approached. "Ma'am, I need you to come down from there right now. This here's a crime scene."

"Did Gideon O'Toole send you here to keep watch?"

"Ma'am, I need you to get down right now."

Ophelia smiled blindingly at the cop, flipped her cell phone open, and dialed Gideon's number. "You should have told me you had someone at Plato's place," she said when he answered. She passed the shotgun to the officer, then swung down the rope ladder with the cell phone to her ear. "I don't mess with your goddamn crime scenes on purpose. Can't you put up some yellow tape?"

"Can't you mind your own business?" Gideon said savagely after a short, awful silence.

"This *is* my business." Ophelia shot a smile edged with just enough allure that the cop stepped out of her way. "He was my friend and he was killed because of me. You did notice the bloodstain, I assume? And the gravel where he was dragged?"

"We have samples and pictures, Ophelia, but we're short of manpower and haven't been able to process that scene yet. I'm under a lot of pressure to catch this guy, and I'll do it better without your interference. Believe it or not, I know what I'm doing."

"Perfect," Ophelia said. "Next time tell *me* what you're doing." She slapped the phone shut, retrieved the gun from the now-docile cop, and marched herself and Gretchen back home.

Several minutes later, she got out of the shower. With a

towel wrapped around her, she pattered into the bedroom at the far end of the trailer. Stopped. Sniffed. Then she kicked aside the area rug that covered the secret compartment in the bedroom floor and yanked open the ten-inch-long door.

The odors of blood and gunpowder leaped out at her. In the plywood compartment lay a small-caliber pistol. The same kind used to kill Plato Lavoie.

CHAPTER NINETEEN 🌷

As if Gideon didn't already have enough going on, Darby showed up at the crime scene in the woods and conned the young cop putting up yellow tape into believing he carried an urgent message.

"I've been looking for you the whole damn day," Darby said.

"I don't have time right now. Art is a grown woman. She can do what she likes."

"Not when she's sleeping with a murderer," Darby growled.

Gideon suppressed a grin. His friend sure had it bad. "Constantine won't hurt her. Which reminds me, you need to send Marissa back to Atlanta before she *does* get hurt."

"Jesus, Gideon, if that's what you think, how can you let your sister go out with Dufray?"

"Why shouldn't she have some fun? I don't think she got much satisfaction with Steve."

"She can have all the fun she wants, but not with him." Darby paused then blurted, "Your dispatcher says Art had a crush on me way back when."

It was then that Gideon noticed the paper in his friend's hand. "You really do have a message."

"I went looking for you at the cop shop, and the dispatcher gave it to me. Said she tried calling, but you didn't answer and it couldn't wait."

Gideon scanned Jeanie's scribbled note. Thirty seconds later, after a flurry of curses followed by remarkably composed instructions to the others at the site, he hightailed it to his Mercedes. "You're a lifesaver, man," he told Darby. "And, yeah, she had a whopper of a crush on you. By all means take care of her, but if you value your life, forget the sweet and innocent crap." The engine chugged alive and Gideon peeled out.

Think. Ophelia's fangs shifted at the smell of coagulated blood on the muzzle of the gun. She sucked them back where they belonged. *Thought one: somebody sure has it in for me.* But that was old news. *Thought two: there's no point planting something if it won't be found.*

She hurried to the kitchen for a gallon Ziploc bag. With a paper towel, she picked up the gun, dropped it in the bag, and zipped it shut. A tiny stain, which might be blood, showed on the plywood floor of the compartment. There would be traces from the recently used gun as well. But the cops wouldn't know if no one told them.

But of course someone had told them by now, the same someone who had pried the thin bottom off the compartment from under the house, stuck the pistol inside, and nailed it hurriedly shut so the tip of a nail peeked through the previously unbroken wood.

How quickly could the cops react to an anonymous tip? Knowing Gideon, way too quickly. He was in a hurry, under heavy pressure to close the case. Ophelia got a hammer from the porch and with a few sure strokes knocked the thin ply-wood out of the bottom, wrenched it off the last nail, and placed it next to the gun. The pressure wasn't only because of the three recent murders. His failure to solve the mystery surrounding Constantine's wife's death must weigh heavily against him. A high-profile case like Constantine's could make or break a cop's career. And if the murder weapon was found in her place? He'd have to arrest her. Maybe he even *wanted* to arrest her. They'd had sex, and he wasn't inter-ested anymore.

Why am I so surprised? Ophelia asked herself. He was following a pattern he'd established in the past. *My father went nuts, my stepdad has guilt trips, and Gideon goes through bimbos.* Women might come and go, but his career was what mattered in the long run. Except, there wouldn't be a long run. Not for him, not for her.

If she survived in jail, if any man who touched her survived . . . *Oh God.* Regardless of whether she lived or died, all hell would break loose. Leopard and Constantine wouldn't tolerate either her imprisonment or her death. Gideon would be summarily executed. The uneasy alliance between the cops and the clubs would be shot to pieces. The peace, the hard-won tolerance in Bayou Gavotte, all would be gone. She had to get herself and the gun out of there. Now.

Thought three: who knows about the secret compartment and hates me as well? The old man who'd occupied the trailer before her was dead. She couldn't recall showing it to anyone but Zelda and Vi.

A low bark sounded in the kitchen. Panic crowded Ophelia, but footsteps on the stairs outside propelled her into action. She closed the little compartment, covered it with the rug, and dumped the Ziploc and the plywood into a big pink shopping bag. Someone knocked on the door.

Ophelia took a deep breath and paced herself down the hall. *No quavering. No fear.* "Who is it?"

"It's me, Donnie. I need to talk to you." Barely suppressed excitement underscored her neighbor's words.

Ophelia slumped against the wall and let her breath out with a rush. Gretchen snorted and placed her head on her paws.

An excuse, any excuse. "It'll have to wait. I'm getting ready to go meet Vi." *With a stop on the way.* She hurried back to the bedroom.

"Ophelia," Donnie called. "Why are all those cops over at Plato's? They're putting up yellow tape."

Ophelia returned with a comb in one hand and her jewelry

box in the other. She glanced out the tiny kitchen window and took another huge breath. Across the road, a crime-scene van blocked the drive. "Plato was murdered this afternoon."

"You gotta be kidding!" The front door rattled as Donnie propped himself against it.

"Of course I'm not kidding." She raked the comb through her damp curls and twisted them into a knot on top of her head, then dumped the contents of her jewelry box onto the table. Earrings. Any pair. Any two even remotely alike.

"Who killed him?" Now Donnie was trying to peer through the curtain on the front door.

"How should I know?" Ophelia rammed in a garnet earring. "I don't have time to talk now." She found a red glass flower, good enough for the other ear, and shoved it into place. A string of the same red flowers went around her neck.

"The cops know who did it?"

"Why don't you ask them?"

Ophelia's heart lurched as Gideon's car came into view. It turned in behind the crime-scene van. She gulped in more air; there was still time to make a run for it. Back in the bedroom she armed herself in a deep-red bustier from the club days, a black silk evening skirt, excruciatingly uncomfortable red heels, and all the allure she could muster. She unpacked the shopping bag, crumpled tissue paper in the bottom, placed the gun and plywood back in the bag, and added more paper, then dropped a red evening bag on top. She grabbed her pocketbook and clattered down the hall to the kitchen.

Across the road, Gideon was talking on his cell phone, staring at her house. He already knew. She ran onto the screened porch for the duct tape and remembered she had finished it the other day on the damaged flowerpots. Damn. She couldn't even tape the gun to her leg. What else could possibly go wrong?

In the bedroom again, she unearthed a net bag with a long drawstring from the depths of the closet, dropped the Ziploc into the bag, broke the thin plywood into jagged strips, and jammed it in as well. She tied the net bag around her waist under the skirt, where it hung awkwardly against her thighs. The soft skirt would never hide the movement of the bag as she walked, so she dug in the closet again for a crinoline she had worn to a Mardi Gras ball and crammed it underneath. No time for more. She opened the front door and Donnie almost toppled into her. Gretchen shot out and down the drive.

Even Donnie, who was usually impervious to everyone but Violet, reeled under the allure. "Ophelia, you sure clean up good!"

"Thanks." Ophelia elbowed him away and slammed the door shut behind her.

"You left the kitchen light on," Donnie said helpfully.

"Didn't I tell you to go home?" She hitched up her skirts with one hand, carrying the shopping bag and her pocketbook in the other, and picked slowly down the stairs. The gun in its net bag thudded against her thighs.

"Going clubbing with Vi? Seems sort of heartless with Plato dead and all."

"Fuck off," Ophelia said. She flung open the door of Constantine's truck.

"Here comes the cop again," Donnie said unnecessarily.

"The cop can go to hell." Ophelia tossed the shopping bag and pocketbook onto the passenger seat.

"Been quite a day for bad news," Donnie said behind her. "You hear about Willy and Lisa? Bankrupt. It was that or selling the house quick, so that's what they did. They're moving out next week."

What? In spite of herself, Ophelia turned to Donnie. "How can their situation be that bad? The house was totally paid for. They could get a mortgage. Willy has regular gigs and still does session work."

"Session work's been slow. Then there's the blackmail."

Gideon came across the road, still on the phone. Donnie went on, "Lisa about killed him for telling me, but someone took every red cent of their savings because of those dirty pictures of Joanna. Burton Tate got beat up so bad he's in the hospital, and his little brother got caught bringing minors into the Chamber, so that gig's dead in the water. They don't even have money for food." He glanced at his watch. "Or gas. Lisa wants me to pick Joanna up at school after band practice and bring Connie to gymnastics. I better run."

"Poor Lisa," Ophelia said. "She loves that house."

Gideon shut his phone and continued up the drive, Gretchen dancing beside him.

"Thought you'd be glad," Donnie said, "the way she's been bad-mouthing you."

"How could I be glad about something so awful?" Ophelia cried. "Where are they moving to? Why doesn't Lisa get a job? Maybe Vi could give her temporary work at Blood and Velvet until they get back on their feet."

Donnie's eyes bugged out of his head. "You want to help them? After they vandalized your place and said all that nasty stuff about you? That's way more than neighborly, Ophelia. That's crazy!"

"Come to think of it, why don't you give Willy some construction work?" Ophelia said.

Donnie grimaced. "Jeez, Ophelia, I don't know about that. He's stoned or drunk most of the time."

"I know, but he's not totally useless. Not only that, it'll move you higher in Vi's estimation. She has a soft spot for people who help others."

"Well," Donnie said, squaring his shoulders, "I suppose I—"

"Wow," Gideon said from right beside her. "You look spectacular." He smiled, sexy and calculating as hell. "Going somewhere?"

Anywhere he wasn't. "Clubbing with Vi." Ophelia climbed into the truck and turned the key.

"We need to talk first."

"No, we don't," Ophelia said, desperately trying to ignore the crashing of her heart against her chest. "I'm late."

"We'll talk later, then," Gideon said amiably. "Mind if I take a look around while you're gone?"

Ophelia turned the key back to the off position. She glared at Gideon, strong and sweaty and so gorgeous that tears came to her eyes, and went berserk. "Goddamn right I mind!" She shot anger and allure in equal parts at the treacherous bastard. "When I told you to stay off my property, I meant it." She whipped her head around to Donnie, gaping a few yards away. "That goes for you, too. Go home!"

"Well, *so-rry!*" Donnie rolled his eyes at Gideon and dawdled toward the property line.

"I thought things had changed," Gideon said, so calmly she wanted to spit. "Honey, I have to do my job." He sounded so confident, so right.

Not right, Ophelia thought. *Self-righteous.* Terror clawed up from her belly and into her throat. That he would trick her, try to trap her . . . "I don't *believe* this. I trusted you. I slept with you, for God's sake!"

Gideon's brows twitched together. "What does that have to do with anything? You go have fun with Violet. I'll check your place out." Complacently, the dog prancing beside him, he continued up the drive.

Ophelia jumped down from the truck, flinching when the gun slammed against her thigh. She picked up her skirts and stormed after him. A spike of fractured wood scraped her through the net bag, enraging her even more. "Get off my property!"

Gideon went around the back of the house. "When you're finished with your tantrum, we'll talk."

"I don't want to talk to you," Ophelia snarled, searching

for an insult. "You are a coward. A sellout, just like everybody says."

Gideon stiffened to ice. "If all you can do is call me names, I will do what I damn well please." He pulled a penlight off his belt, got down on his hands and knees, and crawled under the house.

So he did know about the compartment and the gun. If she'd had the slightest doubt before, she sure didn't have any now. Ignoring the wood jabbing at her thigh, Ophelia uncoiled the hose from the hook at the end of the trailer and turned the water on full. She got down on her knees, adjusted the nozzle to the most punishing spray, and aimed it under the house.

Psyche let out a blood-curdling yowl of rage. "Motherfucking cat!" Gideon roared, and Psyche tore into the open and made for the woods. Gretchen barked and tossed herself into the spray.

"Get away, you idiotic dog!" Ophelia peered under the house and again took aim.

"Damn it, Ophelia!" Gideon sputtered. "What's gotten into you?"

"Do you have a search warrant?" she hollered. Gretchen got in the way again and Ophelia gave her a blast with the hose. The dog grinned and skittered away.

After a too-long pause, Gideon said, "Why would I want a search warrant?"

Stupid, stupid! Think fast! "That's what I'm asking *you*, jerk!" She shot the spray full on him again. "You have no right to be on my property. Go the hell away." He crawled out the front, and she hared around the end after him, gripping the hose.

He still looked gorgeous, damn him, water dripping off his dark hair and the end of his nose. Except for the suspicion and anger, the disgust in his eyes. Misery welled up inside Ophelia. She switched the nozzle off and threw the hose to the ground, put her nose in the air, and swept past him in a blaze of allure. The net bag twirled and swung under her crinoline, crashing into one thigh and then the other. She'd have so many scrapes and bruises, she'd be unable to make love for weeks. But there'd be no one to make love to, would there? So everything was perfectly fine.

She climbed into Constantine's truck, turned on the ignition, and rammed it into gear. Tires spitting gravel behind her, she tore out of the driveway. Gideon opened his cell phone and slammed it shut again, calling down curses in her wet, dead garden.

Gideon felt the neighbor's eyes on him as he coiled the hose onto the hook at the end of Ophelia's house. He waited until Donnie had called little Connie Wyler over, installed her in his truck, and driven away, before crawling under the trailer again. Thirty seconds later—for the anonymous message had been detailed and accurate—he found the remains of the secret compartment. He strode, still dripping, down the driveway and across the road, thinking about the weeping garden, about his chronically disappointed father and his desperately lonely mother, about talking and listening, about patience and trust and love, deciding he would get it right no matter how many times he had to try.

Unless, of course, he was just a sucker, which he might so easily prove to be, but when it came to Ophelia, the grip of instinct was so strong he couldn't fight it even if he wanted to. And of course, he didn't want to. *Christ*, he thought, *I'm a fool for love. Or maybe just for spectacular sex. This is the pits. And I don't have time for it now.*

How had Ophelia known about the gun?

Later, he decided. He opened the cell phone again and dialed Leopard, who answered just as the chief's car parked behind his. "Lep," said Gideon, "I don't have time to explain, but when Ophelia gets there, keep her there until I get back to you. She's not safe anywhere outside club control."

Now to deal with the other side of the problem.

"Looks like we're close to cracking this case," the chief said, before he'd even turned the engine off. He got out of his Cadillac in a white button-down shirt and khaki pants.

Gideon shucked off his shirt and wrung out the water. "Hopefully so."

"What happened to you?" The chief gave Gretchen a perfunctory pat. She stuck her nose up at him and retreated to the cool grass near Gideon's car.

"An accident with a hose." Gideon kicked off his shoes and dropped his wet pants.

"Shit, Gideon, you can't make an arrest in your boxers." The chief nodded at the crime-scene people scurrying to get as much as possible done before dark.

"I can't make an arrest at all," Gideon said. "I don't have a suspect yet." He laid his clothes across the top of the Mercedes.

"Yes, you do," the chief said. "I got an anonymous phone call on my personal cell. The gun's in Ophelia Beliveau's house."

Shit, what a close call. The murderer wanted to make damn sure Ophelia took the rap for his crimes. Did he know Jeanie was Ophelia's sister's friend? That Gideon was Ophelia's lover? "We already know someone has it in for Ophelia Beliveau. This is the same dude."

"You're making it too complicated," the chief said. "The guy in the photo shop—we have a positive ID now—was blackmailing Beliveau, so she offed him. She offed the girl in the shop while she was getting rid of the evidence, and then she shot Plato Lavoie when he tried to turn her in. The woman's a menace. Arrest her."

"That's nice and simple, Chief, but it's not true. Her alibis are solid. She didn't do it." Gideon peeled off his socks and slipped his shoes back on. He took the flashlight off his belt and skirted the path toward Plato's platform.

The chief followed. "They aren't solid enough. She spent

today with one of Leopard's goons. What kind of alibi is that? She's key to this case. Everywhere you turn, there she is."

Far more than you know. Gideon went up the rope ladder. *I must be out of my mind.*

The chief climbed up behind him. "Even if she didn't actually do it, she's an accessory. You have to arrest her." He hung from the ladder, watching the sky. "Almost dusk. The bats should be out any second now."

"Sure she's key," Gideon said. "If she'd trust me long enough to talk it through, I could wrap it all up."

"You're thinking with your dick." The chief stepped onto the platform. "I can't have that."

"I'm not thinking with my dick," Gideon said, relieved that he sounded so much more certain than he felt. For the second time that day, he took in the telescope, the shears, the potato chips, the baskets, the yellow utility knife, the slowly shriveling vines. . . . There had to be something useful here.

"I hear she's really something," the chief said.

"She is." *Enough said.* "What do we know about the photoshop dude?"

"Not a lot. Moved here from out west over a year ago and bought the photo business from the previous owner, who was retiring, and added the print portion of the shop. He's already paid off half his business loan, way ahead of schedule. Single, came to Bayou Gavotte for the nightlife. Couple of on-and-off girlfriends who are also on-and-off with various other men. A few drinking buddies. Parents dead, sister in California. Nothing in his personal life leads to a crime of passion, so you won't clear Beliveau that way. It has to be the blackmail. What are you looking so pleased about?"

"Sure it's the blackmail," Gideon said. "Listen. The blackmailer knew way too much about people for a newcomer. It's one thing to happen upon someone who took pictures of his baby in the bath or even his wife in a naughty pose. He's got a name and number on the envelope and goes from there.

But the guy I caught in the photo shop last night—have you seen my report?—was being blackmailed because he'd had a bunch of high-school pictures restored, including one of an old girlfriend who still lives here in town. He's desperate not to let his wife find out, because she's dying of cancer and he doesn't want her to think he's already moving on. Nobody would know about that girlfriend if they hadn't lived here forever." And the same went for recognizing his sister in a film brought in by someone else and knowing exactly where she was vulnerable. And knowing the chief's personal cell number—but he wouldn't use that card if he didn't have to.

He continued, "Lavoie was blackmailed for years by some-one who used a New Orleans address, but several months ago switched it to our photo shop. The way I see it, Lavoie's blackmailer and the photo-shop guy were in this together. How they found out about each other, I don't know. They had a falling-out, and there you go."

"It's a nice theory, Gideon, but it doesn't mean Beliveau's not involved. Either way, it won't hurt her to sit in jail for a day or two."

Jesus, thought Gideon, thrusting away a chill. "Lavoie was up here making his phone call when the killer came right up to him, stuck a gun to his chest, and shot him." Gideon shone his flashlight into the underbrush. "You can see where he fell, where he was dragged, where he bled and died." He showed the chief the darkening view across the road. "Willy Wyler's, Donnie Donaldson's, Ms. Beliveau's, a little of the woods. Two days ago, all you could see was Ms. Beliveau's place. Plato pruned this to get a wider view."

Not that there was much to see. Lisa Wyler was sitting on her porch, nursing a drink. No one was at Donnie's, because he'd just driven off with Connie.

"Donnie Donaldson," the chief said. "He's done well for himself lately. Used to be a handyman, but now he builds several new houses a year."

Zing. "Unlike Willy Wyler, who I hear is bankrupt." An-

other zing. Gideon opened his phone and dialed Jeanie at home. "Babe, I need you to tap into your gossip tree and find out who just bought Willy Wyler's house. Get into the city records and find out who owns the land for a mile on either side of Ophelia and across the road for the same distance. See if property values in that area are going up, what with the golf course and all." Her groan was loud enough for the chief to hear. "If you want to become a detective, Jeanie . . ." Pause. "Yeah, Darby found me. Thanks." He hung up.

"What do Willy Wyler and property values have to do with anything?" the chief complained. "Three people are dead. I'll lose my job if you don't close this case in a hurry."

The vines, the baskets . . . "Plato Lavoie was up here making baskets while he watched Ms. Beliveau's place. He made baskets to stay calm, to stay sane. He'd seen something that worried him, something he eventually called me about. He went back to the house to dress for work, then came back up here one last time. What was he watching?"

"Damn it, Gideon," began the chief.

"I don't think he usually left the place a mess like this. When I came up the other day, it was spotless." He shone his light across the platform. "Look at those two basket bottoms by the wall. He almost always did round baskets. He was probably the world's foremost expert at making round baskets. He must have been totally rattled to flatten one side. . . ." *Zing.* Or rather, duh. Double duh.

"Beliveau knew Lavoie had found her out," the chief said impatiently. "She caught him by surprise. He tried to call you, but it was too late." He watched the flickering forms swooping and diving across the darkening sky. "I knew we'd see bats here. If I lose my job, I'll have to get some real work, and I won't have time to make bat houses. You have to arrest that woman."

"Plato worshipped Ophelia Beliveau," Gideon said. "If he'd found out she'd killed someone, he'd never have betrayed her, not to me or to anyone else." Zings of instinct flew every which way, too much to sort out. *Later.* Gideon clicked off his light.

"So she's just an accessory," the chief said cheerfully. "Bats are a good omen. Is Beliveau at home?" He craned his neck to see across the road, but darkness was swiftly taking over.

"No, she's not." And by now she should be safe.

"We'll wait till she shows up," decided the chief. "You're slick with the ladies. You charm her into letting you look around, you find the gun, and we haul her in. She confesses who did it, we arrest him, the case is closed, and my job's good for at least the next year."

"If there's a gun over there, it's a plant," Gideon said. "If we arrest Ophelia Beliveau, you might not be alive to enjoy next year. I certainly won't be, and rightly so."

"Gideon, we can't let the clubs run this town! If they want to take care of their own problems, fine, but I can't and won't sit back while club people murder innocent citizens!"

"Bullshit. You want me to arrest an innocent person for your personal gain. I won't do it."

"You'll do what I tell you! And that's goddamned unfair," he added. "You know I care about innocent citizens. I even backed you up about Dufray last year!"

"Ordinarily, sir, I believe in you and I'm proud to go along with you, but not this time. I will not arrest Ophelia Beliveau."

"Goddamn it, then, Gideon, I will!"

"Over my dead body. Sir."

The chief's eyes bulged. "Don't you threaten me, by God!"

Gideon kept his voice level and low. "I'm not threatening you, sir. I'm telling you the truth. My life is on the line in more ways than one, and if the choice is between dying defending Ophelia or dying because I didn't, I'll choose the first option. Somebody's framing her, and I intend to find out who." But if he was framing her, why would he try to kill her? *Bingo.*

The chief paced the platform. "We have to check out this lead. You know that."

"I'll go over there now," Gideon said. "Unless you want to wait for a warrant. But why rush it and risk upsetting Leopard, not to mention Constantine Dufray? If someone planted a gun in her trailer, they want it to be found. They won't take it away again."

The chief stalked to the edge of the platform and watched his beloved bats flash across the sky. After a long silence, during which Gideon shone the light all round the platform and ended with the basket bottoms again, the chief said, "You have until tomorrow morning."

"That's all I need," Gideon said.

CHAPTER TWENTY 🌷

As she opened the door of Leopard's office, it occurred to Ophelia that although she might not have jumped into the fire, she had probably replaced one frying pan with another. And Gideon would be the one who got burned, which was his own damn fault.

I'm a fool, she thought, *but I can't let that happen.*

Nothing but mild interest showed on Leopard's face when she closed the door and slumped against it, knees wobbling. Constantine, in the far corner with his guitar, didn't even raise his head.

"Here you are," Leopard said from the recliner. "Just like Gideon said. You have five minutes to clue me in to what's going down, and then I gotta go."

"Gideon *what*?" She thought she'd drained herself of adrenaline on the way over. Apparently not.

"He told me to expect you. What's up?"

Gideon had guessed where she was headed. He figured he could come and get her anytime he liked. "He wouldn't pursue me here! He couldn't possibly do anything so crazy!" She was shaking now.

Leopard heaved himself off the chair with a long-suffering eye roll, put his hands on Ophelia's shoulders, and steered her toward the couch. "Vi said you slept with him. Why would he need to do any pursuing?"

"To arrest me," Ophelia said miserably. She stuck her chin out at Leopard with what wimpy oomph she had left. "Don't you dare hurt him, Lep. Or you either," she told Constantine. "If he comes, just kick him out. If you sic your thugs on him—"

Leopard rolled his eyes again. "He didn't say anything about coming here, just that you needed to stay someplace under club control for a while. Now, sit down."

"Not till I get rid of this gun." Ophelia fumbled under the bustier to unbutton the silk skirt. "I don't know why he suspects me of killing all these people, but he does. I can tell by how he looks at me. Then this gun showed up in my house, and his boss must be putting pressure on him." With an exasperated cry she raised her skirt, tugged at the crinoline, and kicked it away.

"You're talking crap," said Leopard. "Gideon doesn't give a fuck about what his boss wants." The phone rang and Leopard read the display. Ophelia's silk skirt slithered into a pool on the floor. "This gorgeous vampire chick is doing a strip for us," he said into the phone. Ophelia gritted her teeth and fumbled with the double knot in the drawstrings of the net bag. "No problem," Leopard added. "See you." He hung up, flicked open a switchblade, and knelt to cut the drawstring and take the bag.

"He's coming over?" Ophelia didn't even try to hide the quaver in her voice. She pulled her skirt back up and fastened it.

"Jesus, girl! He just wanted to make sure you got here okay." Leopard tossed the string into the trash and opened the bag. "You've got three minutes. Explain."

She slumped on the couch and did, while he sniffed inside the Ziploc with the gun and replaced it in the net bag.

"More likely he wanted to get the gun out of there so you *wouldn't* be arrested." He shot a glance across at Constantine.

"It should be easy to find out," the rocker replied in his sinister voice, which ordinarily amused Ophelia and occasionally pissed her off, but this time struck fear into her soul.

"Constantine!" she cried, "If you hurt him—"

"By *asking* him," Constantine finished, laying down the guitar. "Cappuccino? No. Irish coffee." He opened the liquor cabinet under the counter.

Leopard unlocked the safe in his bookshelf and slipped the net bag inside. "Gideon says he's got the chief under control for now. Let me know if he wants the gun back. I'm out of here."

Ophelia sprang up. "You'll give him the gun?"

"If he convinces me it's the best move. Maybe he'll be able to trace it. Maybe he'll decide to plant it himself, once he knows who really shot Plato. Come on, girl, this isn't like you. I can't believe the dude's got you so freaked out you can't think straight. He's not turning into another obsessive, is he? Dud in bed, won't take no for an answer?"

"Of course he isn't a dud in bed!" Ophelia swallowed hard, but it didn't help, and a tear rolled down one cheek, and then another. "I really like him, Lep, but he's turned out to be a jerk. Worse than a jerk, and I feel like such a fool, because it was so *comfortable*."

Leopard gaped. "Sex with Gideon was just comfortable? I've never heard anything so boring in my life!"

"It wasn't *just* comfortable," said Ophelia indignantly. "And if you had any concept of what it's like when everyone you've slept with has been possessive or obsessed or all-out insane . . ." More tears escaped. "He was relaxed. It was so good, it was so comfortable, and I felt safe." She almost sobbed. "For once I felt safe!"

"Ah," Constantine said. "And now you don't."

"How can I, after that dirty trick?" There, a little less wimpy now. She sniffled and carefully wiped the tears away. "The sneaky, slimy"—*sexy, Goddamn it*—"bastard smiled at me and tried to get me to say it was okay for him to check out my house. 'Go have fun with Vi,' he said. Right—while he got all the evidence he needed to put me in jail for life. Not that I'd last more than a day in jail anyway without killing someone, and I can't believe he doesn't realize that. Or maybe he just doesn't care." She caught herself on a sob and paced furiously around the room.

"He would have discredited my alibis," she continued. "Reuben works for you, and one of the customers I saw the other day is mega into bondage. The sweetest guy, but who'll take his word for anything?" She clenched her fists and smothered a scream. "I thought Gideon was . . . was really *nice*. I thought he was on my side. I could kill him!" Her fangs slotted down. "But don't you dare touch him!"

Leopard rolled his eyes for a third time. "I'm gone. Talk some sense into her, will you?"

The door closed behind him. Ophelia let out a long, slow breath. "Sorry. I needed to get it out. I'll stop being hysterical now." Pushing her fangs wearily back into their slots, she retreated into the corner of the couch and accepted the brew Constantine held out. "I know you don't mete out undeserved punishment. But I have to be sure, and even then, I can't bear the idea that you would. Hurt him, I mean."

Constantine sipped his own heady coffee. "Do you want an alternative viewpoint?"

Ophelia sighed. "Of course I do. It's just . . . I don't want to hope and then find out he's scum. I'm so tired of fighting myself, of fighting off all those men."

Constantine lowered himself next to her. His dark eyes were unusually kind. "Maybe he was trying to spare you any more worry. He can't stay with you while he's working on this case, but he figured you'd be safe with your sister, and if his boss was harassing him to arrest you, he wanted you on safe ground until he could talk the old man into seeing things his way, which it sounds like he's done. Sure Gideon's under pressure, but he also has a conscience. Whatever Lep says, I doubt Gideon would plant evidence, even if he knew someone was guilty. Do you have any idea of the bribes he refused because of me?"

Ophelia bristled. "You mean he thought you were guilty?"

"I have no idea what he thought, but I do know he refused enough money to set him up for life."

"Then why does he look at me like he suspects me?" She wasn't sure what she saw in Constantine's eyes, so she hurried on. "He looks at me so intently, and he listens, and he watches, and it has nothing to do with sex, and he waits and waits until I just have to say something."

Constantine answered a knock on the door and returned with a heaping plate of crispy oysters and fries. "Contrary to popular opinion, men don't think about sex *all* the time. He has to spare some thought for the murder investigation." He set ketchup and Tabasco on the table. "Help yourself."

"The last thing I need is an aphrodisiac." She ate an oyster anyway. "I can't believe someone wants me dead."

"Maybe they don't." Constantine unscrewed the cap of the Tabasco sauce and poised it over the oysters. "May I?"

Ophelia nodded. "What do you mean?" She squeezed ketchup onto the plate.

"The rhythm's wrong," Constantine said. "Starts with a dead cat, then we have a little vandalism by someone else, which may or may not be relevant, then there's the body in the truck. Then someone fails to kill you but succeeds in killing your garden—"

Ophelia raised a hand. "Except—!" She dipped a fry in the ketchup and ate it. "Except that the poisoning of my garden must have happened before the body in the truck and probably before the vandalism. It takes a while for the weed killer to work."

"Even better. Ignoring the vandalism for now, first there's a threat, then another threat, which also strikes at your livelihood, then another strike at your livelihood, which might also conveniently get you in trouble with the cops. Then someone shoots at you, and then deescalates back into framing you for murder. If he wanted you permanently out of the way, why not shoot at you again?" He ate a fry. "Maybe he wanted to remove the protective cop."

Ophelia sat straight. "You think he was shooting at Gideon?"

Constantine gulped an oyster. "How should I know? It's one way of seeing things."

"My God! We have to speak to Gideon *now*."

But Gideon didn't answer his phone, even though she called over and over while Constantine polished off the oysters and fries and made arrangements to pick up Art and meet Violet at a club.

"Maybe I drowned his phone," Ophelia said. "If Gideon gets shot because of me . . ." It didn't bear thinking of.

Constantine grabbed Ophelia's cell and left a message. "Ophelia's freaking out. She thinks that shot this morning might have been meant for you."

Ophelia lunged for the phone, but Constantine had already closed it. "He knows how to watch his back. Besides, I need you tonight."

"You're coming, too? Thank God!" Artemisia tottered out her front door a few hours later in the electric blue gown and hugged Ophelia. She glanced guiltily at Constantine. "I'm sorry, but you scare me to death, and Vi doesn't understand how hard this is for me! I feel like an idiot in this dress. Are you sure Darby and Marissa will be there?"

Constantine motioned Art inside his current truck, another big hunk of metal. "All arranged."

"Arranged how? What's going to happen?"

"You'll see."

"You're making Art uncomfortable," Ophelia said, getting in beside her. "Look how she's shivering, and it's not even cold."

Constantine pulled away from the curb, heading toward downtown. "It'll be over soon."

Ophelia shot him a glance. What would be over? He was being aggravatingly mysterious, but she couldn't refuse to help someone to whom she owed so much.

"It's not Constantine's fault," Art said. "It's just that I don't know what I'm supposed to do. Dress or no dress, I can't slink up to Dar and vamp him away from that woman."

"You won't have to," Constantine said in his sinister voice.

Ophelia shot him another look, opened her mouth to ask a question, and shut it again.

Art shuddered. "What's he going to do?"

"How should I know?" Ophelia said irritably. "He won't tell me a thing."

"Trust me." Constantine laughed.

Ophelia rolled her eyes. "Art, forget about what Constantine's planning and think about what you want from this evening. Are you sure you want Darby? What if he falls for you and then you break his heart?"

"Of course I want him! I've loved him ever since I was sixteen. I just didn't know." After a tense silence, she muttered, "I should have. I could have, if I hadn't been so dumb."

"Dude might have changed some since then," Constantine said.

"He's still Dar," Art said gruffly.

They entered the Chamber by the employee door, bypassed the haze and heavy music of the dance hall, and were ushered into a cool, dim room with a stage at one end and an array of tables, a few of which were unoccupied. Ophelia muttered something obscene as she took a seat at Constantine's reserved table and ditched her shoes. "Why are we here?"

"For the floor show," Constantine said in that same creepy voice. Ophelia recognized this mood. He wasn't being sinister on purpose. He was gearing up for something highly unpleasant, and it couldn't be just to help Art get her hands on Darby Sims. Meanwhile, all Ophelia could think of was Gideon, the decision she had to make, and the job she had to do in the morning.

Art sat at Constantine's other side. Slow, sultry music

played in the background. Art gazed at the purple and gold decor, the handcuffs daisy-chained across the ceiling, the phallic pillars, and the frankly inviting plaster flowers clustered above. "Any show in this place has got to be all about sex. If Dar's bringing Marissa here, I may as well go home right now."

"Stop fussing," Constantine said. "Relax and enjoy the view."

"What view?" Art protested, and then a waiter dressed in nothing but a loincloth came by to offer drinks. She stammered out, "Rum and Coke," and when the waiter and his pecs and his bare ass had lounged away, she blurted, "This is one of the *respectable* clubs?"

"No one underage, no one gets hurt," Constantine said. "Apart from that, there aren't a lot of rules."

"There's only one table left," Art said. "What if there's no room when they get here? And I still don't see how—"

The house lights dimmed, a row of spots at the back of the stage flicked on, and a tiger-striped couch was rolled onto the stage by two hulking, almost-naked men, one of whom was Darby Sims. A cheer rose. Darby and the other guy saluted the audience with a bump of their bare butts and strolled away into the wings.

Art made a tiny whimpering sound. She flicked her eyes to Ophelia, who shrugged and laughed. A few seconds later, Darby returned with leopard-skin chairs and stools. The music segued into a low bump and grind. In the rear, a female voice piped up. "Take it off, take it *all* off!"

Darby grinned, raised his beautifully-defined arms over his head, and languidly humped the room as a whole. Then he turned his magnificent rear to the audience and sauntered away.

"Oh, my Lord in Heaven," Art said reverently. "Dar has the world's most beautiful butt."

Their drinks appeared, and so did Darby and the other guy with more props. Again. And again. Ophelia drummed her fingers on the table and sipped her Cosmopolitan. Art dragged her eyes away from Darby's nether regions long enough to take a huge swallow of rum and Coke. She choked out a question. "Why's he working in the theater? Gideon said he got a job as a tattoo artist!"

"Not till next week, so he's temping as a stagehand for a night or two," Constantine said.

"I don't *believe* this," Art whispered. "How can he be so comfortable, almost naked, with all these people watching?" She chugged some more rum and Coke.

"He part-timed at a club in Atlanta as an exotic dancer," Constantine said. "That's where he met Johnny and Marissa Parkerson. My sources are more thorough than Vi's."

"How come I never knew?" She raised her mug again.

"Better nurse that drink, Art," Constantine said. "You too, Ophelia."

Ophelia cuddled her Cosmopolitan. "It relaxes me. I'm nervous as hell."

"This makes you nervous?" Art's eyes dimmed as Darby left the stage and the emcee came on. "I'm not sure *what* it makes me. I could watch Dar forever."

Ophelia said around the red straw in her drink, "Your boyfriend-to-be does have an excellent ass."

"Hey," Art said. "Keep your eyes to yourself! His ass belongs to *me*!" Even in the dim light, her blush was vivid. "I can't believe I said that." She glared at her empty glass as if it had done her wrong.

Ophelia hardly noticed the transvestite song-and-dance routine that opened the show. What should she say to Gideon when they next met? If he didn't really suspect her, if he didn't want to arrest her, she still had to explain herself to him, explain why she wasn't safe. Either that, or reject him for good. "Don't do either," Constantine had said on the ride to pick up Art. "Start a new life." But it wasn't that simple or that easy. Constantine should understand that, if anyone.

More drinks came. The trannies pranced off the stage, and Art gazed hopefully at the wings. No Darby. Another revue—this time an abundance of T and A—swung on in their wake.

"Ah." Constantine motioned his chin toward the doorway, where Reuben hovered with Marissa hanging adoringly on his arm. Reuben and Constantine had hardly locked eyes before Constantine's dropped to his drink. "Don't watch them. I don't want her to see me yet." Reuben steered his date toward the empty table.

Art groaned. "Constantine's going to terrify that poor woman by just looking at her."

So that was it. *I really do have no choice,* thought Ophelia.

"I hate this," Art said. "She's not even with Dar tonight. I wish I'd got up the nerve to ask Dar out myself."

"I'm not doing this because of you," Constantine said. "She was never Darby's girlfriend. She hired him to look for Johnny, because he was coming here anyway." He turned to Ophelia. "Look her way. Be sultry."

Ophelia fidgeted with the little red straw. "You are so brutal sometimes."

"Uh-huh," Constantine agreed. Damn him.

"Marissa needs to know whether her husband's dead or alive," Ophelia said. "Maybe she has insurance money coming. Maybe she wants to marry again."

"I can't tie up everybody's loose ends," Constantine said. "Throw out a bit of allure. Enough so she sees you, but don't start a riot." When Ophelia still hesitated he said, "This is for you as much as for me, babe. Do it."

Oh, hell. Ophelia obeyed, turning it up slowly, hating how heads turned her way. Just as the act ended, a startled cry sliced into the room.

"What's *she* doing here?" Marissa whimpered. "I don't like this place." She half-rose, but Reuben's solicitous arm went around her shoulders and pushed her gently into her seat. Every man in the room and half the women stared at Ophelia.

A man at the next table forgot his date entirely and surged forward, but stumbled back in a hurry when Constantine spun his way. Art wrapped her arms around herself and looked miserable.

Ophelia said, "Good enough?" and returned grumpily to her Cosmopolitan. "Damn it, Constantine, I'm trying to think. I have a decision to make."

Constantine pried the drink from Ophelia's grip and signaled to the waiter. "What decision? You're head over heels for the dude." He glanced sideways at Marissa, leaning now into Reuben's protective embrace. "We'll let her stew for a while."

Art said, "I wish I could go home." She took another swallow of her drink. "I wish I could go home with Dar."

Ophelia retrieved her Cosmopolitan and guzzled some more. Constantine took it away again. "Cool it," he said quietly. "You've already decided in Gideon's favor and know it."

"You should marry him," Art said. "I need to marry Dar."

"Not *that* decision," Ophelia said. "I have to *tell* him."

"You haven't told him you love him?" Art bit her lip. "I need to tell Dar, but I'm so scared."

"For God's sake, why?" Constantine rolled his eyes. "Let it go and move on."

"Let him go?" Art said. "I haven't even got him yet." She drooped over her drink. "If he doesn't love me back, I *will* have to move on."

"What if I end up marrying him?" Ophelia said. "I won't be able to live with myself."

"You won't have to live with yourself," Art giggled. "You'll live with Gideon. Happily ever after."

Constantine blew out an incredulous breath. "Do what you have to. It's your funeral, babe."

"Hey," Art said, "I'm a modern woman. I won't die just because some gorgeous dumbass doesn't love me." Tears trickled slowly down her cheeks and into her rum and Coke.

"What if I'm wrong?" Ophelia whispered. "Even if he's not scum, what if he doesn't understand? What if I can't trust him? I'm still not sure he wasn't going to arrest me today."

"His funeral, if he does," Constantine said. "He's a good guy, and he's right for you. Why burden him with your baggage? Leave it be."

"Nobody with an ass like that could possibly be right for me," Art sobbed. "I worship Dar's beautiful black butt! Oh, my God, did I say that out loud?"

The waiter set coffee and walnut cake before them, and Constantine got rid of Ophelia's Cosmopolitan for good. Art's rum and Coke disappeared, too.

Constantine sat up straight. "Let's ramp it up a little before the next act. This time she gets to see me." He shook his long, wild hair out of its ponytail and turned to face Marissa.

As if on the end of an invisible string, the blonde's head jerked around. "There he is!" she gibbered. "Can't you see? He wants to kill me!"

Constantine let go of that invisible thread and fed Ophelia a forkful of cake. Reuben murmured soothingly to Marissa.

"You set her up," Art said. "She thought she had a date with a hot guy, but he's in cahoots with you. That's so cruel!"

"Look for trouble and trouble will find you." Constantine put a hand on Art's, and she jumped. "Calm down," he said, kind yet cold. "Marissa is not your concern. I'd do it whether or not you were here. Right, Ophelia?"

"Right," Ophelia said ungratefully.

Whatever song and dance was going on up there ended, the house lights came on, and finally the stage hands reappeared, goofing around as they cleared the stage. They set up an array of whips and floggers and finally humped their way to center stage behind two massive naked dolls.

"Hi!" Violet tripped across the room, followed by Donnie

Donaldson. Art raised a vague hand, her eyes devouring Dar, and then Violet got in the way.

"Hey," Art shrieked, leaping out of her chair. "You're blocking my view!"

Dar's head whipped around.

"Go Dar!" Art hollered. "Don't wear yourself out. Save some for *me*!"

The crowd roared. Darby grinned and blew her a kiss, and with an extra bit of bump and grind, set back to work.

Violet and Constantine laughed. Art put her face in her hands and wept.

Chapter Twenty-one 🌷

Realization slammed into Ophelia. She shoved her face against Constantine's shoulder, dug her fingers into his chest, and bit down hard. Her fangs sliced through her lip. She grunted with pain and clung tight.

Constantine always caught on fast. "I know it's funny, but do you have to slobber all over my arm?"

Blood drizzled from Ophelia's mouth, staining his sleeve. She sucked her fangs out of her lip and willed the goddamned things back into place. No way. Not with Plato's murderer only a few yards away.

"Ophelia," Violet asked, "are you okay?"

"She's drunk," Constantine said. "So is Artemisia, hence the complete lack of inhibition."

"That's not like Ophelia," Violet said. "She must be horribly stressed, and no wonder, poor angel."

If I was drunk before, I sure am sober now. Ophelia wiped her lip on Constantine's sleeve and licked the cut shut. She pressed her forehead against his shoulder, waiting for the fangs to give up the fight, wondering how she could get away with not looking at Vi and her . . . date. Rage boiled up like lava, hot and relentless, and with it, hurt and chagrin. He'd been a good neighbor, almost a friend. How could he? And why?

"Introduce me to your friend, Vi." Constantine sounded amused.

"This is Donnie, Ophelia's neighbor. He dropped by and wanted to come along."

"Not the vandal, I hope?" Constantine was quivering with suppressed laughter.

"Of course not," Vi said. "Donnie's harmless."

Ophelia hissed and almost sliced her lip again.

"Ophelia, you're not going to barf on me, are you?" Constantine asked dangerously. "I'll only put up with so much."

Artemisia stood shakily. "I'm *definitely* going to barf." She plunged toward the restroom.

"You too, Ophelia." Constantine slung her over his shoulder and followed more leisurely. Outside the ladies' room, he set her on her feet. "That's the killer?"

Ophelia manually forced the fangs into their slots, snarling. "He's with my sister!"

Constantine shook with laughter. "So he is. How did you figure it out?"

"You figured it out. You told me that shot was for Gideon, not for me."

"So?"

"Donnie sent Gideon to the river after me. He's the only one who knew Gideon would be there. He could have driven to the other side of the river and set up in one of the empty houses in minutes. Come to think of it, he built that secret compartment for the man who used to live in my trailer. And now he's got Vi! What are we going to do? Stop laughing, damn it!"

"Vi can take care of herself."

"What if she sleeps with him? I can't let her sleep with a murderer!"

"Oh, I don't know," Constantine said. "There's a certain cachet to it. Look at all the misguided women clamoring to sleep with me."

Ophelia stifled the urge to slug him. "What if she won't sleep with him and he gets pissed off? He's been gaga about her for ages, but she's never shown much interest."

Constantine chuckled. "I foresee an amusing evening. Don't worry, I'll make sure she's safe. You okay now? We can't let the dude know we're on to him."

"I have to talk to Gideon tonight," Ophelia said. *Oh God, yes. Oh God, no.*

She found Art past the worst, but still hunched groaning over the toilet bowl.

"I am such an idiot," Art said, accepting wet paper towels and wiping her face. "He didn't look turned off, did he?"

"He looked thrilled." Ophelia hauled her from the stall to the sink. "Rinse and spit."

"I'll never get rid of this vile taste," Art said, spitting again and again. "What if he—? Maybe he was just putting on an act. I mean, he was up on stage. He couldn't very well yell, 'You disgusting slut.'"

"He wasn't disgusted, and now he knows you aren't turned off by his questionable past either. Everything's working out perfectly." *For you. And I'm happy for you.* "Coffee and cake is what you need. We both need."

"But what do I do now?" Art faltered when they reached the table again.

"You wait for Dar to come to you. I'll cozy up to Constantine, so it won't look like you're with him." *And I won't have to look at Donnie.*

Her vile, worthless, murdering neighbor, thank God, was dividing his attention between Violet and the activity on stage. She motioned Constantine one chair over and plopped down between him and Art, giving him a smacking kiss on the cheek. "More cake and cappuccino! You're a darling." As she dug into the cake, she told herself, *Get sober, build your courage, and go.*

"Um," Art said during a break in the show. "I have a problem."

"You've sobered up and you're thinking straight?"

Art plowed on. "I haven't had sex for a long time. And

when I did, it was terrible. What if I go to bed with Dar and it doesn't work out?"

"Tell him you need to take it slowly," Ophelia said. "Be thankful you're not a vamp. Guys are incapable of taking it slowly with vamps. You at least have the option of easing into it."

"But what if he wants something different from what I want?"

"Negotiate a relationship," Ophelia said. *Negotiate your life.* "Find ways to compromise." Her brain scurried around looking for a compromise with Gideon, but couldn't find one.

"If you start talking about sex you'll end up in bed, so make your birth-control plans now," Violet spoke up.

"There's a condom machine in the restroom," Ophelia said.

"Don't buy the bubble-gum-flavored kind," Violet said.

"Don't buy any flavored kind," Ophelia replied. "You're not going to eat the goddamned thing."

"Not the condom, anyway," Art whispered, blushing again. "I'm such a slut." She took a big gulp of coffee and slunk down in her chair. "And I'm so frigging scared."

Me too, sighed Ophelia to herself.

Later, Art dragged her to the restroom to check out the condom machine. She dithered for more than fifteen minutes before deciding on one ribbed, one lubricated, zero flavored, and one plain. Then she opened the restroom door and blundered right into Darby Sims, dressed now in an old T-shirt and jeans.

The condoms dropped to the floor. "Hey," Art gasped. Ophelia let the restroom door close all but a crack and hovered shamelessly inside.

"Hey," said Darby. "They don't need me anymore tonight." He picked up the condoms. "What, no chocolate?"

"You're the chocolate," Art blurted. "Oh, Dar, I'm so scared."

Darby stuffed the condoms into his pocket. "I'm mighty

nervous myself." He smiled and took her hand. "How about we go someplace and talk?"

Back at the table Ophelia whispered, "Why doesn't Gideon call? What if he's already dead? If he is, I'll kill Donnie myself!"

"That's the spirit," Constantine said. "I'll be your accomplice. On the other hand, maybe he's just busy."

"Maybe he doesn't want to talk to me," Ophelia said.

"Maybe he can't afford the distraction." Constantine laughed.

Ophelia thought and thought and got nowhere, but a cappuccino and another slice of cake later, she knew she was safe to drive. If she was driving into catastrophe . . . so be it.

The music ended. Constantine said softly, "Time to wrap things up. Hold on to yourself, babe. This won't be pretty." He stood and closed his eyes.

Marissa shrieked and clawed out of her chair. "He's killing me!" Her head jerked back. She flailed and fought against Reuben's attempts to hold her, gasping and sobbing. Two bouncers appeared out of the shadows by the wall and lifted her off the floor.

"That should do it," Constantine said. The bouncers carted her through the exit with Reuben behind them.

"Poor darling," Violet said. "Such a lousy date. Tell him to come see me the *minute* he's free. I'll go take a nap and muster my strength. A taste of Reuben is just what I need." She pressed a warm kiss on Donnie's cheek. "Donnie, sweetie, let's do this again sometime soon." She drifted away, Donnie floating behind her.

"That's one true love and one shameless lust," Constantine said, counting on his fingers. "So, Ophelia, how about you?"

True love or death, thought Ophelia, terrified at how much she was counting on. If not true love, at least not being dragged off to jail. Lust, for once, had abandoned her.

She drove Constantine's truck slowly through Bayou Gavotte and along the country road past her forlorn little house. She doused the lights and went up Gideon's driveway in the dark, parking beside the Mercedes. At least he was here. At least he was alive. *At least he can arrest me if he wants.* She stepped barefoot out of the car, expecting the dogs to raise a ruckus, but heard only insects strumming their nocturnal songs.

Since he was alive, that meant she had to talk to him. Or she could just leave again.

She sucked in a deep breath, hurried up the steps, and rapped on the door. Nothing. Low lights burned in the living room and kitchen, but no footsteps and no dogs.

She didn't have to do this. She could turn around and drive away. She could call him with her information, stay at Vi's till everything blew over, and then get on with her life.

What life? No way.

Ophelia skirted the house, but the deck was deserted. The tangled garden beckoned. On midnight walks down the river the previous summer, she'd caught the aromas of gardenia, night-blooming jasmine, and sweet olive. A refuge, Gideon had said. If she restored this garden, it would be a refuge for both of them, but it had better not be from each other.

She heard Gideon's voice and a splash down by the river. A couple more yards along the path, a cold nose nudged her hand.

"Oh, Gretchen," she whispered, "I'm so scared."

Gretchen grinned evilly and danced down the path ahead.

He didn't look busy, ankle-deep in the water, skipping stones while Daisy and Belle milled around him. Weary, maybe even dejected, judging by the set of his shoulders. He hadn't been able to solve the murder. He hadn't been able to arrest her or anyone else. How should she approach him? He'd say the theory about the sniper shooting at him was a lot of bull, and he wouldn't believe her about Donnie.

"Thank God you're alive," she blurted the instant he turned. "I was afraid Donnie had killed you."

Coolly, he asked, "How could he kill me when he's clubbing with Vi?" Which was definitely better than "Trying to pin it on your neighbor, bitch? You have the right to remain silent. . . ."

"Before that. You didn't answer your phone, you didn't call when Constantine left a message. . . ."

"To say what?" Gideon faced the water again. "I was busy. His message confirmed what I already believed, but unfortunately, I have to have proof." He crouched and fingered through the pebbles by the shore.

"You already knew?" Ophelia clenched her fists. "Why didn't you tell me?"

"It didn't hit me till shortly after you left," Gideon said in a tone of patient fatigue. "I was on Plato's platform talking it through with my boss, and everything fell into place. That's why I wanted to have dinner with you earlier. Talking it through is what works for me." He stood and shrugged dismissively. "I spent the evening going after proof. I knew you were in good hands."

"Uh, well, great then. I guess I should go."

Gideon stood and zinged a pebble across the water. "Wait."

"What?" She cringed at the hostility in her voice.

"I need to tell you something." He wasn't looking her way, but she could hardly blame him; she didn't much want to meet his eyes, either. "I have a confession to make."

You?

"Since you're already pissed off at me, I may as well get it over with." Zing, skip, skip.

"It sounds like *you're* pissed off at *me*." Ophelia crossed her arms in front of her bustier.

"I'm pissed off in general," Gideon allowed. Zing, plop. "It doesn't matter. I searched your house. . . ." After a silence, he added, "If you're going to go ballistic, could you get it over with?" The next stone zinged across the river and skipped once near the opposite bank.

Ophelia squelched the urge to stomp away. "Why would I care? I don't have anything to hide." *Not in my house, that is.*

"Don't you want to know why?"

"That's obvious. Because you still suspect me."

"No, damn it, not because I suspect you!" Gideon slapped the last stone across the water and turned, his eyes burning through the darkness. "Why the hell would I suspect you? I know you didn't do it. I've always known you didn't. Now I know Donnie did, which gives me even less reason to suspect you than before."

Ophelia let her arms fall and slowed her breathing. *Okay. For now.*

"I can't believe you thought I would arrest you," Gideon said. "Even if I thought you'd done it, I'd never put you in a cell. I'd find some way, some better way. . . ." He scooped up a handful of pebbles and strode toward the water.

Ophelia followed. Moonlight glanced off the stones and splashed into the meandering river. "What better way?"

"I don't know! Does it matter?"

Unfortunately, it does. "Why did you search my house, then?"

"To encourage him to think I suspect you. To make sure he hadn't planted anything else, and to know what was there already, in case he does plant something."

"Ah. He might kill someone with a vibrator and stick it in my underwear drawer."

"You *are* upset," Gideon said.

"Not really. Now that you've inventoried my sex toys, you know the feather duster will fit right in." *I'm actually fishing,* she realized. *I've never done anything so humiliating.* She met his eyes, but for the life of her she couldn't read what went on behind them. Still nothing to do with sex. Hoping her utter dejection didn't show, she said again, "I guess I'll go."

"Stay a while," Gideon said. "Please."

"Why? What do you want from me?"

"I want your presence. I want your listening ears and your lively mind and your generous heart. I want you with me at the kitchen table or on the couch—"

She crossed her arms again and tried to sound cynical. "Not in bed?" *I'm so pathetic.*

"Of course I want you in bed, but how much talking would we get done? I can't catch a murderer if I'm thinking with my dick."

By the time he had outlined the theory that Donnie and the print and photo guy were in cahoots, Gideon's libido, if not yet controlling his thoughts, had given notice of its intention to do so. As Ophelia curled on the couch drinking coffee, mulling things over, and cussing Donnie out, and then cussing him out even more when she heard how Plato had been victimized for years, Gideon tried to keep his eyes off the bustier and progressed from strained detachment to bemused admiration to downright lust. Which was despicable of him, since Ophelia was shedding tears over Plato and his two D-shaped basket bottoms.

"Plato knew he was in danger," Gideon said. "Maybe he watched Donnie too obviously and got caught. Maybe he got so upset he confronted Donnie. The basket bottoms were a long-shot backup plan, in case he didn't reach me. He'd told me about all his baskets being O-shaped because of you, so he hoped I'd figure it out."

Ophelia didn't look lustful as she wiped the tears away, but she looked desirable as all hell. *Luminous*, Gideon mused, eyeing her in the low light from the stairwell, trying halfheartedly to keep his mind on the case. *Does she give off allure even when she's not in the mood?* Ophelia's mind was definitely where it belonged, and fortunately, she didn't need prompting from him to stay on track. *Heaven*, he decided, not sure whether he meant her ability to take the ball and run with it or to take him by the balls and reduce him to a gibbering fool. He'd mentioned that a search of Donnie's house had yielded nothing to do with the photo shop, and she'd nailed it.

"The trash bags," she said. "He half-filled them with film or prints or CDs, then cushioned them with pine straw and dead leaves. But how will you pick out his bags from among the zillions of other ones in the dump?"

"The orange one," Gideon said. "There was one orange bag in his truck."

"Jack-o'-lantern leaf bag. It must have been left over from fall. You're right, not many people have them at this time of year. There was a beat-up roll of carpet cushion on his truck, too."

Now she sat straight, her eyes wide and delighted. "That's how he carried the body out of the apartment. Remember? There were bits of foam rubber sticking to it." Her luscious lips curved into an unrestrained, blinding smile.

"Oh God," he said thickly. He gripped her by the shoulder and kissed her hard. "Amazing woman." He kissed her again, and she laughed in her throat and tongued him back.

She drew away. "Let's get back to the detective thing. I can't have sex with you tonight."

"You started your period?"

Ophelia shook her head. "I just can't."

Gideon tangled his fingers into her curls and licked at her lips again. "If it's a birth-control issue, I have condoms upstairs. But we already fucked that one up this morning."

"I've been trying the pill for a month or two," Ophelia said, drawing away again. "Apparently it reduces sex drive in some women." She grinned ruefully. "Not me, so far."

Gideon groaned. "Don't smile like that if you want me to back off. If it's not birth control and it's not lack of libido, what is it?"

"It doesn't matter," Ophelia said. "Tell you what. I'll get you off, and then you'll be able to think straight again, or at least be temporarily incapable, so we can keep on talking this through." She slid off the couch and went straight for his fly.

"Are you offering me a hand job, or . . ."

She smiled at him again, flashing those glow-in-the-dark razor-sharp fangs. "Scared?"

Holy shit. "Hell, yes," Gideon said. "Go for it."

CHAPTER TWENTY-TWO

Afterward, Gideon mumbled, "Can't do detective work when I'm comatose, either." A few seconds after that, his low, steady breathing told Ophelia he was asleep.

She stood and went slowly upstairs. What had Constantine said? *Don't burden him with your past.* She peeled off the red bustier and let the silk skirt fall to the floor. *Leave it be.* In the hexagonal shower, Ophelia stood for a long time under a cool spray, eyes closed, imagining a life with Gideon, free of the past. It felt damned good.

It also felt like a fantasy.

She toweled dry and rooted in Gideon's dresser for something to wear. Now, *that* felt right—comfortable, as if going through his stuff was fine. She found a well-worn green T-shirt, pulled the silk skirt back on, and went onto the back deck to indulge her fantasy, just for a while, and plan her twisted garden.

When Gideon came out an hour later she was long past fantasy and into the reality of clearing the honeysuckle and Virginia creeper from what had once been a bed of roses. "I'm partial to vines," she told him as he came up beside her, "but they require firm control. It's a miracle a few of your mother's roses survived. She chose varieties that do okay in this climate, but still, under this sort of onslaught . . ." She shook her head. "I don't mess with rose gardens in south Louisiana. Too much work. Black spot, mildew . . . You need to get rid of the wisteria next to the house, too."

"It's impossible. I've tried everything short of digging it up."

"That's what you have to do," Ophelia said. "Dig it up."

"Maintaining a rose garden is too much work, but digging up wisteria isn't?"

"It's a matter of choice," Ophelia said. "If you don't want a rose garden, you just don't have one. If you don't want wisteria, you have to prove it. Even then, it might come back."

"I don't not want it that badly," Gideon said.

There was an uneasy silence. After a while, Ophelia said, "The honeysuckle and Virginia creeper will have to be dug up, too, and the soil sifted. Then you need to plant something besides roses." More silence. She babbled on. "A pergola would be a nice feature. Some of your mom's plantings will recover with a little care and pruning—the camellias, gardenias, azaleas . . . I'd suggest periwinkle or Asian jasmine on the slope toward the river, English ivy in some shady areas beside a meandering flagstone path, maybe trumpet vines against the deck. And some potted plants on the deck itself, of course. It's awfully barren as is."

"Art gives me potted plants for my birthday," Gideon said. "But they always die."

Another awkward pause. Ophelia stripped off her gardening gloves. "We need to finish our talk so I can go home. I still don't know why Donnie has it in for me. He's crazy about my sister. He should want to stay on my good side." She gathered her secateurs and shears and headed up the stairs to the deck.

"He does want to stay on your good side." Gideon followed Ophelia indoors. "He also wants you to move back to town and sell your property—to him. I've been through the city and parish databases. Donnie's been buying up property along this side of the river, almost to my place, and for a ways on the other side of yours, for the past several years. You and Willy were the only holdouts, and now, with the new golf course and the upscale subdivisions across the river, land prices are likely to go up." He opened the fridge and proffered Ophelia a beer.

"No, thanks. I already drank too much tonight, and I have to drive home." She scrubbed her hands at the kitchen sink and dried them on her shirt.

"Coke, then." Gideon popped one and handed it to her, then led the way to the futon couch. He patted the cushion beside him.

Ophelia sat at the other end of the couch, out of reach. She took a swig of Coke. "The real-estate agent told me my property value was increasing, but I didn't care because I wasn't planning on selling. Donnie's offered to buy my place a couple of times, but I can't afford property in town unless the value goes up a lot more. Also, I've wondered about starting a small nursery, and for that I'd need my land even if I did move back to town."

"Did you tell him that, too?" Gideon moved closer and swallowed some beer. Couldn't he take the hint and keep his pheromones at a distance?

"I might have. Yeah. A couple or three weeks ago."

"That was the last straw for Donnie's ambitions. It's one thing to buy and build a single lot at a time; he's been doing that for years. It's another entirely to develop a whole subdivision. What with the classy subs going up across the river, he figured the time was right, but he couldn't have a couple of holdouts right in the middle of his development." Gideon grinned, but behind the smile he was giving her that suspicious look again. No wonder he didn't want her to move in. No wonder he wasn't asking her to take care of his garden. He still suspected her—but of what?

He went on acting cool and perfect, the detective so very much in charge. "With Willy Wyler, he figured he could wait it out—the guy's got major drug problems and his wife's too proud to work, so they were going down the tubes without any help from him. Even if Willy hadn't sold to Donnie, it wouldn't have been catastrophic, because his house is comparable in value to what Donnie would build. But an old trailer, no matter how refurbished, no matter how pretty its garden, would never do.

"When those nasty pictures of Joanna showed up at the photo shop, he put the squeeze on Willy even more. Encouraged Willy to believe you took the pictures. Probably egged him on to mess with your place, too. He figured if you got hit with enough—dead cat, dead garden, vandalism, accusations of child abuse and even murder—you'd either get scared or you'd end up in jail and sell your place to him to raise money for a lawyer. He may not have planned to kill his cohort at the photo shop, but once he had, where better to dump the body than on you? And who was ready with plenty of ill-gotten cash to rescue you? He was, of course."

"He thinks if he gets rich he'll have a chance with Vi," Ophelia mused. "Men are such fools." *Including you. And if you aren't, it's even worse.* She stood up to get away from his suspicions and his hormone bouquet. "I have to go home."

"Wait," Gideon said, standing as well, way too close.

Ophelia closed her eyes to block out his delectable aroma, which didn't help at all.

"Don't go," Gideon said, in that slow, lazy voice that had drawn her in from day one.

She headed for the door. "We've pretty much talked this out. Try the Taylor Road dump first. Donnie has a key to the back gate, so he can get in and out easily. He took me there once to dump a whole truckload of trash because I was too broke to pay the fees. The bastard," she added under her breath. "He's always been so helpful, and none of it was real. I can't believe I actually liked him, sort of."

"Taylor Road it is," Gideon said. "First thing in the morning. In the meantime, sweetheart, please stay."

"Why? I already said we're not having sex tonight." She picked up her gloves and tools.

"I don't want to have sex tonight," Gideon said, and then

stopped. "No, of course I do, but not if you don't. Sex or no sex, I want you here with me. Is that so strange?"

Ophelia rolled her eyes at him, one hand on the door handle. "I get it. You think I'm in danger if I go back home. Well, now that I know who I'm watching for, I'll do just fine."

"Sure you will, but why should I be alone here and you be alone there? Why not sleep in the same bed?" She said nothing, and Gideon threw up his hands. "I don't get it. I thought you liked me. Turns out I'm just another sex toy. A bimbo. Pretty damn ironic, wouldn't you say?"

Ophelia stared at him, swaying with surprise. "What?" she asked faintly.

"What else am I supposed to think? You don't want to talk to me, you're always trying to get away, and the only thing about me you've shown interest in is my dick. I suppose I should be flattered that a vamp wants me for her boy toy, but the fact remains, I want more."

Ophelia put the gardening tools down before she dropped them. "What do you want?"

"If I tell you, you'll freak out and leave."

Ophelia made an incredulous face. "You're into kink?" She leaned against the blessed firmness of the door. "I don't believe it."

"The only kink I'm into is you, and I'd rather not talk about sex in any form if you're not in the mood, because even when I'm pissed off at you, I want you to throw me on the rug and fuck me senseless." He made a disgusted noise. "Probably even more when I'm pissed off. I'm turning into a love slave. Me!"

Ophelia laughed and bit her lip so she wouldn't lick it. "Then what do you want from me?"

His eyes burned into her, and she squirmed under both the scrutiny and her mounting desire for him. Damn. "Promise you won't leave?" Gideon said.

Her heart thumped against her chest, hard and then

harder. She sucked in a breath. "I'll hear you out before I decide whether to leave."

"All right," he said, looking strained and determined and adorable. "I want you to move in with me. I want you to sleep with me every night." He stopped, his eyes scouring her again, and took a deep breath and went on. "I want you to sit beside me and talk to me and live with me. And marry me and have kids with me." He paused. "And while you're at it, fix my goddamned garden, if you like."

Ophelia said nothing, mostly because she couldn't. Again, she closed her eyes.

"See, I knew it," Gideon said. "It's too soon, just like Lep warned me. You think I'm just another crazy guy under your spell. If you give me a chance, sweetheart, some time to prove it, you'll see that I'm a lot more than that."

Ophelia came slowly back across the room and sank onto the couch.

The weeping garden. That tangled, twisted garden, all hers.

The man just asked you marry him, and all you can think about is a bunch of plants?

"We hardly know each other," she said stupidly.

"That makes it even more fun." Gideon sat next to her and took her hand, pressing kisses on her palm. "Honey, you don't have to answer me now. Just think about it."

"I'm so confused." Helplessly, because she wanted to and because there was nothing else, she leaned across and kissed him. The kiss deepened and grew, and then she was on the couch under him, her arms twined around his neck, his hands insistent under her shirt, his lips pressing hot kisses down her throat.

"I love you," he said roughly. "That's all there is to it. And I'd better go take a cold shower right now if we're not having sex tonight." He raised himself on one elbow. "Why, again, aren't we having sex? Don't tell me you don't want to. I won't believe it."

"It's nothing to do with not wanting," Ophelia began, but by then his hand was under her skirt and hard on her thigh. "Ow!" She recoiled. Damn.

"What the hell?" Gideon sat up. It took him half a second at the most. "You had the gun hidden under your skirt, on a strap or something, right? You wore a crinoline to bulk it out so I wouldn't be able to tell." He stood and paced across the room. "Jesus."

Ophelia shrugged it off. "I was in a hurry, and I'd run out of duct tape."

"Your walk was awkward, but I attributed it to the heels. You really were afraid of me." He ran his hands through his hair. "Damn."

"It's only a couple of bruises."

"Take your skirt off," Gideon said.

Five minutes later, flat on Gideon's bed and naked from the waist down, Ophelia wallowed in love and guilt. He had taken her explanation with admirable calm.

"This won't do." He eased a splinter out of her thigh and dabbed the tiny tear with an alcohol-soaked cotton ball.

"Ow! Skip the alcohol next time." She poked out her tongue. "My spit works better."

"My, my," Gideon said. "What an unusually flexible woman you must be. No wonder that vibrator doesn't impress you."

Ophelia chuckled. She sucked his middle finger into her mouth and pushed it out again. "What won't do?"

He wiped her saliva across the cut and got back to work with the tweezers. "You can't marry me if you don't trust me."

"I haven't said I'll marry you." She watched his dark head bent over her thigh and longed for innocence. His warm breath tickled her pubic hair. *Well, not that kind of innocence.*

"But you want my garden," Gideon said, "and marrying me is the only way you'll get it." He tugged on the second splinter.

"There are other gardens," Ophelia said, horrified at how easily he had read her, hoping she sounded indifferent.

"But you want mine," Gideon said with a panting little laugh. He leaned closer and licked her. "And I want yours." He sucked gently. "But not if you don't trust me."

Ophelia put her hands behind her head and wriggled languorously. She ran her tongue over her fangs. "Trust doesn't happen overnight."

Gideon withdrew and picked up the tweezers again. "What I don't understand is, why shouldn't you trust me? I haven't given you any reason not to feel safe with me. Even Lep and Constantine are on my side."

She sure wasn't about to explain, so she tried for cool and supercilious again. "I'm supposed to fall in love with you because they approve?"

"No, but you might consider trusting me because they do." Gideon eased out another splinter. "Whatever happened to you in the past," he said, flicking the splinter across the sheets, "is over."

Ophelia stiffened, and fought to let the tension go. No use.

"Whoever fucked with you," he said, "is history."

Ophelia winced.

"In the interest of moving forward . . ." His eyes were fixed on her thigh. "You need to get rid of him. Give me some spit." He spread Ophelia's saliva over the tiny wounds. "He's fucking up your future. Dig him up or bury him, do whatever you have to, and then go forward with me."

Ophelia tried to lie still—*Control it, control yourself*—but her body and spirit curled away from him. "I don't want to talk about this," she whispered. *Please.*

"We don't have to talk at all." He disappeared into the bathroom with the alcohol, cotton balls, and tweezers. Above the skylight, stars winked through quivering oak leaves. Gideon returned and stripped off his clothes.

Oh, good, thought Ophelia, watching him with mingled

relief and desire. *This I can handle.* She eyed his erection and licked her fangs.

Gideon brushed featherlight fingers past the bruises on both her thighs. "Is this why you didn't want to have sex, or was it just the embarrassment factor?" Without waiting for an answer, he slithered onto his belly and tongued her clit again. "You like this a lot," he said after a minute.

How could I not? She realized with astonishment that she was whimpering. This adorable man was *good*. Incredibly, achingly good.

"And you get hot faster than any woman I've ever been with—"

Get on with it then, will you?

"And you come easily—"

Not if you're talking the whole damn time!

"And yet, you're not really relaxed." He pulled away and grinned at her. "I have an idea."

Ophelia gaped at him, throbbing in the cool air that had taken his place. "I don't believe this. You're a tease."

"Don't you just love it," Gideon said. "Fusion, that's the answer."

Five torturous minutes later, lying almost motionless under Gideon, his penis hard but quiet inside her, Ophelia was still fighting his ridiculous fusion idea. And him.

"It feels good," Gideon laughed. "You need to relax some more."

She squirmed. "Is it cheating to clench my vaginal muscles?"

"The point, my sweet one," Gideon explained as he kissed her, "is to sense everything. To notice every point of contact." He shifted his weight and trickled a toe along her foot. "Our toes tantalizing, our thighs pressed together. Our bellies pooled in pleasure. Your sumptuous breasts against my . . . uh, manly chest. Spread your arms." He laid his arms along hers and twined their fingers. "A thousand sizzling erogenous zones, feeding, spreading, firing together."

Ophelia groaned and thrust her pelvis against his.

"Patience." Gideon touched his tongue to hers and flickered over her fangs. "Relax and savor it."

"Why the hell can't you just fuck me?" Ophelia cried. "Forget the stupid bruises. I want to get jammed!"

"Some other time," Gideon said. "Tonight it's slow and easy."

"This is so slow it's almost dead," Ophelia growled, panting and heaving, but although she was strong, he was stronger. "Stop the sex guru thing and act like a normal guy. How many other women have you put through this torment?"

"None," Gideon said. "I read about it in some book, but I never wanted to merge with anyone until you came along."

A tiny, happy spark flared into life in Ophelia's belly. *He really does love me.* "It's a terrible idea."

Gideon touched his lips to hers and whispered hot and softly into her mouth. "Relax into me. Envelop me. Fuse with me, love."

"This is in*sane*," Ophelia moaned. Gideon's mouth came down hard in a demanding kiss with some blessed movement in it—*oh God, thank God*—and eagerly she kissed him back, pouring all the passion she didn't dare feel into that kiss, sucking him into her, sucking her into him.

"Oh," she said, whelmed in astonishment and delight, as the flare in her belly welled into exquisite light. *You really do love me.* She tightened her fingers against his and every muscle seared down her outstretched arms, down her arched back, down the quivering length of her legs. *And I love you.* He shifted his hips a thousandth of an inch and glory unimagined shot through Ophelia. *Finally.* She clenched her vagina around him, let go, and clenched again.

"Calm down," Gideon said. "We haven't fused properly yet."

"I can fix that," Ophelia snarled. She sank her fangs into his shoulder.

Gideon rocked hard against her, gasping and laughing. "Took you long enough."

Ophelia tried to retort, but the blood was too good and the fuck was too smooth. She closed her eyes and let the moving fusion be, one two three slick golden strokes. She withdrew her fangs, quivering with the effort. "Wait."

Gideon laughed, spilling pleasure through her with a slow relentless grind. "I thought you wanted to hurry up." His hot breath melted into a groan. He gripped her ass and rolled them over together, gazing up at her with heavy-lidded eyes, the breath hissing through his teeth. "Bite me again, Ophelia."

His hands traveled possessively across her ass and she writhed against them, writhed against the golden pressure of his penis filling her. "I can't talk with my fangs inside you." She touched her tongue to his and licked his mouth, licked her lips. She giggled. *I never giggle. What the hell has gotten into me?* "We need to talk."

Gideon ran his fingers up the crack of her butt, spreading their slick juices. "Talk later."

"But this is *important*," Ophelia mocked. She squeezed down onto him, buried her face in his aroma, caressed his neck with her fangs, traced his earlobe with her tongue. She drew slowly away until only the tip of him played at her opening. "Sex can wait."

Gideon slid a hand in between them and went straight for her clit. Ophelia shuddered out an ecstatic moan.

"You had something to say?" Gideon laughed.

Ophelia writhed speechlessly against his fingers.

"Or you could just shut up and fuck me," he said. "I never did go for too much talk."

Ophelia squirmed away from his devastating touch. "So that's how you did it."

Gideon splayed the hand across her hip and grinned up at her. "Did what?"

She slid off him and folded her arms. "Kept your bimbos from talking too much. You fingered them speechless."

"Shit." Gideon propped his head on his hand and frowned at her. "I'm a jerk, right?"

"You're a darling." Ophelia slithered up against him and kissed him. "You gave them the best time they ever had." She slung a leg across his hip. "But it has me really, really worried." She laughed, drunk with love. Insane.

Gideon rolled on top of her. "Uh-huh." He plunged his tongue into her mouth and scraped it on a fang. Ophelia moaned and bucked under him. His eyes burned dark and devilish into hers. "You sure do look worried." He chuckled and kneed her legs apart.

"Wait," Ophelia said, panting and gasping, drenched in euphoria and sex. "I'm not like your mother and sister, and I'm not a bimbo either. Usually, I don't talk all that much."

He nuzzled down her neck, paused at her armpit, trailed his tongue across her breast. "Could have fooled me." He laved the nipple and sucked gently.

She rubbed herself against his knee and moaned again as he traveled to the other breast. "I have to get more than the bimbos, not less. If I don't talk, will you never finger me speechless again?" Her laugher dissolved into a wavering cry as he drove deep inside her.

"The garden"—he panted, thrusting into her again— "and the finger, for you only, forever, when you marry me."

"All right," she whispered, arching hard against him, accepting him to her very core. "I'm scared out of my mind, but . . ." *I love you.* "I don't have any choice."

"Excellent." Gideon's voice broke harsh and breathless in her ear. He surged into her, golden sweet and demanding. "Now what about *my* perks?"

Ophelia settled her fangs against the sweet spot where his neck joined his shoulder. "Fuse with me, love," she said.

* * *

In the still gray light of dawn, Zelda braked her bike in front of Ophelia's porch and tried not to grimace at its occupant. After all, Joanna was half the reason she had come. "What are you doing here? Where's Ophelia?" She glanced at the house. "The kitchen light's on, but there's no truck in the drive."

Joanna Wyler stood slowly. Her face was puffy, and her eyes were red.

Wimp, thought Zelda, and immediately felt a pang of remorse—or maybe it was just the toothache that had kept her up most of the night.

"I don't know," Joanna said belligerently. "She didn't answer the door, so I guess she's not here." She stuck out her chin and clamped her lips together.

Zelda had to give the girl points for effort. She tried to sound a mite less judgmental. *Embrace the vamp destiny,* Violet had drummed into her head over the years. If that included mentoring wimps, so be it. "Then why are you sitting on her porch?"

"None of your business." Joanna's lip quivered. "I've got as much right to be here as you. Ophelia's my friend. She doesn't hang up when I call to apologize. She doesn't beat me up."

"I didn't beat you up." Zelda motioned toward the rear of the trailer. "Let's go inside."

"You would have if Rick hadn't made you even madder," Joanna said, following her.

"That's probably true. I'm not saying you didn't deserve it, but I need to control my temper." Zelda stashed the bike against the wall beside the screened porch. "I apologize for losing it, and I accept your apology for being such a worm, and let's forget it."

"Okay." Joanna sounded wobbly and surprised. "Thanks."

Psyche came out from under the back stairs, complaining. Zelda shoved a wood shim between the screen door and frame, popping the hook open, and dug her keys out of her shorts to unlock the door. Psyche made straight for her food dish, and was followed in by Joanna. Zelda shut the door and put her hands on her hips, which were no curvier than the day or the week or the year before. Some things showed no sign of change. "But you still have to say who took those pictures."

Joanna looked hopefully around the room, as if Ophelia might be there after all. "That's why I came to see Ophelia."

"Okay," Zelda said sternly. "But you have to tell your parents, too, so they stop spreading lies."

Joanna clenched her fists and screeched, "That's what I'm going to do, as soon as I see Ophelia. Stop being mean to me!" Psyche yowled and Zelda rolled her eyes, and Joanna wailed, "Even the cat hates me now!"

"Feed her and she'll be your friend forever," muttered Zelda. "The cat food's under the sink." She made a pass through the trailer, stopping in the bathroom long enough to find the clove oil. "Maybe Ophelia left early so she could work while it's still cool. How long have you been waiting?"

"Forever." Joanna blinked at the kitchen clock above the window. "Two hours."

"Two hours ago it was still the middle of the night," Zelda said. "She always feeds Psyche before she leaves in the morning. Looks as if she didn't come home last night." *Looks as if she's sleeping with that cop, like Mom said she would.* Zelda flexed her aching jaws and tried not to feel abandoned. Ophelia deserved a nice boyfriend, but couldn't she have waited a few more days? "Why didn't you go back home?"

"I hate it there." Joanna fingered Ophelia's earrings, scattered around the open jewelry box on the kitchen table. "You don't understand. You have a mother you can talk to."

"Not necessarily." Zelda bit her tongue at this appalling disloyalty. The pain was apparently getting to her. With a heroic effort, she stopped herself from telling Joanna to keep her mitts off Ophelia's jewelry and set about rectifying her flub. "Definitely not at this time of day." She opened the clove oil and dabbed it on one inflamed gum.

Joanna dumped the rest of the jewelry onto the table. "Why not?"

"She's up till all hours at the club. Last night she didn't get to sleep till after four a.m. I couldn't go busting into her room at five." Zelda spread clove oil on the other swollen gum. "I've been up all night with a toothache. I came to see if Ophelia had a better painkiller." She flexed her jaw again, enjoying the cool intensity of the clove oil, knowing it wouldn't last anywhere near long enough. "Don't worry," Violet had said the day before, "just like that you'll sprout them, easy as pie"—but all things vamp were easy for Violet.

"Time to fess up," Zelda said a couple of minutes later, after Joanna had arranged most of the earrings in pairs. "Who took the dirty pics?"

"I'm not telling you," Joanna said. She pushed aside a pile of unmatched earrings. "I'll wait for Ophelia. She won't laugh at me."

"Why would I laugh?" Zelda said. "There's nothing funny about some disgusting dude taking pictures of you." She cocked her head to one side. "Was it some *cute* guy? You'd better be careful, girl, or you'll end up pregnant. Is that who was trying to get you to have sex?"

"Nobody's trying to get me to have sex." Joanna set aside a pile of displaced backings.

"Don't be naive. If he took dirty pictures of you, the next thing he'll want is sex." Zelda scooped the mismatches to her side of the table. "Was it Gabe Tate? You've got the hots for him, along with every other idiot at school."

Joanna flushed, her eyes wide and shocked. "No! I wouldn't!"

"Good. He's scum. He got kicked out of the Chamber for bringing in underage girls." Zelda fingered an earring with a red glass flower, wondering where its mate and the necklace that matched them had gone. "Was it some dork? Is that why you think I'll laugh?" She put the earring on. The only other red earring was a dangly one with a garnet. She set it aside in favor of blue ceramic beads.

"Your earrings don't match," Joanna said. She cringed at Zelda's blighting look.

Another pang of compunction assailed Zelda. "Don't be a slave to convention," she said almost kindly. "Who took the pictures?"

"I can't tell you," Joanna said. "I really can't."

"Chicken," Zelda said, and Psyche hissed. "See? Even the cat thinks you should tell me. I know! Was it a girl?"

"No! I'm not a dyke! Stop asking me!"

Zelda huffed. She pressed her hands to her jaw and said through her teeth, "Listen. You don't need to be scared anymore. You have *me* on your side. I'll go with you to confront whoever took the pics. I'll go with you to confess to your mother. I'll say hi to you in the hall at school. Whatever it takes."

"You'll say hi to me in the hall?"

Zelda's head began to hammer. "Grow up, Joanna. I'm not the queen or anything. Sure I'll say hi, but what does it matter?"

"Do you swear not to tell anyone else? Except Ophelia, because I'm going to tell her anyway."

With difficulty Zelda refrained from rolling her eyes. "I swear."

"And you won't laugh?"

"I don't know whether I'll laugh! What does that matter, either? Have some self-respect!" She clutched at her throbbing jaw. "Just tell me who took the pictures."

Psyche hissed again.

"All right," Joanna said. She squeezed her eyes tight shut. "I did."

CHAPTER TWENTY-THREE 🌷

Gideon woke shortly before dawn. He yawned and reluctantly withdrew his arm from Ophelia's warm curves. If she was always such a tumultuous sleeper, he foresaw a sleep-deprived future. He yawned again, showered, and headed downstairs to start the coffee.

Two minutes later he heard Gretchen first, a low, uneasy whimper from the upstairs hall, followed by that long, eerie keening that had freaked both man and dog in the car only a few days earlier. Gideon tore up the stairs three at a time, losing the towel around his waist, shoving the whining Gretchen to the side as he leaped through the bedroom door.

"Oh God, no, I didn't, no please, no please!" Fangs flashing, claws flailing, Ophelia flung herself back and forth across the sheets.

Gideon launched himself at the bed and wrapped an arm hard around her from behind. "Ophelia, sweetheart, I'm here. Ophelia, it's me. It's okay."

"I didn't mean to, you bastard!" she wailed. Desperation shattered into sobs as her eyes sprang open. "Oh. It's you. Damn." She slumped against him, drawing in harsh, shuddering breaths. "Damn," she moaned softly.

"'Damn, it's you?' That's all the thanks I get for rescuing you from your bad dream?" He laid his cheek on her hair. She smelled of sweat and sex, of grief and anger and fear.

Ophelia struggled to sit up. "It's a night terror, not a dream, and you didn't rescue me, you idiot, you just endangered yourself. That was why—or one reason, anyway—why I . . . Oh, Gideon, how can I marry you?" Her voice shook. "If I hadn't woken up, I could have killed you!"

"Wait a minute. You were afraid you would attack me in your sleep?"

"I *told* you I wasn't safe." She pushed away from him and stood up. "I have to get away from here. I have to go home."

"Have you attacked anyone else when you were coming out of that lousy dream?"

Ophelia scowled. "Night terror. And no, I haven't, because I haven't slept with anybody since . . . since forever."

"You wouldn't have killed me." Gideon stood as well. "Thanks to me, you slept through most of the night."

"Your ridiculous fusion theory doesn't deserve *that* much credit." Ophelia went into the bathroom and slammed the door.

Gideon opened it again. "It's not a theory anymore, but a proven method. It's foreplay to earth-shattering sex, as we demonstrated last night."

Ophelia turned on the water and stepped under it without waiting for it to warm up.

"So mind-blowing you need a cold shower just thinking about it. Maybe I should get in there with you." He did. "Whoops, it's already warming up. Whatever shall we do?"

"I'll work it off." Ophelia said, sounding a little less unfriendly. "Maybe you should do the same."

"Ah, so you admit the sex was earth-shattering?" He searched her face for the hint of a response. "Mind-blowing, at the very least?" When the corner of her mouth twitched, he leaned in to kiss it. "A hell of a lot of fun?"

"It was phenomenal," Ophelia said. "Once I got my fangs into you." Her fangs slid down and she pushed them promptly back into place. "But then," she added with studied obnoxiousness, "it's always great once I bite."

"Oh, but this was better." Gideon slid his arms around her from behind and nipped at her neck. "You bit *me*."

She leaned back into him and closed her eyes. For a brief, blissful moment he savored the response of her breasts under his hands. He ran his lips up the line of her jaw to her ear. Then she peeled him away. "It doesn't mean I can marry you." She took the washcloth and wrung it out.

"Yes, it does." He handed her the soap. "Apart from the fact that you accepted my proposal last night—"

"I wasn't thinking straight," Ophelia said. "I must have been insane."

"Apart from that," Gideon went on, "the sex, earth-shattering though it was, only put you under for the first hour or so. I'm what kept you asleep the rest of the night."

Ophelia lathered up the washcloth, wariness crawling across her features. "What are you talking about?"

Gideon leaned against the tiles. "You were on the verge of that bad dream all night. Every time you started tossing and moaning, I pulled you close and told you everything was all right, and you calmed down again. The dream didn't get hold of you until I left the bed."

"Night terror," Ophelia said, a hint of desperation in the way she scrubbed herself.

"Night*mare*," Gideon insisted. "You know it and I know it. If you don't want to tell me about it, fine, but don't lie to me."

Ophelia clamped her mouth shut, shackles of tension surrounding her, keeping him at bay.

Gideon strove for tenderness. "You may not trust me awake, but asleep you do. You feel safe with me when you're asleep. Doesn't that say something?"

Two tears rolled down Ophelia's cheeks. "Give me some space, damn you," she whispered. "This is my problem, not yours."

Gideon's heart twisted. He folded his arms, because it was all he could do to not grab her and envelop her and keep her safe. "Anything that affects you, affects me, too."

"If you don't share a bed with me, this one won't affect

you." She raised her face to the shower and washed away the tears. Wearily, she said, "I know you mean well, but this time *you* need to trust *me*. This is something I have to deal with myself." She stepped out of the shower.

"Okay," he said heroically. "Your call." *At least until Donnie Donaldson is behind bars.* "Your shorts and underwear from yesterday are hanging in the laundry room. You want to borrow another shirt?"

"*You* took the pictures?"

"Yes." Joanna's voice was stony. Her eyelashes flickered, but she didn't open her eyes. "Laugh already. Get it over with."

"That's actually quite cool. Crazy, but cool all the same. What, you set up a camera on a tripod? Timer and all?"

Joanna opened her eyes a crack. "Yes."

"You have a lot more guts than I gave you credit for," Zelda said. "Were you going to put them on the Internet?"

Joanna's eyes popped open wide.

"Just kidding," Zelda said.

Joanna shuddered. "If anybody sees those pictures, I will seriously die. It's so unfair! All I wanted was to develop them and look at them. See whether I look sexy or just stupid. They weren't supposed to go to the photo shop! They were black and white, and my dad used to do photography, so he has a darkroom and chemicals. I had it all planned."

"How'd they turn out?"

"I don't know," Joanna groaned. "My dad wouldn't let me see them."

"Your *father* saw the pics? Death by embarrassment, with no mitigating factor. Are you going to try it again?" She chuckled. "Lighten up, will you? Just kidding."

Psyche backed away from her food bowl, hissing, her fur standing on end.

"What's wrong with her?" Joanna said.

Zelda raised a hand. "Shh." She listened hard. Muffled

sounds came from under the house. "There's a man out there."

"I don't hear anything." Joanna eased off her chair to look out the small kitchen window. "I don't see anybody. How do you know it's a man?"

Duh. "Look at Psyche."

"Maybe it's a male *dog*," Joanna said.

"He's not breathing like a dog," Zelda said. Whoa. Vampire hearing was definitely cool.

"You can't hear somebody breathing outside," Joanna scowled. "Stop messing with me."

"Hush!" Zelda listened to soft kissy noises, awkward footsteps, and a grunt. Definitely male. "Stay here."

Joanna whined, and Zelda flapped her hand irritably. More footsteps and a scraping noise came from under the floor at the far end of the trailer. Zelda sneaked down the narrow hallway.

Bang! As she reached the bedroom, a blow shook the floor. She stifled a curse, but Joanna, the fool, shrieked as another bang sounded directly below Zelda. Shit. She listened hard. The breathing under the trailer had quickened with alarm.

After a few seconds Donnie Donaldson's voice came clearly. "Here, kitty, kitty. Come on, Psyche girl. Got some food for you." Zelda heard him stagger out from under the trailer. He stomped up the steps to the front door and knocked. "Ophelia, you home?"

Zelda returned to the kitchen as Joanna let Donnie in. "She's not here," Joanna said. Psyche skittered across the floor toward Zelda.

"That's what I thought," Donnie said. "She didn't come back last night, no truck in the drive this morning, so I figured I'd feed the kitty. But I see you already took care of that." He put a bowl of bacon scraps on the floor and wiped his gloved hands on his overalls. "She'll eat this sooner or later. What are you two doing here?"

Zelda reached for the cat, but Psyche scurried past her down the hall. "Waiting for Ophelia. What were you doing under the house?"

"Trying to feed Psyche, like I said. She holes up under there."

"Then what was the banging noise?" Joanna asked. "It sounded like a gun!"

"Hammer." Donnie indicated his tool belt. "Nail sticking out of one of the supports for the back deck, so I knocked it back in."

"It didn't sound like it was under the back deck," Zelda said. "It sounded like it was under the other end of the house."

Donnie gave her a patronizing look. "Hearing's not that accurate, Zelda girl."

Mine is. A spasm of pain slashed through Zelda's jaw. "God, this hurts. Toothache," she explained for Donnie's benefit. "Maybe Ophelia has something that'll help."

"I have painkillers," Donnie said. "How about you two ladies come to my place and give me some advice."

"About what?" Joanna asked. Zelda hurried down the hall, clutching her jaw.

"A little present I'm making for Violet. She went out with me last night, you know," Donnie added complacently. "Well, of course Zelda knows. She saw us leave for the club."

I also heard her at two a.m. with Reuben. "What are you making?" Zelda called from the bathroom. She opened the cupboard, found nothing, and tried the bedroom.

"You'll see," Donnie said playfully. What a dork.

Zelda opened the dresser drawers and saw stuff she wasn't supposed to see—not that Ophelia would really care—but no meds except ones she'd already tried.

"Does your mom know you're here?" Donnie said softly to Joanna, but of course Zelda could hear it just fine. "I didn't think so," he said. "I bet she doesn't approve of Zelda either. Well, if you two come on over to my place real quick, before your mom wakes up and notices you're gone, we'll make it our little secret. Unless you want me to . . ." His voice drifted to a silent question mark, and Joanna whimpered. "That's a good girl," Donnie said. He raised his voice. "Come on now, Zelda. I got some real good painkillers from the dentist."

Secrets, thought Zelda. *That sounds icky.* And Donnie sounded more than icky, he sounded almost dangerous. And then she remembered something. She kicked the area rug aside, and there was the secret compartment Ophelia had shown her ages ago.

"Just a minute, I found some Midol!" she called. She got down on her knees and pulled the compartment open. Inside lay a pile of photographs held together by a rubber band. No time to look at them, but the top one said it all: naked, silly Joanna, one arm over her breasts and the other spread across her pubic hair, a nervous grin on her face. She shut the compartment and pulled back the rug back to cover the little door.

Horrifying conjecture spun through her head as she popped the Midol bottle open and spilled out a couple of pills. What if Joanna had lied to her? What if Donnie had taken those pics? That would be one hell of a secret. Ick. *Ick!* Why were the pictures in Ophelia's secret compartment? She tried to think, while Psyche stared reproachfully from under the bed.

Donnie's footsteps came down the hall. Zelda grabbed a purple vibrator from the top drawer and set it on the area rug, shut the dresser drawer, and hurried into the hall. "I need some water to swallow these," she said, pushing past Donnie, who promptly turned and followed her way too closely.

Joanna looked imploringly at her as she came into the kitchen. What the hell was going on? Zelda took a glass from the cupboard, filled it with water, and swallowed one of the pills. She left the pill bottle on the table beside the glass and grinned brightly at Donnie. "Are you going to give us breakfast?"

He blinked and did the tiniest double take. "Sure."

Oh, crap, thought Zelda. *Now, that's even ickier.* But it distracted him enough that when he went to open the door, she was able to scoop the little pile of mismatched earrings off the table and into her pocket.

At the bottom of the front stairs she dropped the second Midol. It showed up blue against the dead grass. At the driveway she dropped one earring, not daring to look down and see what color it was or whether it showed against the gravel, although Donnie seemed preoccupied with shepherding them to his place as fast as possible. Across the drive she dropped another on the dirt at the verge. "Wait," she said, "My flip-flop came off." She kicked it on again while noting with relief that this earring at least was yellow and definitely visible.

Another yucky thing: Donnie smelled bad. Fearfully, freakishly bad. Every instinct told Zelda to run, but she couldn't let silly, helpless Joanna go with Donnie all by herself, even if she'd done it before and had been lying all the time. Zelda hummed a tune and let another earring fall on Donnie's lawn, and another at the bottom of his back steps.

Inside the house, Donnie shut the door and locked it. "Upstairs, girls," he said.

"What are you making for my mom?" Zelda preceded Joanna up the stairs, Donnie right behind them, panting heavily. *Old guy, out of shape,* thought Zelda, or maybe, *Disgustamungo! He's turned on. But he has no idea who he's dealing with.*

It turned out that he was neither. He was in plenty good shape to knock both of them on the head as they reached the landing. Zelda saw Joanna crumple to the floor, and after that everything went black.

Gideon's cheerfulness almost did Ophelia in. Not that he didn't have plenty to be pleased about. "We're building a good case against Donnie. He's got questionable financial records, and he offered cash for Wyler's place, closing this afternoon. Hopefully we'll find the trash and the carpet cushion, but there's sure to be trace evidence that links him to at least one of the murders. In the meantime, I want him behind bars before he kills someone else. The chief's not ready to cooperate. He says he can't go around arresting respectable business owners he's known forever—the kind who might get elected to city council—just on suspicion."

"Why should Donnie kill anyone else?" Ophelia asked, deciding Gideon wasn't really cheerful. He was being phony-nice, just like when he suspected her. Which he was doing again now. She glared at him indignantly. "Stop that!"

"Stop what?" Gideon's dark eyes were bland above the rim of his coffee cup.

Ophelia bit aggressively into the muffin slathered with peanut butter that Gideon had insisted she eat. "Stop looking at me like you suspect me. It makes me not trust you again."

"Until I figure you out, that's how I'll look at you," Gideon said. "It means I care."

With difficulty, Ophelia swallowed the chunk of muffin.

"Donnie will kill anyone he sees as a threat," Gideon said, back in "Good Day Sunshine" mode. "What are your plans for today?"

"Work," Ophelia said.

"At home? At a customer's?"

Ophelia swallowed again. "Both. Don't worry, I'm not planning on threatening Donnie. If you need me, my phone will be on." She washed the lump in her throat with coffee, but it didn't go down. She fought for some other topic. "Art left the club last night with Darby Sims."

Gideon broke into a genuine smile. "That's good news! They should have gotten together years ago. Did Constantine get rid of Marissa Parkerson?" Ophelia gaped, alarm bells clanging, but Gideon merely chuckled. "Art was kind enough to inform me she wasn't sleeping with him, so I knew something else was going on. He scared the shit out of the poor woman, I suppose."

"Something like that," Ophelia said. "It really bothered Art."

"Not you?"

It was impossible to figure out how he meant that. "It wasn't pretty, but I'm used to Constantine. It's never any use arguing with him once he's decided what to do."

Gideon was so cheerful he almost bubbled over. "If Marissa's husband was such a screwup, she's probably better off if he really is dead."

Too bad "dead" didn't solve it for her. "Uh-huh." Ophelia stood. "I have to go."

"Sure you do." Gideon blew her a huge, sparkly, sinister kiss. "Have a great day."

Ten minutes later, Ophelia pulled into her driveway. Donnie's truck, empty now that he'd disposed of all the evidence, and spanking clean to boot, sat next to his house. The front door of the Wyler Colonial slammed open, and Lisa scrambled out with a backpack in one hand and a bag lunch in the other, yelling "Joanna!"

Ophelia drove Constantine's big blue truck past her trailer and the greenhouse to park behind the chipper at the farthest compost pile. She hefted a shovel and a spade out of the back of the truck, and her spare shotgun from the cab, and set to work.

It was too much to hope she'd be left in peace. Lisa hollered for her daughter again, and shortly afterward Ophelia saw her banging on Donnie's door. She slogged grimly away at the compost pile and listened to Lisa's shrill whine. "She left without her books! And her purse! She never forgets them. Did you see her catch the bus?"

The rumble of Donnie's voice was too low for Ophelia,

but clearly the answer was negative. Then Lisa shrieked, "She was *where?*"

Rat, thought Ophelia, with a silent apology to self-respecting rodents. But of course he wouldn't stop until he'd uprooted her, too.

She threw the shovel beside the pitiful pile of dirt she'd managed to move, picked up her shotgun, and walked out past the chipper. "Joanna's not here, so you can damn well back off," she said when Lisa reached the greenhouse, but the woman's careworn face wrenched Ophelia's gut and she softened her tone. "Sorry, Lisa, but I haven't seen her this morning. I just got home myself."

Donnie sauntered up behind Lisa and clamped a hand on her sagging shoulders. "Told you," he said, sounding patronizing and patient. "I said Joanna was here *earlier*. I figured she went back home, but maybe it was already time for the bus. I don't watch out the window all the time, you know."

He chuckled. Ophelia gripped the shotgun by the barrels and approached them, glancing from Lisa's miserable face to Donnie's smug one, longing to put the bastard away for good. *Like that worked before.*

"Now I have to drive all the way to the middle school," Lisa whimpered. "I can't afford the gas. I can't afford anything."

"I'd take it for you, but I don't have the time today. How about I advance you a couple of bucks?" Donnie pulled out his wallet and magnanimously handed Lisa two dollar bills.

Ophelia bent her head to fiddle with her advancing fangs. She had to remember not to be threatening.

"You'll have cash today after we close," Donnie told Lisa. "Shouldn't you be packing?"

Ophelia's fangs strained to emerge, and she willed them to be still.

"To go where?" Lisa quavered. "Some friend you are, stealing our house out from under us the moment we're down. Willy was so upset he never came home last night. He's a lousy husband, but usually he comes home."

"I'm doing you a favor," Donnie protested. "You can find someplace else to live."

Snake, thought Ophelia, and apologized silently to snakes. *I will make you sorry.*

"But I love my house." Lisa hauled in a deep, sobbing breath and flicked away tears.

"This is a lot of cash for me to lay out," Donnie said. "You should be grateful."

Maggot, Ophelia thought. Then she remembered all the hard-working bugs and other creatures who deserved her respect, whose handiwork she would be especially grateful for today. She put on a sweet smile. "You're buying Lisa's place? You don't need to waste your hard-earned cash, Donnie. Remember what I said last night?" She turned to Lisa. "Hold off on the deal for a day or two. I'll talk to Vi about getting you a job. Even if your credit's shot, it's not hard to get a loan on a house you own free and clear." A tiny light of hope showed in Lisa's eyes. Ophelia smiled at Donnie again. "Right?"

Rage filled Donnie's face. Ophelia bit her lip to suppress a rush of pleasure, drawing blood. Which also felt damn good, even if the blood was only her own.

"They've already signed a contract," Donnie said.

Ophelia propped her gun against her chest and spread her hands. "What's a contract between friends? Tear it up. Lisa, when you get back from the school we'll make some calls."

Lisa hurried away, her shoulders straighter, but Donnie lingered, following Ophelia toward the compost pile. "Why did you have to tell her that? She's trash. Good riddance."

Ophelia set her gun down and picked up her shovel. She tossed a shovelful of compost. "You're the trash, Donnie, as Violet will tell you herself when she hears about this."

"I didn't do nothing wrong. They're broke, they needed to sell, and I made an offer."

She slung another shovelful and glared at him. "You took advantage of someone else's misfortune. You can forget about getting together with my sister. It won't happen."

Another satisfying flash of hatred answered her. Donnie planted his legs apart and rocked on his heels, watching her, giving her the creeps, but no way would she let that show. "Why are you moving dirt from one pile to another?"

"I'm turning compost for my new garden." *Ha!* "I'm so glad the old garden was destroyed. It's given me the impetus I needed to try something new and different and fabulous. I have *huge* plans." She threw a shovelful more or less in his direction. "Funny, isn't it, how a catastrophe can turn into something wonderful?"

Donnie snarled, "Or something wonderful into a catastrophe. You never know." He clomped away. Ten minutes later she heard his truck start up and burn rubber onto the road.

Ophelia returned to work, mildly uneasy about what Donnie might do, but before long she was so much more uneasy about what she herself was about to do that it hardly mattered. *I will not think about it,* she told herself. *I will just do it, and it will be done.*

She shoveled and sweated and repeated this mantra as she dug deeper and deeper. She heard Lisa and Connie leave; she listened to birds and distant dogs, and wondered why Psyche hadn't come begging for food. Eventually, though, she had dug deep enough and she knew it. Nausea rose in her gullet, but she thrust it back down. The time had come.

She climbed out of the hole, got her water bottle from the truck, and took a long swallow, but it didn't wash away the sick disgust. She took a good look around. Lisa hadn't returned, nor had Donnie. No cop cars stood in Plato's drive, and only light traffic passed on the road. There wouldn't be a better time.

She set the water bottle down, sucked in a deep breath, and donned the gardening gloves she had left at the rim of the hole. She scraped earth from around the big bone she had just exposed. The human bone.

I'm sorry. But I didn't start it, and I never meant it to end this way. I may be a vampire, but that doesn't mean everything's my fault.

Tears sprang uselessly to her eyes. She wouldn't willingly do this to a mole. Finally, she wiped her tears and firmly closed the door on that and any other faltering thought.

"I have no fucking choice," she said out loud—and turned the key on the chipper.

CHAPTER TWENTY-FOUR

Zelda woke in darkness to the sound of blubbering close beside her. She was propped in a sitting position between the sobbing someone and the corner of a tiny dark room, with only a thin line of gray light showing under the door. The room stank of old shoes.

She lifted her head and was greeted by a headache that jostled for attention with the throbbing in her gums, the ache in her shoulders, and the blood in her mouth. Zelda focused on the blood, which tasted incredibly good. She ran her tongue across her gums and scraped it on the tiny sharp tip of a fang. "One down," she muttered, and then, "Oh, crap." Her hands were tied behind her back.

"Zelda!" Joanna bleated right next to her ear. "Thank God you're awake. I'm so scared!"

Zelda's feet were tied together as well. "Crap," she said again. "You're tied up too, right? I don't *believe* this. Donnie knocked us out, tied us up, and dumped us in a closet full of stinky old shoes. This is like some terrible movie, and I'm the TSTL."

"The what?"

"Too stupid to live. There's always a girl like that in bad movies. I *knew* there was something weird going on. I *knew* I shouldn't go into Donnie's house with you, but he likes my mom and I've known him forever, and you looked so miserable, and . . ." Zelda yanked at her bonds. "And I'm an idiot, so I came with you and Donnie anyway."

"I'm sorry." Joanna started to cry. "It's my fault. You were just trying to be nice."

"Yeah, well, there's nice and there's stupid, and I turned out stupid." Zelda yanked again, and the muscles in her shoulders screamed. *Double idiot. Use your brain.* "Don't cry, Joanna. We're in this together and we'll get out of it together."

"It's so dark in here," Joanna said. "I'm sorry, but I'm really, really scared."

Zelda could see okay. She felt a rush of sympathy for Joanna, helpless and generally in the dark. "Donnie took those pictures, right? He was threatening you, so you made up the thing about taking them yourself. It's okay, I'm not mad at you for lying to me."

"I wasn't lying! I did take them myself. He caught me taking them."

"Eew," Zelda said. "That is so gross." She pulled her knees closer to her chest and pushed them forward again, sliding a fraction of an inch along the closet floor.

"Donnie is a nosy, disgusting pig." Joanna's voice quavered indignantly. "He doesn't just look out his own windows, you know. Sometimes he looks in ours, which is how he caught me. I hate him. He took the film and told me he'd send copies of my pictures to all the boys at school if I told on him. And as if that wasn't bad enough, he got them developed and made sure my parents saw them." Her voice rose in panic. "What's he going to do to us?"

"Nothing," Zelda said firmly. "We're going to get away." She shifted her body closer to Joanna and rolled her hip in the other direction. Her key chain dug into her butt. Yes! "Don't start crying again. I've got a plan."

Below them a door slammed. Joanna jolted out a gasp. "It's Donnie!"

No duh. "Shh!"

"Maybe he went out!" Joanna whispered. "Maybe—"

"Nope." Zelda could already hear him on the stairs. "He's

coming up. Pretend you're still unconscious. Don't move, don't say a word."

Heavy footsteps approached the closet door. Another of those ghastly pangs shot through Zelda's gums, and she bit her tongue to stay still. Blood taste again. Nice. She hauled her senses away from the blood and toward the danger she and Joanna faced, wondering what she would do if he tried anything. Bite, she thought, bite hard, and if she got the chance, rip him open. She shuddered at the violent, vampish thoughts.

"Anyone awake in there?" Donnie asked.

Joanna stifled a sob.

"I'm real sorry, girls." Donnie sounded almost sad. "I didn't want to have to lock you up. I don't want to have to hurt you."

Bang! The wall of the closet shook, and a desperate wail tore out of Joanna. Her body vibrated against Zelda's. What the heck was going on? *I'll kill him for scaring Joanna like this.* For a second, Zelda contemplated the positive side of a vamp temper, but a series of bangs almost split her head open. She bit her lip hard to stop from shrieking. More blood.

"Awake now?" Bang! "Y'all weren't supposed to be in Ophelia's house," Donnie said. Bang!

Joanna crumpled against Zelda, valiantly muffling her sobs, and then Zelda figured it out. The old creep was nailing the door shut.

"It's not my fault," Donnie said. "I'm real sorry."

Rage coursed through Zelda, and her gums throbbed and quivered and heaved. She shut her eyes tight, *tight*, and the wave of torment passed. *Easy as pie?*

But Violet hadn't been locked in a closet with someone hammering right next to her aching head at the same moment her fangs fought to slot down for the first time. At the thought of her mother, Zelda almost wept, too. But, no. Later. When they were out of here she could cry all she wanted. She licked the blood where she had bitten her lip and leaned comfortingly, she hoped, against Joanna.

"I have to run an errand, girls, but I can't have you getting out while I'm gone." Bang! "I'll be back real soon." The heavy footsteps clattered down the stairs. A few seconds later a door slammed below.

"Shh!" Zelda listened hard. "There goes his car. Now's our chance." She bumped forward, heedless now of noise. "Move over toward where I was, only with your feet in the corner and your back to me. *Quickly!*"

Joanna snuffled hard and did as she was told, but it took forever to squeeze around in that cramped space. Zelda backed up and squished sideways. "Get your fingers into my pocket. Right here." She bumped her hip against Joanna's butt. "Get the keys out. There's a knife on the key chain. We'll cut the ropes."

Joanna groped toward the pocket.

"You can do it," Zelda said, when after the third try Joanna started crying again. "Just keep trying. That's all it takes, just trying and trying until it works."

"It's so hot in here." Joanna's fingers flailed at the pocket's edge. "It's so stuffy. We're going to suffocate!"

"We will not suffocate. I will gnaw my way through the walls if I have to, but we have plenty of air for now. Just keep. On. Trying." Zelda took a deep breath. *I will not lose my temper. Or my cool.* "Maybe if I lean over you won't have to reach in so far." *Please, please, please.*

Joanna heaved and shoved and strained, and got nowhere. "It's no use," she wailed. "I can't do it. I can't see, and my shoulders hurt, and my fingers are going numb, and my wrists are killing me!"

That's because they were bleeding. "You don't have any choice," Zelda hissed. "Just keep trying. Focus. Concentrate. It's not all that hard!"

Joanna screamed and thrashed and banged her bound feet against the floor. "How do you know how hard it is? You're so fucking perfect! Can't you get scared and cry like a normal girl?"

What?

Embrace the vampire destiny, her mother would say. *Give her what she needs.*

Since the alternative to sacrificing her cool was likely embracing death instead—for both of them—Zelda jumped on it with gusto and relief. "What makes you think I'm not crying?" She let her voice tremble, now that she could. She had to, if it would comfort Joanna. She sniffled. "Just because I don't cry a lot doesn't mean I'm not scared. Besides, I'm saving it for later."

"Saving what? You're talking about sex now?"

Zelda gave a snort of near-hysterical laughter. "Not my virginity, dummy. My *tears*. I'm saving them for when we get out and I can hug my mom and cry buckets." She allowed herself a sob and then bit hard. Blood again. "Try again. Please. You are the Queen of Persistence, and your subjects bow down to you in awe."

Joanna let out a tiny giggle, and sniffled hard and tried again, and a minute later the keys clinked onto the floor.

"Perfect! You saved our lives!" Zelda slid her butt forward, hooked a finger into the ring, and closed her hand around the knife, giving thanks to Constantine for providing her with this miracle tool. She felt around the edges of the little knife, slipped off the safety, placed her finger on the button, and popped the blade smoothly open. "Back-to-back, now." Several agonized minutes of sawing later, the rope binding Joanna's hands gave way. "Now you cut mine. It doesn't matter if you can't see. Do it by feel, and don't worry about cutting me." Zelda held still and waited and prayed, and it took too long, but eventually it was done. "Good job!" She flexed her fingers and eased her tormented shoulders, then grabbed Joanna's raw, bleeding wrists and spat on them before Joanna could stop her. "Slather it in. It'll help, I swear." She sawed through the ropes holding their feet. "Now we get the hell out."

Zelda rammed the knife into the drywall and set to work.

* * *

Gideon laid the second maple tree gently beside the first on an old blue tarp in the trunk of his Mercedes.

"That woman has bewitched you," the chief said.

"Uh-huh." Gideon laid the third maple tree beside the others. "Sure feels good."

"Gideon, I'm serious. I mean what I'm saying."

Gideon got the fourth tree. "You want to meet her, sir? If you see her, you'll understand."

"Goddamn right I'll understand," the chief said, "because I'm a normal man just like you. I did some nosing around last night, and you know what I found out? She's a vampire." Gideon raised his brows and quirked his mouth into the beginnings of a smile, and the chief said, "Damn it, boy, don't give me any sass. You think that vampire gene business is hogwash, but I'm older than you, and by God, I know better." He cleared his throat. "Slept with one, back in the day."

Wonders never ceased. "All the more reason for you to understand how I feel about Ophelia, sir." Gideon wrapped the blue tarp over the trees and unwound a coil of yellow nylon rope.

The chief glared. "You've slept with her?"

Gideon secured the rope to the trunk latch. "With all due respect, sir, my personal life is none of your business."

"You're having an affair with a *suspect*? Are you out of your cotton-picking mind?"

Gideon wound the rope around the trailer hitch below the license plate and tied it off. He straightened and faced the chief. "She's not a suspect, sir."

The chief threw up his hands. "My best detective seduced by a vamp." He stole a glance at Gideon and grinned in spite of himself. "Helluva lay, huh, boy?"

"She's going to marry me," Gideon said.

The smile morphed into an almighty scowl. "Jesus Christ, Gideon, that's just what I was afraid of. You can't marry a woman you've known for three days just because she's good in bed! These vamps may be hot as all hell, but they've got vicious tempers, and they're almost always associated with criminals of one kind or another."

"The underworld offers them protection from the crazies and lowlifes that won't leave them alone. I can offer her the same sort of protection. I know my own mind, and I know she's right for me. And since you know so much about vamps, you also know the county jail would not be safe for Ophelia."

"Where the hell else am I supposed to put her? I can't leave a murderer on the loose. Even Leopard and his goons have to understand that."

Gideon raised his eyes to heaven. "She's not a murderer. If she were dangerous, Leopard would have taken care of it by now." He opened the passenger door for the chief. "How about you ride with me today?"

"Donnie Donaldson isn't a murderer either," the chief protested. "He's a solid citizen. All you have are theories, Gideon, and not one ounce of proof." He got into the Mercedes.

The third anonymous phone call must have been coming into the station right at that moment, because they hadn't been on the road more than a minute when Gideon got the dispatcher's call. "Is the chief with you?" Jeanie asked. "He'll probably kill me for calling you instead of him. It's the same anonymous creep again. Wants to know why we haven't searched Ophelia's house."

"That's it?"

"Also why we're letting a murderess run around loose. *Murderess*. What a word. It's straight out of gothic romance. He was on a pay phone in Hammond."

"Which means he's at least twenty minutes away, closer to thirty," Gideon told the chief, hoping like hell during the whole drive to Ophelia's place. Yes! Donnie's driveway was empty.

"That doesn't prove a thing," the chief said.

"It doesn't eliminate him, either." Gideon pulled past

Ophelia's house and parked beside the first of her compost piles.

"Damn," the chief said when he saw the bat house askew against the greenhouse. "Not a bad-looking bat house. The vandal do that?"

"There aren't any bats in there, only wasps." Gideon got out and opened the rear door for his dog. Gretchen leaped out and took off toward the chipper.

"Tsk." The chief wandered toward the bat house. "I could have helped her with that. Damn shame she's going to jail."

"Now who's lost their objectivity? If there's something in her house, it's another plant. And if you had let me put someone on surveillance here . . ." But the chief wasn't listening, so Gideon didn't waste his breath. He untied the ropes holding the trunk and unloaded the trees.

The chipper choked to a halt. "Goddamn this fucking machine to hell!" came Ophelia's furious voice, followed by a panicked roar. "No! Gretchen, put that down!"

Gideon surged forward at a run but stopped short. Fangs full down, Ophelia grappled with Gretchen in the dirt, ripped a bone from between her jaws and tossed it into a hole behind her.

What the fuck? "Gretchen. Come here."

The dog scrambled to obey. Ophelia picked up a shotgun from beside the chipper, her eyes flickering here and there, a wave of vampire energy and terror slamming into Gideon. Gretchen skidded to a halt beside him, whimpering. Ophelia leveled the gun in their direction.

Déjà vu, except this time Ophelia wasn't acting cool.

The chief, still by the greenhouse, threw himself to the ground. "Get down, damn it!" He groped for his gun.

"She won't shoot me," Gideon said in a loud, clear voice. "I can't say the same for you, Chief, so you'd better stay put."

"What the hell do you want?" Ophelia's voice shook with rage and fear.

"Gideon," the chief implored.

"I mean it, sir. Gretchen, *stay*. Guard the chief." Gideon picked up two maple trees and walked calmly toward Ophelia. "Having problems?"

Ophelia backed toward the chipper, her shotgun wavering in the general direction of the chief. "Why are you here?" she croaked. "Why did you have to come?"

"To bring the trees." Gideon tried a light, carefree voice. It wasn't easy, faced with fangs full down and another blast of allure. "Sorry we surprised you, honey. It's understandable that you'd be in a state of nerves, but . . . Ah, I see you've already dug a hole."

Ophelia lowered the gun and leaned trembling against the chipper, her face pale with misery, her eyes empty of hope. Gideon walked right past her, eyeballed the big thigh bone in the hole and a few others poking up. He set one of the trees down on top of them. He put the other tree on the ground beside the hole. Jesus Christ. He sure hadn't figured this one right.

He went right up to her. "You couldn't have waited till later?" he said in a low, savage voice, unable to contain his fury at her recklessness, his fear at her peril. "He's been here for two fucking years, hasn't he?"

Ophelia gaped. "You knew?"

Sort of. But there was no time to explain.

Ophelia's whisper was harsh, but her eyes betrayed her. "When was I supposed to do it? I can't run the chipper at night!"

Gideon found his voice again. "You couldn't have waited a day or two till this other fiasco was over? Until you were a tad less likely to be caught?"

Ophelia's knuckles whitened around the barrel of the gun. "You were supposed to be at the dump this morning. If you knew, why did you come here?"

"I didn't know, but . . ." It wasn't the time to bring up the trust issue again, but by God she would hear about it later. He signaled to the chief to stay back and forced himself to speak low and calm. "I assumed Constantine had killed him."

"He was on tour at the time."

And she'd been all alone. "What happened? Did Parkerson attack you? Rape you?"

Ophelia drooped. "He tried."

Gideon let out a long, harsh breath. "Then he got what he deserved." He let that sit. "But you can't put him through the chipper."

Ophelia shuddered. "No." She closed her eyes. "But I wanted you so badly, you and your garden, and I've been stuck out here by myself with him and those awful dreams for so long. . . . I couldn't think of any other way." She shuddered again. "I guess it doesn't matter now."

"You're right, it doesn't. This is one hell of a mess." Gideon put an arm around her. She cringed and curled into herself, but he pulled her closer anyway and deposited a kiss on her hair. "I need you to vamp the chief."

"What?" She looked blank. Almost absent. Damn.

"You've got to get him on your side." The chief was getting to his feet now, scowling in their direction. Gideon picked up a sizeable twig and poked it tentatively into the chipper. "Do whatever you vamps do. He's obsessed with bats, which might be useful. Take him on a tour of your bat houses and go heavy on the allure." *Wake up, girl,* he wanted to say. *Don't go all emotional on me now.* "He thinks you've bewitched me."

"And have I?" She sounded desperately sad.

"No doubt about that." Gideon stifled his impatience with a smile. "Listen, honey, the chief's a stubborn old fart with a one-track mind. He won't buy my theories about Donnie, and this morning there was another anonymous call saying to search your house. If you can arouse the chief's chivalrous instincts—"

"Unfortunately, that's not all that will be aroused," Ophelia said.

"I'm not asking you to sleep with him." Gideon resisted the urge to shake her. "He knows you're a vamp, he's been with one himself, and he knows enough about vampires to be wary of their legendary tempers. Trust me, if you can show him you're a desirable, sweet-natured woman who values his advice about bats, he'll want to shift tracks." He took her by the arm. "Perk up, Ophelia. You've dealt with this for a long time. You can't afford to give in to your emotions now." He guided her toward the chief. "I have to go make some calls."

Her eyes flicked miserably toward the grave. "But, Gideon, what about . . . Gideon, I know you're a cop, but do you have to get involved with this? Don't you understand what it means?"

"I don't have any choice," Gideon said.

CHAPTER TWENTY-FIVE ❧

Hemmed in by trust and betrayal, Ophelia hustled the police chief to the river, tossing out allure and making no effort to control her fangs. In the clearing by the water, she relented long enough to let him appreciate the bat houses, because his enthusiasm was so genuine. After a while she led the march toward home. Time to dump the chief back on Gideon and get on with going straight to hell.

Gretchen had other ideas. "I don't want your dumb dog along," Ophelia had told Gideon, but he'd said, "Please take her," visibly controlling his annoyance, and she still didn't know why she'd gone along with it. Why help him safeguard the remains that would send her to prison? "Get out of my goddamn way," Ophelia told the dog four times along the track and once more as they finally neared the end of the woods. "Stop trying to comfort me, damn it." Gretchen bumped her flank gently against Ophelia's.

"Don't burden him with your past," Constantine had said, and now she knew why.

Gideon was a cop. He'd found evidence of a homicide. True, she'd been defending herself. True, it hadn't been her fault. Still, he had no choice but to report it. Except that he'd promised she'd always be safe with him. And she had believed him, even in her sleep.

Gretchen jostled Ophelia again, and the chief hollered something tedious about stopping or shooting. Asshole. Tapping her toe on the dirt track, Ophelia waited for the old man to catch up. In this mood, she doubted she could have sweetened him up even if she'd been trying. Briefly, she considered bopping him on the head—gently, just to get him out of the way—and going on the run. But setting aside the loneliness of such a life, she shriveled at the thought of being caught and dragged back to Gideon in chains, so to speak, after he had—*get this*—trusted her. It would be more dignified—she almost laughed—to give in now. To disregard the simmering rage since he had waved her and the chief toward the river while he leaned uncaringly on his Mercedes and made his calls.

It didn't make sense. It felt terrifyingly wrong. And some foolish part of her, deep inside, still wanted to trust him. A wasp sailed by, and she envied its life uncomplicated by murders and incomprehensible cops. Didn't he know what would happen to him after she ended up in jail?

No. For the umpteenth time, she shut out that horrifying thought. *We'll see each other in hell.* She stifled a hysterical giggle.

The chief came up beside her, wheezing. "Where is that damned Gideon?" he gasped. "I should fire him: sleeping with a suspect, disappearing in the middle of a murder investigation, leaving me in the clutches of a vampire—" He grew more and more incensed, and the wasps had picked up on his mood. One zoomed out of the wonky bat house, and then another.

"I've hardly vamped you at all," Ophelia said. "You're in a lot more danger from these wasps than from me. All Gideon wants me to do is convince you that I'm innocent." She shifted the shotgun on her shoulder.

"You'd look a lot more innocent if you put that gun down."

"We already discussed this, mister," Ophelia said. "I don't trust you any more than you trust me." She grinned at him, fangs and all.

"Don't do that," groaned the chief, wiping his brow on his sleeve.

Ophelia stuck out her tongue, making the old cop shudder and hurry away toward the greenhouse. Gretchen stuck out her tongue, too, and lolloped in the direction of the chipper and the gruesome hole in the earth. Idly, since it didn't matter anymore what Gretchen dug up, Ophelia watched her go. Over the top of the chipper, past the last of the compost piles, poked the tops of three young Japanese maples, two upright and one bent, in a tight row.

A tiny door of hope opened in Ophelia's mind. She tried to shut it again, but the door was open and she desperately wanted it to stay that way. He'd said she should trust him.

From over in the direction of the chipper she heard him, a muffled curse the chief would never catch, and the soft click of a car door.

The older man's voice interrupted her scurrying thoughts. "After you spray the wasps," he was saying, his eyes on the bat box hanging askew on the vandalized greenhouse, "clear out all the empty nests. Then I'll take a look at the inside and see if you need to redesign the roosting spaces." He shook his head. "I don't know why I'm telling you this. You're going to prison for the rest of your life."

"I'm *innocent*, you dumbass cop. I'll clean it out after the wasps leave on their own. I don't kill anything I don't have to." It about killed *her* not to look toward the chipper.

The chief snorted. "You can't go around with a gun in your hand and fangs in your mouth and say you don't kill anything."

"Of course I can. It's the truth." If only she could see what Gideon had done.

Donnie's truck pulled up in the driveway next door. The idiot chief gave the murderer a friendly wave. "Where the hell is Gideon?" he said again.

Any minute now the chief would find Gideon, but Gideon might need more time.

Ophelia whipped her shotgun into position and eyed Donnie down the sights. "How about I put him out of his misery now?" Donnie froze halfway from the truck to the porch. The chief swore and went for his gun, but Ophelia shot him a mesmerizing smile. "He'll suffer a far worse fate at Leopard's hands. Consider it a mercy killing." Donnie edged toward his back stairs.

The chief dragged his gun out of its holster, hands shaking, fighting her allure.

Ophelia lowered the shotgun. "Calm down," she told him. "I'm not really going to shoot him. It was just a joke." Donnie sprinted for the door.

"Lousy joke," the chief growled as Donnie made it to safety. "Where the fuck is my detective?"

Ophelia answered with another dazzling smile. "Who knows? I need to freshen up. Come and wait for Gideon at my place. It's getting hot out here."

The chief melted under that smile. "Shit," he said, "I can't believe that after all these years, an old man like me—"

"Some things never change." She herded him toward the back stairs, riding high on hope and trust, when she caught sight of the bike.

Zelda's bike, stashed to one side of the porch.

Zelda was here? Since when?

Ophelia hopped up the back steps. The hook on the screen door had been popped, and the shim lay where Zelda must have dropped it. Ophelia hurried indoors. "Zelda?"

Only Psyche answered, with a querulous meow. The skin on Ophelia's scalp prickled. Why were her earrings lined up in pairs on the kitchen table? And the Midol on the counter . . . She hadn't put it there. Psyche showed up in the entrance to the hall, spied the chief, and spat.

"Sit down," Ophelia said. The chief must have started thinking straight again, for he only reluctantly obeyed. "Don't touch the cat. She hates men." Ophelia made a quick pass though the house: living room, spare bedroom, bathroom, her own room.

"Where are you going?" The chief blundered down the hall, pursued by Psyche's furious yowl.

Ophelia ran into him in the doorway of her room, the vibrator in one hand and the shotgun in the other. "Zelda wouldn't come here to fool around with my sex toys." Gideon wouldn't have left this kind of mess, either. The chief flushed deep red as she shoved the purple vibrator into his hand. "It has to mean something," she added, figuring it out even as she spoke. She whirled, kicked the area rug away, and knelt to open the secret compartment.

"That slime!" She grabbed the pile of snapshots. "That unspeakable lump of shit!" Ophelia shoved the shotgun under her arm, snapped off the rubber band, and leafed through the photos. She glared at the gawking chief. "I can handle being accused of murder," she said, slapping the photos into his unoccupied hand. Murder wasn't far from the truth. "But this child-abuse crap really burns me up. God only knows what harm that sleaze bucket has done to Joanna."

The chief stared at the photos with Christmas-gift glee. He avoided Ophelia's eyes, his gaze flicking toward her shotgun.

"No, I did not take these photos," Ophelia said. "No, I didn't know they were here, no, I will not put the gun down—and where the hell is my niece?"

She stormed down the hall past the cop. Zelda wouldn't just walk off. Not only was there nowhere to walk to except the river, and she knew Zelda wasn't there, but Zelda would have left a note. She spied the unfamiliar bowl on the floor holding scraps. Where had it come from? Not Zelda. Ophelia thought about calling Vi. Best not to start a panic yet.

"Ms. Beliveau." The chief came into the kitchen. "I need you to stop right there." He dropped the photos on the table and yanked at his gun, his other hand still clamped around the purple vibrator.

"You look ridiculous," Ophelia said.

Psyche hissed and swiped at the cop's leg. He yelped and swore at the cat. "Ms. Beliveau—"

"I have to find my niece." She wrenched open the door and leaped down the steps. A solitary Midol stared up at her, blue against the dead grass. "How did that pill get there?"

"Ms. Beliveau, I don't want to have to get rough with you."

Ophelia turned with a brilliant smile. "Then don't."

The chief wavered in the warm spring sunshine. Two doors down, a white Lexus drove up. Lisa Wyler jumped out and plunged toward them, waving her arms. Ophelia spied the first earring, then the yellow one at the verge of the drive. She strode across her dead lawn and the driveway, toward Donnie's house.

"Ms. Beliveau!" thundered the chief.

The third earring glistened in the sun on Donnie's trim green grass. Ophelia's heart thumped frantically and her fangs slotted down hard.

"She's not at school," Lisa sobbed, crossing Donnie's yard. "Did she come back here?"

Hell. Ophelia pushed her fangs up. "I haven't seen her, Lisa, but I'm afraid—"

A hard hand gripped Ophelia's arm and the cool muzzle of a gun jabbed into her back. "Ms. Beliveau, you're under arrest," the chief said. "If you so much as look at me, I'll shoot."

"You're right," Zelda said from her perch on Joanna's shoulders. "The tile stops here." She licked a bleeding finger and pounded a hunk of drywall down into the bathtub, then started with the knife again. Her hand howled with the pain of fighting the knife against backer board and tiles, jamming it into closely spaced studs in the front and one end of the closet, knocking against exterior wall at the other end, and finally trying the backer board again. Joanna had done her share of messing with the walls, and it was Joanna who had suggested Zelda sit on her shoulders and try the top of the wall, which might not be tiled. "Thank God one of us is thinking straight. When I get pissed off, my brain short-circuits." She grunted, forcing the knife sideways to widen the hole. "I'm so mad I'm ready to bust."

"I'm just plain scared," Joanna said.

"I used to think I was a patient person." Zelda bashed at the drywall, and another hunk fell away. "I used to think I had self-control."

"I used to think I was a wimp," Joanna said. "So did you. But I'm not a wimp. I'm just scared."

"Rightly so." Zelda changed hands, braced herself, and smashed her bruised fist against the last bit of wallboard. "That's it. Here I go." She folded the knife, dropped it in her pocket, and hefted herself to a standing position on Joanna's shoulders.

"Oh God," Joanna said. "I'll die in here alone."

"You won't be alone for long," Zelda panted. She slung one leg through and toppled sideways, scrabbling at the hole to slow her descent, landing with a thump in the tub. "So far, so good." She headed straight for the window, which faced in the direction of Joanna's house. "No cars at your place. I'll be right back." From the only room across the hall, the view was similarly bleak: no vehicles in Ophelia's drive either.

Zelda skittered downstairs and through the main floor a mile a minute. No phone. One locked door. Probably Donnie's office, where of course his phone would be. She kicked the office door, yelped, and Joanna wailed wordlessly from above.

"Coming!" Zelda bounded up the stairs to the room where they had been confined. An ornate chair and dresser, a king-size bed covered in a red velvet spread. Ick. Obviously it was Donnie's room. The decor was a parody of Blood and Velvet, and a picture of Violet dominated the dresser. Tears jumped into Zelda's eyes, immediately superseded by sick fury at the thought of Donnie anywhere near her mother. Her emerging fangs, which had been mercifully quiescent for a while, throbbed angrily. She cast around the room for a way out of this mess, her brain pulsing with thoughts of vengeance and bloody murder.

Aha! Donnie had left the hammer on the bedroom floor instead of stowing it back in his belt, which showed how rattled he must be, because he never went anywhere without a hammer. Zelda couldn't bring herself to feel the least bit sorry for him. She jammed the claw of the hammer under one of the nails in the door. "I'm going to get you out. Would you believe Donnie has a picture of my mom in here? He's so vile!"

"Did you call the cops?" Joanna asked.

"I couldn't get into his office, where the phone is." Zelda wrenched hard and her biceps screamed, but the nail came partway out. "I swear, he will never touch you. Or my mother." Her fangs bucked inside their slots, and the tip that had already broken through tore a little farther down. Zelda took a deep breath to quell the pain. "I am vampire," she whispered to herself, verging on maniacal laughter. She savored the small trickle of blood from her torn gum. "I will prevail." Rising confidence and fear clashed inside her.

"Go to Ophelia's or to my place," Joanna squeaked. "Go call the cops while you can."

Next nail: jam, wrench, wrench. "And leave you alone in here? No way."

"I'll be okay." The quaver in Joanna's voice said that she definitely wouldn't.

"You'll die in there alone, remember?" *Crap. My big mouth does it again.*

"Zelda, don't be mean to me! I'm trying!"

"Sorry," Zelda panted. "I know you are." So much for patience. So much for tact. "I'm the one who's losing it." The third nail came out. "Oh, shit."

"What?"

"I just heard Donnie's truck." Joanna stoically cut off a whimper, and Zelda's heart squeezed. *Patience and tact, step aside. Fury is taking over.* Zelda narrowed her eyes at the nail in her hand, at the closet, at a scattering of unused nails on the floor . . .

Got it! "I'll nail the bedroom door shut." Zelda drove the first nail into the closed bedroom door at an angle where it abutted the frame, just as Donnie had done with the closet. "Then I'll get you out." Second nail. "Then we'll make a plan. He can't stop both of us." *He sure as hell can't stop me.* Bam, bam, wham! Third nail. By the time Donnie slammed the back door shut, the fourth nail was in. She dragged the chair across the room and whacked more nails into the top and the other side of the door.

Donnie's footsteps pounded up the stairs. He rattled the door handle, but the door didn't budge. Yes! He spat out curses and banged on the door, and Zelda whammed home another nail. "Go away, you old creep," she hollered. "How dare you have a picture of my mother?" She hauled the chair to the closet as Donnie's footsteps thumped down the stairs.

"Here's the strategy," she said, yanking at the highest nail. "He'll break the door down eventually. Our plan is to get past him. Discombobulate him enough that we get out and down the stairs. If we manage to hurt him, great, but the focus is on getting at least one or both of us away."

"We can't get out the window?"

"Last resort," Zelda said. *Two more nails.* "It's a long way down, and you can't run away if your leg is broken. Oh, why isn't Ophelia here?"

"Or my mom." Joanna sniffled.

Zelda bit back her opinion of Joanna's mom. "Weapons," she said. "This hammer, for one." She wrenched at the last nail. "The bedside lamp." One last yank, and the nail slipped free. She opened the closet door, and Joanna stumbled out.

She grabbed Zelda and hugged her tight. Zelda hugged her back. "We're almost there."

Donnie was on the stairs again, so she let go. Her fangs quivered and her heart rammed against her chest. "Any weapons in the closet?"

"Stinky old shoes?"

"Sure. Bring them all out." Zelda yanked the lamp cord from the wall. "Bash him with this. I'll take the hammer. The shoes are the second line of defense."

Joanna took the lamp. "Zelda, your mouth is bleeding!"

"Don't I know it," Zelda replied, clutching her jaw with her free hand as her fangs fought for freedom and Donnie commenced his assault on the door.

"You have the right to remain silent!" said the chief.

Ophelia spoke through clenched teeth, through quivering fangs she could barely suppress. "And you have the obligation to shut up and help me!" The gun at her back didn't budge. "Here comes a hysterical mother. That's two missing girls! Can't you see?" She pointed with the shotgun, one by one. "Pill. Earring, Earring, Earring." And one more earring by Donnie's back steps. "Zelda and Joanna are in there!"

Lisa panted to a halt. "Joanna's at Donnie's?"

The chief brandished the purple vibrator, jabbing the gun into Ophelia's back. "Ms. Beliveau, that's the stupidest attempt to divert my attention I've ever seen. Drop the gun."

"Maybe you should holster yours, since you know so little about gun safety. If I drop it, it might go off." She heard frantic hammering inside Donnie's place. What the hell?

Lisa stared. "Is that a vibrator?" She snickered, but the smirk faded. "Who are you? Why are you pointing a gun at Ophelia?"

The chief reddened and threw the vibrator down. He moved around beside Ophelia, trailing the gun across her back, and grabbed the shotgun. "I'm the chief of police, ma'am, and Ms. Beliveau's implicated in three murders. I need you to go on home. Ms. Beliveau's a dangerous woman. No telling what she might do."

"Goddamn right I'm dangerous," Ophelia said. "Donnie's the murderer, not me. All I want is to rescue those girls before Donnie kills them, too." She shuddered with impatience. "Come on, Lisa. Stand up for me!"

"Bullshit," said the chief. "I saw those nudie pictures in your house—"

"Where Donnie planted them. He knew about that compartment. He made it for the guy who lived here before me." Lisa Wyler was dithering between Ophelia and the cop. "For cripes sake, Lisa, we've been through this already. You know I wouldn't hurt Joanna. Donnie was in cahoots with the creep who blackmailed you. He took all your savings, and now he's taking your house. He even encouraged Willy's drinking binges. What have I ever done to you? Go break down his door." She raised her voice. "Tell him the cops are here. Demand to search his house for your daughter—"

"Shut up!" The chief stuck the shotgun under his arm and clicked the radio button on his phone. "I need backup. Beliveau's place. Send at least one female officer, and quick."

"There are children at risk," yelled Ophelia. "Make sure it's a woman with brains!"

"Goddamn it, girl!" the chief bellowed. An indignant squawk issued from the radio and the gun in Ophelia's side wavered. "No, not you, Jeanie. You know I wouldn't yell at you. It's Ms. Beliveau. She's a vicious criminal, and she's making a ruckus for no reason at all."

Crashing, smashing noises and a shrill scream came from Donnie's house. Damn, *damn!*

"Give me a break," Jeanie said. "Backup is on the way. Hold tight, Ms. Beliveau."

"Goddamn it, Jeanie," the chief roared.

"Thank you!" Ophelia called.

A window on the second floor of Donnie's house splintered and a gilded lamp plummeted to the ground. Its red lampshade bounced and rolled away. "Help!" Joanna shrieked. "Call the police!" The cop's gun wavered even more.

"Asshole!" Zelda hollered. A shoe came through the window, followed by a cry of such agony that the world stood still.

Ophelia knocked the gun out of the chief's slackened grip, seized the shotgun, and made for Donnie's back door. She smashed the window with the butt of the shotgun, reached in, and opened the door. She leaped up the stairs and lunged through what had once been a bedroom door.

"Stay back!" Wild-eyed, a cracked picture frame on his head, blood smeared on his scalp, Donnie Donaldson tightened an arm around a thrashing Joanna. In his other hand he gripped a screwdriver. "Put the gun down. I'll skewer her, I swear." His voice shook, and so did the hand that held the screwdriver.

Ophelia laid the shotgun gently on the floor. Joanna's struggles slowed as she fought to breathe against Donnie's deathly clasp. An old sneaker fell from her hand. Zelda rose from her knees, a trickle of blood running over her lip. "It's okay, Joanna," Ophelia said. "Donnie doesn't really want to hurt you." Lisa's voice, shrill with hysteria, rose through the window. "Your mom's down there, and so are the cops. It'll be all right."

"Nothing will ever be all right again." Donnie's voice broke. "Would you believe my asshole of a partner wanted to blackmail you for sex? I gave you so many chances, and you still screwed everything up. Why couldn't you just sell me your land, you stupid, stupid bitch?"

Because . . .

No. This was not her responsibility. This was not her fault.

"You should have told me about your plans, Donnie," Ophelia said sadly. "We would have worked something out." But no, it wasn't her fault. Ophelia widened her eyes at Zelda, crawling bloody-mouthed up from the floor, shiny new fangs extended, eyes on fire. Oh, shit. "Zelda, it's okay. Stay down. You don't have to do this."

Donnie's eyes flicked to Zelda. He yelped, stumbled backward over a sledgehammer, and dropped Joanna. She hit the floor with a thud and a crack, and her eyes slid shut. Donnie seized the sledgehammer and scuttled backward.

"He scared my friend," Zelda sobbed. She licked the blood off her lips. "He *hurt* her. She may even be dead."

"She's not dead," Ophelia said. "She's just unconscious. Stay out of the way."

Donnie gripped the sledgehammer and eased sideways toward the bedside table. Shit, again. Where were the cops when you *needed* them?

"Let me go to my baby!" Lisa sobbed from below.

"Ouch! Get us some backup!" roared the chief. "Male backup! Somebody sane! Some crazy woman's clobbering me with a vibrator!"

"He has the hots for my *mother*," Zelda snarled. "I'm going to rip him apart."

"No, you aren't." Ophelia slotted down her fangs. *I survived this. I can survive it again.* "I am."

Donnie eased open the drawer in the bedside table, and Ophelia crouched to spring.

"The hell with that," Gideon said from the doorway.

Donnie pulled out a handgun, and Gideon shot him dead.

CHAPTER TWENTY-SIX 🌷

Joanna and her mother had gone to the hospital in an ambulance. Donnie's body went in another ambulance to the morgue. Two sorts of backup had shown up: two cops, one the promised female, and Constantine.

"Gideon called me," the rocker said with a twisted grin. "Thought I might be needed."

The police chief, now Gideon's fervent supporter, wandered through the scene, rehearsing his statement to the press. Ophelia mothered Zelda until Violet arrived, and then walked quietly away to inspect the maple trees Gideon had planted. His car still stood next to the chipper. She looked at the car and the trees again and wondered, but when Gretchen bounded over to snuffle eagerly at the trunk of the Mercedes, she knew for sure.

Ophelia gave a short statement to the female cop, and Zelda, holding a tissue to her mouth, gave an even shorter one. "This is it, Gideon?" a member of the crime-scene crew quipped. "No more bodies for a couple of days?"

Zelda flexed her jaw and surreptitiously fingered her fangs. She huddled on Ophelia's steps beside her mother, whose white lace top was streaked, liked Ophelia's, with Zelda's blood.

"They're not supposed to rip out of your gums like that," Violet said over and over again. "Poor sweetie. My poor, poor baby."

"There was no choice," Ophelia said. "It was a case of sprout her fangs or die."

Violet shuddered but said, "Stop playing with your fangs, Zelda, or the cuts will never heal. Your saliva will handle only so much."

"Be thankful she didn't have to use them," Ophelia said.

"I'm thankful neither of you had to. Ripping people apart is simply ghastly. Not that I've ever done it, but I can imagine—"

Actually, you can't. Ophelia and Constantine exchanged glances, and Constantine winked. And then laughed.

Finally, Gideon beckoned to Ophelia. She walked away with him, guiding him a lot farther from the others than he deemed necessary. He had a lot to learn about living with vamps.

"Everyone can go home now," he said. "We'll get signed statements later. Our guys found a couple of trash bags of photo-shop stuff at the Taylor Road dump, right next to a roll of carpet cushion and some computer equipment. I'll make sure no one's secrets get out. Art's job is safe, and Andrea and her kids can come home."

Ophelia breathed him in, his scent and his strength, and waited for whatever came next.

He held out the keys to his car, to his house, to his entire future, and spoke very low. "Unless you have something urgent to do here, why not take my car—by yourself—and go dig up my mother's rose garden?" Apparently he mistook the reason for her hesitation, for he added diffidently, "Unless . . . You have other resources to take care of things, if you'd prefer."

Ophelia glanced at Constantine, lounging darkly in one of the plastic chairs, a little smile hovering on his lips. She turned away, feeling Constantine's smile grow. "You don't have to do this," she told Gideon, not meaning it at all.

"Just don't plant daisies," Gideon said.

* * *

In the light of the full moon, they lowered Johnny's bones into the hole Ophelia had dug in Gideon's garden. "I couldn't leave him to Constantine," Ophelia said. "Maybe I would have, if he'd been in town when it first happened. But now . . ." She tossed in a shovelful of dirt and stopped to lean on her shovel. "Constantine might have dumped him in a swamp. I couldn't do that."

"Most people don't end up under a beautiful garden," Gideon said. "Johnny is being cared for far beyond his deserts, and eventually Marissa will be able to declare him dead and move on with her life." He threw one shovelful after another into the grave. "Constantine already played a highly useful role."

"He's always been a good friend to me, but I didn't want this"—she gestured with her shovel—"to be Constantine's problem. Only mine." Ophelia sighed. "And now it's yours."

"Ours," Gideon said.

When the grave was full, Ophelia led the way back toward the house. "I still don't understand. You're a cop. You have to take homicide seriously. You're not supposed to cover it up, even if you think it was self-defense. I appreciate it, but . . ."

"Do you have a better solution?" Gideon asked.

Ophelia propped her shovel against the deck. She shook her head.

"Even if I didn't take into consideration my own skin and yours, how would justice be served if you went to jail?" Gideon asked. "Even if you survived that, even if Lep didn't kill me and possibly my boss, you'd spend endless time, and money you don't have, trying to prove it was self-defense, and even then you'd probably end up serving time. As it is, the only person I can't help out is Marissa Parkerson, and frankly, weighing things in the balance, I just don't care. I do my best to work things out fairly for as many people as possible. No way I'll follow rules and procedure if they make matters worse."

Ophelia raised her eyes to Gideon. It had to be said: "I'm not a trusting sort of person."

"You mean I *still* haven't earned your trust?" He didn't sound upset. He chuckled as he set his shovel next to hers and went to free the dogs from their pen. "Even if I weren't such a trustworthy guy, you've got me by the balls now in too many ways to count."

"It's not right." Ophelia rinsed her hands long and carefully under the outdoor tap. "But I still want the garden. And I want you."

"And my finger. Mustn't forget that." Gideon followed her up the steps to the deck and pulled her onto his lap on a bench by the wall. She leaned uneasily against him. The night breezes sighed and the milling dogs subsided one by one onto the deck.

"It's not going to be easy," Ophelia said. "It's never going to be safe."

"Works for me," Gideon said. "Tell you what. You don't have to trust me, but I get to glare at you suspiciously anytime I like."

"It's a deal," Ophelia said, smiling a little now, twining her fingers into his and relaxing into his embrace.

For a long time they stayed there, in love in a twisted garden, and at last the sun rose on a brighter day.

So you like vampires? You're not alone.

Don't miss the part steampunk Victorian
historical, part futuristic thriller

Crimson & Steam
by
Liz Maverick

. . . He found her on a stretch of Santa Monica Boulevard, just inside an alcove. She stood frozen, silent, her face obscured by shadow. He grabbed her by the shoulders and spun her toward some dull light oozing from a nearby store's half-broken bulb.

"Coward," she spat. "Do I have to make it really easy for you, so you can't refuse? Should I just rip my clothes off and beg?" She pulled the tie holding together her wrap blouse, and the fabric cascaded away. "Do it. Here in this alley, Marius. Please."

"Jillian, don't!" Marius's blood raced. Exposed neck, pale shoulders, pink-tipped breasts—all delicate flesh and the black lace of her transparent bra. He'd never seen Jill this way. He'd only dreamed of it.

"I will. I'll beg," she continued. "I'll do whatever you need to make this okay. I'm not afraid of what we have. Why the hell are you?"

She pulled the hem of her skirt up and leaned back against the brick wall. Marius tried to wrench her skirt down, but she was pulling out all the stops and rudely pressed her palm against his groin. "Don't try to tell me no," she murmured. "I know what you want. I know what I feel."

"Stop, Jillian. Stop!" Marius begged. He forced himself to ignore the pulsing of his erection in her hand and grabbed the ends of her shirt, tying them together as best he could. Without thought, he closed his eyes and pressed his mouth to the crown of her head. "Please," he whispered. "I never meant to hurt you, and—"

"'Hurt me . . . ,'" Jillian echoed.

She reached into her pocket and pulled out a switchblade. Flicking it expertly open she said, "Hayden gave this to me. Hayden, your worst enemy. At the time I thought it was a really shitty birthday present, but it always seems to come in handy." Transfixing Marius with her stare, she held the knife to her neck. "Could you resist me if I made myself bleed for you? I know what it's like when you smell blood. That means my blood will make you insane, if you feel half of what I think you do for me. You won't be able to stop yourself, and it won't be your fault." She swallowed hard. "I'm not afraid."

"Enough!" Marius roared, baring his fangs. The switchblade clattered to the pavement. "Enough." He took her face in his hands. "This isn't you. This is not who you are."

Jillian slowly pulled free and backed up, collecting her weapon.

"Do you think this helps?" Marius continued, unable to contain himself any longer. "Do you think I feel no pain? I watch you run around with Hayden Wilks, and you think it doesn't kill me? He gets to have you in every way that I cannot. It makes no difference that I understand why you're with him, that I know you don't love him. It doesn't matter, because . . . yes." His hands dug into Jill's shoulders as he struggled to stay in control. "I can feel you. Do you understand? I can sense you. I know when he's with you, when he's touching you, when . . ." He had to look away. "Knowing I could make you feel so much more, that my feelings for you go so much deeper, that you've given yourself to someone who doesn't deserve you because I'm not allowed to have the life I want to live . . . It makes me feel like dying sometimes. You must understand how much I care about you. But—"

"But not enough," she interrupted. Then, with a hitch in her voice she added, "Soul mates aren't supposed to end like this."

Marius dropped his hands. "I'm sorry."

CRIMSON & STEAM
by
LIZ MAVERICK

The Shattered Sylph

L. J. McDonald

SHATTERED

Kidnapped by slavers, Lizzie Petrule was dragged in chains across the Great Sea to the corrupt empire of Meridal. There, beneath a floating citadel and an ocean of golden sand, lies a pleasure den for gladiators—and a prison for the maidens forced to slake their carnal thirst.

Despite impossible odds, against imponderable magic, three men have vowed Lizzie's return: Justin, her suitor; Leon, her father; and Ril, the shape-shifting but war-weary battler. Together, this broken band can save her, but only with a word that must remain unsaid, a foe that is a friend, and a betrayal that is, at heart, an act of love.

ISBN 13: 978-0-8439-6323-6

Gayle Ann Williams

NO SAFE HARBOR

With her badass rain boots, her faithful dog, and the ability to predict the monster tsunamis that have reduced the US to a series of islands, Kathryn O'Malley isn't afraid of much. Cut off from all society, she takes to the airwaves as Tsunami Blue, hoping to save something of humanity as the world around her crumbles. But Blue should be afraid—because her message reaches the wrong ears.

Now she's the target of ruthless pirates known as Runners who want to use her special talents for their own profiteering—as soon as they can find her. Blue's only shot at survival lies with the naked stranger who washes up on her rocky beach. A man who might just be working for Runners himself. Torn between suspicion and attraction, the two will have to navigate a surging tide of danger and deceit if they hope to stay alive.

TSUNAMI BLUE

ISBN 13: 978-0-505-52821-6

ELISABETH NAUGHTON

THERON—Dark haired, duty bound and deceptively deadly. He's the leader of the Argonauts, an elite group of guardians that defends the immortal realm from threats of the Underworld.

From the moment he walked into the club, Casey knew this guy was different. Men like that just didn't exist in real life—silky shoulder-length hair, chest impossibly broad, and a predatory manner that just screamed dark and dangerous. He was looking for something. Her.

She was the one. She had the mark. Casey had to die so his kind could live, and it was Theron's duty to bring her in. But even as a 200-year-old descendent of Hercules, he wasn't strong enough to resist the pull in her fathomless eyes, to tear himself away from the heat of her body.

As war with the Underworld nears, someone will have to make the ultimate sacrifice.

MARKED

ISBN 13: 978-0-505-52822-3

Dorchester Publishing is proud to present

⊰ PUBLISHER'S PLEDGE ⊱

We GUARANTEE this book!

We are so confident that you will enjoy this book that we are offering a 100% money-back guarantee.

If you are not satisfied with this novel, Dorchester Publishing Company, Inc. will refund your money! Simply return the book for a full refund.

To be eligible, the book must be returned by 5/30/2010, along with a copy of the receipt, your address, and a brief explanation of why you are returning the book, to the address listed below.

We will send you a check for the purchase price and sales tax of the book within 4-6 weeks.

Publishers Pledge Reads
Dorchester Publishing Company
11 West Avenue, Ste 103
Wayne, PA 19087

Offer ends 5/30/2010.

☐ **YES!**

Sign me up for the Love Spell Book Club and send my
FREE BOOKS! If I choose to stay in the club, I will pay
only $8.50* each month, a savings of $6.48!

NAME: _____

ADDRESS: _____

TELEPHONE: _____

EMAIL: _____

☐ I want to pay by credit card.

☐ **VISA**   ☐ **MasterCard**   ☐ **DISCOVER**

ACCOUNT #: _____

EXPIRATION DATE: _____

SIGNATURE: _____

Mail this page along with $2.00 shipping and handling to:
**Love Spell Book Club
PO Box 6640
Wayne, PA 19087**
Or fax (must include credit card information) to:
610-995-9274
You can also sign up online at **www.dorchesterpub.com**.

*Plus $2.00 for shipping. Offer open to residents of the U.S. and Canada only.
Canadian residents please call 1-800-481-9191 for pricing information.
If under 18, a parent or guardian must sign. Terms, prices and conditions subject to
change. Subscription subject to acceptance. Dorchester Publishing reserves the right
to reject any order or cancel any subscription.